The Sealed Knot

CLARE CLARK

Copyright © 2022 Clare Clark

All rights reserved.

For Sarah, with thanks

CONTENTS

1. To Hell or to Connacht **1**

2. From This Day Forward **8**

3. Raspberry Wine **18**

4. Lord Protector **28**

5. Break And Prevent The Designs And Combinations Of The Enemy **43**

6. A Wager **44**

7. Anything Your Heart Desires **56**

8. Fire Will Spread **70**

9. Insurrection Is Intended In This Nation **76**

10. To Have And To Hold **77**

11. Pot Luck **90**

12. A Grave Discrepancy **105**

13. The Road **107**

14. After He Had Patiently Endured **116**

15. A Lesson **121**

16. Others **132**

17. The Mermaid **142**

18. On þinum worde snottor **151**

19. Treggredick **159**

20. To The Greenwood Gone **169**

21. Dragoons **179**

22. The Present **187**

23. The Insolencies of the Liberty of Soldiers **197**

24. Speaking Bluntly **206**

25. Minerva **212**

26. A Sealed Knot **226**

27. The Protector Was Inexorable **234**

28 Carnage **235**

29. The Dawning Of The Day **244**

30. The Goodness And Loving Kindness Of The Lord **254**

31. Masks **255**

32. Four's A Crowd **267**

33. The Message **279**

34. Springing Sooner Than The Lark **289**

35. Mission Bells **304**

36. White Gold **318**

37. Hardened Resolve **327**

38. Son Of A Bitch **335**

39. The Past Is A Foreign Country **347**

40. The French Are Very Much Short With Us **360**

41. Light and Dark **361**

42. The Painted Chamber **374**

43. The Rotten Core **389**

44. Great Expectations **397**

45. Takes One To Know One **402**

46. The Score **410**

47. The Beginning **421**

ACKNOWLEDGEMENTS **431**

1. TO HELL OR TO CONNACHT

28 May 1657

He strides through the black camp, boots squelching in churned mud, blade thudding lifelessly against wet leather. Stiff bodies already back from the sortie dissolve quickly enough into the drizzling darkness before him, but adrenaline still floods his veins with fire. His senses are still alert for threat. Somewhere, a drum is still beating.

A posse of infantry, huddled as close as they dare to one of the burning braziers, raise enthusiastic cheers as he passes but he ignores them. These are familiar swine and he is deep in the muck and shit and swill with them, but their snorts in the aftermath of fighting are as foreign as the land. A wave of disgust follows in their wake, but he is close now. Close to the freedom of solitude. Close to silencing the screams with some restless measures of whisky. Oblivion.

There's a commotion outside his tent; shouts and crying from a jumble of voices and tongues. He braces himself as he approaches, hand hovering instinctively over the hilt of his sword.

"Sir!"

"What?"

"Sir, with compliments from Major-General Cromwell."

The expressionless eyes of the company cook glance up before he shuffles back to reveal three bodies, a welcome line of indiscriminate shapes and features, wet hair plastered onto heads bowed down. One weeps silently, her angled shoulders quivering with the effort of control. His dark eyes flick to see another broad back heading towards its own tent, arm slumped heavily on the slight shoulders of an emaciated woman. His fist curls, blood pounding and he glares down at O'Donnell.

"I thought I'd been totally fucking clear."

"But I've to follow orders, sir. Himself says as how I'm to be makin' sure yer enjoyin' yerself, after yer performance today with the tories. Says ye've earned it." *Don't fucking blame me.* The cook shrugs as resentfully as he dares and gives a small shove between the shoulder blades to the first sodden, skinny spoil. It's a noisome task, but O'Donnell would be as ruthlessly efficient in distributing bounty in the aftermath of battle as he was slopping out the grout before it. "Yer preferin' another, sir?"

He stills, unclenching his fingers with conscious effort before pushing wordlessly past into his tent. Some dim reflex has him turn back and gather the canvas to permit her entrance, some habitual scratching at the door of civility that males him flinch. White tendrils of fog and sunken wood smoke wind around their ankles, like snakes coming to explore a mammal's burrow. Then the flap collapses back down, trapping them with the sordid smells of wet canvas, wet mud, and damp, acrid fire.

He lights a candle, once and then twice as it gutters in the cold air. Turning back, he can see she's shivering violently, bare legged in her thin shapeless dress. *Is it colder than usual?* He snatches up his heavy woolen cloak, draping it brusquely about her shoulders. It's been dark and bitter and wet for as long as he can remember. In the flickering light, her bones stand out disturbingly, thrusting odd shapes through her pale skin as if she were a half empty sack of twigs. Her collarbone pushes a line of vivid white from a deep hollow and her eyes are ringed with an exhausted black, as if someone had pressed coal-dirty thumbs into the sockets.

"Blood," she says suddenly, and it takes him a moment to realise she is staring at the roughly bandaged wound on his thigh. "On yer leg, sir. Blood. I'll clean it."

"No. It's fine." His voice is cracked and harsh; he barely recognises it. He turns to his trunk, sitting deep and uneven in rotting mud that never dries, and he swipes up an unfinished cup of whisky. It was poured earlier. *Before.* A superstitious ritual to give him something to return for. Knocking back the remaining dregs, the heat eases his throat.

Outside the wind changes suddenly and the side of his tent whips inwards, straining against a gust that forces muffled song and low, throaty laughter through the rain sodden canvas. The song is melancholic now. The men will take their rest where they can find it, mired in mud and frustration. Victory would make them nostalgic for their women at home; it would kindle a bone deep need for the feel of a warm body. *Dangerous.* He swallows an unreasonable irritation. He'll need to escort her safely back to whatever desperate hovel they'd found her in. Oblivion is marching further away with every passing minute.

"What's your name, girl?"

He cringes inwardly at the paternalistic tone. *Girl.* Beneath the waste of poverty, she was no more than, what, five years younger than him? In the flickering flares of candlelight, she could be ten years older. The lines on her face speak of a strain that should have been accumulated over several lifetimes. In any case, no woman would welcome being patronised while she waits patiently to be assaulted.

"Neala Kielty, sir."

"Kielty?" He shakes his head with a small wry smile of recognition, a pricking of painful memory, and murmurs quietly to himself: "A coincidence."

She looks up at him then, hesitant but not afraid. "It's no coincidence, sir. The other girls, outside, well Dervla was mighty nervous of ye, on account o' yer size, she thought... then Mary was swiftly sayin' she's heard the stories of ye an' so forth. It wasna so hard to be next in line, sir, when we was reachin' yer door."

She waves absently back towards the battered entrance and, in spite of himself, the corners of his mouth quirk, his muscles relax a little. *Neala Kielty is alive.* Something to drink to. He pulls a bottle out from under the narrow camp bed and balances a second cup on the top of his sword chest.

"Then welcome, Mistress Kielty, to my humble abode," he says, sweeping an arm about his campaign tent with a faint grimace: "We'll have a whisky, wait a quarter hour or so, and then you can go and tell Dervla that she was right to be concerned."

Her tentative smile freezes and, as her brow furrows, he kicks himself, ploughing long fingers back through the knotted waves of his black hair. *Bastard.* He's suddenly conscious that he must look terrifying. Out of the rain, the stale sweat of exertion is drying on his skin and it feels like a hardened paste, thickened with other men's blood and dirt, painted on his body like the tattoos daubed on the pagan warriors who stalked this land before him.

"I'm sorry. You're hungry? I have some bread, I think."

"Do I not please ye?"

He pauses for a moment, bottle poised mid-air, genuinely confused by the hurt in her eyes when he'd expected relief. *She fears the consequences?* Sure, in this topsy turvy world, it's illegal to lie with an Irish girl and every invading man guilty of fornication risks a flogging… but in the year since his arrival, Harry Cromwell has proved himself a practical man, if a nervous one. He spins in a world of shadows, reading rebellion in every furrowed brow, but steps neatly over lower level criminality where it can be traded for higher-placed support. Westminster won't court martial every single one of his officers, provided every single one was guilty. *Damned if you did, damned if you didn't.*

He frowns. Most likely she fears being pushed back outside to run a treacherous gauntlet through the drink-addled bodies of his soldiers. This time of night, in shadows black as pitch, she'd be worth the risk of the whipcord lash for the rank and file. He shakes his head as he pours two generous slugs of whisky and holds one out to her.

"Mistress Kielty, Neala, you're safe."

"I know," she says quietly, shrugging her pointed shoulders, taking a sip.

"I'll see you to your bed. You'll be back with-" he pauses, downing the whisky and pouring another, free fingers tugging again through his hair. "Nothing will come of this."

"I know." With small, purposeful movements she places her cup down and shrugs off his heavy cloak, laying it carefully across the chest before it can fall to the dark earth. "Sir-"

"I'd never take a woman served on a platter by my company's quartermaster," he adds, turning away to swipe his snapsack from the bed.

"Sir, I came to ye of my own willin'."

"We both know there's no such thing as free will for you in this Godforsaken place," he continues mildly, issuing a hollow laugh, feeling inside the bag for the remnants of a hard-baked loaf. "Nothing you do is willing, Neala. I'm the victor, you're the vanquished. I'd have you beaten and starved, your children sold into slavery, your menfolk killed and your holdings confiscated-"

"*He* would... *Ye* wouldn't."

He continues rummaging, ignoring her words and a sharp, high-pitched scream outside: "There's no difference. We're one and the same. You're here because two or more of my men marched you into camp with a knife at your back. It was only a knife because lead shot is too expensive to waste on you."

His fingers find it finally, and he holds the blackened meal outstretched. She glances at it briefly: "I know how to be hidin' fro' yer men, sir. I came to ye because I wanted to. Ye've saved him. Again. We owe ye... I owe ye."

"You owe me nothing. I don't know what you mean," he says carefully, his features hardening as O'Donnell's low grumble passes too close by the tent, his job done. All this infernal noise, but if someone hears her whispers, this knife-edge will cleave them both in two. He sits heavily on the edge of the cot with a hiss. The adrenaline is wearing off and until the whiskey takes hold, he can feel the wound in his leg as a fresh and brutal stab. "Don't speak like this. I mean it, Neala. Enough."

"I have only the one thing to say, sir."

He looks up at her then. Her mouth is full, wide, almost too large for her face, and her eyes glimmer from within the smudges. She might have been pretty, once. Long pale hair falls loose down her back and from this angle there are faint undulations to her body, echoes of what might have been in more abundant times. *Before*. The half-starved body is a flicker of the woman it might have been, but it was woman still.

He understands it. It's as old as the urge to raise a weapon in the first place. Filled to the brim with blood and sweat and horror, a victor will seek remembrance of his humanity, or at least an echo of it in the pretense of a willing love. Whore or widow. Wife. He knows the men don't ask questions. Sometimes there's no reliable oblivion in the recurring nightmares of sleep or the teasing paranoia at the bottom of a bottle. Never peace in the rambles of ancient philosophers, he thinks ruefully, with a mental glance at the single book buried deep in his trunk, a hangover from a courtly education. No peace, save that to be found in a woman's arms. There a man could forget himself and his brutality, indulge in the fleeting fantasy of redemption. A warm body is too easy a thing to need. An unspeakable weariness washes over him with the pain and he rubs a hand over his face, unable to look at her any longer.

A jug of cold water and a bowl sits by the candle, beside a filthy cloth. Slowly she picks it up and kneels before him. His jaw tightens but he sits still as she gently peels back the battlefield bandage. His breeches were torn by the blade and she teases loose scraps of cotton clear from livid flesh, working silently until the ragged edges of the wound emerge clean, before wrapping round a fresh dressing from his snapsack. It's the best she can do, in the circumstances.

"Thank you." He stands stiffly and touches her face, unable to stop himself acknowledging, receipting a debt paid. "It's time. Let's go."

"I was meanin' it, sir. I came of my own willin'."

Suddenly, she leans forward to cup him, a move at once awkward but insistent. He startles, flinching as her thumb rubs his flesh. His fingers come tight around her fragile wrist to pull it gently away, shamed that the surprising warmth of her hand has made his breeches uncomfortably tight.

"No, Neala, stop it. I mean it. I don't need this."

Undeterred, her free hand reaches to stroke his roughened jaw, drawing his eyes down to hers. Her pupils are too large to tell the colour ringing them in the dim light.

"I know that, sir," she whispers, rising awkwardly onto the balls of her bare feet to get closer. "But I do. I've been needin' to thank ye the only way I can. Ye saved him. Ye saved me."

"Not for this-"

Her lips are as soft as they look, and her whisky-tinged tongue flicks delicately across his teeth. She's gentle but generous, rousing his body with the playfulness of a familiar lover and wearing down his mind with the heady gift of, what, oblivion? Redemption? *Forgiveness?* It's a compelling promise, no matter if his soul is beyond saving.

She unties the thin leather cord clinching the neckline of her dress, letting it gape open, wriggling against him so that it falls from her shoulders to pool on the floor. She lifts his hand and places it on her breast, letting him feel the urgency of her tight nipple, erect and dark against translucent, blue-veined skin. A logical part of his brain nags that it is a consequence of cold, not arousal, but his desire gathers its own pace.

"If..." he starts, self-loathing washing through him as he lets her wind her thin arms about his neck, stretching out her naked body tight against his.

If.

The die is already cast. ☐

2. FROM THIS DAY FORWARD

28 May 1658

"Dearly beloved. We are gathered here-"

There was an echoing thud and then an interminable pause, as the Minister bent to fumble among his black skirts for the service book he'd been clutching.

His white head bobbed low in a shaft of morning sunlight and thick glasses slipped down his nose, clattering onto the stone floor. A few irreverent titters came from the children crammed into the front pews and a mumbled lament rose from the flagstones: "Oh sweet Lord, give me strength… each will have to bear his own load."

Jack raised an exaggerated eyebrow and leant in towards her. "I shall find my load easier to bear if you'd stop eating pasties, my sweeting," he whispered, unable to hide the grin, and Tara stifled a snort of outrage as she squeezed his hand, willing him to swallow the giggle she could feel bubbling up within him.

She stared down at his fingers, struggling to retain composure. They were loosely interwoven in her own and he rubbed his thumb along hers. Not long now. He would lift her mouth to his lips, graze her soft skin against the permanent blonde stubble that clung stubbornly to his cheek. She smiled at the thought, a queasy anticipation deep in her belly. Standing where the altar rail had once been, the scent of incense and cacophony of organ long since expunged, the barren stone was at odds with her excitement. She had, dare she admit it, a not unpleasant countenance underneath unruly curls, but it was nothing short of a miracle that Jack's clear blue gaze had landed on her, and God knew she was ready for a happy ending.

He was a foreigner to Petersham, like she had been. Yet while she'd spent three years scratching a living on the very edge of the sleepy settlement, he'd walked straight into its heart. He arrived in the depths of winter, when few risked the exposures of travel, but when he took up apprenticeship on the common with Robert Butcher, she caught glimpses of him in the darkness, flashes of a golden head and broad grin against the endless greys and browns of the village. He had fair height and a solidity born in manual labour, but he moved playfully, like a baby wildcat, languorous and mischievous in equal measure.

Every girl of marriageable age had vied to catch his eye. Every caring mother had found need to buy extra cuts of meat so they might happen to mention, in passing, to kill the time as he filled their baskets, the virtues of their dear Mary, their steadfast Joan, their exemplary Bess. Still, she'd made him work to convince her... but when the frosts finally thawed so too did her determination to stay alone. She glanced up to see the light make a halo of his shaggy hair. He'd fallen with the snow like the Christmas angels of her childhood, before that ungodly festival of light went the way of the others. and when he put his arms around her, there was nothing to do but agree to be his wife.

Mary, Joan and Bess remained bemused. Behind her, their pinched faces peered between empty cressets, the air heavy with their disappointment. The whole village had turned out in judgement for the spectacle. It was a matter of much whispered consternation that the aloof outsider would dare steal the most eligible bachelor from under their noses. *Why her?* There were few enough ineligible ones to go around, since the war...

Might they have been friends, in another life? Was the hardness always in their faces, or had the years petrified them? It was like a contagion, this bitterness of being left behind. Seven years since the war and the world was picking itself up again, but how could you recover from an abandonment by fate? It wasn't your fault, but it twisted trusts and devoured hope, until all that was left was a demand. This is mine. *Mine...* my borders, my Protector, my man, my future. *Not yours.*

Jack was just amused, somehow finding the coin for the reckless extravagance of a new brown leather jerkin for him and a new dress for her. Slippers in matching pale-yellow silk. *Let's give them a good show!* When she tried it on yesterday evening, free of the usual grey wools and coarse dowlas, the outfit had lifted her from her cottage world, but now she couldn't shake the weight of their stares so easily.

She glanced guiltily back to see Ned Gibbons sneak peaks at her from behind Jack's shoulder. Their wedding rings were still clutched in his sweaty fist, presumably, ready for his cue, but his simple features were busy, vacillating between unwholesome appreciation of her gown and unholy worship for his fellow apprentice. She tugged at the edges of her stays, breaking the spell of his gaze. The Minister cleared his throat awkwardly, preparing to continue.

"Today, in the sight of-"

Another thud, louder, more urgent, and Tara started as the heavy church doors at the back swung open at speed, smacking back against freshly white-washed walls. The violence unsettled a nest of roosting thrushes in the rafters, but their protesting twitters were lost in heavy footsteps and the harsh metallic clang of armour. *Weapons.* She looked at Jack and felt a swell of nerves to see confusion cloud his eyes.

"It's the new Earl," hissed Ned, gaping wide-eyed at the uncompromising, black-clad stranger already striding down the aisle towards them. "Abi said he was expected any day... God's blood, he's shoulders like a drayman."

"What the Hell is going on?"

His eyes were obscured by a wide brimmed hat, but the demand bounced along clean walls and a woman in the second pew hurriedly crossed herself, a private invocation against the possibility of eternal damnation. Silently the congregation turned its questioning gaze forward to the Minister, still fumbling to hook his glasses over each ear, and then back to the aisle, as if following the shuttlecock in a particularly slow-moving game of battledore. Another man, also armed, filed into the vestry, treading enthusiastically close behind his master.

Jack came to first, his mouth instinctively forming its most disarming grin: "Come, sir, tis our wedding day! Join us, pull up a pew, you and your friends are most welcome. As yet you've missed naught."

The reference to the slow start was meant to ease tension and on cue a snort escaped from his best man, but it echoed hollow and Ned shifted uncomfortably on the balls of his feet as the stranger drew to a halt beside him.

"Fielding, I suggest we retire, unless you relish the idea of a floor show. You, and you," he added, a cursory nod in the direction of Jack and Tara, "Now."

The minister jolted into action, nodding and backing away across the chancel with a nervous half bow towards a woven curtain covering the entrance to the small vestry. He held it awkwardly aside to permit entrance but Tara tugged hold of Jack's sleeve to stop him following, and fought an urge to scream.

"No!" Whatever this was, it was happening too fast.

"Don't even think about it…" Jack whispered, his voice unusually stern. He shrugged her loose so he could follow and motioned to Ned to stay put. "We'll sort this privately."

"Jack!" she hissed at his back, "We're not dogs to be ordered about."

"And yet you will come to heel." The stranger's black cloak brushed past and she caught his profile. A rush of incongruous memory, glazed in summer sunshine, snatched at her breath. *You?* His deep hazel eyes were unwavering as they appraised her without any hint of recognition, and in the emptiness of his gaze she felt a faint, childish stab of a sun-bleached desire to please. *You.* Her head dropped to focus on an ancient divot in the flagstones under her feet, her heart pounding, but the girl inside squared her stance. *That was all before.* Before war, before betrayal. Before murder. *You.* Gabriel Moore was all grown up.

Her fists clenched as shock turned to fury but he was already at the curtain and barking back at his servant, impervious to the excited rustles of the congregation behind them: "Wortley. No interruptions."

The man nodded, lank hair scraping about his shoulders like trodden straw, hand resting meaningfully on his sword hilt, and her neighbours fixed their eyes downwards.

Breathe. Time started to move again and she followed hurriedly into the vestry where Gabriel Moore was ready to preside over the claustrophobic court.

"… not consulted" he was saying, low but firm.

"Lord," Fielding started timidly, wringing his hands but quite unable to hide the fact they were shaking. "Forgive me, I didn't know you had arrived with us, I thought the big house still shuttered. Your predecessor had no interest in our petty matters… Tara Rivers is of ample age; it surely matters not that she is unrepresented."

Tara frowned momentarily at the unflattering reference to her stubborn spinsterhood and Jack smirked, but Gabriel replied without sharing in the joke: "I'm here now, Fielding, and nothing will happen in this village without my permission. That is my right. I've made my feelings very clear to the bishop in Kingston." He paused to let the words and their implications sink in. "Perhaps you're prepared to risk his distemper by continuing with this spectacle?"

Tara frowned: "Yes, of course he'll continue with the spect- with my wedding! Who on earth do you think you are?"

"*Sweeting*," said Jack again, warningly, between closed teeth.

"Bishop Staunton will have you in cholera-ridden Newgate in no time," Gabriel continued, ignoring her entirely, "You'll be back administering last rites to the miserable faces of criminals, fearing for your life from some fair means but mostly foul ones…"

"No, my Lord" Fielding said quietly, casting a nervous glance towards her. "My child, patience is a virtue, The Earl of Denby is right to remind me. In my ignorance, I have ridden roughshod over local tradition and offended him. Still, I am sure he will grant blessing. As our Lord in Heaven Himself once said, "It is better to-"

"No."

The verdict bounced around the small room and Jack cursed violently under his breath. He turned to brace himself against a bench, eyes glowering as he stared sightlessly at Fielding's cluttered work surface.

"No, what?" Instinctively, she reached for Gabriel's wrist but beneath his leather gauntlet, she felt the muscles of his forearm tense and dropped her hand.

"No." The firmness carried more than a hint of anger; the Earl was frustrated to be surrounded by village idiots and Fielding shuddered. "Tamara Villiers will not marry this man."

All three stared at him blankly in a heartbeat of silence.

"Stop it-" Tara stammered. No-one in Petersham knew her real name. Not even Jack. She bit her lip until she could taste the metallic tang of blood. This was nothing to do with some archaic administrative error; Gabriel Moore knew exactly who she was.

"There has been a mistake, my Lord. This is Tara *Rivers*." Jack spoke calmly as he finally turned around, his handsome face wrinkled with an almost comic air of confusion.

The Earl lowered his voice, but it carried the seriousness of his threat: "Jack Ludlow, get out now or I'll inform the authorities of your night-time poaching in Richmond Park. I'll have you horsewhipped and hanged at Kingston within a week. Fielding, go back to your ragtaggle herd and tell them the show is over."

"Oh God..." she whispered, feeling the breath escape her chest as if she'd been winded by a punch.

"Villiers? Is *that* your name?"

"Jack, please, I can explain, let me explain, you love me, we will-"

But he'd already retreated against the curtain, momentarily wrapping himself in its voluminous folds as he tried to escape. Fielding sprang forward to assist at his muffled curse.

Jack can only have been three inches shorter than the intruder but he was literally getting smaller as she watched, paralysed by rising panic. It was all slipping away. Her whole future. Not a half hour previous, life was finally certain, normal even, but the promise of simple contentment wavered like a mirage and she felt a flick of cold air as the curtain fell back into place. Then Jack was gone and the Minister's awkward apology echoed around the nave. Everyone could leave. The wedding was cancelled.

Barely holding back hot tears, she started to follow Jack but Gabriel put a restraining hand on her shoulder: "Not yet."

"Don't you dare touch me." She spun around, shaking off his fingers and lashing out with an instinctive fury, but a punch had no impact. She followed up with a series of frustrated jabs, attempts to shove him away that left him unmoved. After a moment, he captured her wrists tight, holding them down where they could cause no more irritation.

"Stop it," he growled, "Stop it Tamara, damn you. Just wait a moment."

"Who the Hell do you think you are?"

Her chest was heaving but her voice low, so that it wouldn't travel back along the bare stone walls to the congregation. There were no peeling bells to drown out the mealy opinions of her neighbours as they shuffled slowly out into the morning sunshine. Mary and Joan and Bess were wide-eyed with a frenzy of speculation and icy drifts of bitterness reached them, settling like snow about her feet.

Praise God Jack has escaped; I always knew she had bewitched him.

"You remember me," he said, impervious to the damning chatter.

Lied about her name, Ned says! A bigamist, I'll wager! Cold wench.

"I won't stand for this," she spat, eyes prickling.

Didn't I tell you there was something rum about that superior shrew?

"Then take a seat and we'll discuss it." He walked her forcibly back a few steps until she came hard against a stool draped in Fielding's spare cassock, where he half pushed, half lifted her onto the perch.

"What are you even doing here?" she demanded, sliding back off the moment he released her wrists and pacing around him, eyes narrowed and hackles raised like a cornered mouser. "Your family seat is in Hereford."

"Old King Charles granted me Ham House a decade ago for services rendered to his son."

Services rendered before the war.

She froze, seeing him clearly for the first time. Unusually tall and solid, his body had fulfilled the gangly promises of youth. Under the hat, brows and shoulder length hair were dark, his jawline hard and nose straight. Cheek bones were broad, prominent, but his cheeks were hollowed slightly by a tiredness that cast sunken shadows around his dark eyes. It was the only hint of vulnerability in features that were almost aggressively attractive. From a thick leather belt, a sword fell heavily against thigh-high boots. Breeches joined at the waist with a black doublet, fastened by a row of balled silver buttons that ran up to his neck and down each sleeve. No ruff, as was normal at court, but a white linen undershirt was just visible, folded over at the collar. Every expensive inch the civilised squire. Only, given the services he had rendered since Charles Stuart was beheaded, every inch was evidence of complicity... ornamental veneer on a callous murderer.

He confirmed it: "Parliament saw fit to ratify the gift after-"

"After you betrayed our King!" she interrupted. "Don't make it sound like you polished boots or, or collected cabbages for the war effort... You killed Ralph. The least you could have done was fall on your sword for this Godforsaken regime."

"Lower your voice, Tamara, for Christ's sake-"

His jaw tensed but she continued, green eyes flaring: "Your corpse should be rotting in the muddy corner of some field."

He dropped his hat onto the bench and ran a distracted hand through dark hair that fell back in waves to hide his eyes. "I am apparently resurrected."

"Like Jesus, I suppose. You always were a sanctimonious-"

"Like *you*," he interrupted mildly, turning to lean back against a stone column. He looked at her thoughtfully as he ran a hand over rasping stubble. "You disappeared from the face of the earth three years ago, after the Penruddock roundups."

Tara shrugged, her own arms folding, refusing to elaborate, and after a moment he continued: "It doesn't matter. Your uncle begged me to bring this fiasco to a halt. You can't marry a butcher's apprentice."

"It's of absolutely no bloody concern to either of you whom I marry. Besides, why on earth would Eddie ask you? He wouldn't beg *you* for anything, you turned your back on us all a long time ago-"

It was Gabriel's turn to shrug. "You cannot think I'd be here if I were not obliged. I met him yesterday on the road outside Reading."

She frowned, Reading was a long way from his home in Exeter: "The both of you can go to Hell, I–"

"Be careful what you wish for, Tamara, that's looking more than likely." His tone softened slightly as he continued: "Edward Villers was under guard. He was arrested in Salisbury three days ago at some Quaker meet. He was on his way to the Tower."

"Arrested." she murmured flatly under her breath. There was no need to ask why. Non-conformist preaching was a minor irritation in Cromwell's side, not a capital crime. But treason… As far as her uncle was concerned, when one war in England ended, another began. It was a miracle, perhaps, that it had taken this long, Cromwell's network of spies would have been watching him for years. Especially since the Penruddock debacle.

"Our Lord Protector sees a country bristling with plots and conspiracies, threats of invasion and uprising. His Secretary of State John Thurloe is an efficient creature; he put London's known royalists under house arrest two months ago. Now he's rounding up suspects in the provinces. Do you remember Dr John Hewitt from court, the old king's chaplain?" *Vaguely*, she thought, fighting against a rising bile. "He denounced your uncle after Cromwell questioned him personally."

Eddie arrested. So not just Jack, then. *Everything*. It was all over. She'd come once again into the bright sight of the authorities to fathom the evidence. Attend the trial. Petition for the defence, if Eddie were even allowed one. *Witness the execution*. She blinked.

"Tamara?"

"It's Tara now," she said softly. "I'm no longer a Villiers."

"You're Villiers another day yet," Gabriel pointed out, reasonably.

"And you're still a traitorous bloody bastard," she flared.

"Temper, temper." The start of a frustratingly familiar curve softened the corner of his lips. "We're in a church."

"For my *wedding*," she retorted blankly, stiffening again.

"You're not serious," he laughed suddenly, but the sound was hollow.

"What on earth were you thinking? He's a butcher's apprentice, and a petty criminal! Pretty hopeless at it too-"

"Enough. I'm going -"

"You're not," he interrupted testily, pausing to raise an eyebrow when Fielding poked a cautious nose around the curtain only to hurriedly let the fabric fall back down. "You're coming back to Ham House while I decide what to do with you."

"You don't get to do anything with me... I'm not a child anymore, in case you hadn't noticed."

Gabriel took in her clenched fists, the fury etched across her brow, and sighed inwardly as he turned to retrieve his hat. There was no time to argue about it: Hyde would be waiting for him in Kingston, hopefully with more detailed orders than he'd received so far. "Wortley!"

"I mean it... I'm not coming with you."

"Then by all means, save your objections for the new Earl," he replied sardonically. "He's freshly arrived from a long and bitter war in Ireland. Here's an idea! Go wait for him at Ham House. No doubt he'll be entirely disposed to listen to your complaints at length, having certainly nothing better to do this afternoon."

The curtain drew back and Tara spun to face the greasy leer of his servant, but she was too slow to dodge his firm grasp on her elbow.

"Get your hands off me!"

She squealed in surprise when the dirty fingernails dug deeper, pinching her flesh, and Gabriel's tone lowered dangerously, any hint of civility evaporating. "*Gently* Wortley. Lady Tamara Villiers is my guest, for now. Put her in the gallery to wait for me. *Alone*. I'll be back presently."

3. RASPBERRY WINE

The warhorse danced restlessly, hooves falling haphazard on the cobbles. In the narrow streets, the shouts and bangs of Kingston's shuttering market rattled the beast with echoes of battle, only amongst the sweaty, densely-packed throngs there was no blessed release of charge. The promise of an open road shifted his black, muscular bulk in zig zags along the well-trodden trail to Richmond. With a tight rein, Gabriel was still in control of Rowley's broad shoulders and snorting nostrils, but only just.

His fingers squeezed the leather in imperceptible warning as they came close to unsettling a slow-moving cart stacked high with freshly printed newssheets. Then his jaw tightened as its back wheel toppled into a pothole. With an audible hiss, he steered around the abruptly static obstacle, passing close enough for a glimpse of the Government-sponsored headlines.

The Mercurius Politicus was full of promise for the breakfast table tomorrow. England's civil conflict had been spilling across the continent for years, but tensions increased dramatically two months ago when Cromwell renewed the Anglo-French alliance. Charles Stuart, the exiled heir to the English crown, if indeed there was still such a thing, was already declared King of Scotland and sworn ally of Spain. The two forces were now apparently directly pitted against each other at Dunkirk, where a French siege of the fortified port had just begun, with the Spanish garrison scrabbling for reinforcements.

Gabriel frowned: this was old news already. Of more immediate consequence was Edward Hyde's revelation about Cromwell's squadron of twelve frigates, scouting between Ostend and Flanders. Along the east coast, Spanish transport ships had bobbed about at anchor for weeks, filled with Stuart troops and the silent threat of invasion. A rebel plan to seize Yarmouth for a bridgehead had been uncovered with a violent wave of arrests, drawing parliament's attention to the remaining South Coast harbours large enough to welcome a King. Plymouth. Falmouth. Lyme Regis... The Lord Protector was busy bolstering garrisons in anticipation of menace, just as the royalist traitors were busy preparing to provide some.

Only if Hyde was right, and it was a fair bet the news he brought to Kingston was more reliable than the officially sanctioned propaganda, Cromwell's frigates had done more than scout. The enemy coalition was entirely destroyed. There were no more Spanish transport ships. There could be no invasion. Anyone still planning to receive the king would be vulnerable now. Restless and ripe for plucking. He could find them. Little wonder Villers had been arrested now, with a little leverage over the old Quaker, there was no telling how many radical layers would unpeel.

Town slowly ceded to fields and the market traffic thinned but after another hundred yards his charger was skirting awkwardly around a handcart piled precariously with worn clothing. Its nervous retinue scattered for cover against the hedgerow. Tsk! He hissed at the flattened ears as two mongrels took their lives in their paws to defend their master's honour, snapping angrily at the dancing black ankles.

With some relief, Gabriel turned onto one of the long approach drives to Ham House. He shifted to dig his heels into the sturdy ribs but Rowley needed no encouragement. Flesh quivered under his coat, picking a ripple of chestnut red in the setting sun, and his long legs snapped forward as if the sinews had been winding up tightly all afternoon. There was relief in speed: they were home, finally. Free, for now. For a moment, he felt a kinship with his horse, its hind legs scattering gravel and dust to obscure the path behind them.

Rowley slowed to a trot as they reached the front of the mansion house, Gabriel's muscles adjusting automatically to the change in rhythm. They were both breathing heavily; the light was fading into blue, and cooler air misted before them as they clip-clopped through the brick arch entrance to the stables. The yard had been still and a groom approached at the sound of hoof beats, nodding a welcome.

"Everything alright, Donn?"

"Aye, grand altogether Milord. His Highness looks ready fer a drink."

"He's not the only one," Gabriel murmured, kicking his leg over Rowley's back and jumping down.

The younger man snorted with the horse, his loose red hair shimmering as he took the bridle over its ears and led him with a familiar smack on the rump towards the middle of the yard, where Rowley nosed eagerly towards a water trough. Gabriel watched him a moment. Rowley sensed a kindred spirit in exile, displaying gentleness in the hands of the slim limbed groom that he otherwise steadfastly refused to reveal. For all his easy manner though, Donn was scarred. Picked up by the army outside Galway as a scrawny boy, he'd watched his father pay the ultimate price for refusing to submit to the Commonwealth, and was roughly used for nearly four years to translate Lord Deputy Fleetwood's zealous orders into Gaelic sermons and threats.

When Gabriel found him, Donn had outlived his purpose and was facing lazy accusations of theft and a choice of hangman's rope, transplantation to the barren wastelands of county Connacht, or slavery in the West Indies. He could take no credit for the stroke of pure, dumb luck. The Lord Protector's abrupt replacement of Fleetwood gave him the chance to intervene, and during the short power vacuum until Henry Cromwell arrived, he was just important enough for his demand for a stable hand to constitute an order. He was under no illusion then that he was only marginally preferable to certain death, however the boy had grown up fast. He was possibly now one of few men he trusted.

"Ye've a thirst fer whisky, Milord?" Donn was grinning as he flung the contents of the pail over Rowley's sweating haunches. A grateful whinny echoed around the yard as steam blossomed into the air.

"At least they didn't count the barrels as well as the bogs, eh?" Gabriel replied with a rueful smile. It was an old joke. Preparing for re-distribution to Protestant settlers and army creditors, Cromwell's survey of confiscated Irish lands had duly counted the muddy fields and ramshackle dwellings with staunch scientific detachment, but it never got a handle on the real gold. His horse, his groom and three dozen barrels of whisky made for unexpected souvenirs from that Hell. Although little doubt that if it ever came to a choice between him and his mount, Donn would have little compunction in installing Rowley in a comfortably appointed stall before turning to see if his master needed any assistance.

Heaven knows he needed it now, he thought with some wry apprehension, turning finally to leave the yard and crunch along the gravel pathway at the edge of his vegetable gardens. His vegetable gardens. It still seemed incongruous, improbable... wrong. It was also a somewhat scenic route towards the back door of the kitchen, and the irony of his cowardice didn't escape him. Cromwell himself had praised his heroic comportment under attacks from the tóraidhe rebels who roamed the hills in increasingly patchy numbers but still managed to do serious damage to English settlements. And yet still he hesitated to deal with Ralph's fierce and frustrating baby sister. This wasn't what he had signed up for.

He frowned, pausing to stare unseeing over a bed well-stocked with culinary herbs.

She was right. She wasn't a child anymore. Raised by traitors, her back to the wall in a world where no one could be trusted, she hadn't been a child for a considerable time. He remembered her father Gregory Villiers well from his years at court, before the war, a fervent and committed man, blindly loyal to the King as the storm clouds of revolution gathered. Before he died, Gregory had been key to a rebel organisation in the south west, dedicated to resisting the Commonwealth and resurrecting the monarchy. The Sealed Knot. There would have been no room for indulgence or weakness. Nothing spare to maintain a household that wasn't as deeply mired in the treason as him. It was inconceivable Tamara had not played a part in it. Was she a part of it still?

He hadn't expected compliance exactly, but time certainly hadn't tempered her tendency to stubborn argument. He could still hear Ralph diplomatically explaining it would be better to let his seven-year-old sister, skittish as a kitten with enthusiastic claws, join their game rather than bear the brunt of her tantrum at being left out. Time may heal but it'll never change, he thought ruefully, remembering her, muddy and tousled and scratched by undergrowth, heels kicking out from the side of a nursemaid anxious to return the girl to a more appropriate sedentary activity.

He could still see Ralph astride her, tickling mercilessly until her tears of laughter conceded his sap whistle. It was crucial to their soldier game but neither himself nor Charlie had managed to liberate the instrument from her tight grasp by persuasion alone. Some fledgling sense of honour prevented them from snatching it but Ralph had laughed at their feeble attempts, cocking one eye at his sister: "Tatty Angel, come now, give it to me or you know what'll come next."

She'd squared her stance then, all pout and petulance, but her features betrayed the faintest unease. "You don't dare. I want the whistle. It's my turn."

"You'll beg for mercy," Ralph threatened, trying not to laugh. She squealed delightedly then and run across the lawn, auburn curls flying. She was no match for her older brother but by the time he had tackled her to the grass both were giggling so much that neither noticed the whistle was squashed beyond all recognition under her skirts.

The game was more mature now; he needed to liberate a damn site more from her grasp than a childish toy. He ran a distracted hand back through his hair before continuing. In many ways, he thought, it was exactly the same.

Coming through the brick gateway through to the private lawns at the back of the house, a soft body hit him hard without warning, ricocheting to land with a thump in the gravel at his feet.

"Hell's teeth, I didn't see you coming."

Her mumbled curse in response didn't sound pained and he offered a hand to pull her up, but she ignored it and scrambled ungraciously to her feet, tripping on the edges of her pale yellow gown as she tried to straighten.

"I told Wortley to see you to the gallery, what are you doing here?" He kicked himself mentally. Keep it civil. "I'm sorry, Tamara..."

"I told you. It's Tara."

"Tara..." Be nice. If he was going to convince her to stay with him until Edward Villiers' trial, to unlock the organisation Cromwell feared above all else, he needed her cooperation. "We should talk." He frowned as she curtseyed deeply, caught a wobble and barely stifled a giggle at her own clumsiness.

"You know the word then, my Lord. '*Sorry*,' he says, finally. Sorry for this... whatever this is." The giggle turned to hiccups and then to glare as she fought to be serious.

"You're drunk." Gabriel hung his head and gritted his teeth, forcing down the irritation. He'd been considerably longer with Hyde than he'd intended but he'd left very simple instructions with Wortley, and Tara herself for that matter. Looking down, his eyes rested on the trowel in her hand. He asked again, as calmly as he could: "What are you doing?"

"Some bastard destroyed my wedding this morning and had me locked up here-"

"You're not a prisoner-"

"-before disappearing into thin air! Apparently, he hadn't the courage or decency to die in Ireland for his precious Lord Protector, but saw fit to install himself in Ham House, in Petersham, of all blasted places… he loves the chance to play master of all you survey, just like his father."

She moved to jab his chest hard with the point of the trowel so he disarmed her, throwing the tool into the lawn. "Enough, Tara, stop-"

"Oh," she frowned momentarily then leant in as though ready to share some juicy titbit of gossip, "and you'll love this, apparently he is above the law! Unlike my uncle, who's in chains and very much subject to it… You'll forgive me then if I grew sick of your blasted ancestors staring down at me, imperious superfl- supercili- bastards. Bloody staff too. I'm leaving. That's what I'm doing. I have things to do. I-" Her breath hitched, tears clearly close to the surface, and she waved expansively towards a far corner of the lower bowling lawn, where old Robert Gardener stood, watching her progress from a safe distance in the fading light.

He waved at Robert, standing him down, briefly wondering whether being threatened by a drunken woman brandishing garden tools would convince the help Ann had managed to hire to stay. There was by no means a full complement of staff ready to turn the shuttered mansion into a home; Fleetwood's summons had left only time to send ahead for Ann, his father's old housekeeper. He cringed mentally from habit, anticipating another lecture from the fierce crone.

"You heard him! Get gone and be buggered!" she shouted with some hiccupping satisfaction as Robert tugged his forelock towards them, but shooing him away revealed the bottle of raspberry wine she'd pilfered from the long sideboard in the gallery. Instinctively, she tried to tuck the bottle back between her skirts, holding her eyes briefly to staunch sudden tears and allow her brain chance to catch up. What had started as a medicinal shot to calm her nerves had turned, over the last few hours, into an impatient mission for oblivion as her entire life unravelled. The movement made her head spin. "Oh, God," she whispered as the wetness spilled over her lashes.

Gabriel frowned, running his hand back through his hair: "When did you last eat, Tara? Did Ann not bring you supper?"

She tried unsuccessfully to bat him away as his fingers sought her chin. "That's not your concern. Your sideboard was well stocked. I'm well-watered," she retorted, a fresh giggle bubbling up at his question. Suddenly inspired, she sang a line from a lusty drinking ballad that presented itself: "*A Vintner of no little Fame, Who excellent Red and White can sell ye...*"

"Right now, you stumbling around my garden like a fisgig is my only concern. You haven't eaten anything all day, have you? Odd's fish, you're an idiot," he pulled the bottle from her grasp, setting it down. "This stuff could fell a horse. If you're going to down an entire bottle, at least don't do so on an empty stomach."

He didn't wait for an answer. He bent down, gathering her against his chest, muscles tensing as his arm swept behind her knees and lifted her clean from the ground, pacing back into the house. Through the warm haze of alcohol, she was vaguely conscious of screaming and she flailed her loose limbs, hitting the door frame with an indignant *oomph* and kicking out at a plinth in the hallway. He grunted in annoyance at the echoing smash as a large vase hit the tiled floor and the furry body of a mouser snaked away into the shadows with a startled meow. His arms tightened but, having braced herself for the torrent of anger that didn't come, she submitted and allowed herself to be carried up the stairs, only barely aware of his barked orders to bring food, his steady heartbeat and her own soft but tuneless rendition of *Oyster Nan*.

She must have passed out. She woke into candlelight, under the damask cover, wearing just her shift. She groaned and opened her eyes to see her dress was hanging on the back of the door, the ties of the stays evidently yanked loose by someone who didn't appreciate the difficulty in rethreading the ribbon evenly.

"What did you do?" Tara scrambled up and drew her knees protectively against her chest as Gabriel turned from the window. The sudden movement made her head throb and the room spin violently.

"Nothing. My housekeeper made you more comfortable," he said patiently. "You want to be sick?"

Nodding hurt too much, opening a vortex in her brain, and her face blanched as a wave of heat and then cold rolled nauseatingly through her stomach. He crossed the room and held up an empty chamber pot to the side of the bed, gently gathering back her hair as she retched into it. When she'd finished, he held out a cup of water to swill the foul taste and waited until she spat it out.

"I want to go home."

"You need to sleep this off first, and fill your stomach with something more substantial than home brew." He retrieved a wooden tray from the top of a chest and placed it down beside her, its weight depressing the mattress a little. The soup was still steaming, and smelt sublime. She took a few mouthfuls, shame galvanizing as her body recovered from its queasiness. How could she have been so stupid?

"Thank your cook," she muttered, unable to look him in the eye.

"Raspberry wine, is it, the chink in your armour?" The curl to the edge of his lips hinted he was more amused than antagonised, but somehow that was worse.

"Too much on an empty stomach." She spoke with as much dignity as she could muster before shifting the tray down and rolling away. Still as pathetic as the girl who begged without pride to join their games. "It won't happen again."

"Glad to hear it, how will you fight me with neither the strength nor the wit?"

With the last of her energy, Tara tugged out a bolster pillow from behind her and flung it towards him but he dodged the missile and it thudded harmlessly against the closing door. She flopped back onto the pillow with a groan. Sleep was pulling her inexorably under, the vague promise of a whole head and a clear mind to come in the forensic light of a morning still hours away.

It was a fitful oblivion, peppered with familiar nightmares of her father on the scaffold but also spiced with dreams of Jack. He was with her now, holding her close, hiding her eyes from the court's judgment on Eddie. He covered her ears but she was an intimate acquaintance of the silences and the screams, having lived and relived them a thousand times. It wasn't enough, but she was grateful for his trying, and now she was running her fingertips along the hard lines of his scalp, dragging her nails along the raspy stubble on his jawline.

She didn't need to see it, she could feel his warm smile as he knelt before her in the long grass of the riverbank and pulled her down, bending his head to kiss her lips as his hands found her shoulder, the nape of her neck, pulling her closer, deeper against his body. His lithe arms felt hard, tense underneath her fingers. His hair glinted gold, pouring molten light across her skin, the last strains of a sunset highlighting strands of red chestnut in her own dark curls, a maternal legacy that shimmered in dying light.

Jack.

Morning already? They were in the bedroom of her childhood home. She couldn't remember how they had arrived at Weycroft Hall, but instinct told her to be quiet, nervous of discovery. He was so hot to the touch. It was worth the risk. Besides, mama and papa would both be engrossed in their plotting. It was strange, come to think of it, that she might be worried her parents would find them. She frowned. *They were both dead.* Weren't they? Both dead, she was sure. Should she check? Were they laughing?

She must have paused too long for he seemed irritated. Without warning he pushed off the childish cot and stood apart, tapping on the floorboards with the blocked heel of his boots. Then just stamping impatiently. She frowned at him again, now terrified, reached out to pull him back, to beg apology for her distraction, to recapture the softness of his touch. He was all that mattered, now. All she had. *He was everything.* But he was slipping through her arms, turning away. Stamping.

"What?" she spat out tersely, her voice croaking and her eyes puffy and damp with tears.

"Milady, it's fast approaching dawn and the Earl has requested that you go to him in the library."

Tara's eyes slowly made out the form of the serving girl's head where it floated uncertainly around the door, silhouetted against the palest light. It must be before 5 o'clock. There was the briefest moment of recognition, mundane reality ready to pierce what remained of her dreams, but she rolled over and bunched up her eyelids again firmly. Her own head felt similarly unconnected. It throbbed from the wine she had swallowed, while her stomach ached from the wine she had retched back up again. "No."

"Milady, I'm sorry but he said to say that if you didn't get up and go to him now, he would come and get you."

"*Christ's wounds,*" she whispered with a frustrated grunt and the maid flinched at the curse. The Gabriel Moore she remembered would follow through on the threat and defeat, before breakfast, was not a good start to the day. There was a lot to do. "Fine. Tell the bastard I'm coming."

The girl had left a single candle and as Tara lifted it from the floor, she saw a scrap of paper pinned beneath. A note in Jack's small, uneven hand: *Always, my sweeting.* Hurriedly she pulled open the door and peered into the chamber outside: "Stop!"

But no one was there. She was on her own.

So was Eddie.

The sudden sober thought sat her up. She groped for her dress on the door, running her hand along the seams. She would go to the Tower and see him, to make sure he was fed... but with a charge of treason there was no hope of access without speaking to Cromwell himself. She took a deep breath. Her fingers found the placket and then the purse sewn inside. It jingled reassuringly as she fingered the small roll of notes and counted the coin, satisfying herself that the frugal horse remained intact. Twenty-four shillings. Four pennies. Not much. Not enough to be confident she could cover Eddie's board. Would the Society of Friends help their preacher? Possibly, although since the Quakers prided themselves on their imitation of Christ's poverty, it didn't bode well. It was not sufficient surety to post bail, in the unlikely event the Lord Protector would be convinced to offer it...

One step at a time.

In a grey light, she hurriedly rethread her stays and arranged the skirts, patting down the hidden placket so it was once more inconspicuous amongst the folds of fabric. Her slippers were waiting by the door and she winced momentarily at the excruciating thought of Gabriel or the unseen housekeeper pulling them off and neatly placing them there, all the while with her singing about the willing seduction of Oyster Nan at the top of her voice.

But it didn't matter. *Not really.* She could help Eddie. Marry Jack. She tucked the note into the top of her stays, partly to keep it safe but mostly to feel the promise pressing against her heart. The feel of the rough paper cut through the haze of hangover like sunshine on a grey day and for the first time since she had arrived at the church yesterday and met his clear blue gaze, she smiled.

4. LORD PROTECTOR

"I'm going to Whitehall; I have business with the Lord General." Gabriel glanced up at her momentarily through falling black hair before bundling a series of papers on his desk and rolling them into a carry tube. Back in London, Charles Fleetwood had summoned every senior office within spitting distance and though the purpose was as yet unclear, he knew Cromwell had questioned the loyalty of his army. Fresh from distinguished service overseas, there was a fair chance he was needed for fire-fighting closer to home.

"You woke me at this ungodly hour to wish you God speed?"

"I had you roused," he replied patiently, head cocked to one side as he ran his fingers back through the loose curls, gathering the hair at the nape of his neck and swiftly winding around a length of cord to keep it neatly back, "because you're coming with me."

"To London?" Tara closed her eyes and dug a knuckle into her forehead, hoping to massage a pinprick of pain loose while he raised a dark eyebrow at the ridiculousness of the question.

"Drink some coffee. I daren't leave you alone in my house, with all the temptations about."

"The wine? It's safe this morning, I assure you."

"The wine to guzzle, the treasures to smash. The gardening implements to threaten my staff. I think it's better I keep you close." He paused while she slumped painfully into a carved chair. "Besides, I presume you want an audience with the Lord Protector to discuss your uncle? I'll get you access-"

"I'll make my own way to London," she flashed, as if she would consider doing anything else. "I'll get an audience with Cromwell on my own merit."

"They've doubled the guard at Westminster in response to recent threats; my name will do you no harm if you want to get past the gates. In any case, you were planning to walk?" Gabriel didn't wait for her answer; he blew out the candle on the desk and headed out to the stables.

In the pale mizzle of dawn, Donn had readied a sedate chestnut mare for his hungover charge. Gabriel took a deep breath as she pointedly ignored the groom's offer of a mounting block and somehow hauled herself up onto the horse with one foot in the stirrups, settling herself awkwardly. She was to ride side-saddle but made no move to hook her leg over the pommel, to use her knee for a better purchase. Here again was the stubborn child he remembered. He fought to swallow a rising irritation as she shifted uneasily, then without ceremony he came alongside her horse, lifting her leg over the pommel. Her breath hitched in surprise but his touch was no-nonsense, practical and swift, and he'd mounted Rowley before she could formulate a protest.

"Let me be clear," she said, slowly to hide the wobble in her voice when her own horse fell into step with his of its own accord. "I don't need a guard. And if you're so damn worried about your precious ornaments, I'll gladly pay for the damage. Jack will-"

"You're not my prisoner, Tamara-"

"*Tara-*"

"But you are my responsibility, *for now*. The swiftest way for you and I to part company is to hand you back to Edward Villiers. So, while there's a chance for bail I'm taking you to the Lord Protector."

She shifted in the saddle, seething. Her mount responded with a skittish lurch and she gave an involuntary yelp, immediately ashamed as Gabriel silently brought Rowley alongside and tugged gently on her reins, bristling when she realised that his fingers on the leather, holding on a little longer than necessary, were intended as instruction. She hadn't sat on a horse in years. There were usually sufficient options by way of carts, coaches or gigs to make her way without the trouble of aching thighs or a sore arse.

And this cool spring was a fickle mistress. A dark grey sky weighed heavy with a sense of foreboding. But the gentle swaying motion of her horse started eventually to settle her nerves, despite the drizzle dampening her cloak. A muted silence descended above the regular hoof beats, broken only when Gabriel gave a functional overview of their journey. After an hour or so, he leant over with a breakfast of bread and fruit from his saddle bag, but she kept the hood of her cloak up.

* * *

Whitehall Palace was a sprawling, maze-like complex of irregular warrens and burrows built haphazardly over the centuries. They approached from the east and the armed guard on the main gate recognised the Earl of Denby immediately. Eager to please the war hero, he took her into his personal custody as Gabriel turned Rowley towards Horse Guards Yard and the army grandees. Tara followed as he led her past the Banqueting House and straight through The Court, until they came to doors opening onto a wide panelled hall that echoed with the regular tick-tock of a grandfather clock. The guard disappeared then but another man stood doorkeeper behind a reception counter with an air of imperious self-importance, and she took a deep breath before interrupting his paperwork.

"Lady Tamara Villiers. I need an audience with the Lord Protector."

The secretary nodded indifferently as he dipped his quill in an inkpot and slowly added her name to a ledger. He paused to peer at her above small, neat pince nez, his black feather hovering above a space in the second column, "You arrived with Commander Moore?"

"What has that to do-?"

"What is your business?"

"It's personal," she said firmly, unwilling to have her story précised for posterity by such an unsympathetic scribe. "And important."

"It always is." Impassively, his eyes flicked towards an open door. "Wait in there. His Highness may not see you today. He has a great deal of correspondence and there were a large number here before you."

"I might be here until tomorrow?"

"It won't have escaped your notice that tomorrow is the Sabbath," he added, still focused on his ledger but with an eyebrow raised with mild reproach.

The waiting room was full of impotent gloom and low-level grumble. The proportions were generous enough originally, but it had been haphazardly subdivided and the light of a miserable day struggled to make an impression through the one remaining opaque window, set high on one wall. Aside from some dark panelling, it was largely unfurnished and weary petitioners paced its worn wooden boards, the draft raised by their shuffles causing the candlelight from two wall sconces to flicker. Others had long since tired of moving, seemingly collapsing down without care wherever they had last stood. She stepped over a protruding leg, whose elderly owner leant back vacantly against the wall, and perched down next to him.

"How long have you been here?" she whispered towards an immobile pile of limbs and linen on her other side. It was cool despite the number of bodies, and a chill passed over her damp skin.

"Four days," came the weary reply, and Tara smiled politely until she realised the woman was not joking. The huddled form looked up with a resigned shrug before adding unnecessarily: "Our Lord Protector is a busy man."

"*Clearly.*"

The regular beat of the clock in the hall dragged, as if it was actively engaged in slowing down time rather than measuring it. Tara's fingers worried a loose thread on her stomacher as impatience festered with nervousness. It had been years since she'd seen Oliver Cromwell. A few insistent coughs echoed around the room but, ever cautious, no-one dared fire an angry flare at the inconvenience of waiting. After a while, it looked through the high window as if the rain had finally stopped but the change in the weather did nothing to lift the mood of the room. For the most part, no one amongst the wretched company could envisage actually delivering their petition to the Protector, let alone being released into the real world. She released the thread for fear she would eventually work the seam loose, but her cold hands found industry pleating and pressing the silk of her skirts to the rhythm of the passing seconds. Underneath, her foot tapped an uneasy time.

The best part of the afternoon had passed before the secretary peered myopically around the heavy door into the gloom. "Villiers?"

"Yes?" Instinctively, she smoothed the creases into something more presentable as she stood, willing life back into awkwardly numb legs.

"Lady Tamara Villiers?"

"Yes."

"The Lord Protector will see you now." If the officious secretary sounded mildly shocked that she had been permitted an audience, her fellow petitioners were astonished. Open mouths gaped and she offered a brief apologetic shrug as she followed him from the room.

The little man moved at a surprising speed and she was forced to trot behind him to keep pace back across The Court, through Scotland Yard and up a series of stone stairs. They tripped along a disorientating maze of uneven corridors that seemed to span several buildings, approaching the oppressive private sanctum of the labyrinth. Then without warning, he stopped and knocked on a heavy oak door, nudging it open to usher her inside.

She knew immediately that he had been waiting for her. He stood calmly gazing out of the window, his silhouetted bulk a portentous, anonymous black. It was a dramatic lesson in power; the intense rays of the late afternoon sun were able to slice through the thunderstorm but having reached the most powerful man in England, they were forced to bend around him.

Tara squinted as she took in the simply furnished room: a large writing desk with a grand carver on one side a simpler chair on the other and, over by the fireplace, an uncomfortable-looking settle. A large but simple wooden cross was hung on the wall behind his seat, a somewhat heavy-handed reminder of the sacrifice of service. She bunched her fists at her sides, steeling herself for the battle ahead.

"My Lord, I come to cast myself on your good grace and mer-"

Cromwell interrupted with a weary sigh, silencing her with a hand but without turning. "I nearly didn't permit you entry, Lady Tamara Villiers. Can you have any idea how many women make claims on my days to petition? Divers women crying out in their multitudes for their slain and imprisoned husbands or kin. They will not understand how hard the sacrifices have been for anyone besides themselves."

"I don't need much of your time, my Lord." Despite knowing that he had positioned himself for effect, it was still disconcerting to face a faceless enemy and she raised her hand to shield her eyes. Slowly the back of his doublet materialised, the mundane details of leather belt and breeches making man again from Minotaur. His hair was cropped closely around his head, but unruly kinks haloed in the rays of sun had undermined his attempts at control. "I am come about my uncle."

"Of course you are." He stared sightlessly out of the opaque diamonds of the window over White Hall. Heavy rain had started to fall again, heralding the arrival of thunder clouds that rolled ominously towards them. He didn't seem to notice the guards on the main gate lean mutinously towards a tree for shelter, and he let the words roll absent-mindedly across his tongue, sounding momentarily like a serpent. "Edward Villiersss."

"My Lord, I'm told he was arrested by soldiers in Sailsbury a few days ago. There was a Quaker meet-"

"So?" The question sounded innocent, as if he could not imagine a complaint arising from this fact.

"So, my Lord, it is no secret that my uncle has committed himself to the followers of Fox and adopted the Quaker path to God," she started. "But you cannot be concerned with his preaching. You have spoken publicly of a refusal to pinch men's consciences, so long as they are Protestant."

"I have indeed," he conceded, non-committal. "But your uncle offends me not by his enthusiasms, though they are troubling. He is a traitor."

"But you must surely remember-"

"Must I?"

"He was acquitted at trial near three years ago, after Penruddock's folly. There can be no legal basis for his current incarceration."

"I don't appreciate your tone, my Lady. You presume to be a lawyer? Perhaps you come straight from years of private study at the Inner Temple?"

"No," she stumbled briefly, "I, I."

"*If* we were still training lawyers and *if* by some topsy turvy turn of events you were one of them, you would know that my government has taken great pains to support habeas corpus after the years of tyrannical detention on the whim of that foppish despot." He had finally noticed the weakness of the guards and tapped a sharp finger against the window, a warning that dereliction of duty would not be tolerated. They snapped to immediately, backs against the gate, standing a little taller, puffing their chests out a little further to catch the raindrops.

"Forgive me, my Lord," she said, hurriedly, acutely aware now that she risked being dismissed without even uttering the speech she had so carefully formulated. "I know you to be a merciful, understanding man..."

"I am. You must remember I showed considerable mercy to those convicted of the Penruddock conspiracies."

"I... You did, my Lord." She remembered the vacant look in her father's face when the usual penalty for treason was commuted to beheading. If she failed today, would her uncle share Gregory Villiers' fate? Her hands were shaking again and she pushed them between the folds of her skirts.

"And you'll understand the need for caution when our nation's security is at stake," Cromwell continued. "Charles Stuart stays safe in Breda, growing fat on the donations of his snivelling sympathisers in Europe, while those runts he left behind continue to plot for mischief. Any threat to our order demands appropriate handling."

"It is appropriate to lock an elderly man in a rat-infested hell hole," she snapped. "You could kill him..."

"Is it not appropriate to protect my realm from a popish invasion intent on restoration of the old order?" He roared back, his heavy breath misting the pains before him. She could feel her heartbeat pound as he added, more calmly: "Dr John Hewitt gave us your uncle's name. I heard it with my own ears and am given to understand important new evidence will be found."

"New evidence of what, exactly? My Lord, your interrogators went to extraordinary lengths in '55 to implicate my family. There was no evidence then-"

"Has Edward Villiers not assumed your father's role? Does he not now command the Sealed Knot?"

"The Sealed Knot died with my father."

"I am not so convinced. If there's evidence of treason to be had, my Postmaster General John Thurloe will find it. If not, then… scabrous vermin!" Silence fell as Cromwell became apparently engrossed in a new domestic drama playing out by the gate. Through the glass, it was a mime. A woman on her knees, beseeching a guard, hands raised as if in prayer, her head firmly lowered in supplication. "Extraordinary lengths… You would say I acted illegally three years ago?"

"I do not mean to imply that torture-" Tara swallowed dryly, a sickness rising from deep in her stomach. He was running rings about her and her sure footing was being sucked away; the righteous outrage she had stoked into a persuasive speech in the waiting room below was no more than quicksand. She scrabbled against the sinking feeling and the sneaking suspicion that she was expected to fall to her knees and beg like the woman outside. Her fists unclenched and clenched again. Quietly, carefully, she said: "But there are ways to apply pressure without drawing blood. Eddie was walked; he didn't sleep for days on end. He-"

"I take no offence, my child," he interrupted gently, although she still could not see his face. "Desperate times called for desperate measures. I suppose the most important question is whether one would say times are more or less desperate now than they were three years ago?"

"I don't-"

"On the one hand, of course, most of the old royalists have been persuaded to our cause."

"You do not persuade a man by killing him."

He shrugged and she flinched: "On the other hand, my Treasury coffers are empty. My army is infiltrated by enthusiasts all of sorts; my people perish with plague. Estates lay ruined. Mothers weep and sons, ignorant and impetuous, have their empty heads turned by treason. We rely in no small part for our nation's prosperity on the pagan gods determining Viking trade deals… We fight wars on fronts from Hispaniola to Dunkirk and our closest ally is France, our oldest foe. And all the while the upstart Stuart threatens to march into my country at the head of a papist army-

"Forgive me, Miss Villiers. I'm not a young man. I pray every second of every day for this country and trust that He sees the goodness in it. But still our destiny hangs in the balance. Is it appropriate to let it turn to dust?"

Tara swallowed the implication in silence. Eddie would not survive the brutal treatment a second time. Her legs felt weak suddenly and she sunk onto the ladder-back chair in front of his desk. He took an audible breath and rapped at the window again for the guard's attention, shooing the prostrate woman aside with an impatient swipe of his hand.

"Bloody vagrants," he muttered to himself. "Nonetheless, as I say, Thurloe will soon be in Exeter and will expiscate what he needs. Where exactly is your uncle now, Tamara?"

Another test, and she stumbled again: "I hear he is in the Tower."

"You *hear* it?" Cromwell seized on this nugget and turned to face her for the first time, his brows furrowed in innocent question. His eyes were bright, watery, but his skin was glazed with the glistening sheen of fever. He looked old and against his pale face, the distinctive warts seemed larger, casting dark shadows against the pallor. "You came to see me on hearsay?"

"I haven't seen him for a while." She tried hard to keep her tone level, remembering her last meeting with Eddie, bruised and broken in the hours after her father's execution. Get out Tammy, get clear of this place and do not look back. Keep your head down.

"Whyever not?" His face was a study in earnest confusion, his frown deep, forcing a line of warts to prominence on his forehead. "Forgive me. Of course, you have been with your husband."

"No," she started, suddenly aware of a large bluebottle circling the Protector's head, knocking itself senseless against the panes of the window before crawling up the wall. "I do not have a husband."

"How peculiar!" he replied casually, following her gaze and taking a moment to roll a parchment on his desk into a weapon and thwack the insect flat, a small circle of red blood marring the otherwise white wall. "But Edward Villiers is your only living family, is he not? Where are you been if not safe at home in Exeter with him?"

"I don't see what that has to do-"

"Answer me! Where have you been since the Penruddock trials?" A bushy eyebrow raised with the burst of anger.

Tara took a steadying breath; if this was not to degenerate into a disastrous shouting match, there was nothing for it but to offer up the answers. Through gritted teeth she conceded the truth: "Richmond."

"Richmond, Surrey? Not fifteen miles outside London!" A wry smile brightened his face. "Alone?"

"Yes, alone." She said, increasingly impatient. Without being conscious of it, she tugged on a loose tendril of hair and wound it about her finger, finding some measure of calm in the repetitive action. She prepared to start her speech again. "My Lord, I come to appeal to your mercy-"

"And yet," he interrupted, as if the thought just occurred to him. "In the absence of your uncle, who is your protector?"

She smiled sweetly, feeling her footing back along a path of unconvincing flattery. "Why, of course, you are, my Lord"

"So very charming." He smiled to himself in response and moved closer to stand by the chair, lifting her hand in cold fingers and raising it to his lips. Her nose wrinkled with the acrid wave of stale sweat but she met his eyes directly. "But I enquire as to your legal protector. There must be some male presence. Especially with your uncle a traitor. Apologies, of course he is not convicted, as yet."

He let go of her fingers with apparent reluctance, and sat himself down on the other side of the desk. "I hear you arrived with the Earl of Denby."

Tara started, confused by both his interest in the fact and the irrelevance of it. "The Earl of Denby was travelling in the same direction, that's all-"

"You are not wed..."

Always, my sweeting. The note was still against her heart and it burned. *Soon, I will be.* She looked away, staring into the empty fireplace to regain composure.

"My apologies, I didn't mean to embarrass you."

"I am not embarrassed."

"Good." He pulled across a wad of paper and selected a sharp quill from a feathered pot. It dipped into a ready inkpot and was tapped carefully against the side as he continued slowly: "You are certainly handicapped by Gregory Villers's legacy, but it beggars belief that you should not have been carried off by a single red-blooded Englishman in the last three years. I know of course that your father was deeply mired in the old king's court… he was advisor, yes? I admit I was curious to know what happened to his daughter after the trials. You seemed so… innocent. You struck quite a chord amongst my Devonian militia."

Tara winced. "My Lord, I know you to be a merciful, understanding…"

Cromwell waved airily, dismissing her speech, his finger scratching a spot behind his ear thoughtfully. "I consider my role to be a paternal one. Though it grieves me, I am quite incapable of jettisoning all but the most wretched of my subjects. I was born to this, ordained by God."

"Like a King?"

The question was out before she could stop it and Cromwell's brow furrowed. He would need be a fool to think that malicious whispers about him taking the Crown would not provoke rumbles, multiply dissatisfaction in the minds of radical soldiery. The Lord Mayor of London called it A Humble Petition, begging him before parliament to establish his own hereditary monarchy. He could feel the bile rising; there was nothing humble about it. Since then, the Crown had been a spectre at every damnable feast; the implicit implication that kinglessness was anarchy. *Many good men are repining at everything*, he'd warned Harry in his last letter. *Wretched jealousies are amongst us; the spirit of calumny turns all into gall and wormwood.*

He closed his eyes. *If the Lord did not sustain me, I were undone; but I live, and I shall live, to the good pleasure of His grace; I find mercy at need. Lord direct, and keep me Your servant.* True, the people of England understood their duty to a king. But he demanded universal obedience as Protector and the People of God obeyed, basking in his freedoms and justice. Why would he take a title that betrayed the whole purpose of the last decade? Besides, it was a matter for God's judgment. Providence would determine, as it did often so dispose. What fault his, if he had been preferred and lifted up amongst men? The will of the Lord will bring forth good in due time.

She was stock still and, calmly, he sat back to survey her, cool eyes running over her body, prising at the edges of her stays, following the curve of her waist and hips until his frown cleared to reveal a face set in decision. He'd been waiting to haul Villiers in for years, driven by a compulsion to tie up the frayed ends of Penruddock's uprisings. When Hewitt's evidence had finally given him enough to act, his instincts had been correct. Sooner or later, his oldest son Richard would inherit his crown, it was his fatherly duty, for the good of the Commonwealth, to ensure loyalty, to buy support that might survive the life of his own ravaged body. And to have Tamara Villiers before him… it was as if the Lord had presented him with a purse of shiny gold coin. Such currency should be wisely spent. Two birds, one stone: punish Villiers and put another able man into Richard's retinue. Well, his eyebrows conceded wryly, let those without sin cast first.

"You're a handsome woman," he said determinedly, a hint of cruelty about his lips signalling an end to niceties. "I see a fresh blossoming heart and a musical glib tongue, likely not entirely uninteresting to men. You must turn thoughts to making a match."

Tara struggled for the diplomatic language in which to wrap her temper: "With respect, Lord Protector, I can think of nothing beyond the fate of my uncle. I know you to be a merciful-"

Cromwell waved his hand in the air again, impatiently batting away the conversation he had never intended to have before settling himself down to the real business in hand. "First we will see you safely settled. Your uncle would agree that his orphaned niece should not be left to fend for herself on the meat market of marriage, eking out a living, only God knows how, from some backwater hovel. You are an heiress of noble birth, liable to be courted by all manner of desperate delinquents."

"I'm not a child, my Lord, and I am nothing to a bounty hunter. I'm a competent sempstress. I support myself well enough since my family's property was-" stolen. She stopped herself making a bad situation worse. "removed after the war."

Cromwell inclined his head. "Your portion certainly lies in desperate condition however I'm sure that the sequestration committee is not so hard-hearted as to refuse a request from me. Most disgraced royalists are granted access to at least a fifth of the rents received since the confiscation of their estates. The Villiers' estate was in Dorset, if I am right, Weycroft Hall, was it not?"

"My father refused charity."

"Your father was reckless as to your future. He was a proud fool," he snapped. "As is his brother."

"My uncle is in prison in fear of his life."

"I have told you that will be dealt with."

"You have told me nothing of the sort!"

Cromwell ignored her outburst and the scratch of drafting filled the room, quill sending spiders scrawling over the clean page with alarming speed. "I will override the sequestration Miss Villiers, but you will be overrun with suitors, tempted by the form of your…" He paused, running his eyes back across her body, "by the substance of your lucre. You must secure protection from a respectable man as a matter of urgency."

"I am not here for a bloody marriage portion!" Her temper flared now, like rum thrown on a fire, but her voice, raised in frustration, met a wall of silence.

His eyes narrowed in warning: "Calm yourself. 'Tis nothing to me. I will see to it that a match is found befitting your status. Someone powerful. You will be kept in comfort. In fact, I have the very man. Blackstone! Send Tollemache in! Now!"

Tollemache. Tara froze as Cromwell refilled his quill, tapped away the excess ink. "No, no… *no…*"

But he continued, muttering as though to himself: "Someone loyal, deserving, grateful, despite your tainted past…"

She didn't need to turn to know the brutish form, Silus Tollemache's leering face was etched on her brain, but some morbid compulsion drew her to turn. He'd been younger then, of course, but while his black hair had thinned, the thickness of neck and waist and wrist was still there. The torso was still barrel-like. Cromwell motioned for him to sit and with noisy exhalation he landed heavily on the settle behind her. He was here as an observer and his low whistle told her what exactly he was observing.

"Miss Villiers." Cromwell demanded her full attention for the business ahead. "You need male protection to negotiate your way in this world. So, what's it to be? Marriage or mistress? Or perhaps you would rather obliging

Magdalene?"

"You'd get six pence a bout perchance, as a common jilt!" Tollemache's interruption betrayed impatience. He'd been kept waiting. Her skin prickled, a shiver running along her spine. "You'll from hence to Exeter Kate's on Bow Street, eh? They too know how to dress their meat!"

Cromwell nodded at her thread-pulled gown, sharing the joke in a way that made her flesh crawl. He pulled a fresh sheet of paper in front of him and his pen scratched away: "Forgive Sir Tollemache, he has singular tastes. But I am sure he can be civilized yet, in the right hands."

"I sincerely doubt that," she hissed, all pretence of civility falling with his ultimatum. She leaned forward, bracing herself against his desk. "It's a stark choice you present my Lord, slave or whore."

"Calm yourself," Cromwell warned, with a sideways glance under hooded, rheumy eyes. "I merely understand that in today's world 'tis as hard a matter for a striking woman to keep herself honest as... as for a bee to keep from the nectar. Do not let a cross or proud disposition squander an opportunity to make a respectable wife, before you grow further in years but not in men's liking. Soon they will not welcome you warts and all."

He smiled self-depreciatingly, tapping the refilled quill again, and she was boxed in, losing the battle. Retreat. Regroup. Buy time. She started carefully: "Forgive me, Lord Cromwell. I am grateful for your interest. This is a man's world... I do at times feel myself abroad in foreign lands, unable to understand... but I simply desire at this time to-"

"If all she desires is of this length, she might soon lose her desires," snorted Tollemache, but this time he was silenced by a glare from the Protector, who had left his chair and come to kneel by her side, apparently touched by her contrition. She swallowed the flinch as he placed his large hand on her thigh, heavy fingers stroking through the fabric of her gown with a thoughtful grunt. His eyes flicked back towards Tollemache and whatever they saw there contained an understanding.

I am worth something here. It was an advantage. She pressed home: "My Lord, I'll be better able to consider my own fate when I'm assured of my uncle's."

"Of course," he said, looking up with a smile that didn't reach his eyes. "We will strike a deal. You indulge my pastoral concern. Permit me to envisage your future. In return, I will see what I can do for your uncle. This sounds fair, does it not? Now leave us, we have important matters to discuss."

He didn't wait for a response, but it didn't matter. He'd outflanked her again with only the whisper of a promise and of course she would agree to it. He stood awkwardly, pulling himself up on the ladder-back of her chair, the cool air perhaps exacerbating a rheumatism, pausing to scratch thin, dry lips across her forehead. He seemed still older suddenly and a vague limp undermined his gait as he walked back around his desk.

"Together we will ease your uncle's condition," he said, handing over a shaky permission letter granting access to the Tower. "I've made exception to my orders that Edward Villiers must not receive visitors. Go to him tomorrow and tell him the good news about our bargain. God speed," he added, moving to hold open the door for her to leave.

5. BREAK AND PREVENT THE DESIGNS AND COMBINATIONS OF THE ENEMY

To my son Henry Cromwell, Major General of the Army in Ireland
Whitehall, 29 May 1657

Son Harry

How difficultly I was persuaded to give you your commission, my son! How insistent you were to prove yourself! And now I have seen your letter writ to Mr Secretary John Thurloe; and understand you are very apprehensive of the behaviour of some persons around you.

I am satisfied of your burden. Without question, busy and discontented persons are working towards new disturbances. We are informed that the old Enemy Charles Stuart is forming designs to invade Ireland, as well as other parts of the Commonwealth; and that he and Spain have had a great deal of correspondence regarding raising a sudden rebellion.

It is necessary that you put my Forces into such condition as to answer any fall-out from this. Contact as many Garrisons as there may be in Ireland and get a considerable marching Army into the field. Put it in the most proper and advantageous place for service to break and prevent the designs and combinations of the Enemy. It is time to harden your steel.

You write of needing help. I had your captain Gabriel Moore recalled to London for reasons of national security and am resolved to execute plans for his use abroad in another direction. But know your Protector shall not be found wanting. I shall send you additional men, just as soon as some can be found who are fit for the trust.

I commend you to the Lord and rest your loving father,
OLIVER CROMWELL

6. A WAGER

Outside, heavy clouds made the dusk a leaden, velvety grey and she turned her face to the heavens to let her breathing calm and the first fat drops of rain pound against her skin, coolly washing away Cromwell's touch.

"You," she said simply, resisting the pull to turn towards the large figure leaning patiently against a column behind her.

"Me. We have a long ride; you'll want to avoid getting the lining of your cloak wet."

"Why are you still here? I met with Cromwell. The situation is settled."

"Settled?" he asked, with a careful tone of mild interest

"Surprised?" she snapped, planting her feet flat on the cobbles, eyes narrowing. What if he had taken orders from Cromwell all along? That surely made more sense, she thought. What if he had been sent to deliver her for this match to Tollemache, free of the inconvenience of Jack? "Villiers is a powerful name still. But now I no longer need it, or you."

"Don't be so bloody stubborn, Tara, let's go."

"I'm going to the Tower."

"Not now, you're not. It's late, no-one will be permitted entrance now. We'll stay in London tonight and you can go first thing tomorrow. I know an Inn in Southwark."

"I'm to marry Jack, I won't-"

"Don't flatter yourself," he interrupted with a raised eyebrow, and the coming storm left no room for argument. Gabriel had mounted Rowley and was leading her horse towards a mounting block against the Palace gate as the rain picked up its pace. She cast her eyes up to the window of Cromwell's office and saw the murky bulk of Tollemache silhouetted in candlelight. *Better the devil you know*, she muttered under her breath, leaning in to take hold of the wet saddle.

The narrow roads of the Westminster warren were largely empty, only the occasional servant scurrying between tall, misshapen houses, feet shod with iron pattens that clapped noisily on slippery cobbles. Now heavy, the rain prevented speech. It poured down from first floor overhangs and Tara peered out though the water sheeting from her cloak's heavy hood without seeing; the noise of horse hooves picking over sticky mud was enough reassurance that her mount would follow Gabriel's brooding lead.

She shivered, feeling a few cold trails of rain slide along the edges of her hairline. The interview could not have been more disastrous. She could see it now. Her speech, her hope to somehow shame the Protector into releasing his prisoner was shambolic. Bur Cromwell knows Edward Villiers cannot be killed quietly, she told herself. And at least she now knew that she had something to trade. All the while she could prevaricate on the deal with Tollemache, Eddie would live.

It was a foolhardy plan for the purchase of the most precious commodity, time. The man had surely lost the most part of his influence when the hated rule of the Major Generals was dismantled a year ago, but it was hard to be sure. What did Cromwell stand to gain by rewarding him now? And it was not clear when the trial would take place. The High Court was busy with traitors; the newssheets reported that one hundred and forty commissioners had just been summoned to deal with the backlog. How long did she have? Two months? Three? Six?

They made plodding progress along the Strand, skirting brand-new mansions, dressed in pale stone, that squatted in lawned grounds. Where developers had found opportunity, the humbler Tudor tenements had been turned to rubble, construction sites still gaping ugly black holes like missing teeth. The war was over here; the brave new world rising in glory. They passed by the Exchange shopping centre with its well-dressed double galleries; the gleaming grandness of Somerset House and into the straggling thoroughfare of Fleet Street. It was rammed with traffic from interconnected alleyways and clogged with bottlenecked carriages. At the end, St Paul's spire stabbed at the clouds with reckless hubris, inviting God's judgment. And as if in reply, the dark skies grumbled ominously while the rains fell.

Forced to manoeuvre around stalled carts and a heard of turkeys bound for the city's slaughterhouses, it took over an hour to reach St Magnus-the-Martyr. The church stood like a spiritual toll booth, funnelling hooves and heels onto London Bridge. It was a lifetime since they had passed through that morning. It was getting late now, most shops were closed or closing for the curfew. Small fires had been lit for shopkeepers to warm themselves after a full day in chill air and the bridge reeked of wood smoke. Tara peered up at the dense, teetering homes and had consciously to resist an urge to pick up the pace. Several structures still bore the scars of a fire that had broken out two decades earlier and threatened to bring the whole bridge down. Smudged walls and blackened beams told a cautionary tale. So too the freshly spiked heads of traitors on the southern bank.

Southwark Cathedral stood with more grandiose, brick-safe permanence and they passed it and the putrid tanneries to head along Borough High Street in sodden silence, until Gabriel reined abruptly into the yard of The George coaching inn. Her mount followed without question, drawing to a grateful halt as Gabriel slid from Rowley's broad back and handed his reins to a ready stable boy before moving to unbuckle the day bag from her saddle.

Sounds of laugher and argument seeped from the windows, carried on flickering lamp light out into the drizzle. It looked blessedly warm and dry, and her wet skirts slopped against the leather saddle as she lifted her stiffened leg over the pommel. "It's busy," Gabriel grimaced through the rain, moving to steady her awkward dismount. "I'll arrange separate rooms, but I suspect we'll have to share a table if you can stomach it."

The bar room was a claustrophobic stew of bodies marinating in air heavy with pipe smoke, sweat and laughter. She coughed as her lungs accustomed to the heat and Gabriel smiled to himself as he kicked the door shut behind them and left her at a small corner table by the fire to organise the rooms. If she had seriously spent three years in her own company on the edge of Ham, a cramped and common London tap house would seem as foreign as France. And perhaps on neutral soil she would be amenable to a truce.

Tara unhooked the clasp of her damp cloak to hang it beside the inglenooks and shifted uncomfortably as lazy stares skimmed the fabric of her pale dress without shame. In the whirr and din, cat calls rose from gruff throats and she craned to seek him returning, followed closely by a serving girl wearing a besotted grin and carrying two shots of whisky and two cups, ale for him and what smelt like raspberry wine for her.

He swung his leg around the stool, raising a toast to the girl's low-cut linen bodice: "Kirsty's an angel. She's juggled some patrons and found us two rooms."

Tara nodded and sat awkwardly as the girl, her eyes scanning Gabriel's face for approval, placed two trenchers on the table. They were heavy with a mutton potage that had been spooned onto flat bread sippets. The smell of thyme and parsley made her mouth water and Gabriel waited for Kirsty to light the candle between them before then sliding one plate closer to her.

"Eat," he said simply, holding out a knife, handle first.

"She really don't like you much, sir," chanced Kirsty when Tara hesitated to take it.

"Impossible. Everybody likes me." He turned to wink at Kirsty, earning a delighted giggle.

Tara frowned at the foreplay but her eyes fastened on the copy of newsletter poking from the girl's apron pocket: "May I?"

"If you want more current intelligence, you need only ask," Gabriel said quietly as she liberated the paper in response to an indifferent shrug from their waitress, who headed back to the bar with a daintier step than she'd arrived.

"Ask you for intelligence?" Tara asked mildly, her tone clearly indicating that she sincerely doubted intelligence in the literal sense was his strong suit. She read aloud to herself from the front page: "Our Commonwealth's frigats are yet riding up and down, waiting for that opportunity to attack the pretender Stuart, which I suppose they will not have in haste."

Gabriel shook his head and skewered a chunk of meat onto his knife, refusing to rise to the bait: "The coalition's ships have already been destroyed."

"How do you know that?"

"It doesn't matter." he shrugged. "But you won't read about it in your rag. It's not common knowledge, yet."

"Why...?" She started, before the realisation dawned. The Mercurius Politicus was nothing more than a mouthpiece for Cromwell; everything in it was there for one reason only. She answered her own question: "Because Charlie's troops will have ensured landing points were available before they set sail. Royalists in every port along the south coast will be ready to rise up to support an invasion."

Gabriel nodded: "And all the time the traitors think the Stuart ships are en route, they will continue to plan for such an uprising. For those furthest from London, official news that they are on their own won't reliably reach them for another fortnight or longer-"

"-and so the authorities suppress the truth to buy time," she finished. Cromwell's spies had bought themselves weeks to investigate and arrest conspirators; and any rebellion that went ahead would face the highly-trained, highly regimented new model army alone, with their backs to the clear blue sea. "Hence the rush of round-ups; the sudden interest in my uncle."

"Hence also why garrisons have been quietly strengthened all along the south coast. After the Yarmouth plotters were exposed, His Highness is not taking any chances. There's a well-armed militia in every key port, ready to quash any doomed uprising that slips through the net. Isn't our Lord Protector clever?" He nodded at her trencher, his tone softening. "Eat, Tara, while it's hot. And down this: it will bring the colour back to your cheeks."

She toyed briefly with upturning the cups, pushing back the plate and demanding to be shown immediately to a room, away from the rabble and his disgusting carousing. But she was, in truth, bone cold and hungry and, loathe as she was to admit it, the distraction of company, even his, was welcome after a hopeless afternoon locking horns in Whitehall. After a moment's hesitation, she downed the whisky, shuddering at the foul-tasting liquid before taking up the knife to tuck in.

He watched, abstractly, seeing for the first time that the girl he remembered was now a woman. Without her heavy cloak he was struck by the softness of her hair, long dark auburn waves gathered back but partly dragged forward after a day's friction inside her hood. The loose tendrils were still damp. They curled tightly around her neckline and unconsciously she twisted one around her index finger as she ate. A nervous tick, he supposed. He could faintly discern long limbs and swollen breasts beneath the simple gown. Her skin was pale, clean, pink. Her mouth looked soft and he shifted uncomfortably. He looked up and saw the blush spread across her cheeks.

"You're hungry?" she said practically, motioning towards his untouched trencher.

"*Ravenous*," he said softly, kicking himself almost immediately and cursing the warm candlelight. Most women knew the words to that particular script but she turned away and he murmured an apology, rubbing a hand over his face: "It's been a long day, I'm sorry."

"What were you doing with Lord General Fleetwood?" she asked, changing the subject with a perfunctory tone. "Is there a good reason you were recalled from Ireland?"

"I had to compose a loyal address," he said simply, his attention moving to the meat juices soaking into the dumplings. He eyed his knife with unreasonable suspicion then skewered a chunk of meat, swallowing quickly.

"A what?"

"A statement... of Loyalty to, and Warm Affection for, Oliver Cromwell as Lord Protector, who is after all empowered by the Lord and working with Him to safeguard the State." He declaimed with emphasis, chasing a dumpling around his plate. "I expressed Support for the existing constitutional arrangement of Government resting with a single Person and a parliament, together with other Provisions ensuring liberty of conscience, guarding against a perpetual Parliament, and so forth, though noting that if specific Amendments were necessary the Army would not interfere... Then I pledged continuing Support for the Protector and invited him, in turn, to depend upon the Army."

"Sounds like sycophantic claptrap," she judged, lips pursed.

"That's the general idea," he agreed with a non-committal shrug. "You may have noticed His Highness requires regular flattery. Even the City of London managed to stop counting its money long enough to present its own address. If the army holds out much longer, it'll start to get awkward."

A hint of that familiar smile curved the corners of his mouth but his expression was inscrutable. Was the general idea to be sycophantic or merely sound it? There were no more clues as he ripped apart the bread sippet to mop up what gravy was left on his plate. Did he believe it? She watched him for a moment, eyes hidden beneath falling jet-black lovelocks that shone almost red as they picked up the flames of the fire. Nothing. Tara exhaled with the wasted effort of understanding and sat back a little to take in the surroundings.

Slowly, what had initially seemed chaotic resolved into a well-ordered universe. There was an air of comforting routine about the conversations. At the next table, a maker in good humour took halfpennies to conjure rhyming verse about his cup companions. In a nook on the other side of the fireplace, two white-haired men were locked in a slow-moving game of chess. She had spent so many long winter evenings in playful combat with Ralph, in between their stints at court, before he left to fight, huddled in front of the inglenook in Weycroft Hall.

"Do you play?"

She nodded, thankful for the possibility of distraction, from the past as much as the present.

"Come then, my Lady, a truce in our war, for a battle of wits." He didn't wait for confirmation and his eyes sought out Kirsty at the other side of the taproom. The girl understood and raised an eyebrow in response, bending lasciviously forward to retrieve a spare game set from behind a row of ale barrels.

"That would hardly be fair, sir, while you're so completely disarmed."

He looked at her in surprise, then a burst of hearty laughter made him suddenly younger, carefree even. *The boy I knew.* A faint dimple formed in his cheek, the dark weight that usually clouded his eyes evaporating, and Tara started as a full set of carved pieces spilled onto the table before them. Kirsty had dropped the game, all fingers and thumbs, and was scrabbling to retrieve pieces from the flagstones before they rolled away. Gabriel bent to collect the last scattered pieces, excusing the girl with a relaxed nod, and she backed away with cherry red cheeks.

His eyes flicked up as he began to arrange the figures, hers white and his black: "Humour me then, Tara, for the sake of our childhood games."

"Knowing the kind of man you've turned out to be?"

"You thought me a god once," he teased, without rancour.

"At that time, everyone taller than me was a god," she retorted, softening incrementally. "Besides, that was before you turned into a common thief and stole my whistle."

He smiled at her warped recollection, organising the pietons into neat battle lines. "Then take pity on me – it's my birthday. Twenty-eight today. Prince Charlie and me both in fact. Did you know that?"

"No... I didn't," she said, unsure if she remembered this or not.

"The coincidence piqued King Charles' interest all those years ago and convinced Queen Henrietta there was a certain alignment of fates. Added to my father's connections and rather tenacious ambition... it was enough to get me gainfully employed at court while he took up residence as an advisor."

The gainful employment of a whipping boy. Charlie's own backside was protected by philosophy, the divine right of kings, but Tara did clearly remember wincing as Ralph told her of the consequences when the young Prince's unscholarly memory exasperated his Latin tutor. She relented: "You think you can take another beating?"

Gabriel grinned, sensing victory. "Such confidence! What a shame our more over-zealous puritan friends have outlawed a harmless wager, or this could get interesting."

"That's purely academic since I have no money. I suppose you'd say I should be grateful to the sequestration committee for the lack of temptation." She waved an abstract hand at the insignificance of wealth but stopped when she saw the start of a large, lop-sided smile.

"If you have no moral objection, we needn't play for money... I'd like to hear the end of that tune you sang so loudly for us all yesterday. My housekeeper was particularly outraged. How did it start again?

As Oyster Nan stood by her tub, to shew her vicious inclination;
She gave her noblest parts a scrub, and sighed for want of... what was it now?"

Copulation. She sighed for want of *copulation.* Head to one side, she eyed his obvious amusement as he sang sweetly, biting her lip to stop a smile spreading. He was laughing at her, but she deserved it. Besides, she was tired and the whisky was warming. There would be other battles. The poet at the next table cheered the bawdy tune, tipping his ale jug.

"Fine. But here is the deal. You win, I will tell the whole sordid tale. But I win and you… you will tell me why Ralph had me stitch FIVA onto his breast pocket of his finest doublet."

Gabriel looked up, brows furrowed with a gentle question. "You want to know that?"

She nodded, thinking back to Ralph's solemn request. Ornamenting the fine, sober black wool with her brightest onion yellow thread had earned her a resounding smack and the confiscation of her needlework box. Yet, pleading the rules of a secret society, of which only Gabriel and Charlie were the other members, Ralph had refused to tell her what her sacrifice was in aid of. Seventeen years on she was still none the wiser. It had always niggled.

Gabriel paused before holding out his hand and she laughed as he solemnly shook her fingers. "Deal."

"I probably shouldn't ask why you have such rhyme in your repertoire in any case," he mused after a while, making an opening gambit by shifting forward a black pieton onto a white square.

"You shouldn't." She echoed his move on the other side of the board, feeling a faint stab at the thought of her father's royalist cell in Devon, unsuitable company for a young lady in any normal circumstances.

"But I'm sure it makes you very popular in the Kingston taverns."

"*Alas, said she, we're soon beguiled by men to do those things we should not.*" She gave what she hoped was an enigmatic smile as she softly picked out another teaser line of the song and he laughed again, two pieces sliding along the squares in quick succession. Enabling moves, a clearing of the foot soldiers before either could start to make serious damage to the other's officer class. He moved his bishop as Kirsty loitered, busying herself wiping down a stool covered in split ale. A thankless task and a reasonably pointless one, Tara thought, given the state of the men hovering nearby. They were close to collapsing on the floor, never mind waiting for a presentable table.

Another few moves and Gabriel had pushed his last starting pieton into the field, catching Kirsty's eye as he looked up to indicate his turn was complete. Tara watched, shifting a pieton forward as his eyes flicked across their cups and the girl grinned, the colour rising again in her cheeks. Back at the board, he pushed another random foot soldier forward so she swiftly claimed the black bishop. He frowned momentarily before continuing the assault, pushing a rook amongst her heavily defended line.

"You consider yourself to have a winning way with ladies," she said, ignoring the ambling threat of his piece. A white knight flashed across the board and she took a gulp from the refreshed cup in front of her. It was a good move, from this position she had a choice of two more black officers to take, and she tried not to smile. She continued gently: "I remember, before the war, Mama said it was nigh on impossible to find an eligible courtier's daughter who didn't expect to make a match. And yet against these odds you are unencumbered. You must have some dreadful personal habits."

"Dreadful," he replied, deadpan, as he pushed his rook sideways, squaring up to take a prisoner. "Women are finickity creatures."

She raised an eyebrow, briefly unsure how seriously to take the confession. "I know you weren't raised by wolves. Perhaps you've lived alone for too long," she concluded dryly.

"So have you, or you wouldn't leave food unguarded for so long," he retorted, his knife suddenly moving in to purloin a dumpling from her plate. He laughed as she batted him back, then, after a moment, elaborated: "A man needs three square meals and a roof for a discerning love life. Ideally also a career that doesn't involve getting shot at regularly."

"Have you been with the army all this time?" she asked, frowning. The war in England ended seven years ago after all, after the Battle of Worcester, when Ralph lost his life and Charlie his country. On the victor's side, a man of Gabriel's rank might have been expected to take his place in Cromwell's court and find profitable industry without risking injury.

He inclined his head slightly, eyes back on the board. "Eight years, all told. The first two in my father's regiment ensuring Cromwell's victory in the war... the last six as a captain in Galway."

"Why didn't you go back to Hellens Manor with your father, to bask in the glorious light of the Moore's ascending star?"

"It's true, when war looked certain, Lucius was quick to jump from the Stuart's sinking ship and scramble aboard Cromwell's raft... he was set to be rewarded with a key role in the new government... but he was badly injured at Worcester... and when he died, I went... to... Hell...." He slowed as he moved a second rook sideways to endanger her queen and she glanced at him, pausing before responding, before offering platitudes of condolence. His tone lacked self-pity and his features were unreadable.

"Well, I feel for the men you command now," she muttered caustically, her white knight sweeping in enthusiastically to further up the casualty rate of his troops.

"They're more use to me than a wife," he shrugged, eyebrow raised as he took her noble but self-sacrificing horse with a lone black pieton.

"Yes, well, that wasn't my observation. Obtaining a wife and having a winning way with ladies are not the same thing at all," she chided. "No matter," she added gently, taking custody of his queen on the other side of the board. "I can save all my sisters from your foul habits."

She was momentarily gratified to see him startle at the move. He leaned back and a grin softened the contours of his face as he looked at her, creasing the corners of his eyes and making them glow with humour. Kirsty's bobbing interruptions had begun to get tiresome. She was back again to refill his tankard and he glanced up, ready habitually to reward her attention with a relaxed smile, but it fixed when he spotted behind her shoulder, at the barrels in the corner, the same large figure that had lingered behind them along the Strand and then again as they crossed the Thames at London Bridge.

He looked back to the board, completing a move at random. "The Irish have a saying," he said distractedly: "There is no feast like a roast, and no torment like a marriage."

"Am I to take comfort in that?" Tara asked softly, claiming one of his unguarded knights without fuss.

He started, admonished, then moved a last pieton recklessly forward and watched her face for a glimmer of understanding: "If there had been another way, Tara."

She snorted, wrapping up pain in a practical air as she captured his rook, and he let the matter slide, feigning interest in the last throes of the match while he weighed up how best to deal with their uninvited companion. It was too late to drag her back to Petersham, or even on to another inn. The food and the game had revived her a little, but dark smudges were forming under her eyes; she was exhausted and, in any case, they'd never get away with their horses unnoticed.

This didn't feel like another of Thurloe's lazy reporters. To begin with, he was clearly not used to subterfuge. An innocent passer-by or a practiced spy wouldn't linger in the rain; too wet… and too damn obvious. Yet this man had been waiting, on the bridge. *For him or for her?* In his late forties maybe, he was enormous. Strong. Likely a career soldier. Bulky arms flexed as he lifted his ale, bare forearms ending in large, calloused hands. His clothes were filthy but functional. There was a cutlass hanging from the sword grip clinching his belly and a long dagger glinted from the top of his boots. Beneath lank, greasy hair, his face was thunderous. He chanced baleful glances towards Tara but turned away when Gabriel flicked his gaze in the direction of the bar. *For her.* Whoever he was, whatever it was he wanted, this was personal.

"I see you're not a master tactician after all." Tara raised amused eyes, interrupting his assessment as she swooped for his last bishop and claimed victory over his king. "Check mate!"

"Congratulations," he muttered, forcing a brief smile that didn't reach his eyes.

She waited a moment, but her prize was not forthcoming. "Come on then. *FIVA.* What did it mean? Tell me! Come on, I've earnt it - tell me!"

"Not now, Tara. Calm yourself a minute-"

"You really think I need another man telling me to be calm today?" She frowned. His lips had formed a tight line and the playfulness had evaporated. She hadn't expected him to be a sore loser, but evidently any show of geniality from one of the more famous soldiers in the Commonwealth was an act. The imperious commander was back, and she was unforgivably foolish to have let her guard down. Worse, it had been shamefully frivolous, fiddling while Rome burnt about her.

"I'm going to bed," she said bluntly. "Happy Birthday."

She stood then, downed her drink, swiped her cloak and the candle and strode determinedly to the stairs. Kirsty hurriedly intercepted her, waving airy instructions for the direction of her room, and Gabriel started up to follow, but sunk back down to his stool. He picked up his cup to down the dregs in a conscious gesture of utter indifference. Kirsty was already looking back at him, and she smiled when he motioned for another drink.

If he was going to set a trap, he needed bait. ☐

7. ANYTHING YOUR HEART DESIRES

Hot, grumbling irritation propelled Tara up the narrow stairs and along a first-floor gallery, open to the night air and overlooking the yard. But by the time she had found the door at the end and slammed it behind her, the heat had dissipated and she was as cold and empty as the simple, whitewashed chamber.

There was a fireplace but no fire and the shutters were ajar. She shivered at the chill but made no move to shut out the night air and trap the smells inside. Instead she leant back against unyielding oak, closing her eyes in a futile bid to shut out drunken noise from downstairs. Not that a backdrop of rabble and laughter was likely to keep her awake, she had never been so bone weary, but there was still too much to work through before she could sleep.

Letting her eyes accustom to the faint moonlight, she put the light on top of a simple stool by the bedside. A tatty tester superstructure virtually filled the room, a somewhat incongruous grandiosity for the tavern. Then she threw herself fully dressed onto its sagging wool-stuffed mattress, hoping that the burning smell of the mutton wax candle would soon expunge the reek of its previous occupant. Inn beds were none too clean at the best of times and even the Earl of Denby's coin could only achieve so much at short notice. The bed's old rope gave little resistance. She tried not to think about the numerous dark stains spotting the aged linen coverlets as she sank into them, reaching awkwardly behind to loosen the ties of her stays.

It was a providence, she told herself practically. Furnished with Cromwell's pass she could go to Eddie first thing, taking useful intelligence from the interview: being denounced was not the same thing as being discovered. Likely the authorities were keeping him close while they hunted for evidence to corroborate Hewitt's desperate confession. The spymaster Thurloe was ruthlessly efficient, but Eddie's treason was her territory. They had been close, once, learning well enough in the aftermath of war and rebellion how to speak volumes without using words. If he could tell her something, anything, she might yet be able to help.

She closed her eyes, swallowing a sudden swell of pain at the certainty that she had to push all thoughts of Jack as far from her mind as possible. What was he doing now, she wondered bleakly... Drowning his public humiliation in a Kingston tavern perhaps, ably assisted by Ned. Mary and Joan and Bess would be eager to commiserate too...

None of this was her fault. But when this was over, when she could explain, what would Jack make of her gamble with Cromwell? *Madonna or whore*, she thought bitterly, the illusion of leverage in Whitehall evaporating. Cromwell understood perfectly: given the right choice, every woman was a whore. He had sat from the start like a corpulent spider, spinning his web in front of her eyes, puffed with confidence that his prey would tickle the signal line and wrap herself up in the sticky thread for his taking.

Would she be ashamed to tell Jack that she had offered herself on a platter to save her uncle? She would be ashamed to tell Gabriel...

Did he already know? The boy she remembered was a proud creature, quietly self-sufficient. But they had been playmates then; who was he now, other than her enemy? She honestly had no idea. She tried to think dispassionately. Becoming a man had made him superior, arrogant. Most likely he understood the rules better than most. Kirsty downstairs clearly understood them too. His mood had changed when he looked to the bar and there was nothing to see except that girl.

Good luck to her.

And yet after everything, covered in mud and reeking of wet horse... he couldn't, surely... He wouldn't... The throbbing deep in her belly spoke its intimate rebuttal and she groaned aloud before tugging the bed curtains half closed and pummelling the pillow in frustration.

It was pitch black when she opened her eyes again with a start. Of course, the candle must have burnt out after she finally drifted off into a troubled sleep. It was silent now and she was still so tired. Everything ached from the ride, limbs stiffened by the chilled air.

A hissed expletive filled the room, the sound of a shinbone hitting a hard wood corner and making the heavy bed scrape an inch across the floor.

"*Gabriel?*" She scrabbled to sit upright, the muscles in her thighs complaining strenuously even though the tiredness was instantly forgotten.

"Ha!"

Through a fog of confusion, she didn't recognise the voice at first but there was no mistaking the menace. The bed curtains were yanked back. She felt a strong hand around her ankle and screamed as it dragged her forwards into a shaft of moonlight that fell across the bed. A large face appeared and a sweaty hand clamped across her mouth. Tollemache.

Her heart was pounding and fear sliced through her spine, making her limbs uncooperative as she flailed wildly, trying to get away. Her mind somehow clawed its way back through the rush of blood to reason. She would have to get out the way he'd come in. Her eyes darted to the door and the heavy wooden bar that served as a bolt, still resting in two arms either side of the doorframe. How on earth?

"Where the Hell do you think you'd run to, Miss Villiers?" He spat angrily, pushing her back into the sagging mattress and leaning forward to pin her hands to the pillows above her head. Long fingernails dug sharply into her wrists and she squirmed, panicking as his rancid panting came closer to her mouth. Waves of sickly-sweet ale hit her. "Promises were made! You're betrothed to me, and here I find you holed up in a drinking house like a common whore, calling for your lover!"

"What promises?" Her hollow acquiescence to Cromwell's deal was supposed to progress at an entirely different pace. She glanced frantically around the gloom of the room for another escape. The window. The shutters were still ajar; he must have climbed in that way. She dragged her eyes back to his, willing speech, biding time. "No promises were made! Let me go!"

"Muddle-headed doxy, you're mine now."

"You bastard, I will never be yours-"

"Ha! You do know me then, you teasing bitch. I knew you would. It was me that broke the uprisings in '55, me. Cromwell promised me your title and your body then as reward for snaring Penruddock's snivelling traitors. He'll deliver this time.

"Two decades of loyal service," he continued, between puffs of foul air as he tried to put a stop to her struggling twists. "Two decades I've waited for the coin to retire and the wench to warm my bed. I'll not wait longer! So much for the raggabrash you ride with, eh? I might not be able to marry you in the eyes of the Lord tonight, but I'll taste the wares before I buy. Perhaps it's for the best He doesn't watch..."

He yanked apart his jerkin and ripped off his linen shirt to reveal a heavyset torso, broad expanses of pale, flabby flesh blackened with thick, rough looking hair. "In five minutes, we'll be common law man and wife."

A cold chill of understanding ran through her. Cromwell had made a bargain for Tollemache's support when her father was executed, when a titled orphan should have fallen in the confusion under the Lord Protector's care and custody. Her uncle had thwarted that deal, but Cromwell had been expecting her the moment Edward Villiers was arrested. She was far too old now for a formal wardship of course, but now she would come willingly, thinking the sacrifice a worthy one to save him. Her fate was sealed the moment she rose from the dead and entered Whitehall. *Did Gabriel know?*

"That's right, my little turtle," he leered, misreading her horror as he fumbled to open the rope knot holding his breeches in place. "It was me in '48, I liberated your castle and its mistress," he added with a sneer. "I've been there your whole life."

"Oh God." The words croaked as she was paralysed by a memory buried so deep, she'd almost convinced herself it was a nightmare. Not the Penruddock trials then. Earlier. *It was him.* The siege, during the war, when Weycroft Hall and all its inhabitants... She hissed aloud a promise she's kept inside for a decade: "I'm going to kill you."

As he laughed, her free fingers patted the stool until she grabbed at the candlestick just within reach and swung it towards him but her rushed aim was poor and he caught it easily. It turned in his hand until her twisted fingers dropped the weapon, and then he lifted it high to feign a swing at her head, demonstrating the ease with which he could do her serious damage. It landed heavily on the pillow beside her and she winced, a scream escaping.

"Go ahead and scream my lovely, the punters might as well know you're having a good time. Who knows, you might even enjoy it. Your mother did." A cupped hand slammed hard into her sex, causing her to yelp in pain and shock.

"Sir, is everything alright?" A timid knock came from the door. Silus paused a moment and craned his head towards it.

Kirsty? Tara exhaled. *If she's outside my door, she isn't...* An unstoppable wash of relief was followed immediately by the sound of her screams for help.

"Get gone... you fucking wench. Unless... you've come to join us!" Silus was bellowing in bursts now. The awkward exertion was taking its toll, and Tara took advantage of his momentary distraction. She rolled to scrabble off the bed but he caught her ankle pulled her slowly back towards him, his hollow laugh impervious to the kicks of her free foot and the twists of her body. Her skirts gathered around her waist as she was dragged closer. Then he straddled her, pushing her deeper into the straw mattress with his bulk until it creaked alarmingly, his knees pinning her arms against her body.

She could barely breath and she gasped mouthfuls of air into the top of her lungs as he ripped her partlet aside and tugged sharply down on her bodice, exposing flesh. He bent to run his sour tongue along the ridge of her breasts and upwards towards her earlobe. She thrashed wildly and, when the chance came, she bit down on his finger. He snapped it back with a yell.

"You like to fight, Miss Villiers? This is even better than I could've hoped for! Let's get the blood really pumping," he sneered, raising his hand to strike her and letting her feel his hardened cockstand jammed against her crotch. "This is for your whore mother and your traitor father and the walking dead man in the Tower. Yours will come later."

"Take your fingers off her or I will take them from you."

Tara opened her clenched eyes to catch sight of a blade glinting in the singular shaft of light. Carefully, slowly, Gabriel was motioning with his sword and Tollemache sized the threat up over his shoulder. He sighed as if this was no more than a minor irritation, but still he swung his leg over, removing his bulk from her body, drawing himself up to his full height. But before she could move free, he pulled Tara roughly towards him, holding her firm against his front like a shield, indifferent to the kicks of her bare heels against the thick leather of his boots. With one hand free, he pulled his cutlass from its sheath, which still dangled from the leather at his waist.

"Be still, my little flitter-mouse," he hissed in her ear, running his tongue along her jaw and flicking the lobe while she squirmed. "We wouldn't want to clip your wings."

Time slowed immeasurably as Tara felt her heart pounding against her wrists, caught together across her chest and held fast by thick, calloused fingers. The rank sweat from Silus' bare chest seeped slowly against her back, mixing with her own. She bit down hard on her bottom lip, trying not to let out a whimper.

"Tara."

Deceptively calm, Gabriel's voice reached through the hammering in her chest and she searched the moonlight to focus on his face. He was angry, really angry, and the brutal determination etched on his features cut her to the quick. He looked merciless. For an absurd moment she was almost afraid for the bastard behind her.

"Go upstairs to my room, bolt the door and wait for me."

She nodded and Tollemache gave an impatient grunt, tightening his hold and curling his lips into something resembling a smile. "I'll not let this bitch run. When I've let your guts around your heels, I'll mount her like a dog."

There was barely enough room between the walls to raise their swords properly but neither man was prepared to let practicality stop them. Tollemache swung first and there was a loud clunk of metal as his momentum drove hard into Gabriel's blade, sliding along to a forceful stop at the hilt cup and locking them together. She was dragged forward as he moved and felt the shudder run through his chest at the impact. She kicked back again futilely with her heels as Gabriel strained to withstand the weight of the man.

"Woof," he sneered, spitting saliva onto Gabriel's leather jerkin.

Without warning, Gabriel twisted free and, unsupported, Tollemache's sword fell heavily down, threatening his own leg as Gabriel drew his own blade back across the man's shoulder. He was rewarded with a pained grunt and Tara was shoved forcefully aside. She scrambled across the bed to the door, one arm pulling her ripped partlet back across her chest as she fought to lift the bolt on the door.

With space now between them, Tollemache recovered and swung heavily. Gabriel deflected this blow and one or two more but he was driven back by the sheer force of his opponent until the backs of his knees hit the window frame and it snatched his balance so that he toppled sideways, the wooden shutter breaking his fall as he swiftly rolled a sword length's away. Tollemache took advantage of the fall to lurch after his quarry; Tara had lifted the bolt but before she could open the door he grabbed her by her hair and she squealed as he flung her back down on the bed. She scrabbled up to the headboard, pulling her knees up to protect her chest as his attention turned back to the fight.

"Enough. I warned you," Gabriel growled.

He lunged as he stood and Tollemache misjudged the direction, his cutlass wavering impotently to the right. Then he let out an ungodly cry as the blade sliced through his left hand, peeling off three fat fingers that fell to the floor with plopping sounds. He followed them in descent, landing heavily on his knees with an expression of pure shock, clutching his damaged hand to his chest.

"Stop! I'm important!" His panicked eyes screamed defeat and he drew an awkward elbow over the beads of sweat plastering his hair across his forehead "I can get you anything... anything you desire."

"You no longer have anything I want." Gabriel raised his sword high but he caught Tara's eyes, wide with fear and horror, and something stopped him bringing it back down into the notch between the man's neck and shoulder blade. He grunted in frustration as he lowered his weapon, shaking his head in a moment of disbelief.

"Wise move!" Tollemache spat saliva on the floor. "I am Silus Tollemache."

Gabriel shook his head with a bitter smile. It was a well-known name; Silus Tollemache had enjoyed dizzying control of the West Country's militia, taxes and morality for a time. His aunt had written about the shuttering of playhouses, the new laws against drunkenness, sexual licentiousness, even swearing-

"Fucking listen to me! I'm a Major General! I have the Lord Protector's confidence!"

The Tollemache his aunt described used any miserable crime or petty grumble to offer trial by fight in the street. Facing a traitor's death at the hands of his tightly controlled court, most would opt to take a beating and pray that it was over soon. At first, Cromwell called men like him a necessary evil in the frontier lands, awash as they were with the King's supporters, but the violence was finally too much even for the Lord Protector.

"The Major Generals were dismantled," Gabriel said quietly. "Perhaps you didn't get the message."

A hiss eased out under Tollemache's breath. "The Villers wench is mine, by order of Cromwell. She pledged herself."

Gabriel snorted in disbelief but his eyes flicked briefly in question to Tara's pale face and then to the door as it opened an inch. The innkeeper peered gingerly around the frame, floundering at the sight of Tara in ripped undress and Tollemache on the floor, half-crawling half-sliding to back himself into a protective corner. His eyes widened as the large man blanched, suddenly vomiting the ale-swilled contents of his stomach down his naked chest. He cried out as the regurgitated alcohol met the blood seeping between his remaining fingers. and the innkeeper turned his appeal direct to Gabriel: "This is a respectable and genteel establishment, sirs. I don't need a hurly-burly-"

"Your name, sir," Tollemache panted.

"Gabriel Moore, Earl of Denby."

Tollemache's eyes flickered. Ireland was something of a pet project for His Highness and everyone knew of the brutal victories across the sea, hard won by the swords of Fleetwood's men, hard preserved those of Henry Cromwell. He'd underestimated the defender of Villiers' virtue. But then his own brutalities were closer to home, and he had the weight of the Lord Protector's will. "Don't be a damned fool, Moore. Cromwell promised me this wench. She's nothing to you, and you come between a man and his betrothed at your peril, when the union is blessed from such heights."

"You're too late, Tollemache, she's already my wife."

Gabriel's calm response cut through the fight more effectively than his blade. He sheathed his sword, bent down to the bed and scooped Tara into his arms as if she were no more than rag doll.

"You won't leave my sight again," he promised, although something in the tone made Tara doubt the words were for her benefit. Then he paused at the door, where the innkeeper's wide eyes were busy assessing torn bed curtains, flapping, smashed shutters, an overturned stool and a mattress smeared with blood. "Send the bill to Whitehall."

His scent was a deep musk, mingling with the sweat of the fight and leather, and she let herself breath it in as he strode along the gallery and up another flight of stairs, letting it wash away the stench of Tollemache. Gathered into his solid heat, she buried her head into his neck for fear sobs of relief would rack her body. Strobing shafts of moonlight from the balcony caught his features but the hard lines of jaw and nose gave nothing away.

Gabriel's room on the second floor was a mirror image of her own, but Kirsty had been a little more diligent in her duties. A low fire was lit in the grate and a candle burned by the bedside, casting a gentle pool of light. He sat down at the foot of the bed and tugged at a blanket, ready to set her on the mattress and wrap her with it, but she stayed curled tightly on his lap.

The vulnerability took him briefly by surprise and he started awkwardly. "You're a damnable fool... I don't know what exactly you promised Cromwell this afternoon but I can guess. How could you be so bloody stupid?"

The words had immediate effect. Pushing hard against him she fell awkwardly out of his lap and staggered to the opposite wall, yanking together the edges of her torn bodice and hugging her hands tightly around her chest. Her narrowed eyes flashed: "How dare you! I made no promises! I had to get him to consider my uncle's case."

Gabriel laughed at that, but there was no humour in the sound. "To *consider* it? You traded an empty promise of shuffling paperwork for an entire lifetime as brood mare to that hulking toad? Jesus Christ, you certainly drive a hard bargain, Tara, Cromwell didn't stand a chance!" He shook his head, incredulous.

"It's none of your business what I said, or didn't say. My options were pretty limited. I'm on my own and-"

"You are not on your own!" He shouted back in frustration: "*I am here!*"

"What earthly use would I have for you?!"

He raised an eyebrow with irritating calmness to remind her exactly what use he had just been: "I took you to Whitehall to weep and petition. That is doing your duty by your kin, just like every other woman in that blasted waiting room. This? God's blood, how could you be so damn stupid, to dangle yourself before that bloodthirsty brute. You're not half as clever as you think you are. Once you're his wife, who do think can help you then?"

"It won't come to that. I was buying time. I won't be his wife."

"By God if you were my wife, you'd know it," he muttered, exasperated, springing up from the mattress to pace towards the window.

"Don't you dare talk to me like that," she spat. "I am pledged to Jack and we've done a good deal more besides-"

"Witnesses?"

"No! Of course not…" Tara tailed off. Without ceremony or proof of consummation there could be no binding commitment. Yet.

"Well then," he retorted sardonically, "as far as Tollemache is concerned and shortly the Lord Protector too, that's exactly what you are. Mine."

"Enough!" she yelled, viciously forcing the hair back out of her face so that her words would hit its target unimpeded. "Whatever this is, it ends now. I have tolerated your company for no better reason than… than *shock*, but I will not have you near me another second."

"Fine! Then keep the room. Tollemache can come back to finish the job in more pleasant surrounds."

"Isn't that why you brought me here in the first place?"

"What?" He roared at her then, temper finally snapping as he ploughed shaking hands back through his hair and backed away. "Don't you dare think for one minute that I have anything to do with that bastard. I just risked my life to pull him off you."

She squealed in frustration but in the silence that followed an errant thought began nagging for her attention. "You wouldn't be able to hear anything in my room from here. Why did you come for me, anyway? And how did you get in?"

Gabriel flinched. "You're on my watch, Tara, it's my job to know."

"That's not an answer."

He glanced at her then, the hint of a pout on her lips and chest heaving with barely controlled anger, and dropped his head: "He followed us from Whitehall. He was in the tap room. Your room is above a lean to and I had a hunch he'd make use of it, come in through the window. After you went to bed I waited in the courtyard for him to make his move. I had to-"

"A *hunch*? You dare to lecture me on stupidity and all the time you used me as bait!"

The fuse was burning bright and her anger flared, mingled with incredulity. There was no mistaking the brute's intention or his talent for violence; even if he had wanted to stop him, how could Gabriel be so damned confident he would be able to? Her mind paced through the alternative outcomes, coming unstuck on a certain dark fate each time. Her one bargaining chip for Eddie spent because the Earl of Denby's self-righteous swagger took the gamble. Once news escaped of her undoing, she would have nothing left. Even Jack. Assuming she could still avoid being shackled to the monster, it wasn't possible he would still want her, already used by it.

"... completely different!" Gabriel was shouting, defensively, when she focused back on him. "That little scene was going to play out sooner or later. I had to bring it to a head where I could control it. Let's just be grateful I'm better at this than you are, lying on your back with your legs spread wide and your skirts around your waist!"

Tara strode towards him, her nose an inch from him as she yelled back: "You fucking lobcock! You had to play the damn hero but what if, what if he'd fastened the shutters behind him? What if you couldn't have got in? Everything, ruined, *everything!* I have no other cards to play, nothing else they want!"

"Why you?" He asked suddenly. "What is it about you Tara? You know that bastard, don't you?"

"Tollemache arrested my father," she said, backing and turning away, her anger dissipating in the shock of memory and a shiver of chill running over her skin. "After the Penruddock uprisings in Cornwall, he was in charge of rounding up conspirators."

"It's more than that," he insisted.

"Not enough for you that my father was beheaded on his paltry evidence?" She glanced back over her shoulder. "He ravished my mother and had her hanged for witchcraft. Enough now? This is what your war did... it let loose monsters and your Lord Protector raised them up."

"My God...," he whispered. Adrenaline still pumped through his chest and it mingled uncomfortably with the tenderness rising beneath. "You're shaking-"

"I'm fine."

"I meant it," he said gently, only faintly aware that his normal detachment was abandoning him again, as swiftly as it had when he watched Tollemache shift his bulk in through her darkened window. "You're not on your own."

"No... not you. I won't..."

He turned her towards him, his long fingers tilting her chin so she could see the promise in his eyes. "Nothing will hurt you while I'm here."

There was no tentative question of forgiveness, and no toleration of debate. The gentleness in his voice didn't mask the undercurrent of command and hot tears spilled across her cheeks. "I'm not crying."

"You're cold and you're exhausted, but you're safe now." He pulled her into his arms with a whisper and despite the warring in her brain her body was ready to surrender, calmed by the heat of his touch. "Ssshhh. I have you."

Just this once. Slowly, incrementally, her body relaxed, letting him brush away the tears with the pad of his thumb. His hand slid to the nape of her neck and he pulled her in beneath his shoulder, pressing her against the solidity of his chest until the strong and regular beat of his heart calmed the noise and the fear in hers. His hand moved in a slow stroke of comfort down her spine.

Just this once. She was so tired. *Just this once.* They stood entwined together for some time until her breathing slowed, and finally she let herself be lifted and laid down on his bed, watching through closing lashes as he lay heavy blankets across her.

"Sleep," he urged in a whisper, bending down to lay a chaste kiss on her forehead. "You're safe, Tara. FIVA,.. we meant it to stand for *viam inveniam aut faciam*. I will find a way or I will make one."

He watched the corners of her mouth curl with the faintest hint of a sleepy smile. As a boy, Ralph was obsessed with the alp-crossing exploits of Hannibal. Inspired, the boys swore oaths to each other and selected his defiant words for the motto to their secret society. They tattooed "FIVA" wherever they could, the bastardised acronym was testament to their seriousness in the face of any parental oppression.

They were bloodthirsty would-be warriors then, with no sense of the true cost of such an oath. He understood it now though, and the simple truth of it was like a brutal kick to his stomach. Two days ago, the image of Tamara Villiers was buried deep, no more than a stubborn, impetuous child. And now? A stubborn, impetuous woman was a dangerous thing. But so was duty, and his oath was already pledged. He hovered by the bed a moment, watching until her breathing slowed to a steady tempo, then sat down silently in a high-backed chair in front of the fading fire.

* * *

Clanging and banging rose from the kitchen early as the innkeeper's wife started to prepare for the new day. Gabriel stifled a groan. Reaching out a hand to rub the back of his neck he shifted his balled cloak against the hard chair, briefly wondering if it would be possible to find a new position for another few minutes of precious rest. He had slept with a soldier's wakefulness, one ear hearing every creaking floor board in the corridor or grunting exchange of words in the courtyard, ready subconsciously to sort the sounds into neat categories: immediate danger, potential threat or other man's problem.

If he were sensible, Silus Tollemache would be holed up somewhere licking his wounds, but he might just be stupid or determined enough to come back for his prize. If he came, he would not come alone now, and Gabriel wasn't at all convinced that the brute believed his lie about their marriage. He still wasn't sure what possessed him to say that. It was a bad move tactically. At best it made him a target for Tollemache, at worst Cromwell would question his loyalty. He'd have done better to have run the man through.

He would have, without a moment's hesitation, if he hadn't seen the fixed terror in Tara's eyes. She didn't understand that this wasn't a chess game, the damn fool. She'd been right, or course, in assessing exactly where her value lay to the men who set the rules, she'd been schooled in that from the beginning. But was she really hopelessly ignorant of the limits of that power, of the line past which a woman's greatest asset is her utter undoing? Real lives, real blood, real men. He'd seen many kill for a lot less than the promise of quim and cosh. And Tollemache had a decade's hatred burning bright within him.

He glanced over, contenting himself again that she was still in the bed, still deep in slumber. Even unconscious she was stubborn, her body curled into a tight ball, but her hair refused to comply. It drifted out softly across the pillow, flashing streaks of auburn with the slowly rising sun. He closed his eyes against a desire to touch it, to run the silken threads between his fingers. His body ached to cover hers. Not with lust. Not *entirely*, he mentally conceded. It was something more elemental, this desire to draw her in and protect her physically, to hide her beneath his torso, to wrap her up in his limbs. To find, finally, some value in his strength. Some justification for it.

Quietly, he pulled kindling from a basket and prodded the embers of a fire into life. In the faint dawn glow, the night-time fight seemed like a dream. He'd risen once or maybe twice when she'd cried out in her sleep, but daylight made it possible to rationalise the savage need to protect her. There was a history between them, a fondness for the child she once was. His love for her brother. Any man would flinch at the idea of Silus Tollemache owning any woman soul and body. But the way she looked at him, held onto him when her guard was down. It weighed heavier than he expected.

He shook himself mentally. His duty was clear. Hyde's instructions were straightforward. Use his Villiers connection to find a way to the West Country rebels. *Find a way or make one.* He grimaced. As secret societies went, the Sealed Knot was a hopelessly complicated tapestry, a myriad cells and chains of command cross-woven with warps and wefts of impenetrable codes and ciphers, multi-coloured with different hopes and schemes. From his cell in the Tower, the traitor would not breath a word to betray his men. But out here, in the open air, this fierce and frustrating woman might speak volumes without ever opening her mouth. He just had to listen carefully.

Like every other command he'd ever followed, he would carry it out. Preserve his distance. Whatever had now to happen between them in the short term, Tamara Villiers' fate was, ultimately, irrelevant. *It had to be.*

At last satisfied that the room would soon rid itself of the chill, he took a deep breath, stood up and stretched with a yawn, letting his sword clatter against the side of the chair, hoping to rouse her without moving closer. ☐

8. FIRE WILL SPREAD

Tara woke with a start. In the paralysing confusion between nightmares and reality her heart pounded and she clawed through her brain for an explanation. *Jack*. He had attacked her. No. *No*. He *saved* her. *No*. Gabriel...

It was morning, and she was in his room. Her chest slowly relaxed as she surveyed his broad back. It must be early, but he was fully dressed already, prodding at the remnants of a fire, his dark hair loosely gathered back.

She was dressed too, although her partlet had long since slipped beneath her shift, necessitating some fast, undignified foraging down her front. A quick inventory: her stays were loose, her stomacher askew and her right sleeve ripped in one, no, two places. Surprisingly little damage, she thought practically as it came back to her: the journey, the rain, Silus Tollemache. Her wrists hurt. She made to sit up and winced, her thighs and backside throbbing from the long hours in the saddle.

"The rain's stopped. We'll breakfast on the road. Be downstairs in ten minutes."

She frowned at the formal tone but he'd already left, swinging his cloak around his shoulders and pulling the chamber door closed behind him. So, the evening's truce was over; the hostilities could re-commence. He was right about one thing. She was a damnable fool.

She eased her stiff legs over to the sideboard, swiped her hair into a loosely gathered top knot and splashed ice-cold water from an earthenware jug into a bowl, scooping it up to wash the night from her skin and with it any remaining trace of Tollemache. The small leaded window overlooked the yard and she could just see the horses being saddled under Gabriel's terse direction. There was no cloth; she dried her face on her skirts, pulled the ties of her stays tight in angry jerks and went to join him.

"I'm going to the Tower of London. In all likelihood Cromwell will revoke my pass when he learns what happened here last night. I must see my uncle."

"Of course," Gabriel interrupted calmly as he checked the girth strap on his saddle.

"Then we part ways-"

"We'll go straight to the Tower now; it wouldn't be wise to wait." He sounded infuriatingly reasonable as he swung his leg over Rowley's back and drew up his reins. "I don't want Tollemache and his men to find you alone."

"Nor *you* alone, I imagine," she muttered as she climbed the mounting block, grimacing as she stretched her leg out over her own mount.

The Tower gatekeeper accepted the Lord Protector's personal letter without any glimmer of interest save a frank assessment of her likely solvency under one raised eyebrow. He took in her dress, once fine, now grubby and ripped. Still unsure, his eyes flicked towards Gabriel, leaning casually back against the outer wall. Apparently impervious to wastage, his jerkin and breeches still looked smart, a respectable and expensive black.

The guard extended an open, grubby hand: "The Governor Sir John Barkstead requires acknowledgement and begs to remind you that the prisoner owes for his board and keep at 18d a week."

Tara cursed Gabriel's continued presence under her breath but fished about in her placket for her purse, counting what coin she had separated out for immediate use into the man's grimy fingers. At last satisfied, he gave a barely perceptible nod to no-one in particular and from a darkened doorway in the corner tower of the keep, a pale, bald-headed, key-rattling warden emerged, blinking in the morning sunshine and stretching out a yawn.

"Only you." The gate guard grunted in dismissal of Gabriel. "Your friend here can wait outside."

She followed the warden, whose growth seemed stunted by a lack of sun, without looking back. And once inside the thick stone walls, the temperature dropped immediately. Lichen made the limestone drip and the floor slippery. She blinked, waiting for her eyes to adjust to the darkness, and grabbed at a slide of rope running down the centre of spiralled stone stairs, focusing determinedly on the practical concern of not losing her footing in the inadequate slippers. Still, she couldn't shake the notion that in their twisting descent, down into the damp and disorientating bowels of the Tower, it was as if they'd slipped through the intestines of a corpse.

Two, perhaps three storeys below street level, the uneven steps stopped and the warden started along a claustrophobic passageway, dimly lit by torches balanced in rusted iron holders. Shivering, she covered her mouth from the stench with a fistful of her cloak, tripping behind the man as they passed a series of cave-like dungeons. Then, finally, they stopped, and the warden motioned towards a particular darkness, handing her a candle before shuffling back.

"Uncle Eddie?" She pushed past the guard, impatient for her eyes to make out the features of a hunched figure on the ground. "Jesus, you look awful."

"They took my hat," he shrugged helplessly as she dropped to her knees beside him, feeling the damp cold of the stone floor through her skirts. A hat would hardly help matters; if anything, it was likely to have made them worse. With the stubborn habit of hat-wearing and the peculiar attachment to old patterns of speech, the Quakers were marked out for radicals. They made people uncomfortable. They made them angry.

"Eddie, you'd still wear your hat in unsuitable places? You know I wasn't talking about your shiny pate." She tried to sound casual, and leant forward to place a kiss on his bald head, feeling the skin like parchment. "Have you enough to eat? To drink? I will try and get you moved, they can't keep you here, you'll catch ill–"

"Oh, Tammy," he laughed hoarsely, giving a dreamy smile. "A man condemned to execution need hardly fear the ague. Wait patiently upon the Lord, whatsoever condition you be in. Here, come, pray with me, Tammy."

He took her hands in his and she could feel the chilled, slack skin draped across bones that tightened silently on her fingers. He began to murmur the Lord's Prayer.

"Eddie," she whispered, trying not to let her impatience taint his quiet devotion. "There's no evidence. Listen to me: you're not condemned. They have nothing. Just don't antagonise them. If they take you to trial, please, don't question the court's authority. Answer them freely, tell them you've nothing to hide."

"Look at me, thou art a clever girl, but you know these usurpers have no authority without the King. The Lord Protector is a tyrant who barely consults his own sovereign parliament..." Edward Villiers opened his eyes slowly and raised a wry brow, his pinprick pupils widening in the weak candle light.

"The guards tell me they've arrested Sir Henry Slingsby, John Mordaunt," he added quietly and Tara stiffened. According to the Mercurius Politicus, those men had been arrested, tried and sentenced to death. It was possible news hadn't yet reached him in the bowels of the Tower and she couldn't bring herself to say it.

"I am not alone, Tammy. Even Dr John Hewitt is somewhere in this place," he continued. "Dost thou remember him from Hampton Court before the war? Thou were a child."

"The King's old chaplain, yes, I know. Eddie it was him. The wretch gave them your name, he-"

"Don't judge him harshly Tammy," Edward interrupted gently with half a smile. "He knew nothing of-"

"That doesn't make it any better!"

"Cromwell's lapdogs can be very persuasive. No, don't fear, it means it doesn't matter, to the bigger picture. But my enemies will not be made fools of again. Well, they're welcome to this hatless carcass. Let His Highness revel in the moment; let him mistake a symbolic victory over old bones for a real one over the hearts of England-"

"It won't come to that Eddie," she said, willing him to lower his voice. She checked the door. "He told me he'll see what he can do for you."

"Thou hast seen him?"

"Of course. I went to him yesterday, as soon as I could after I heard you'd been arrested. He is your best chance-"

"And thou art here now. Traitors are not permitted social calls. So, he was waiting for thee..." Edward hung his head with the implication: "What did it cost thee?"

"Nothing," she lied.

"Like Hell it didn't," he barked suddenly, his dry throat cracking and his chest rattling with exertion. "Oh dear God, I told thee: stay clear, Tammy! After thy father died, I told thee to hide, to go where thou could be safe. Not to draw attention to thyself! Have thou any idea what he plans for thee? What he threatened Gregory with, all those years ago?"

Tollemache. Yes, she had some idea. And forewarned might have been forearmed. She was getting sick of being kept in the shadows. Tara clenched her fists to stop them shaking. "Odd's fish, Eddie, I can't hide forever. I am not so feeble as to stay quiet when they threaten you. I had to go to him and petition-"

"Who brought thee here?" he asked, eyes narrowing.

"I made my own way," she replied awkwardly. So, it was a lie. Gabriel hadn't met him outside Reading. Eddie hadn't begged him to stop her wedding; hadn't expected her to fall under the Earl of Denby's generous protection. She'd managed that on her own accord, she realised bitterly.

Edward thought a minute, drawing himself up and looking at her with a keen intensity as if burning the image onto his brain. Then he pulled her hard into his feeble frame, and it shook from the dry sobs that racked his chest afresh. "It's good to see thee again, Tammy, it truly is. But I promised thy father... I promised to keep thee away from this madness. What have I done? May God forgive me."

"What madness? What do you mean?" she whispered urgently into his whiskered cheek, half an eye flicking back over her shoulder to where the guard waited on the other side of the door. In addition to extortion, Sir John Barkstead was highly prized for his vigilance. She could hear Cromwell's self-satisfied boast now at her father's trial: *There never was any design on foot but we could hear of it out of the Tower.*

"Plymouth. 10 June." She heard a flash of quiet satisfaction in his voice and felt a cold finger of fear run up her spine. "It's time, Tammy. Fire will spread to Falmouth. Lyme Regis. The West Country will welcome its King, line his path to London. Your father's men are ready mobilised in Portsmouth, in Southampton…"

"No," she hissed. "Eddie, the Spanish ships have been destroyed, there'll be no invasion to support them. Do you hear me? Charlie's not coming. The men, they're on their own. The uprising can't go ahead."

His eyes misted with sudden understanding and he froze.

"Thurloe's to Exeter any day," she added hurriedly. "He is looking for evidence. Is there anything in your house to betray you, or them?"

The old man nodded imperceptibly against her shoulder: "Messages I hadn't sent yet…"

She uttered a cry of frustration as the heavy door creaked open behind them. A disembodied grunt echoed in the darkness: "Time!"

"I am to marry, Eddie," she said, pulling back, her voice breaking with the effort of ending conversationally.

"Good God, no, not Toll-"

"His name is Jack. He is a good man. When this is over, when you are free, we will all three live together."

White brows drew together as a new guard pulled on her arm: "That's it, time I said."

"Forgive me Tammy, first you must sing to the sparrow-"

With a grunt of irritation, the guard yanked her away then and pushed Edward roughly back against the wall, silencing any further attempt at speech: "Enough, I said time! Out, girl."

9. INSURRECTION IS INTENDED IN THIS NATION

To the Mayor, Aldermen and Common Council of our City of Plymouth
Whitehall, 30 May 1658

I pray uncypher this yourself.

Trusty and well-beloved, we greet you well.

The enclosed letter came by chance to the hand of my Postmaster General John Thurloe. It was intended for the pretender's court in Brussels, and you can see therein that persons in the Cavalier party are designing to put us to blood.

It hath pleased God to shine light onto their plans. The Enemy intends to invade us very suddenly from Flanders and at the same time an Insurrection is intended in this Nation.

We are taking the best care we can, by the blessing of God, to obviate the danger. We have Twenty-two Ships of War in Ostend to protect the coast. Given intelligence that the Sealed Knot have specific designs on your City in the coming weeks, we could not but warn you.

Take heart. The rebel leaders of the Sealed Knot shall all soon be secure. John Hewitt and Edward Villiers, both great men for them, are awaiting justice in the Tower. I am a civilised ruler, without recourse to the bloody threats of the Stuarts, however I am not without persuasion. They will soon reveal their plans and the People of God shall prevail.

Until then, do what you must. Put arms into such hands as are true and faithful to us and this Commonwealth. Let us hear that you have receipt of this Letter.

I rest your very assured friend,

OLIVER P

10. TO HAVE AND TO HOLD

Gabriel reined up Rowley to a halt in front of St Peter's church and when her own mount stopped abruptly behind his cue, she eased her stiff leg over its back and slid ungracefully to the ground. Less than ten minutes' walk and she would be back where she belonged, making amends to Jack over a late lunch, making plans to get to Exeter first thing in the morning. She slid the reins over flickering ears and offered them up.

"We're done."

"That's the most you've said to me in hours," he mused, slipping out of his saddle and hooking both sets of reins over a wooden stake by the church gate. He glared at two approaching villagers until they thought better of attending to their spiritual needs and turned back towards the common.

"Humble apologies I've not been sufficiently entertaining," she muttered dryly. "I've been a little preoccupied. I'm going home now."

"We'll go home shortly. First we must marry."

"I assume that's a joke," she snorted, turning to walk away. "You must be completely insane."

"I must be," he said, without humour, reaching out as she passed to take her elbow, forcing her to jog awkwardly aside while he pushed open the church door and marched in, scanning the space. It soon echoed with a barked "Out!" and a lone woman, formerly lost in contemplative prayer on the back pew, muttered her reckless irritation as she passed.

"What the Hell?" Tara wrenched her arm free and hissed up towards his shoulder: "Stop it, Gabriel. I'm serious."

"So am I."

"I'm going to marry Jack. And he's less half a mile away, wondering what on earth has happened to me."

"Fielding!" Gabriel yelled towards the empty chancel, before turning to look directly into eyes that flashed defiance: "Even Ludlow will manage to work out what has happened to you once he sobers up. You do remember last night? The result of your damn fool promises to the Lord Protector?"

"I told you. That is between myself and Cromwell." A small fluttering of panic beat its wings in her chest. *Dear God, he was serious.* "It has nothing to do with you."

"It has everything to do with me–"

"Because of your damn fool lie to Tollemache? I do not need you."

Tension radiated as he sought to keep check on his temper. He ran a hand back through his loose hair. "Jesus, Tara, Jack Ludlow? That dalcop couldn't protect you from a rabbit, let alone Silus Tollemache, especially now the brute has Cromwell's betrothal rattling around his thick skull. He wouldn't stand aside just because you've made hay with the village idiot."

"That's our problem, not yours." It sounded hollow even to her own ears.

"He thinks you and I are wed. What do you think he'll do if he finds out we're not? You can't hope to hide again."

"I hid well enough before."

"*I* found you," he shrugged. "And I think you know exactly what would happen. Thurloe wouldn't even need to fabricate a charge; the discovery of his poaching is hardly beyond the wit of his agents."

Tara sunk onto a pew, burying her face in her hands. Tollemache would hound them and have Jack arrested. He would be hanged. After a moment, she looked up and registered him, still talking.

"...you wanted to play at politics without a thought as to the consequences!" He was pacing, hollering again for the minister.

"You can't force me to marry you," she said quietly.

"I'd prefer not to... but the law only prevents forced marriage for the contents of a woman's purse," he replied dryly. "And without Cromwell's whispers to the sequestration committee, which I doubt very much he'll remain inclined to make after last night, you, Lady Tamara Villiers have no purse, let alone anything of substance to put in it. Hell's teeth, think on it," he added, his tone softening as shuffling finally came closer and the curtain to the transept swept open. "Just think quickly."

"Sir! A marvellous surprise to be graced again! You need me, sir?" Fielding approached apologetically, as if afraid to enter his own dominion. Under unkempt white hair he threw a hopeful smile at Tara, clearly unsure whether he was about to be lauded or castigated for his handling of her last wedding. "My dear, are you quite recovered?"

She started angrily: "Have you seen Jack-?"

"My Lady, he is coming-" .

"Marry us, Fielding. Now."

The Minister frowned, cautiously. "My Lord, that would be highly irregular," he started, before his attention was pulled back by Tara's persistence.

"Coming where?" Her hand found his forearm: "Jack, Minister, you said he is coming..."

"To terms, my dear, I believe, with recent events. He was mightily discomforted by your abandonment but..."

"I didn't abandon him!"

"Unusual but not impossible," interrupted Gabriel firmly. "Banns have been read."

"Not *your* banns, my Lord," Fielding pointed out with a nervous shake of his head, adding quickly when he saw the determined set of the Earl's face: "Although of course that's nothing my parish clerk can't rectify. There's an entry of sorts in the register... and. after all, all things are possible with God."

"But I do not-"

"Hell's teeth Tara," Gabriel said quietly, cutting off her protest. "There isn't much time before the news is out. It must be now. Now."

"Have you witnesses?" asked Fielding hopefully.

Gabriel raised an impatient eyebrow. "I will barely have wits by the time you've done your job. Put some blasted crosses on the page. This will be done now in the eyes of God. Name your fee and remember this contract is ordained as a remedy against sinful fornication."

Tara spluttered and Fielding turned a bright shade of puce, pulling out a handkerchief to dab at his shiny forehead. He nodded, darting back into the transept to extract his Book of Common Prayer and, recovering his delicate equilibrium, balanced his spectacles on his nose with considerable solemnity. With the heavy, leather-bound tome in one hand, he turned the pages awkwardly to the correct service.

"Dearly beloved, we are gathered..."

"Fielding," said Gabriel warningly, and the Minister hurriedly rustled through a few more pages before starting again.

"Gabriel Moore, Earl of Denby, do you take this woman for your lawful wedded wife? Will you love her, comfort her, honour and keep her in sickness and in health; and fors-?"

"I will."

"Will you worship her with your body and endow her with all your worldly goods, as long as you shall live."

"Until death do us part."

Fielding nodded and took a deep breath before turning to start afresh: "Tara-"

"Tamara Angela," corrected Gabriel bluntly.

"Tamara Angela Rivers."

"Tamara Angela Villiers."

Fielding glanced at Gabriel with an apologetic shrug. "*Tamara* Angela *Villiers*, will you take this man for your husband? Will you obey him, serve him, honour and keep him in sickness and in health; and forsaking all other to keep yourself only unto him, as long as you both shall live?"

There was no sound save for her shallow snatches of breath. Gabriel was right. Nothing felt real, but he was right. Jack would be on the gallows. She glanced up at the myopic minister, still anxious above all else to please the Earl, and nodded imperceptibly.

It was enough. When Fielding enquired unhopefully about a ring, Gabriel retrieved a plain silver band from a small pocket in his jerkin, slipping it onto her third finger and ignoring her distracted frown. Then, finally finding the book too awkward to hold, Fielding abandoned formality and hazarded a mumbled guess at his final speech about no man tearing anything asunder. He took both their hands, holding them together as firmly as he dared, to mark the end of the proceedings.

"A hymn perhaps?" he added, a little overly optimistically.

Gabriel and Tara replied in unison: "No,"

"A prayer then, by way of blessing: Our Father, who art in Heaven, hallowed be thy name…"

Gabriel's footsteps echoed as he walked ahead down the aisle, pausing only to pull a purse of coin from his cloak and drop it noisily into the collection tray.

She followed numbly as Gabriel strode up the entrance steps and through the grand front door without looking back at her. The black and white floor tiles of the entrance hall made her head spin.

"I would be alone."

"Wortley! Have Ann make up the blue room for my wife." The wiry servant from the day of her wedding, her *real* wedding, materialised from shadows beneath the stairs. He stepped forward with a nasty grin and bowed.

"I hope you can be happy here." He didn't look at her, but Gabriel's tone softened once Wortley had left for the kitchen. His fingers traced papers on the hall table, his head bowed in apparent absorption, heralding a return to the normality of the day.

"Happy?" The word bounced through the empty space, gathering momentum until it brought a wave of anger to crash back across her chest. "Two days ago, I was minutes from an entire lifetime of happiness and then you arrive! Hell's Teeth, my happiness is irrelevant… you bastard roundhead, you stole my country and now you've snatched my future. You killed my brother; your people murdered my family. Now my uncle is on trial again for his life and you've just chained us together like two dead carcasses and, and you stand there as if you- ah!"

He sprung forward without warning, strides eating the distance between them, and her heart pounded as he stopped before her. His voice had lowered to little more than a growl: "Enough, Tara. Three days ago, I was contemplating a simple life of estate management but your uncle pleaded with me to extract your worthless arse from marriage to a feckless butcher."

That lie again. It was obvious in the Tower that Eddie knew nothing about Jack, but someone did. Someone knew where she was, someone had found her before she revealed herself to Cromwell in Whitehall. Whoever was giving Gabriel orders, it wasn't Eddie. She looked directly up at him, unblinking, fists curling and heart pounding: "That *feckless butcher* was an angel compared to you."

"And yet *I* am the one to save you from a lifetime of use by that other butcher you courted so recklessly. I've angered the Lord Protector, jeopardised my position and put a marker on my back. I expect more gratitude."

"Quite the martyr, aren't you? We should ask Foxe to revise his bestseller, so the whole world can witness you forcing me into that damned church."

He glowered at her, his low voice shaking with the effort of control. "The last couple of days have been a huge shock, I understand that, but I warn you, my Lady, do not talk to me like that."

"I will talk to you as I damn well please," she spat.

"You will do as you're damn well told."

Without warning she slapped him hard across the cheek. His long fingers went instinctively to the angry red mark and, for a split silent second, there was confusion in his eyes. It surprised her too and she was shaking as she backed away.

Long skirts scratched the floor noisily as three maids bid a hasty retreat. back through a service door towards the kitchen, each tripping over the other, leaving Wortley exposed and grinning unapologetically. "Forgive the interruption, Milord, I've passed the message to Ann. Also, the fire bush outside says that the chestnut filly you were interested to see is in the stable yard if you want to give it the once over before the sun sets."

"I will do that," he said calmly, his head inclined towards the news of his new horse. "Did Donn bring her here on the rein?"

"Yes sir, but he says to warn you she's not yet broken," he smirked: "She's a stubborn filly."

Gabriel paused, before drawing his hands through the waves of loose hair, pushing it back to reveal expressionless eyes and a mouth drawn in a firm line. His voice was as deceptively soft. "You leave me no choice, Tara. You must learn your place here. Take her upstairs, Wortley. I'll assess the horse and see to my wife presently."

"You'll see to me? What the Hell is that supposed to mean? You'd beat me? You wouldn't dare…" Tara bristled as she read the instructions for what they were, but he ignored her, striding through the front door, her indignation chasing him across the tiles: "You bastard! Don't you bloody dare!"

There was no warning to be gentle this time. She felt Wortley's bony fingers grip her elbow painfully tight as he yanked her to the staircase to the second floor, impervious to her shouts and twists. A maid flattened herself against the wall to avoid hampering their awkward progress, while the late afternoon sun picked up the carpeted treads, and made macabre shadows of the intricately carved bannisters. He made the delighted mutters of a maniac: "You'll be sorry you crossed the Earl. He'll make a pretty mark with his whip; ungrateful witch."

Pick your battles. She stopped shouting and tried to steady her breathing, counting the doors and the windows as they moved through opulent and interconnected rooms. Finally, panting with exertion, he drew her to a sharp halt in front of the same chamber she had occupied two nights previous: "Nothing to say, Milady?"

"If I'm to receive the master, why trouble myself with his mongrel?"

His leering face was too close but she met his bloodshot eyes, forcing herself to show no hint of the fear balling in her chest like a sickness. He dropped her arm and immediately she jabbed her elbow into his ribs, bracing herself as he registered insult and strike. A tiny vein throbbed above his left eye, faster pace than her shallow breaths. Her fists clenched.

"Out the way, now, Mr Wortley." A short woman, clad in head-to-toe black, emerged from some dark corner to unlock the door. Safely beyond her sixties, her dark hair was heavily salted with grey and pulled back into an austere knot, exposing severe, neat features and singular raised eyebrow.

"Ann, is the room not ready yet?" Wortley pushed his charge forward into the pale blue bedchamber. "Milord intends to teach her a lesson."

"That'll be all then thank you Mr Wortley." Ann followed her in, turned the key in the lock behind then and took in her scowl. "Can't say as I'm surprised to hear that it's necessary, you've clearly got a nasty temper. Can you undress yourself?"

"What? Why?"

"'I'm told against all rhyme and reason 'tis your wedding day. You need to remove that grimy gown."

"I don't."

"You do," Ann replied curtly, as she busied herself straightening the rugs and folding up a heavy winter blanket, sliding it into a great linen chest at the foot of the bed to reveal an expensive damask bed cover in pale blue. Tara hadn't noticed the colour, last time. "The old master would turn in his grave at this turn of events. It's in a shaming state, look at it all ripped and dirty. You should have taken better care of it, or have you dresses to spare waiting in your hovel? I've heard talk of you in the village. I imagine you're as pleased as punch to have traded in that butcher boy."

"Get out," Tara shook her head slowly, shaking. "Get out, you bitter-"

"Milord deserves more respect. I'll not go until you're ready-"

"I have no intention of letting him anywhere near me."

"A gowpenful-o'-intentions don't count for 'aught, Milady. You've snatched the mantle of wife-"

"I've done no such thing!"

"And now you'll learn the meaning of the word. In good society, everyone knows that a stubborn malapert woman leads to matrimonial wrack and ruin."

"You think I'd worry about that?" Tara exclaimed, incredulous. "You really believe this is my doing? You think I want to be captive to a monster?"

"He's no monster, Milady, he's a proud man and he won't be made a fool of. You must be silent, obedient, peaceable, patient and studious to appease his choler if he's angry. Come now," she added, motioning to the stays, eyebrow raising higher still: "'Tis your last chance to do it for yourself, or I'll do it for you. I need to get this shaming thing cleaned. I've done it once already remember, when you were idle with wine. I'll see if I can find you a robe somewhere."

She was serious; small but wiry and her mouth was drawn into a firm line. She moved closer, ignoring a slapped hand to take hold of the back fastenings on Tara's stays.

"I'll do it." Tara turned away, cringing, and bit her lip to bring her features back under control as she slowly unpinned the lace partlet, the extravagant something new for her special day with Jack already ripped from Tollemache's attentions. She took her time and laid it carefully on the linen chest, before tugging sullenly at the ribbons of her stays. About the walls were several small oils depicting rural scenes and she tried to focus on one, with a hearty grinning milkmaid, bathed in bright sunshine who sat perched before a Friesian, geese meandering about her like children.

"I've not got all evening, Milady." Ann breathed a sigh of impatience and stepped forward to free the remaining ties with a couple of strong, efficient tugs. Tara grit her teeth as the stays fell away, dragging her filthy skirts down to pool on the floor. With some relief she realised she was permitted to keep her shift, for all the protection the gauzy white cotton offered, and she crossed her arms tightly over her chest, all attempt at dignity evaporating.

"Now, you get the correction over with and you can make amends with a clean slate."

The sickness in the pit of Tara's stomach intensified as the housekeeper unlocked the door. The boy she knew at court was no more than a fleeting moment's memory within the man downstairs; she had no clue what he was actually capable of. "Wait! Where are you going?"

"I'm not about to watch." Wortley was still outside the door and the housekeeper muttered distastefully as she disappeared, laden with yellow silk. "Tell the Earl she's ready."

He shrugged, sneering as he entered the room. "Are you going to cause trouble to Himself?"

"Go to Hell," she hissed, backing away.

He produced a twist of rope from behind his back and she looked about frantically but there was nowhere to go as he got closer. He'd readied a slipknot which he pushed over the first wrist he grabbed, but he didn't notice her bare feet making contact with his shins.

"Get off me!"

Panic took over as he pulled the rope taut towards the tester on the bed, struggling to hook it over the top of the wooden frame and trying to pinion her body hard against a corner post. Too quickly her other wrist was caught, and the bind pulled tight, threatening to draw her up to tip toes. She found just enough purchase to bang her knee into his crotch as his breath got closer to her shoulder.

"Bitch!"

"I'll do worse, you bastard." She felt his fingers tighten on the nape on her neck and closed her eyes, bracing herself for pain, but it was worse. After a moment's pause, as his breathing settled, she felt his grip relax then she froze as he slowly traced a line through her thin shift, down her spine.

"*Get off me!*" she screeched again, writhing to escape his touch. "I'll tell the Earl!"

"Twattling doxy, whose idea do you think this is?" He laughed as he felt lower, under the bottom edge of her shift, calloused fingertips trailing directly over her skin. "I'm to make sure you stay put this time."

"No, no *no no*!" Her screams pierced the still room as she twisted desperately to lose his fingers. "Get off!"

"*Out!*"

She wrenched her head around to see Gabriel's features twisted into rage. His shirt was open at the top. There was a fine layer of sweat over his skin and he swiped his leather riding crop towards the door. The sound made her heart pound and she tugged with renewed vigour against the rope as Wortley hurriedly made to placate his master. "Milord, she's vicious. She punched and kicked me. I had to make sure she couldn't do you no harm. I-"

"I'll manage my own wife, Wortley. Out before I turn my whip on you."

He slammed the door as the man scurried out, the resonating thump unsettling the painted milkmaid's tranquillity and sending her and her cow crashing to the floorboards. Then he slammed his palm on the door for good measure, creating a second shudder that reverberated through the hollow silence. She was panting, but no longer screaming. Over her shoulder, between escaped strands of hair, she could have sworn his hands were shaking but when he turned back to her, his entire demeanour was composed, impassive as a marble effigy.

"We'll start as we mean to go on," he said finally, his voice strangely loud. "You swore not two hours ago to honour and obey and you will do just that."

"Let me go, Gabriel. Cut the ropes!"

"In the hall. You struck me."

"Only I wasn't such a coward as to have you tied up first," she hissed, ashamed of how her voice wavered. "Let me go."

"You'd call me coward?"

With a stab of irritation, she felt hot tears gather and threaten to spill. Her chest heaved with the effort of self-control: do not cry. He'll do it anyway. For all the veneer of civility, he was a soldier and he lived by simple rules. Charlie's whipping boy; he'd think nothing of it. She took another deep breath. Was it better to buy time talking or to get this over with? *Talk.* He looked too strong.

"You're nothing but an ale-house brawler. I'd be better off with Tollemache. Nothing you talk of can be beaten into a woman. I will never obey you! *Ow!*" She yelped as the crop made contact with her bottom, but more in shock than pain, it was not hard enough to hurt. She craned her head to look at him. "So help me God, I hate you. To have your wife tied to a bedpost for a whipping is not just barbaric… it's illegal."

He frowned before meeting her gaze full on, his face set in a hard, determined mask. His voice was still loud: "This is necessary correction. You know as well as I do the law supports me fully. Hate me if you must, but you will learn your place and behave as befits the lady of this house."

"I will not, you bloody lobcock, you lied to me, you said- *Ow!*" Again, the crop made contact and again she uttered an involuntary yelp. But again, it was not the brutal thwack she expected. He was more controlled, more restrained, and the heat that rose was pure sensation. She gulped at the air.

"Count to ten, my Lady. Cry out again and it will be twenty."

Ten strokes. Even as she opened her mouth to scream again the realisation hit her. *No one would come.* No one would ever come for her again. She laid her forehead against the heavy wooden bed post and clenched her teeth, determined not to give him the satisfaction of her tears.

Nothing happened.

After a moment, she opened one eye gingerly and watched as closely as she dared while he tugged a feather bolster away from the footboard and rolled it into a ball, pushing it tight into place against the headboard where she could see it. Then he took up his crop again and hit it, the leather meeting the balled cushion considerably harder than it had found her skin. The sound of the air whistling and the thwack echoed in the room. He glanced at her, eyebrows raised in expectation.

"One." she said quietly, a broken cry barely containing the sob of relief.

Another thwack. Louder still. It would echo along the entire floor.

"T- Two." She squealed this time, her breath coming in ragged pants as she pulled pointlessly against the rope.

He didn't look at her again but with regular measure they counted the hits on the bunched pillow. At ten, he threw the crop against the door, where it clattered to the floorboards, and drew his sword. Then he moved behind her, pinioning her body against the post, and she cried out when he bought the blade down on the rope with a solid thud, freeing her hands. A combination of fear and relief made her legs give way and he caught her as she wobbled, swinging her unceremoniously onto the bed before stripping off his shirt, letting it fall to the sheets before her.

Barely able to look, still her eyes took in the hard plane of his chest and the terrifying breadth of his shoulders. "No... I won't..."

She scrabbled to retreat, kicking against the mattress until she bounced away from him, hitting her spine against the headboard. No, no. She should be abed with Jack, gorgeous Jack, tentatively exploring the lines of his body. This was not going to replace her wedding night. This could not *be* her wedding night. "Please." she begged, finally beyond pride. "Please, Gabriel don't touch me."

The bed creaked loudly as he kneeled on it and swiped his sword and she screamed again, but with a flick he bought the blade down across his left forearm, pumping his fist until red blood pooled at the neat cut. Then he dragged the covers out from beneath them, onto the floor and smudged a small stain of red against the linen sheets. Glancing around, he swiped her partlet, still laid on the linen chest, twisting it into a makeshift bandage to wrap around his arm and prevent the blood seeping into his shirtsleeve.

The bed creaked again as he moved closer and Tara whimpered, her heart galloping and her eyes finally smudged with tears. Still he didn't touch her but his scent drowned her senses. Leather. Horse. He paused for the briefest of moments, his lips brushing her hair as he whispered into her ear: "I've made some necessary adjustments to your virtue, my Lady. Now get dressed, We have guests arriving in an hour."

Pushing himself off the bed, he pulled his shirt back over his head and strode out of the room without looking back.

11. POT LUCK

She wiped her eyes, surprised that they were dry. She must have stopped crying at some point. Her head throbbed with tiredness and yet she still couldn't bring herself to climb onto the bed and succumb to oblivion. Little point if he would fetch her down to entertain dinner guests. Could they really be married?

She looked around the detritus of the room and finally heard the tale it told. Long afternoon sun spilled a deep golden light across the linen sheets that still lay crumpled exactly where she, where he, had left them. As far as anyone in the household would be concerned, the Earl had beaten and bedded his virgin bride; marked his territory and put his seal on their insane union. She had let the devil assume she had lain with Jack and so he had rewritten the past to suit him. *If you were my wife you'd know it.* She was now; consummation in the eyes of the world meant that only death could part them.

The thought was a morbid one.

So was the certain knowledge that Eddie's plans would fail. Everything was over and it was all for nothing. His men were busy now, preparing the south coast for an invasion that wouldn't come. Eleven days from now, without the professional back up of the coalition force they would rise up in Plymouth and be defeated in hours. If the other ports lit fires, they too would be crushed.

Cromwell's retribution would be brutal. She swallowed a lurch at the thought of those who would pay the highest price. There were three main rebel groups under Eddie, each led by a different man she'd once thought of as family. Todd Pengelly, a boat builder from Falmouth, was a gentle and skilled carpenter who'd whittled her a small dog, her only toy after escaping Weycroft Hall. He'd produced it from his shirt sleeve like a magician. With gruff foul-mouthed grunts, Robert Farrier saw to the horses that kept goods and news moving along the highways out of Lyme Regis. In Portsmouth, Mad Mike Evelyn, whose name defied anything but the most accurate character assessment, inspired a band of at least sixty royalists.

A faint smile crept across her mouth. When she last saw him, Mad Mike was all-consumed with love for the printer's reticent widow Lucy Hallowell. She remembered the others riling him for his oft-received baffle; Lucy was nothing if not steadfast in her denial. Was there a chance they were happy together now? For how much longer?

Across the front lawns, between the trees, she caught glimpses of a boatman, drawing steadily past on the Thames' still waters. The barge was loaded with crates from the Kingston market. Life goes on. She let her breath keep time with the rhythmic pushing and pulling of his oar.

She'd have to face him at some point, but this was a big house. She could avoid him for hours, maybe days at a time. Perhaps their meetings would come to be entirely on her terms. She imagined his long, broad body filling a fireside settle as the nervous maid approached: Your wife, sir, is indisposed. She said she'll come when she's good and ready. Would he be denied so easily? At once breathtakingly familiar but cold, she saw his dark eyes narrow and his jaw clench as he feigned an easy indifference. Thank you, he'd say, even as his boots found the carpet and his full stature unfurled. She held her breath as she saw him stride through his house, the opulence bought with wages stained by her people's blood, calling her name... She felt something snap suddenly. There was still a life to fight for. Lives.

Eleven days until the Sealed Knot would raise arms in Plymouth and be destroyed.

She looked about with a practical eye and lifted the lid of the linen chest to rummage for clothes. She eased ugly grey woollen skirts up over her legs, brushing quickly over the two tingling red marks his whip had made on her bottom. She jabbed her hair modestly under a linen cap and shrugged on old fashioned, high-waisted stays over her shift. They were meant for someone smaller.

It was only as she bent to tug on woollen stockings and retrieve an old pair of clogs that she noticed a slip of paper poking under the door. Another message from Jack, surely, only this time she retrieved it gingerly, as if it carried a spider passenger. The paper slipped inside her placket unread, as she eased the door open a crack. The stillness was promising. Clogs and woollen blanket in hand, keeping to the carpets so as to dampen her footsteps, she moved swiftly through the series of interconnecting rooms back to the wide staircase on the east side of the house. At the bottom, she crossed the tiled entrance hall and lifted two heavy oak bars on the main door and lay them carefully to the side before tugging it open. No one was following.

The only problem with the plan, she swiftly realised, stopping and shivering in the afternoon's chill air, is that there wasn't one. Could she go home? She'd instinctively turned towards the village only if she involved Jack… and there was no chance of picking up a coach at this time. In any case, her coin was safely tucked away in her yellow dress, wherever that crone had taken it. She squealed in frustration and kicked at a tussock of grass, finally wrapping the blanket tightly around her shoulders and turning, reluctantly, to the river, weaving through the trees until she found a hollow on the bank. She had to think.

When she mustered the nerve to look, Jack's note was a simple "How could you?" but it spoke volumes about broken promises. Abandoned, Fielding had said. Could he really believe she would abandon him so callously from choice? Jack was a straightforward man. Perhaps there were no words to explain even if she could reach him. He would never understand her words in Whitehall, or how the Earl's status might protect her from the anger of the Lord Protector while his own body offered no shield. Tears pricked as she rearranged the blanket on the damp ground and laid back, watching as the sky coloured to a deep blue. Westminster greyed, faded until it was a foreign fortress keeping her enemies at a safe distance. Was this how Gabriel remembered Ireland?

Her mind hovered between past and present. It took years, after her father's execution, for the grief and guilt to numb; years before she let down her defences to Jack. He spiralled through her mind, twisting and turning, wrapping around painful scenes of her childhood. Then Gabriel emerged from black shadows, dragging a heavy chain of more buried memories. Premonitions of another bloody uprising, of Eddie lying lifeless in the Tower, closed the ever-decreasing circle. Darkness closed in. There was no guarantee, this time, she would escape at all. As if on cue, the sun disappeared and a chill rose immediately in the air. Shivers rippled across her skin.

Eleven days.

Slowly and inevitably, the plan unfurled in her mind like a flower opening its tight bud of petals to the sun. She had to go to Exeter. Destroy whatever connection Thurloe might find to link Eddie and the bands of men readying for hopeless rebellion along the South Coast. Stop the uprisings. Before, when Gregory Villiers had lived, she had made the coded messages to send her father's directions to the Sealed Knot bands. They'd be looking for word. It was time to speak it again. Had the code changed? Unlikely, if it remained unbroken.

Sing to the sparrow, though? With pulse pounding and mind racing, she dug her knuckles into her temple. It meant nothing. *Yet.*

She could buy a horse. No, there wasn't enough coin. Take a horse, from the Ham House stables behind her? Not the unbroken mare, she thought wryly, remembering Gabriel's distraction before he... Would he track her? Thievery was a capital crime. Travelling alone, it would surely be easier to lose him, but the stage would be quicker....

Every now and then the chimes of St Peter's Church carried on the breeze, rolling across the yawning chasm of her black thoughts and reminding her abstractly of the passing time. It was getting dark; every precious minute of solitude was starting to feel like borrowed time. Her stomach grumbled with pangs of hunger and her throat was painfully dry. Miserably, she sat up and started as she saw the middling figure of a man walking across the field towards her, silhouetted in the low light. He came to a stop not five yards away, his thick Irish accent betraying surprise: "Milady! Begad, Milord will be relieved to see ye, so he will."

She took in his clothes, still covered with stubborn wisps of straw. His breeches hinted that they had once been a smart dark green in colour, but they were now faded, patchy, worse for wear. He had a simple matching jerkin over his shirt. She raised her eyes further, seeing roughly tangled russet hair. The stable boy. Ginger stubble grazed his chin, but his face was largely obscured as his hand held his forehead to shade his vision from a bright ray of evening sun.

"Will ye be comin' home with me?"

A fork of irritation stabbed though her: "I'll come back when I'm good and ready."

He stood for a minute, and then slowly crouched down on his haunches. Clearly good with flighty animals, she thought ruefully, looking away, back towards the river. "Milady we've all been right vexed lookin' for ye. Milord sent men to the village an' out to Richmond an' Kingston to ask after ye. I canna believe ye've managed to be hidin' yerself just here."

He shrugged in wonder, his eyes skimming over the dip in the grass where she sat, the angle obscuring the body within much better than she could ever have planned. "Milady, forgive me, but no one's had a glimpse of ye for a couple of hours. Milord was thinkin' ye'd up an'…"

They hung in silence until she took another glance at him. He was young, she realised, maybe seventeen, eighteen. Slim and slight timbered, but for all his gentle demeanour, his limbs looked powerful. His profile was clean, graceful even, neat beneath a startling red that flashed vivid in the sunset. When he returned her gaze straight on, she took in the pale blue of his eyes and then the faint white scar of a brand on his forehead, where the skin puckered and twisted around a "T". Thief. She thought instinctively to recoil, but beneath the mutilation, there was nothing but kindness in his features.

With a resigned sigh, she held out her hand for introduction. "Tara."

"Donnacha Kielty, Milady," he said, unsure at the intimacy of first names, rubbing his hands on his breeches before shaking her fingers awkwardly. "Donn."

"Donn. Nice to meet you."

He sat down next to her and they gazed absently at the river in silence.

"I wasn't hiding, you know. I wasn't sulking like some spoilt child," she said finally. He didn't challenge her, and Tara relaxed a little, breathing out into the space created by his quiet acceptance. "You know what he did to me?"

"Well enough, Milady. Sweet Jesus, we couldna fail in the hearin' of it. I donna mind admittin' it's a surprise to see ye sittin' so comfortably." He chanced a grin at her, and it tugged at her lips, momentarily robbing the memory of its horror.

"Ye know," said Donn. "We have a fine sayin' in Ireland: Ní dhéanfaidh smaoineamh an treabhadh duit. If ye'll forgive the Gaelic, it means ye'll never plough a field turnin' it over in yer mind."

She glanced back at the house and shrugged. "You think I should confront him?"

"Aye, well, ye're well able for it, sure ye are. But, I just meant that I wouldna be thinkin' to sit out here stewin' when there's supper to be had inside."

"I hate him," she muttered bitterly, her traitorous belly grumbling with the mention of food. She tugged a stubborn weed out of the ground and wrapped its stiff stem tightly around her index finger, watching the blood drain from the strangled skin.

"Aye, I'm sure ye do."

She could hate him until the cows came home, said Donn's mild silence, but come they would. Besides there was little practical choice until the morning. Unless she intended to jump into the Thames and swim for freedom. It was a vaguely tempting proposition, her lips were cracking with thirst, but she couldn't swim. She caught sight of the concern wrinkling his forehead. No doubt his own supper had been postponed all the while a search party was convened.

"Fine I'll come back. For you though, not for him."

As they approached the house, Tara could see the Earl pacing along the path to the stables. His body seemed tense, his features clouded, and with the habit of a lifetime she felt a momentary pang of remorse for being the cause of any concern. Up close, however, what had seemed like worry from a distance was no more than irritation.

"Where the Hell have you been? You've led my household a merry dance," he started tersely, dismissing Donn with a curt nod. "We have dinner guests and half my staff are still out looking for you. Ann tells me you left your purse behind and no-one's seen you in the village."

"Would you beat me again?"

"What on earth are you wearing?" Gabriel frowned, momentarily interrupted by the ugly grey wool and coarse dowlas. It was old and hopelessly ill fitting, even by the standards of a world in which clothes were routinely recycled without a sempstress' attention. He nearly asked about its providence but Ham House held any number of random items left behind by its previous incumbents. Besides, Tara had stuck her chin out, bracing herself for an accusation of theft. He led her to the dining room without further comment.

A low fire was burning, and Tara hovered by the door as the maid from the staircase bobbed a nervous curtsey to them both. She had just lit the candles and flicking light glimmered across the embossed calf-skin lining the walls, picking up intaglio patterns on silver foil, and bright cerulean blue. "Sir, Titus Latimer and his secretary John Clifford have arrived; Bul has gone to meet them in the courtyard."

"Thank you, Abigail" said Gabriel, dismissing her. "Have cook prepare something, I suspect our visitors will be in no rush to leave."

Abigail. Of course. With the name, Tara placed her immediately amongst the tapestry of village life. Abigail Hardwick was the woman courting Jack's closest friend Ned, hoping for a new father for her awkward son. Assuming she'd been the one to deliver Jack's messages to her room, could she also be entrusted with a reply? Tara watched her leave with an impotent sense of loss. What on earth would she say? Gabriel moved to a sideboard and poured a whisky which he downed as Abigail returned ahead of two men dressed in fine, respectable puritan wear.

"I trust you don't mind the unannounced intrusion, my Lady," said Latimer, with an excessive politeness not matched by his manner as he moved immediately to take a seat at the table. He was tall and thin, sharp featured. Grey hair was cropped close to his scalp and dark eyebrows were arched so high as to give him an almost continuous air of surprise. His chair scrapped noisily along the floorboards as he settled himself, unselfconscious in his own importance.

By contrast, the smaller man was virtually as round as Latimer was tall. He carried a deep-rooted understanding of his place in the pecking order. If Latimer was the hawk-like predator, Clifford was the prey; his movements hurried and furtive like a hamster. He had small, brisk eyes and ruddy cheeks, although it was not immediately clear whether these were the result of exertion in the saddle or the ale he had no doubt swigged en route to Petersham.

"We were passing though Kingston, my Lord, when we heard tell of your recent nuptials," Clifford started, enthusiastically. "And, well, once we had the thought of the wedding feast it made us fancy for a pot luck."

"And, of course," interjected Latimer, "We beg leave to congratulate your happy return from Ireland."

"It is a wonderful surprise." Gabriel smiled graciously. Fielding will have reported the impromptu wedding almost immediately to his supervisor in Kingston, Edward Staunton. Thereafter it was a short hop to Titus Latimer, whose position in the Westminster Assembly of Divines meant he had likely learnt of Tollemache's reason for complaint. A network of gossiping churchmen put the Mercurius Politicus to shame. He glanced at Tara wondering if she appreciated now the necessity of speed but she showed no sign of having joined the dots. "Do sit with us," he added unnecessarily.

"It has been a while, Gabriel. It would be good to talk. Perhaps together we could unravel some of the threads of rumours wrapping us? I trust you don't mind that I took the liberty of sending your man Wortley to collect a physic I left behind in Westminster?"

"Not in the slightest. My household is at your disposal."

"My Lord Latimer is a slave to his digestion and suffers terribly, being often costive," said Clifford conversationally as he took his own seat.

Gabriel inclined his head in understanding and nodded at Abigail as she set down chargers and glasses, which she proceeded to fill with wine from an embossed bottle. Tara nursed her own glass as the men discussed the endless disruption of building works in Kingston. Like most settlements, the town still bore the slashed scars and bullet pimples of wartime skirmishing. Truth be told, it stood remarkably intact despite the indiscriminate malice of cannon fire and the unmitigated plunder of billeted soldiers. There was a little damage to the church, when parliamentary troops had used it for a stable, but other towns had been laid waste, scarcely one half left standing to gaze on the ruins of the other.

At length, Clifford tired of the practical talk and turned his eyes to her. "'Tis a pleasure, my dear, to meet the new Lady Denby, so flush with love and happiness."

Tara frowned, wondering how best to express the exact depths of her love and happiness, but his attention had moved on again and he produced a series of excited gurgles as a roasted shoulder of mutton was placed on the board before him, surrounded with oysters. She hadn't tasted anything so rich for some time and the smell of strong sauces churned her stomach.

"It's a fine spread, my Lord," Clifford said, eyes firmly fixed on a saucer of claret gravy.

"My compliments to your cook, Gabriel." Latimer agreed, helping himself to a slice of artichoke pie and drizzling buttered ginger sauce over its crust.

"If you would break the mutton, sir, I would have but a morsel," said Clifford hungrily.

Latimer snorted, taking up his knife: "It's mighty hard to hire decent hands for housework these days when able bodies are needed in the fields. Perhaps I should make your cook an offer?"

"Wars have started for less," replied Gabriel wryly, selecting a carving knife,

"Speaking of which, I hear Ireland has been trying for Cromwell's son," said Clifford conversationally as he poured a generous slug of gravy over his meat, but Gabriel declined to answer the rhetorical question.

"I hear Henry Cromwell has begged for support from London, but shall be left wanting," persisted Latimer. "The army must be aggrieved at being cut adrift in that foreign cesspit, without even wages fully paid..."

Aggrieved? With Cromwell's indifference to the shortages, the lack of wages, the army was livid. "I believe there were difficulties in finding men the Lord Protector can trust," he said mildly as he carved.

Latimer shrugged a thin smile, throwing a glance at Tara as he tilted his plate to receive the meat.
"You must be fulsome pleased with your new household, my Lady."

Pleased? Did he dare presume, like Ann, that she had sold herself for gold? Her new household constituted nothing more than a sinister housekeeper, a snarling lobcock of a manservant, a thieving groom and, at the head of the table, a bullying brute of a husband who had ruined the one chance she had to negotiate her uncle's freedom. No. She was not pleased. A rush of bitterness coursed through her veins like bile and she could no more tolerate the company than the food. "I feel sick," she said suddenly, rising from her seat. "I'm going to bed."

"My flittermouse," Gabriel started quietly, his tone amicable enough but the word resurrecting the ghost of Tollemache in warning. "Our guests have only just arrived. You'll sit with us a while longer yet, surely."

"I am tired."

"Still."

In lieu of a reply, she landed heavily back on the chair and took up her knife, stabbing at a chunk of meat and moving it mechanically about her plate while the conversation meandered back towards politics. Her heart boiled in hatred for him every time his voice caught her attention, and then in self-loathing as she remembered that her own recklessness had gone some way at least to forcing his hand. She stayed mute, listening only haphazardly to the discussion heating the table as the guests warmed to their speeches.

By the end of the second course it was late, gone ten. They rinsed greasy fingers in the water bowl and Abigail produced a steamed pudding to more excited snuffles from Clifford. She opened another bottle of wine and she drew heavy velvet curtains to the darkness, enclosing them in the claustrophobic candlelight.

"I sense a greater threat now than at any time since the birth of our Commonwealth," said Latimer carefully when she left. "Cromwell is an old man, preoccupied with bolstering support for his son Richard, and I hear that while he gently ponders his legacy at Whitehall the army grows restless."

"The army trades in action, not whispers," said Gabriel. "Richard is marked for succession."

"Indeed. But he makes for a peculiar commander in chief, does he not? What say the arm-" Clifford started, spluttering as he choked on a mouthful of the sponge.

"Shut your mouth, bespawler, Lord Denby does not want your spittle on his table top," said Latimer firmly, rolling his eyes at the bulging countenance of his secretary before turning his attention back to Gabriel. "The Godly amongst us must prepare to manage a vacuum."

"The army will soon present a loyal address," said Gabriel carefully, "supporting the arrangement of single person and parliament."

"A single person... but not Richard explicitly." Latimer inclined his head thoughtfully, his eyebrow raising ever higher. "God save such a person."

"But what hope have we to forge a lasting Kingdom of peace and worship when the people are so easily whipped into a fury against us?" Clifford asked plaintively, recovering his voice and sucking the sugar from his fat fingers while the fire popped behind him. A shower of golden sparks landed harmlessly on the hearth as a blackened log shifted.

Latimer sighed as his own fingers stroked the stem of his glass: "They are the vipers in our nest, ignorant peasants falsely labelling us pleasure haters, when we mean only to bring the English people closer to God. Their intendment is to poison, to rabble rouse and to destroy. We must cast them out."

"I still fail to see how cancelling Christmas brings the people closer to God," Tara said quietly.

Latimer startled to look directly at her over the candle and Gabriel gave a relaxed laugh. "My wife betrays her roots. The provinces miss their pagan pleasures Titus, as well you know, especially in rural areas far away from the civilising influence of London. It will take time for the people to find paths to new, wholesome activities."

The churchman snorted dismissively and Gabriel continued: "You cannot expect every soul to take so readily to sacrifice, Titus, or you might find yourself without profession."

The men laughed heartily at that, at the very idea that Titus Latimer might be surplus to the moral requirements of the land. Tara opened her mouth but shut it again after a firm look from Gabriel.

"Only, time is one thing we do not have," said Latimer seriously as the laughter calmed. "There are a mere eight years until the dawning of a new millennium. The fifth empire must begin in 1666 but the Devil wills us to fail. We stand on the knife-edge of all Hell unless the King of Kings and Lord of Lords returns to reign with his saints on earth for a thousand years."

Tara opened her mouth but another sharp warning look from Gabriel was enough to silence her. He kept his eye firmly on her as he replied to Latimer: "You fear He may not now be persuaded to come again?"

"This Commonwealth was born in blood and fire, Gabriel. In its salad days, it demonstrated an admirable capacity for truth and godliness but with the loss of strong men like your father, the Rump Parliament and the Nominated Assembly have been shamefully weak. As our nation grows into the dangerous period of adolescence, we must not spare the rod."

Clifford nodded in sage agreement but Gabriel had stiffened slightly at the mention of his father. Lucius Moore was a strong man, undoubtedly, but also a ruthlessly efficient one. He'd left behind an unusually profitable estate in Hereford that his only son left resolutely untouched, but other parts of his inheritance were not so easy to sidestep. During the war, Lucius had cultivated a secret garden of contacts, each carefully selected and nurtured to ensure practical and economic survival no matter which way the wind blew. Now it was a tangled undergrowth of weeds who all, to some extent, looked to Gabriel to honour the pledges and allegiances of his father.

Evenings like this one were to be endured from time to time when he returned to England. With the constant threat of imprisonment and the random disappearances of his enthusiastic Fifth Monarchist colleagues, Latimer was here for airy confirmations of military support that Gabriel was neither capable nor inclined to give. Heaven help them all, he thought ruefully, if the King of Kings was actually persuaded back to Earth by Titus Latimer in the anticipation of back up from the army, only to realise that Gabriel had been bluffing.

Clifford poured himself another glass of wine, clumsily knocking over a pillar candle as he leaned forward. He cursed, patting at his smouldering sleeve as it rolled from the table still lit and Gabriel moved to retrieve it before the flame caught at the curtain. The bottom had been misshapen and he extinguished the wick between his fingers, plunging the company into darker shadows before starting afresh with another candle from the sideboard.

Taking this as an acceptable cue finally to leave, Tara stood. Titus Latimer looked up at her properly for the first time, licking his thin lips. "Come my Lady. I am very interested in your upbringing so far from the Capital's enlightenment, do sit down and chew the fat with me."

"I would rather chew my legs off." She smiled sweetly, her eyes firmly meeting his gaze.

Clifford paused with his spoon in mid-air and muffled a snort as Latimer's face slowly fell, but seeing the warning signs, he busied himself draining his goblet while his master's lips curled into a polite smile. "I do hope you are never called to answer for that tongue, my Lady, it clearly has a mind of its own."

"Sincere apologies, my Lord, I meant only that I am cursed with such abundance of happiness that I simply could not touch another morsel. What a joy to be married to such a kind and honourable man," she said blandly, firmly avoiding her husband's cold glare.

"You are cursed, I see, with an overabundance of wit," replied Latimer bluntly. "Women should no-"

"Tara." Gabriel interrupted firmly. "It has been a very long day and you are overwrought. Go to my bed. We'll discuss this later." It was an order and she wasn't such a fool as to defy him openly again. She nodded a curt goodbye and walked away from the table and the candlelight, willing herself not to run. As she felt her way along the unfamiliar passageway outside in the dark, the men's voices carried past her.

"Where did you say you found her, my Lord?" asked Latimer carefully.

"I don't believe I did. We were close before the war. Her brother and I played together in court and she fancied herself meant for my wife, as children are wont. Our paths diverged and her family were destroyed by the war. And when I returned from Ireland, she came to me begging for help, believing herself trapped in an unsuitable match with a lowborn butcher. I was taken with her, now she is full grown," he laughed, permitting the men to share the lusty joke and she shuddered. "Perhaps I got a little carried away, but it's done now."

Latimer was clearly pondering the information; it was a while before he spoke. "Gabriel, I speak only in the absence of your father, our very dear friend-"

"A great man, God rest his soul," added Clifford

"- and the rumours reaching my ears of late are distressing top me, as I believe they would have distressed him. Is her uncle not the conspirator villain?"

"He is," confirmed Gabriel openly, no allegiance or treason to hide. "At least, he will be when the latest trial is over, I am sure of it."

She could hear the lightness in his voice and fought to stop herself bursting back into the room and raising merry Hell. She hovered, waiting for Latimer's response, but the pounding of her heart made it difficult to hear: "…take my pastoral duties seriously and for the sake of my friendship with your father I'll speak plainly. Could you not find your loyalty compromised? Are you not concerned about bringing a viper into your house?"

"Titus, I am as loyal to the Commonwealth now as I have ever been," said Gabriel, relaxed. "Tamara's estranged from her uncle. She may be kind-hearted enough to petition His Highness and express dutiful filial concern for his well-being, but she will not be the first offspring of a transgressor to find a place in our Godly kingdom."

"Your marrying her was a selfless act, truly one of pious charity. I applaud your generosity. We must strike out the godless but in youth there is hope. If we educate and integrate, body and soul, we might yet avoid more bloody civil strife. Still," he added softly on an exhaled breath, "Your work is very much cut out for you."

"Surely there were many offers from more respectable families of a beauty with unripe youth and dowry?" mused Clifford. "Your father-"

Gabriel laughed. "Don't your pulpits preach words of Solomon on this topic? You would know better, of course, but isn't a wise and a discreet woman better than wealth… her price is far above pearls: for house and possessions are the inheritance of the uncles? Forgive me, I forget the lines."

"But a prudent wife is of The Lord," finished Clifford with a flourish.

"And yet, in your father's absence, you will not mind me pointing out what we have witnessed this evening," said Latimer thoughtfully. "Tamara Villiers is neither wise, discreet nor prudent. Her heart sings with anarchy. She seems to have no understanding of her place-"

"St Paul was also unequivocal to the Corinthians," Clifford interrupted: "'I do not allow a woman to dictate to a man, but to keep quiet." Of course, I paraphrase, but our gentle Lord in Heaven expects your instruction to be firm." The eagerness in his voice left no doubt as to the naked enthusiasm with which the man of cloth would provide firm instruction and in the darkness outside Tara's cheeks burned at the memory of earlier.

Gabriel's tone lowered. "You are talking about my wife. She will do and think as she is told."

Clifford must have picked up on Gabriel's warning as he added hurriedly: "Of course, I don't doubt it. Well, I congratulate you. She is more than tolerably fair."

"She is."

With a sigh, Latimer took up the interrogation: "The Devil packages temptation in all manner of fine forms, Gabriel. She is surely possessed-"

"Of a wilful nature, nothing more."

"Her mother was a witch." Latimer lay the insinuation softly, and the hairs on Tara's neck stood up.

"I was surprised to hear that. Angela Villiers was a remarkable woman," said Gabriel in a measured tone. "To look at the work of your witch prickers I had thought that the Devil choose only to be conversant with silly old women who don't know their right hands from their left."

"'Tis indeed a great wonder," returned Latimer coolly.

"People said the Virgin Queen's mother was a witch." Clifford shrugged conversationally between bites, clearly trying to relieve some of the tension freshly filling the room.

A silence descended, lasting perhaps a second too long, before Latimer laughed suddenly. "Come now, she may have the body of a weak and feeble woman but I barely think that comparing the Earl's new wife to a tyrant monarch whore will help us. He has put his... faith in her, and we should do likewise."

"Gentlemen, in my father's absence I am grateful for your counsel and concern. But rest assured that like all the Kings and Queens, Tara's unfortunate past will soon be very much dead and buried." The impatience in his response relented as he paused for his guests to anticipate the satisfactory execution of another royalist traitor, and Tara's fingernails dug crescent moons into her palms. "I have every confidence she understands that her path to spiritual and temporal rehabilitation depends on her bending to my will and authority. In everything."

Latimer sighed deeply, tapping his empty glass for a refill, contented finally after his questioning. "Then through you, Gabriel, she will, God willing, find salvation."

"Amen."

12. A GRAVE DISCREPANCY

Extract from a report of a speech by Oliver Cromwell to the Government on 31 May 1658, annotated by an observer.

[*His Highness looks now at the Paper again and says to himself: "The Revenue stands at 300,000 pounds." Then he considers a Note on the Current Expenses. He frowns, wondering at the contrast of the two figures, not having Arithmetic enough to reconcile them!*]

"This is exceedingly past my understanding; I have as little skill in Arithmetic as I have in Law!"

[*Laughter from the room.*]

"These are both great sums; it is well if I count them to you."

[*He looks again on his Note.*]

"The present charge for the Forces both at Sea and Land is 2,426,989 pounds. Yet the whole present value of the revenue in England, Scotland and Ireland, is about 1,900,000 pounds."

[*A grave discrepancy!*]

"If the present Government has at its disposal 1,900,000 pounds; then the whole sum by which it comes 'short' of the present charge is 542,689 pounds."

[*His Highness must be mistaken. Arithmetic suggests he is short by 526,989 pounds.*]

"There is a clear necessity, for preserving the peace of the Three Nations, to keep up the present established Army, also a considerable Fleet for some good time. This is of vital importance until it shall please God to quiet and compose men's minds, and bring the Nation to some better consistency.

"Large swathes of the forces have been unpaid for some time. They pledge loyalty but they grow restless and dangerous at a time when we need utmost focus on the defence of the realm."

[*His Highness alludes to recent threats from royalist cavaliers in the Sealed Knot, though he seems too delicate to say it.*]

"Men ask: how long will they carry on the War, and what further sum will the Government need for carrying on the same? But let me be plain, if Money be wanting, this whole business will fall to the ground - all our labour will be lost. Will we all make sacrifices for the future of our Godly Nation."

[*Cheers from the room. Parliament votes in the order of wage payment for the armed forces, though it has done so before. It remains to be seen if the quantity of money is forthcoming.*]

13. THE ROAD

"Ann! Ann!" Gabriel paced across the entrance hall towards the kitchen and the only sounds of activity in the house.

The housekeeper closed the creaking door to the bread oven as he entered and put a floury finger to her lips: "Sir! Stop all your whoobub! It's not long since dawn. Your guests are still sleeping! I'll send Abigail to attend you."

Gabriel caught the heavy kitchen door as it swung back towards him, briefly admonished. He'd all but forgotten the blasted rakefires. They'd kept him from his bed until the small hours, despite constant promises of imminent leave-taking. He'd only left them when Latimer finally dozed off in front of the fire, replete with wine, and Clifford's heavy jowls crashed down onto the table of their own accord. With some surprise he'd found Tara in his chamber, exactly where he'd told her to go. She was sleeping unconvincingly when he climbed in beside her, too tired to fight. But he felt her absence before he opened his eyes to morning, enseamed in the sweat of his recurring nightmare, and sure enough the side she had so sternly occupied was cold.

He took a deep breath and injected a more controlled tone into his voice, despite the pounding in his chest. "Where is she?"

The old woman frowned momentarily, as if there could be any number of missing women on any given morning: "I told you yesterday sir, that cook's daughter was nearing her time. Still a youngster herself if you want my opinion. Word came in the night that the babe was coming and she went to be what use she could. Lucky thing the girl kept her legs crossed until after dinner-"

"I'm not looking for the blasted cook." His irritation snapped: "Tara Villiers, Ann. Moore. My wife."

Ann raised an eyebrow calmly, wiping her hands on a cloth. She pursed her lips. "I haven't seen her. One night whittled, the next insolent. You were right to take a whip to her. Your father would have done the same. Mind you, I did see first thing she's been rifling for her yellow dress in the laundry, though it's still too damp-"

His mouth tightened and he turned without another word, swiping two spare rapiers from the sword chest in the hall and sliding his pistol into its holster on his belt. If he was surprised yesterday evening to find her missing, there was no blasted excuse to be caught off guard today. *Fool.* He'd pushed her too far. She'd left, and quite possibly taken with her the one chance he had to find out how Edward Villiers communicated with the rebel Sealed Knot cells.

He headed straight for the stable block, where Rowley had already been led from his stall and Donn was leisurely tightening his saddle. The groom looked up with a confused smile as Gabriel strode into the yard, pewter buttons on his leather jerkin still undone, and yanked a waiting bridle from the top of Rowley's half door, pulling it swiftly over the horse's head himself.

"He's a bit fresh, Milord, I thought to take him out down to the village."

"No need, Donn," Gabriel interrupted with a cursory nod. "He can stretch his legs with me."

With that he was solidly in the saddle, Rowley sidestepped a few paces with a snort as Gabriel took control. He squeezed his legs and the horse responded immediately. They clattered out of the yard leaving Donn squinting behind them and Gabriel gave the beast his head to canter along the river path, where they might not be hindered by early market traffic. Tara would be on foot. No doubt heading to the nearest stage post to pick up the first coach to Exeter.

* * *

The nervousness fluttering across her chest was purely the product of a fraught few days, she told herself practically. There was plenty of time before the 6 o'clock stage and the road was practically empty but she grew increasingly self-conscious as she walked, unable to shake a vague sense of unease; the feeling that she was being watched. After the last couple of days it was natural to feel wrong-footed, she reasoned, consciously slowing her breathing.

And it was nonsense. Aside from the rabbits that lolloped haphazardly across her path, she had encountered only one soul, whose dishevelled clothing suggested he was more late-to-bed than early-to-rise. The reveller had barely acknowledged her, his head clutched in hands as if he could still its pounding by willpower alone. She gave a brief, sympathetic smile as he slumped back into a ditch; the memory of the raspberry wine still recent enough to make her cringe.

She cut down through the trees to follow the river and minimise the chance of another encounter. The only man likely to come after her now was safely in bed and, given the state of the dining table she had glimpsed this morning, almost certainly dozing off his own morning fog. By the time he roused, she would be free from him, hurtling out of the county on the Portsmouth Road. Still, there was no reason to risk a breadcrumb trail of witnesses.

She forced herself to walk steadily in the crisp early air, listening to the rhythmic swish of her skirts dragging on the pebbles. The yellow gown was still damp, but at least Ann had put her purse safely back inside. More rabbits darted before her here, and overhead, a cacophony of enthusiastic warbling stressed the dawn. Still, every whisper of leaves, every creak of a branch felt a potential threat. Her hair was twisted up and a chill ran across the back of her neck. Twice she spun in the path, arm raised against an imaginary attacker and twice she turned back, feeling beyond foolish to be waving airily at imaginary spirits.

Since when were you afraid of your own shadow?

"Ah!" She spun around again as the thundering hooves drew terrifyingly close.

Gabriel slid smoothly from Rowley's back, filling her vision and blocking her path ahead: "Bloody bobolyne! Where the Hell do you think you're going?"

"Hell's teeth!" she yelled back, willing her heartbeat to calm the blood that stiffened her arms, curling her fists into balls. "You scared me!"

"You damn well should be scared! These paths are not safe."

"I have been perfectly safe here for years. It took only five minutes in your world to be attacked, bartered and beaten, and it was you doing the beating!" she cried.

Gabriel folded his arms and thought for a moment, his brown eyes narrowing. "Would you like me to take my whip to you again?"

She lifted her chin and met his eyes. "If you ever even think about doing that again I'll poison your wine."

"Tara, if you knew where I kept my wine, it seems highly unlikely that there would be any left for me to drink."

A hint of a grin played suddenly on his lips and she let out a wail of frustration, pushing him aside to continue pacing to Kingston. "For God's sake, go away! I don't want your company."

"Please," he said gently, reaching out to put a hand on her elbow and stop her marching past him. "You need to stay close to me, at least until we know what Tollemache will do."

"No. I don't need you for anything."

"And I do not need to explain to my guests and my household why my wife has taken herself off again without rhyme or reason!"

"Bastard."

"Bastard husband dear, master of my world, light of my life, etcetera," he retorted mildly, his eyes busy scanning the path ahead and behind before they came to rest on her glare. "You were leaving for Exeter I take it, for Edward Villiers' house?"

She swallowed her surprise and nodded, keeping determined eyes firmly on his. "I must... secure the house, and collect his valuables before they are stolen. I need to bring him clothes."

He looked at her impassively then drew a hand back through the loose waves of this hair. Decided, he set off along the path, clicking his tongue to bring Rowley into step behind. "Come on then. If you must go, I will make sure you get there safely. Besides, I have an aunt and uncle not far from Exeter, they will be pleased to meet the new Lady Denby. We'll call it a honeymoon."

They walked in awkward silence to Kingston where the town was gradually unfolding into life, ground floor shutters swinging up to reveal ready trade counters, filling the cramped passages with the smells of bread, fish, meat and the hollers of advert. He left her standing on the market square with Rowley before disappearing into The Druid's Head to make arrangements and the beast nudged her shoulder bag with increasing impatience, smelling promise in the lumps of bread and cheese she had filched from Ham House kitchen for her breakfast.

"Don't even think about it," she hissed up the long black nose, down which the only answer was a supercilious look and a loud snort.

When Gabriel finally beckoned them through a brick archway into the courtyard, Tara's spirits rose slightly. He handed her a mug of hot coffee and explained he'd left a message to be carried back to Ann. Then he pointed towards a small roan as it was led from the stable block chewing blankly on a mouthful of straw. "All yours, my Lady. I'm assured he's placid."

She frowned, hesitantly. "Why not the stage?"

"After the recent rain? We'd be lucky if our coach didn't sink up to its belly in mud before we got as far as Guildford. We'll do better on horseback."

She raised an eyebrow but nodded silently, handing the empty mug back to a stable lad before clambering reluctantly into the saddle, taking small comfort in the fact that the beast looked unlikely to move quickly without considerable encouragement. Gabriel's jaw had tightened but his tone was excruciatingly calm as he mounted Rowley and sat solidly in his own saddle: "Let me set the pace, Tara. We'll be deep in Surrey if not Hampshire by nightfall."

And with that, they started out, following the morning sun and the main road south in silence. Placid was not quite the right word, Tara thought, or it lease it wasn't the whole story. She quietly christened the stubborn beast Jankyn as she yanked its head back up again for the umpteenth time in the direction of Rowley's shimmering hindquarters. He trudged along for the most part, hooves squelching in the sticky mud, but stopped dead with irritating regularity to tug on juicy looking clumps of weeds at the roadside, in all as utterly indifferent to his rider as his namesake clerk had been to the Wife of Bath's assumed dominion. After a couple of hours, the muscles in her arms ached with overuse, but conscious of the tension along Gabriel's erect spine some distance ahead she thought better of complaining.

Despite Jankyn's shortcomings, they reached Guildford around lunchtime, where he dictated a short comfort stop, disappearing for provisions and reappearing with tall leather boots. She pulled them on with relief. Not a bad fit. Likely more by luck than judgement, she thought uncharitably as he packed his saddlebags.

"How much do I owe you now?"

"Let's see," mused Gabriel with all apparent seriousness as he mounted. "The boots were 30 shillings. The beast was 20 pounds although with any luck we might recoup some of that cost with deposits from the soap boilers or glue makers when he's finally beaten you... Oh, and there's the 3d-odd for the morning coffee and sundry pastries. I'm assuming you still have a sweet tooth?"

"I'll repay you," she said, frowning as she calculated the cost and wondered at the near depleted contents of her purse.

"I know," he shrugged. "Until then, let's just add it to the ledger, my Lady."

By mid-afternoon they had picked up the old drover's way, high along the hogs back, and Tara could not shift a sense of unease. Rolling glimpses of Surrey, stretched out lazily and lush between the branches of beech and elm that lined the road, but she knew the tales as well as most. The countryside was a dark underworld in the years since the war; a bleak place of cruel and indiscriminate desperation. It was a place where scores were settled, the result of grudges too personal and deeply felt to be swept aside by parliamentary order that the war was over.

Leaving the safe anchor of another bustling market town they were adrift again, happening haphazardly upon island rocks of ramshackle homes. Most seemed populated entirely by women, the infirm and children, who swarmed out as they passed, their grubby hands outstretched. Reluctantly, Tara noticed Gabriel's easy manner with those they encountered. He was gentle and democratic in his approach, collecting information she didn't know they needed easily as he dispensed jokes and coin, consciously unravelling the unnerving effect of his stature, his horse, his long swords and his two pistols, one holstered either side of Rowley's long neck.

He slid down and squatted down next to a beggar dragged to or deposited at a crossroads outside Farnham, in a spot clearly judged a promising pitch for passing charity. The man's legs were folded under him but both arms were lost from just above the elbow. He was hunched in the shade of an oak, but it had been a slow day and his wooden bowl sat empty. Now familiar with the patter, Tara led the horses to a verge of tasty looking grass nearby and waited.

"I'm no common mumblecrust," the beggar began warily, glancing up more from habit than reason. "Lieutenant John Tinkler."

"I'm a friend, John Tinkler." Gabriel swallowed silently as he saw the empty sockets where eyes had once been, hollow livid flesh beneath dropping lids. "You're a soldier."

"I am," said the man, his back straightening a little, "albeit army-beggared."

"An old Ironside?"

"No. I served the late King as a cannonier and fought the prince's quarrel valiantly. I lost my way at Pontefract."

"You're a long way from Yorkshire, Lieutenant. Water?" Gabriel held his bottle up to the man's lips and without hesitation the beggar took it between his teeth, dragging a cooling swig into his throat.

"Many men are far from home these days, sir," he said when the bottle was lifted gently away, and he wiped his mouth with the dangling sleeve of a stump.

They sat in silence a moment, Gabriel momentarily distracted as he watched incredulous as Tara passed too close to her horse's rump and narrowly avoided a sharp kick in the shin from the miserable beast. "It doesn't seem as you've had much company today," he said at length.

Tinkler shrugged. "I meet divers people every day. I like to ask about their divers destinations."

"Anyone going to the West Country?"

"Not this week, sir."

After a moment Gabriel stood and slipped a sixpence into the man's bowl. "I will leave another by the trunk of the oak tree behind you, beneath the docks leaves, hidden from thieves. You must be more careful who you tell your tale to, John Tinkler, unless you mean only to live on the charity of those compassionated to you as his late majesty's servant."

"Most days, sir, I would not live at all."

"We'll stop here for the night," said Gabriel, startling Tara with sudden speech.

She looked up. The afternoon was already blending into dusk. She'd lost hours to uneasy thoughts and barely noticed their steady progress along the bridleways, let alone their arrival at a straggling thatched village. "Where's here, exactly?"

"Lasham. We're in Hampshire."

"Where is everyone?"

"Laying low… it'll be rufflers…. The soldiers."

"Why would the people hide from soldiers?" she asked, feeling hopelessly foolish.

"They haven't been paid for many months," he replied simply. "They're getting desperate… they're terrorising the countryside."

They crossed a small green, with no sign of life but a murder of crows that squawked with indignation at the interruption, flapping large black wings and resettling heavily as they passed to the single hostelry. Jankyn followed Rowley through a narrow gateway into a small courtyard of the Swan, before stopping abruptly. A lad emerged from the gloomy stable block to greet them, breaking the eerie spell of abandonment.

"I've pushed you too hard," Gabriel observed with a perfunctory glance over Rowley's haunches as he unbuckled the saddlebags. He gave Rowley's nose a quick rub as he walked around to offer his hand and help her dismount. "A journey like this on horseback is not for the faint hearted."

"I am not bloody faint hearted. You can save that kind of compliment for more deserving women."

He saw the battle as plain as day between her instinctively stubborn refusal to accept help and the potent ache in her thighs but his reflexes were quick. As soon as her fingers met his he pulled her towards him without pause, sliding one arm under her cloak for purchase to lift her clean from the horse.

"You'll be sore tomorrow," he started, softly, chiding himself as he took her weight. He was used to this, but of course she had not ridden so far in a very long time, if ever. Her backside would be screaming. He gently set her on the cobbles.

"I'm fine," she lied, stifling a shiver.

"You're exhausted." All day, the only times her face had turned to his was in glowering irritation but she was finally too tired to keep up the fight and the transformation caused his dark brows to furrow. He turned away abruptly, shaking off the urge that came from no-where to press his lips upon hers, gently but with increasing insistence; to hear her moan softly as he trailed soft kisses from her mouth along her jaw line to her neck.

"You need a hearty meal and a decent night's rest," he murmured, as much to himself as to her, swinging his bag onto his shoulder. He was thinking irrationally. *It's not real.* Once he had a route to the men, this would be over. He shook his head and went on into the tavern to arrange for adjoining rooms, leaving her to follow awkwardly behind, her legs seizing in protest at the movement.

14. AFTER HE HAD PATIENTLY ENDURED

A crowd spilled from the Aldgate alehouse into the night, shouting and jostling for position around two men as they circled one another in patchy moonlight, each stripped to the waist, slick with sweat despite the chill air.

"Come now sir, play fair!" An older man dared the general mood, trying to sound lighthearted. "'Twas just twattlers talking. The lad has no chance!"

"How much fairer do you want, God's blood?" came the gruff reply as the large, thickset man took a broad swipe at the other, hitting him hard under the rib cage. He grunted from the exertion, pushing back the hair that fell randomly across his pate and spat into the dusty road as his opponent doubled over, gasping for breath. "I fight single-handed! If his heart is innocent, he will surely prevail!

"You lot really want me to spare this snivelling traitor?" He turned to the jeering crowd that swayed from its usual excess of ale and waved his damaged hand aloft, wrapped in bandages. For the briefest of moments, he felt the street sway with them, the ground shifting underfoot. But his righteous stance found purchase on the compacted earth. "This man has all but confessed a desire to topple our glorious republic! He'd have you enslaved again by the tyranny of kingship!"

And to his pathetic quarry, shifting over the dirt in slow motion, arms protectively clasped across his stomach and his mouth wide, gasping at the air like a floundered fish: "And you, would you prefer the justice of the courts?"

It was a rhetorical question. No man in his right mind would want the authorities involved in an accusation of sedition, especially one bought by Silus Tollemache. He may no longer be a Major General but he was still a force to be reckoned with. The Lord Protector was an old man; traitors reasoned he was treading water until the cavaliers crawled back to the capital. And crawl they would, on their bellies, like serpents into the Garden of Eden, poisoning and infecting the purpose of the Commonwealth, the righteous rule that Godly men like Silus had already given long, bloody years of their lives to protect. Jumpy London magistrates were erring on the side of caution, but Eden relied for its future on men like him.

In any case, there was no chance for the traitor to reply. An uppercut swiftly followed, the fist moving at speed before his body, meeting his jaw. The crowd roared its approval as another punch met its mark. No one wanted to join their neighbour.

The smaller man had yet to land a hit. He gave the painful impression that he'd never landed one in his life. Dark hair was plastered to his forehead with sweat while bloody circles were forming on his wiry torso, blackening over the pox scars that already covered his body. He stumbled back as his head jagged from repeated blows. But he was still standing. Just.

"Come now, Cooper, you worthless poltroon!" Silus jeered, his eyes drinking in the awe and, he was pleased to see it still, the fear of his audience. "Stop acting the pigeon, boy! Will you answer my fists and prove your innocence or are you as wet as your mother's legs when she dreams of me at night?"

Guffaws rippled across the crowd and he grinned. There was pleasure to be taken from the sophisticated crowd of the capital. His West Country charges, backwards farmers to a man, were more likely to take a sharp intake of prudish breath at such a joke. He was a presence to be reckoned with in the east as well as the west. Perhaps he should settle here with his new wife. Whatever the lobcock Moore had said, Cromwell would resolve the situation. His exemplarily patience, a virtue for which he was not recognised, would be rewarded.

And so, after he had patiently endured, he obtained the promise. It was payback time, and by God he was ready for it. The breaking of Penruddock's traitors, the status of Major General bestowed and then stolen away. Cromwell owed him. The Villiers bitch had spiced his fantasies since he caught glimpse of her pale face as a child, eyes wide, hair thick and loose and plump lips forming a silent "o" as he emptied his seed into her whore of a mother.

He had come close three years ago, but somewhere between the conviction and execution of the traitor Gregory VIlliers he lost sight of his prize and, like an animal, she'd gone to ground. At first exhilarating, the thrill of the chase had quickly muted to the dull thud of frustration. The things he would do. He wouldn't be interrupted again. The thought nudged at his groin, rousing life. Even whores had their limits, but wives. He licked his lips, tasting the faintly metallic tang of blood. The cooper's blood. Silus paced slowly around the dizzy man, his right hand whipping up more deafening cheers, his left still strapped into a ball. He played to the audience, taking his time. He was enjoying this. No point ending it too soon.

Suddenly his cocky berth was not quite wide enough and the quarry finally saw its chance, lunging in wildly and landing a jab squarely on the fat, ugly nose. For a second it looked as if it might just be enough to floor the goliath; he wavered gently and the crowd held its breath. But a second later came the sickening realisation that he wasn't wavering, he was laughing, literally shaking with laughter. Silus held his sides as the guffaws rocked his body and his victim paled, stepped backwards, trapped by his neighbours, swollen eyes searching in desperation for a gap in the crowd. He should never have hit back. Everyone knew it. Take the beating and crawl away. The contact would cost him dear.

When his throaty laughter had run its course, Silus took a single step and swung his right arm with exaggerated showmanship. His balled fist made contact with the man's temple and Gilbert Cooper, assistant barrel maker, father of four, smallpox survivor and suspected royalist pamphleteer, crumpled comatose to the dust. The entertainment was over and the crowd called the victor's name. People patted his wet back, as if appreciative for the distraction, before filing back inside. The cups would be lined up on the bar.

With a triumphant sneer, Silus bent forwards to gather his breath and let beads of sweat drip down his nose onto the street, palms flat against his mud coloured breeches. Who dared to say he was getting too old for this game? Who dared steal his property and think to make him look a fool before the Protector? He glanced over at the cooper's head, laying at an awkward angle to his torso, dark curls spread like a halo, and pictured the form of Moore in his place.

"Si-Silus To-?" A small voice came from his elbow.

"Who wants to know?" Silus stood to face a thin, dirty scrap of a boy of no more than thirteen years. He was all shaking limbs and stutter, and Silus narrowed his eyes in irritation. He should be enjoying this moment, not playing nursemaid to a mewling brat. "Well? Spit it out!"

The boy stumbled over his words, clearly terrified of the man he had spent the evening searching the taverns for.

"Sir, I'm John Hardwick, sir. I've been sent from Petersham with an urgent message from Bulstrode Wortley"

"So?" The growl was indifferent but Silus' interest peaked. Wortley was Thurloe's man, buried deep in the household of that bastard Moore. Arrogant fool had no idea. Not so clever after all.

"Sir, I... Sir. Wortley sends word that-" The boy yelped and stammered as Silus grabbed his shirt and pulled him in closer to his rancid pants, shaking him by the shoulders. "That- That-"

The message was not forthcoming and impatience descended in a red mist as the teeth and torso trembled. The threat on Silus' sour breath misted around the boys' head: "Cut through this circle with the straightest path, boy, or by God I'll put you on the road to Hell."

The child gulped at the air and words tumbled out between them. "Sir, she's left."

"Who?"

"T- Tara. Tara Villiers."

"And where's she bloody gone to, you wretch?" Silus growled before suddenly releasing the boy's shoulders, stroking his tattered, grime-encrusted jerkin smooth. He took a deep breath. It might be worth playing it gently, to get more out of the messenger than Wortley or even Thurloe ever intended.

"Devon. Likely... t-to Exeter, sir."

Silus' lips curled into a thin smile. He spent years keeping order in the western wilderness: those were his people, that was his promised land. If she was running, it was straight into his arms. As good as his word, Cromwell would send him home to receive her.

But this was no place for such a sensitive discussion. He spat into the dust again, ridding himself of the warm blood that swilled around his teeth, and motioned for the boy to follow him as he headed into a nearby doorway, giving a vicious kick to the still prostrate cooper as he passed for good measure. ☐

15. A LESSON

After a cursory breakfast they were back on the road, in the same strained silence as yesterday. But after a couple of hours on the highway, Gabriel reined off into woodland, onto an altogether less well-travelled trail. Jankyn plodded blindly behind without hesitation, blustering immediately through leaves and scraping Tara's leg against a tree trunk.

"*Really?*" she exclaimed, as much to Jankyn as to Gabriel as the horse stumbled, hooves slipping on soggy layers of leaf mulch. She tugged hard at her skirt where the grey wool had caught on rough bark and rubbed at the chafed skin on her calf.

"We need to leave the main roads in case we're being followed," he explained, as she contorted forward to avoid more low-hanging branches.

"I doubt very much that anyone would want to follow us."

"The landlady at Lasham had word from London to make ready for a party of important government men. They're due to arrive tomorrow," he started, pausing when Tara made a dismissive snorting sound: "It sounds as though Thurloe is heading to Exeter already, looking for evidence of your uncle's conspiracy. That or Cromwell has sent Tollemache home empty-handed."

"Or it's pure coincidence," she said primly. *Eight days.* Not long enough for paranoid detours.

"Perhaps, but I imagine you'd prefer to avoid running into Thurloe and I can certainly do without bumping into your aggrieved suitor," he replied reasonably. "We have at least a day's head start. We'll take it steady and follow the River Test, camp at Mottisfont Abbey tonight then cross the river and pick up the road to Salisbury tomorrow. We won't lose time."

The forest closed in tight around them, accepting their bodies into its protective arms, and Tara slowly relaxed for the first time in days. The air freshened with the resin smell of sap and sunlight dappled through the branches, casting flickering shadows on their shoulders. Clusters of hawthorn flowers looked like fresh snow and a carpet of late bluebells was as thick as sea foam, dampening the sounds of movement. The gentle whispers of leaves and bird song blended slowly into a harmonious charm, punctuated only by the occasional staccato snap of twigs underfoot, gentle whickers from the horses and then, suddenly, a desolate scream.

"A woman!" Tara started in the saddle, causing Jankyn to spring sideways, ears flattening.

"No…" Gabriel had already pulled Rowley up next to a giant, twisted oak and he was sitting stock-still. He put out a hand for silence and she steadied her mount as best she could so they could listen. Gradually, the rhythmic murmur of a man's voice reached them.

"Singing?" Tara looked at Gabriel, her brows furrowed as he slipped out of the saddle and slung his reins loosely over a branch.

"It's Psalm 17," he said grimly as he pulled his sword. "In the war… we'd sing it as we came into a battle. Stay here. Keep your head down."

"Gabriel…" she started, sliding stiffly down from Jankyn and squealing as he turned a long nose to nip her arm.

"God's blood Tara, be quiet." He pulled her abruptly out of the beast's reach. "Listen to me, Stay put but if I'm not back within a quarter hour, get on Rowley. Ride as fast as you can along the route we agreed. West. Get to Treguddick Manor, on the road south of Exeter. *Treguddick*. Find my uncle Sir Henry Godolphin or his son Tom. They'll keep you safe."

"Where are you going?" Rowley whuffled quietly as his master disappeared through dense foliage, following the direction of the tuneless voice. She looked to Jankyn for the same understanding but he just snorted contemptuously before dipping his head to yank at the abundant ferns.

"*...thou that savest by thy right hand them which put their trust in thee from those that rise up against them. Keep me as the apple...*"

He approached silently from the north, the footing slippery over the exposed roots and upturned rocks that led to a small clearing, and he dipped down behind a large boulder to survey the scene. Two men, one armed with a worn crossbow, were sat on tree stumps with their backs to him, their swords sheathed and their posture listless. One of them, safely into his forties, had his eyes cast to Heaven, and he was singing the psalm with the lazy air of habit.

Gabriel craned further around the boulder and took a sharp intake of breath when he saw what they were doing. A third, white-haired man was tied upright to a large standing stone before them. It was a fitting theatre, he realised, some ancient ruin of a standing circle now engulfed by the forest. The sacrifice had already been shot twice, bolts protruding from an arm and a leg like the paintings of early martyrs. He was panting with the effort of containing the pain and two thick streams of blood ran to pool in the mud in front of him.

"*... They are inclosed in their own fat: with their mouth they speak proudly...*"

"You heard Boyle here, you worthless luberwort" said one of the aggressors conversationally as he wound the crannequin with a creaking click, click, click, and slowly laid a fresh bolt into the notch behind the lathe. "Where's our coin?"

"*... in our steps: they have set their eyes bowing down to the earth; Like as a lion that is greedy of his prey...*"

"I swear, Alswood, I swear it... I don't know, I've not had it, I swear it. Please. We fought together... from the start. Turnham Green... Newbury... We are brothers in arms! Brothers!"

"*... disappoint him, cast him down: deliver my soul from the wicked, which is thy sword. From men which are thy hand...*"

"Last chance, Sergeant." Alswood stood and swung the tiller forward, catching the weapon with practiced familiarity and pointing it squarely at an undamaged leg. His finger stroked a crude trigger. At this range, the arrow would find its mark with bone-splitting force and Gabriel winced, his fingers tightening on the hilt of his sword. It crossed his mind, to go silently back to Tara and lead her safely away, but the blood pounding against his bones knew that wasn't an option. The soldiers were highwaymen; what began in the war years as sanctioned requisitioning had ended for many as a routine of violent plunder and itinerant thievery. These men had pistoled, slashed, rent and brained for a wage once. Now they did it because, blank eyed and hungry, there was nothing else they could do better.

> "...*O Lord, from men of the world, which have their portion in this life, and whose belly thou fillest with thy hid treasure: they are full of children, and leave the rest of their substance to their babes...*"

"Boyle, please. I haven't got it! The money never arrived! My orders came direct from Whitehall to be patient!"

Taking advantage of the distraction, Gabriel came up swiftly behind the crossbow holder, the sharp edge of his blade resting against the side of the man's throat. "You heard him; he hasn't got your money. Let this go."

Alswood twitched, breathing heavily through gritted teeth as Gabriel pulled a second blade and poked his back in warning. Boyle stopped singing, his bloodshot eyes widening as he slowly drew his own sword from the safety of its sheath. "This isn't your business, stranger. This leasing-monger owes us army wages. We were promised 8d a day for the last two years if we served His Highness and this man now tells us he hasn't the cash. This is justice."

"This is murder." Gabriel flicked the point of his sword forward into the cross bow to dislodge the bolt so that it fell against a stone with a small metallic ting. He motioned for Alswood to drop the weapon and shuffled them both forward until he could stamp on the lathe, splintering it and rendering it permanently impotent. "Must I teach you justice?"

"You would try and kill us both for seeking what is rightfully ours? We've others from the regiment on their way here too. Twelve men in total."

"I've killed more for less."

Boyle ran at him then, eyes burning like embers and sword suddenly high. Gabriel immediately spun Alswood around to face the onslaught, ducking to avoid a head-level swipe and twisting to ram his bent shoulder into the oncoming ruffler's naval. Momentum dragged Boyle's weight forward and he became airborne momentarily, rolling over Gabriel's back to land heavily against a boulder.

There was no time to check he was down: when Gabriel stood, his heel slipping momentarily on leaf mould, his captive had recovered a blade and it clashed heavily with his weapon, instinctively raised in parry. Three swipes met in even force. Four. Five. Finally, a badly judged feint led the man too far forward and Gabriel twisted, ducking again until he could reach the man's back. He sliced along the inside of his knees so that Alswood fell down with a holler and turned to thrust his sword without hesitation straight through the man's chest, yanking it back out as he slumped forward to the ground.

Gabriel stepped forward, bringing his bloody sword down on the ropes that held the Sergeant captive. Chest heaving, he took the man's weight, settling him onto the ground with a rough exclamation at the extent of the damage. It was worse than he thought. When he pulled back he looked the man directly in the eye: "The bolt in your thigh…"

"I would be shriven. I have sinned," whispered the man as his head fell forward with a vague nod at the bloody body of Alswood lying before him. "I slept with that loiter-sack's wife. It was worth it," he offered a half grin, briefly displaying blackened teeth before frowning and his voice cracked into a whisper. "Listen… there's another… crossbow."

Gabriel's head spun instantly round and his stomach lurched to see Boyle was gone. He scanned the forest for a sign. Nothing.

"Where?" he snapped but it was too late, the man's lungs hissed with the last ragged expiration and he slid forward, landing heavily against Gabriel's arm. With an unceremonious yank he was free and back on his feet, sprinting back to where he had left her.

Tara stopped dead, leaning quickly back against the broad trunk as a second bolt whistled past the oak with a gentle pshht to embed in a tree beyond her. Her heart was pounding and her head too full of terror to think clearly. No sign of Gabriel. No bloody sign of him. Just Rowley, his ears flattened, eyes rolling as he stamped the ground, dancing uneasily but refusing to leave. Jankyn was chewing fatalistically on the green offering of the forest floor, either oblivious or indifferent to the threat.

"I've plenty of bolts, lovely," came a cold voice, clearly audible above the click-click-click of a reloading weapon. "You ain't hidin' for long… What say we come to an arrangement?"

She closed her eyes tightly a moment, willing calm, a decision, a plan. A sentence. She could think of no words to appease him, of no sound but screaming and for a split second she thought she was. A hand came down firm on her mouth and her eyes shot open.

"Tara, it's me," he whispered. "Breathe. I need you to trust me. Stay still and keep him talking. Draw him closer. Do you understand?"

She nodded, strength flooding back into her limbs with his feel of his heat and she called out, tentatively at first: "What... what kind of arrangement?"

Without hesitation, Gabriel reached above her to a large knot and, taking hold, scrambled quickly up the gnarled trunk until he could pull himself onto a broad branch. From there he rose to standing, disappearing further up and around the giant oak. A bird flapped its wings indignantly at the invasion and a small shower of trigs fell at her feet,

The disembodied voice laughed, confident. "What say you come here and find out?"

"What say you come here and show me?"

It was a moment or two before the ruffler replied, but when he did the threat was terrifyingly close, just around the trunk: "No rash moves, girl, remember I can stick you-"

The sword dropped from the branches like a plumb line to enter the man's skull, the sound nothing more than a whisper and the soft crack of an eggshell. With a gentle thud, Gabriel landed on the ground behind the body and moved to wordlessly gather Tara up and lift her back onto Jankyn's saddle. She took the reins mechanically with numb fingers, barely noticing that he had left to drag the body back between the leaves, leaving a bloody trail that he kicked over. She didn't see him extract his sword or return or mount Rowley.

"They were expecting company. We need to put some distance behind us, Tara, now. Hold on."

She barely registered the flick of his crop on Jankyn's rump or the fact that the beast broke into a reluctant canter behind Rowley. She just leaned forward instinctively and gripped hold of the edge of the saddle until her fingers turned white. The horses picked a blustering path through the forest and she turned her face to one side to avoid whipping branches and showers of leaves, not seeing where they went.

It was a long while before Jankyn came to halt, heavy snorts rattling through his barrel-like chest, his flesh shuddering in waves under a sweat-darkened coat.

Gabriel broke the silence, reining Rowley around before her. "What is it?"

"I have to stop," she mumbled, teeth chattering.

He looked at her a moment before turning to survey the spot, Rowley's hooves prancing obediently into a small clearing on their right, a little back from the path and mostly hidden by a row of chestnut and oak trees. Defensible. The clearing itself was ringed by willows, and beyond it the glitter of water sparkled between branches.

"We're still on the River Test, and by the looks of it this part is tidal, which means we can't be far from Mottisfont," he said as he returned: "That's good. We'll stay here tonight."

He swung one leg over Rowley and jumped down, slipping off the tack and swiftly hobbling the horse before patting its rump encouragingly towards the grass and pausing to look at her. "Are you still sore from the saddle?"

"No," she lied quietly, sliding slowly down and turning to unpack the saddlebags.

Her stiff, shaking fingers struggled to unlock the buckles and he caught a glimpse of darkened skin at her wrists. The onset of bruising from the meaty paws of Silus Tollemache or maybe even Wortley. He swallowed a lurch of self-loathing. Even if Tollemache conceded his prize, she would be at the mercy of any other thug. If he hadn't killed the man, the ruffler was ready to prove the point. Did she realise the danger?

"Tara?"

Her murmured response was dismissive but he pulled her gently towards him, sliding his fingers into her hair and tilting her head up. He expected immediate resistance; he deserved nothing less, but in the first heartbeat, when his mouth met hers, there was surprise but not anger. A softness in the tiredness of her limbs. A moan escaped between them, barely audible, and he gathered her closer, taking her weight, encouraged by a small shudder that betrayed the instinct coursing through her body. He tested for limits only to find her lips parting, to let his tongue explore and tease, and without warning a searing ache coursed through his veins, galvanising his muscles, tightening his hold on the nape of her neck as he hardened.

She lifted her fingers to lace tentatively into his own, and his eye caught the purpled stain. It was almost painful to relinquish her swollen mouth but the damage was an ugly jolt back to reality and he pulled back. With a thrill of self-disgust, he cocked his head, watching though fallen strands of dark hair, waiting for her to open her eyes and register his grin. "You were supposed to fight me off...

"Wait, Tara, wait," he urged as she quickly took a step back, frowning as she spun from him. "You can't be at the mercy of any-"

She gave a hollow laugh, frozen with the exhaustion of always being one step behind: "That was to prove a point?"

"I'd have you better able to defend yourself," he said, as evenly as he could manage. "Tollemache's not known for his graciousness in defeat. I should not have let him walk-"

"He lost three fingers," she snapped, following his gaze and tugging on the long sleeves of her gown to cover the marks.

"Not from his sword hand. You were right, Tara, in Southwark," he started, turning to take his saddle and sling it over a low hanging branch. "I took a risk. If I hadn't of been able to get inside your room... you were his for the taking."

Tara stared at him blankly. *Tollemache's for the taking.* Or Wortley's. Or the rufflers'. *Or his.* She was supposed to have screamed and kicked his shins and clawed at his eyes the moment he touched her, like she had when others tried.

"You could not fight me off," he said, reading her thoughts, stamped plainly in the reddening of her cheeks. "Even if you'd wanted to."

"You smug, gargell-faced, bastard... I'll run you through."

He grinned at that, sliding two rapiers from the sheath in his saddle and holding one out to her, balancing the long, sharp blade between his thumb and forefinger. "Be my guest."

Still reeling, she hesitated before wrapping her fingers around the hilt. Beneath an elaborate protective cup, the weapon felt beautifully balanced but she let the blade drop heavily to the floor. "I'm not playing -"

"It's not a game."

"You want me to hurt you?"

"I want to show you how."

"You know full well there's barely a man I meet who is not larger, or stronger-"

"You can use that to your advantage. A man's bulk makes him unstable."

"Leave God to protect me," she mumbled stubbornly.

"What if God is late again? I can't help but notice He often takes His time. And I might not always be here," he added quietly, running his hand back through his hair. He tapped her steel with his own blade before taking a step back, his voice hardening: "Raise your weapon."

"I might hurt you," she said, unconvincingly. The will might be strong but the chances were not great, she thought ruefully, watching as he raised his own blade, his movements as fluid and self-assured as water.

"And I thought my loving wife would relish the opportunity!" He was still laughing at her, she realised with a flush of anger that raised her sword arm. It tipped into action when he added, in mock seriousness. "Don't pout, Tatty Angel."

Only a few people had ever been tolerated to use that: Mad Mike Evelyn. Ralph… and then only when she'd been laughing too hard to fight him. She lunged but without the slightest effort and only the faintest movement he deflected the blade and it fell from her hand. Tara cursed, bent to pick up the weapon and lunged a second time, swiping the blade towards him like a particularly ineffective scythe.

Again, the blades clashed and her weapon rattled to the ground. This time, he jogged around and slapped her backside with the flat side of his blade, causing her to yelp in surprise. "Don't rush," he replied calmly as she growled in exasperation. "Watch me closely. Imagine you're leading a dance. Dictate the pace. You're wasting your energy."

By now, she was really trying to draw blood. For a third time, the sword hit the mossy forest floor. A fourth. A fifth. A sixth. Countless times. He'd barely moved, she noticed, while beads of sweat gathered on her brow and slid down the backs of her thighs every time she stretched, swung and lost the blade.

"Watch for clues in the angle of my blade. Point up. Stay light on your feet."

"This is stupid!" she screamed finally between pants, glaring at him as she wiped her face with the back of her sleeve. "Congratulations, you're the better soldier. What an enormous bloody surprise. I've had enough."

Gabriel's chest shook as he struggled to contain his laughter. "Using a sword is as much about feigning attack as attacking. If you look confident enough, if you have the measure of the weapon and can hold it well, a man might think twice before coming at you. I'm not expecting miracles, but I want you able to buy yourself time for God to arrive."

It sounded reasonable but the effort was far outweighing the reward. Nearly half an hour had passed and the exercise was getting substantially harder; she could barely hold the sword aloft any longer and her breathing was laboured, her chest too constrained by the binds of the stays. She bent to catch her breath. Her cheeks were pink from exertion and her hair tumbled about her shoulders, the old linen cap long lost in the forest. A runnel of sweat slid down between her breasts, tickling like flies' feet and with an irritated hiss she swept her fingers down over her skin.

She glanced at him, one eyebrow raised, and slowly he moved behind her. "May I?" His long fingers covered hers as he angled the tip towards an imaginary adversary and he slid a solid, muscular leg between her thighs, forcing her stance to spread a little. His warm breath was on her neck and when his hair fell forward to tickle the sensitive skin it rippled.

"A man with bulk like Tollemache will be dragged along a set path. His feet will tell you the direction; watch them and take the cue to move right or left. Remember how I twisted the blade from your hand? I was aiming to flick it from *here*. Do that and now you can sweep at his arm, like so, and cause a little damage to his flesh even if he will not relinquish his weapon.

"Always aim for the torso. If he's wearing body armour there are weak points where a blade can get purchase. If you have chance to pierce his chest from the front, aim for *here*, or *here*." His body moved with hers, taught and alert as he stretched out her arm to the imaginary adversary.

"You're small and fast. Move around him." He ran a hand down her back to illustrate his point: "Once you're at his back, aim for here, the kidneys. Push up."

"I imagine you know a lot about planting a blade in a man's back," she muttered, flicking her eyes over her shoulder. "Very chivalrous."

"Chivalry can fall on its sword. Tara," he growled, choosing to ignore the dig. He dropped his hold of her. "If a man would try to hurt you, I would have you stab him in the back, slice across his eyes and lop off his cock. Now, again."

She must have closed her eyes for now he was opposite her, ready to attack again. She raised her sword arm, pointing the tip at his chest. This time he lunged as aggressor, his eyes with a cold gleam. For all the world, he was going to run her through. Almost instinctively, she echoed the earlier parry he'd demonstrated, and while it was not quite practiced enough to pull the weapon from his hand, she deflected his blade so that it missed her body entirely. Momentum dragged him forward to follow it, and in a split second she had twisted around, bringing her weapon back in between them, the tip finding his crotch, forcing his body to stop abruptly an inch from hers.

Their eyes met and without warning he grinned, and electricity cut through her like sudden light through the branches.

16. OTHERS

He extracted a pistol from a holster next to his saddlebag and, after a second's hesitation, she moved closer to watch as his long fingers loaded it. It was a doglock pistol, the type Ralph carried that summer in Weycroft Hall, before he joined Charlie's troops. He retrieved a single lead shot from his pocket and bit the top off his powder cask, tapping a small measure of powder into the pan.

"I don't want to carry a gun."

"I don't want you to either," he agreed. "This is dangerous enough in the right hands. In yours, I'd fear for both our lives."

She snorted and he glanced up at her with a gentle smile as he finished priming the weapon, his movements efficient and practiced: "But we need to eat this evening." He sparked a flame on a match cord and flicked back the dog safety catch, his eyes scanning the forest. "See to the horses and build a fire," he added, in the habit of command.

"Sir, yes sir," she muttered, tugging her forelock as he disappeared between the trees.

After leading Rowley and Jankyn down the cool water of the river, she unbuckled a small sack of oats from Gabriel's tightly packed saddlebag and started to relax, enjoying the nudge of their velvet noses. The threat of the rufflers was long gone. Late afternoon sun dappled the clearing, lending a vivid orange and yellow warmth to the scene. The grass looked greener than any lawn she'd seen; the ferns when she brushed against them were softer than the brittle leaves of the seemingly endless Petersham winter.

THE SEALED KNOT

It was more than a new county, they had stumbled straight into a new season, bursting with life and promise. There were still some wild bluebells on the forest floor and an early elder was coming into bloom, its perfumed tones rising through air otherwise heavy with scent of wet earth. Bird song filled her ears, the happy homecoming trills of sparrows and tits returning to roost for the night. It made too little sense to explain it to herself but despite everything, she felt more alive than she ever had. Dirty, hungry, tired, aching, laden with armfuls of branches, she could almost taste the freedom in the earthy magic of the clearing. She sat back on her heels, tucking the flint and steel back in the placket of her skirt, proud that the fire had taken so readily and was building nicely.

A single shot shattered the stillness. The horses whinnied and she held her breath until Gabriel emerged silently from the wood, a hare hanging lifeless from his left hand. He dropped to his knees before the fire, pulled a knife from the scabbard on his belt and stripped back the pelt. He sliced away chunks of flesh, skewered them on the two swords and placed sizzling into the flames.

She watched without comment, wondering abstractly at the unsentimental efficiency of his hands, compared to Jack's more haphazard approach to butchery. The few rabbits he'd brought home she'd prepared herself. He patiently twisted his sword, heating the meat evenly, and at last satisfied he pulled several cooked chunks from the blade with a large dock leaf, handing it to her to eat with her fingers. It smelled delicious and her stomach rumbled in appreciation as she nibbled slowly at the hot edges.

After a while he glanced at her: "Why were you in Petersham, Tara?"

She looked up, surprised by the question. "The man who built Ham House was a friend of my father. I remembered him talking about the village. It seemed like as good place as any. I didn't know you were granted the estate. I wasn't there waiting for you, if that's what you meant."

"It wasn't," he smiled. "I meant, after your father's trial, why not stay with Edward Villiers in Exeter? You were close-"

"He told me to go," she said truthfully. Eddie had pleaded with her to leave his world for fear that she would perish within it. They were both too stunned by grief and fear in those dark days to think logically; Petersham could have been any town or village in the country, so long as it wasn't Exeter. And of course, it wasn't just treason that Eddie had her running from, although she didn't know it then. It was also Tollemache. She glanced at Gabriel. A line had deepened between his brow but he didn't say anything.

"Eddie was too busy with the Society of Friends and his Quaker preaching to take on a niece," she added hurriedly. "Besides, I couldn't go home to Weycroft Hall. It was empty. We were besieged during the war."

"Tollemache," he hissed and she nodded.

"The estate was ruined. Crops and cattle neglected... woodland felled for quick profit. My father left jointures, debts... he refused to show contrition to the authorities or pay Cromwell's composition tax. And he wouldn't beg at the sequestration committee for the charity of a grant from his own assets."

"So Weycroft Hall was confiscated," Gabriel finished thoughtfully.

"It was stolen. Everything..."

"Not everything." He picked up her left hand, ignoring her flinch, and slid off the silver wedding band, handing it back so she could see the whisper of an engraving inside: Ralph, ad victoria, Mama 1645. She gasped as he continued: "Of course, many thought it was justice making those who'd willingly dismantle the new government paying for its furtherance. After Penruddock, the Major Generals' decimation tax on known royalists financed entire militias to support the regular army."

"It was tyranny... there's a faint line between taxation and plunder," she reflected blankly, wondering at the ring. *To victory*. It must have been a gift that last summer in Weycroft. A charm for good luck. She glanced at him and pushed the ring onto her middle finger, forcing it over her knuckle for safety. "The sequestration committee did not pursue justice with its fines. And there are scores being settled even now, up and down this entire country. Personal, petty jealousies, legitimised by a..."

"You're an intelligent woman, Tara," he interrupted gently. "Do you seriously think your uncle's arrest is a score being settled? Cromwell believes that he commands a section of the Sealed Knot."

She let her head fall; the tack of the conversation was too dangerous. After a while she raised her eyes to his, her gaze firm. "How does it feel to have spent so many years settling Cromwell's scores? Are you proud to have turned your back on your prince, on all of us?"

Gabriel's jaw tightened and he ran a hand back through his loose hair before answering: "Conscience is not easily ignored, Tara. It's like love; it can't be bought or sold. We each of us believe we're right... only history will know which was correct."

"You really want us enslaved to the whims of this mad man?" she said incredulously, momentarily forgetting her wariness. It had always seemed entirely understandable that men followed the Protector for power or privilege, but conscience?

"The Lord Protector takes direction straight from God," he shrugged.

"That just makes him unpredictable! To talk to God is prayer, but to have Him talk back is insanity. Cromwell is a murderous hypocrite, he-"

"Be careful," Gabriel warned softly, reminding her again of his allegiance. Dark strands of hair had fallen forward to cover his eyes and the ground gave way a little as she cursed herself again for forgetting. There was no telling what Gabriel would report back to Thurloe, or Cromwell; how much of her own conversation by the campfire would be used as evidence to convict Eddie?

"Besides," he added, changing his tone with the subject, "A man is a slave to whatever has mastered him. God, coin, woman, it's all the same."

He took a deep breath and lay back on the ground, staring up at the sky as he trotted out the snippets of battlefield speeches he had stood through, weapon in hand and heart pounding fast in anticipation of combat: "And as we all know, Cromwell has healed the nation's divisions and saved its soul. He has rehabilitated the ignorant to bring them closer to God and he has rightly ground the royalists under foot, every last one an ungodly, debauched, degenerate rake. Cavaliers defile women; they defile the church and the country..."

"Pah!" she interrupted, feeling the bile drown her promises to herself, her voice full of bitter sarcasm as she stared at him, incredulous. "Stuff of puritan fairy tales. Souls like those rufflers? Or perhaps you were talking about my brother? Ralph was always so keen on murder and defilement-"

"Ralph was a good man," he replied evenly, sitting upright again, the broad line of his shoulders tense and still, his arms resting on his knees.

"What the Hell would you know about being a good man? There is only one way you could have my brother's ring-" Her voice sounded strange and she swallowed quickly, bringing her features back under as careful a control as she could muster.

"At the Battle of Worcester... we were like children," he started quietly.

"Is that how you grant yourself absolution for killing him? You tell yourself you were too young to know any better?"

Gabriel wasn't looking at her but at the flames, and his fingers stroked his temple. "I didn't mean that. I was 21, a man by any standard... I meant that only boys walk into battle armed with enough arrogance to think that their time will not come. It was a game we'd played many times. We were not weighed down with ghosts on our backs as well as swords in our hands." He hung his head, his features strained. "Me, Ralph, Charlie... Each of us were stuffed full of duty and honour; too damn righteous to fall prey to other men's ambitions-"

"You sacrificed your honour the moment you declared against the King. You deserved to die. It should have been you," she said shakily.

"Barely a day goes by that I wouldn't agree," he whispered before looking up suddenly. "Do you know what makes fighting if not easy then, at least more... more normal?"

She shook her head slowly, arms hugging tightly around her knees, as if she could draw herself into an impenetrable ball.

"Partly it's the drilling," he started, staring back at flames that played along the straight lines of his nose and made red light dance in the stubble on his jaw. "By the time you've spent months in the company of your commander's barking orders, the noise of battle will fade into the background and you hear only his words, his will. And partly it's the sacrifice. A soldier only needs one weapon; the army fashions a man's body as it might take a lump of softwood, and chisel and scrape and oil until it will do whatever it must for whatever purpose that musters.

"But mostly it's the anonymity. Wars rely on foreign hordes of Frenchmen or Spaniards or Moors, intent on ugly conquest. Dark skinned or ash light, brutish or fair, it doesn't matter as long as they are the other." He glanced at her then before continuing, trying to read understanding in the tense lines of her body: "Only in.. in our war, there was no other. Same tongue, same clothes. Some officers had sashes but most men used bloody sprigs of leaves to mark out their allegiance. Those field signs don't last long once you step out of formation. Same accents, same families, same history. How can you swing your sword at a man in the heat of battle without knowing, really knowing, if when he turns you will see your enemy or your brother?"

"It can't have been so hard, you stayed with the army."

"I couldn't do anything else," he said with a small shrug. "But after Worcester, I knew I had to find the other, an enemy so fierce and brutal that I could lose myself in blood; be cleansed in it. Ireland had a reputation for delivering such men."

"And was it easier?"

"Yes," he said simply, frowning in surprise at the confession. "For a while."

"Tell me what happened in Worcester, Gabriel. I need to hear it. All of it." Her voice was quiet but firm, and there was a moment of silence before he flicked his eyes to her and nodded imperceptibly.

"It was cold for early September. Rain had fallen all night. I pulled on my breastplate as the drums began beating and rubbed a handful of dirt over the steel to dull the sheen," he glanced at her hurriedly. "I'd already killed a man - for a war with no fronts, it was easy enough to find an enemy, still my father thought it was time for a real test…

"We camped less than a mile from the city gates and had the advantage of numbers, some eight thousand more men than those mustered under Charlie's banner, but everyone around me was subdued; I wasn't the only one expecting to find friends. The men filed slowly out of camp singing psalms, like the one you heard earlier. It raises the hairs on the back of your neck.

"A vanguard moved forward, forming a row that dissolved into the drizzle until the only sign they had ever existed was a line of bobbing lights, like fireflies." He grimaced, nearly a rueful smile when she frowned. "We lit our matches at both ends and marched with the fire smouldering. It's a pretty tell-tale in the dark, but a pistol is no use without a fuse."

"You attacked that morning?" He saw her shoulders rise and fall, and knew that she was fighting not to cry in front of him. She twisted the ring on her finger for distraction and he forced himself to stare back into the dancing flames, taking a deep breath and drawing a hand back through his hair, the hard contours of his face lit again by a golden flicker.

"We tried. Cromwell is a fine battlefield tactician and the initiative lay with us. I joined Charles Fleetwood, he was a Lieutenant-General then, and we forced our way over the River Severn on pontoon bridges to breach St John's. Other regiments manoeuvred to encircle the walls to the east of the city and the batter the southern ramparts."

Once across the river, Fleetwood's forces spread out, sweeping its western bank towards Worcester's walls. The line stretched into a thin semicircle and each man found himself alone. As King of Scotland, Charles Stuart had rallied a regiment of highlanders under Colonel Keith and they offered stubborn resistance to the approaching roundheads, waiting in the fields to bitterly contest every hedgerow. Progress was achingly slow and hours passed, the sun dropping back behind heavy clouds before it got so much as overhead.

By now, the home-grown royalists had already retreated behind the city walls, and slowly but surely the battle followed them, snapping tiredly at their heels, impervious to two sorties hurriedly organised by the Prince, who took advantage of his viewpoint at the top of Worcester Cathedral. The city's defences were finally stormed from three different directions as darkness came. Roundhead and cavalier forces skirmished on the streets. Men lay as they fell in the confusion, trodden under prancing horses' feet, their rent bodies falling heavily together in a grotesque parody of the kinship many had shared in life.

"When night fell there was chaos. Thousands of men crashed about the walled city like bumblebees in a jug, drunk on fear and blinded by the dark. The rain fell, picking up the blood, coating the street like oil.

"It was impossible to know friend from foe. I became separated from my men, and ran through a warren of side streets, desperate to come across Fleetwood or… or anyone with an orange sash."

Gabriel ran almost literally into Charlie on the High Street. Breathing heavily, muddied and bloodied features crisscrossed with pale rivulets drawn with sweat or rain, he emerged from an alleyway as the Prince crashed down the road high on a black horse, with Ralph at his side. It was a desperate cavalry charge, they'd lost their armour and Charlie was shouting at the top of his lungs as they clattered heavily toward the city gate, trying to corral his troops and escape.

"Ralph was an excellent horseman. He saw me and skidded to a halt on the cobbles. His mount was straining to rear, eyes bulging and nostrils flaring at the sight of me. My sword dropped but there was no time-

"There's a redoubt on a small hill overlooking Worcester called Fort Royal. Its big guns had been turned on the city, I'm still not sure on whose orders but fire fell suddenly. Great chunks of masonry and lengths of smouldering wood landed heavily into the street around us. We looked at each other just a moment, then the rest of his men galloped down the street behind him and Charlie screamed at me to get back into the shadows.

"It was quick, Tara," he said softly, understanding the hitch in her breath as she bit back the question. "A canon ball struck the gate and a shower of rubble fell from above us. I swear to you he didn't suffer."

"And then what, to the victor the spoils?" She thrust her shaking hand in front of him, Ralph's ring glinting in the firelight.

"I thought to keep it safe," he frowned. "I thought, one day… I thought I'd find you."

She looked at him then and the hot pain stabbed sharp. "How dare you! How dare you mourn him! He was my brother and your bloody battle killed him! And for what? What did his death accomplish? Damn you, you should have protected him! I loved him!"

"I loved him too," he said quietly. "Jesus, Tara, can you really think I went Worcester to kill my best friend?"

She gulped at a breath, hesitating a moment as her mind raced through unconnected violence. She hadn't properly steeled herself against the onslaught of memory and its disorientating vortex spun across her chest. Ralph's death in the darkness of Worcester's streets, her mother… the execution… Tollemache and the killing of the rufflers. The pounding in her chest intensified as she felt Gabriel holding her tight in The George, the possession in his kiss, and, for a moment, there was just him at the beginning and the end of it all.

"I think… I think you're the most dangerous man I've ever known." It was a deliberate punishment, a lack of denial that branded him with guilt, and she watched as it burned through him.

He turned away abruptly, twisting onto his haunches, his shoulders lifting with a deep breath. He retrieved his sword from the fire and cursed the forgotten meat, now charred beyond recognition.

"Oh, I'm so terribly sorry to tear you from your supper, my Lord. Are you hungry?" The question was loaded with mock sweetness and her body snapped to, restless to force home her advantage. She marched towards the tack to find their saddlebags, yanking out the food parcel the baker had so carefully wrapped in Guildford.

The paper ripped and she bit her lower lip as she saw the contents: a hoard of childhood favourites. Gingerbread, jumbles and almond wafers… The smell of warm spices conjured the kitchen at Hampton Court, sitting at the large wooden table giggling with Ralph and Gabriel, waiting for Charlie to be dressed and drinking warm milk for breakfast.

Manipulative bastard.

"With compliments from the staff…" Tara dropped the entire open package into his lap. Flour and sugar dustings spilled out onto his black breeches, sparkling like stardust in the firelight and he uttered a surprised oath as she turned heel and disappeared back between the trees, heading blindly into the darkness as hot tears pricked her eyes.

He was after her immediately, spinning her to face him and backing her fast against a tree trunk, hands firm on her elbows. Her fists beat at him until they had no option but to brace against the contours of his chest the closer he got, her palms flattened against his heart. It was beating hard and fast and there was no escape. No hiding, no chocking down the grief. Tears fell fast, salty rivulets flowing freely down her cheeks, for Ralph, her parents. Eddie, and his men. For herself.

"Forgive me." He released her arms, bending down until his forehead touched hers and she was pinned by no more than the tender gesture. "Please, forgive me."

She knew the darkness behind his broken whisper. Ralph's death wasn't his fault. She knew that; she had always known it with a bone deep certainty that belonged to a simpler world of sharper contrasts, before they were all washed in the guilt of a thousand choices. Whatever man he had become in the service of Cromwell, that day he had been in an impossible place, torn in half between love and duty. An erratic throbbing in her chest urged her to pull that boy close, but they were no longer children and her whole body ached to give deeper comfort.

It would be so easy to tilt her head and find his lips: for reassurance that she hadn't hurt him, to offer apology for striking blame where it didn't belong. To tell him she knew what it was to carry pain, to need a justification for a life mired in blood and regret. To search for the heat that would surely engulf her again when he kissed her back…

Or was this just another of his games, another point he was ready to prove? Remembering the bitter aftertaste of the afternoon's kiss, mortification balled in her stomach and she froze. She was stronger now.

"Don't touch me again," she hissed, shaking with the effort of denial. Her eyes met his, black in the darkness, flashing with defiance and pride. "I'd rather die."

She left him then, pushing past him without another word, walking purposefully back to the light of a dying fire. She clenched her shaking arms and lay down opposite where he had sat, so that the flames would be between them. She pulled her cloak about her shoulders and her knees into her chest. The moss of the forest floor was soft enough and it yielded to her tense limbs. In time they would surely warm under the heavy wool.

She closed her eyes tight, more to shut out the form of his body than the darkness, feeling small and lost beneath the rustling canopy of oaks and chestnuts. The sounds of the nocturnal wood were unfamiliar and under the high cries of bats and nightjars and screech owls, beside the ceaseless creaks and whispers of ancient trees, she slept fitfully. She listened for the reassurance of his breathing, cursing the fact that, despite her anger and frustration and shame, she was thankful to God that he was with her.

17. THE MERMAID

Tara stirred when the dawn sun jabbed its long arms under her heavy cloak and immediately her ears were full of the insistent coos of wood pigeons. The fire was no more than a small circle of scorched earth and a vaguely acrid scent rose from a pile of grey ashes. Gabriel was gone.

Seven days.

Was this man really her husband? The argument came back in fragments. Cold and determined one minute, warm and playful the next. She felt safe beside him, for the first time in years, but it was a mirage, burnt clean by the glaring knowledge he was Eddie's enemy, and therefore her enemy. Where on earth was this supposed to end?

She pushed off her cloak and took a deep breath. Sleep had been elusive. She had laid still, stoking the fires of her anger even as the flames of their campfire died. His kiss had forever stolen what innocence there was in his touch, firing a frightening heat that seared her sense. *Like he bloody knew it would.* How could she play this game without knowing the rules?

Seven days to stop an uprising.

In her dreams he had come to her, his warmth enveloping her in the darkness. She had felt the heat of his kiss track along her whole body. She ran frustrated fingers through her knotted hair, momentarily distracted as she tugged out a leaf and several hard seedpods. It had been days since she'd been able to clean herself properly. After the inn beds and the ground, she must be alive with crawlers. The very thought made her itch and as if to prove the point a small bug landed lazily on her arm.

With decision, she made her way swiftly through the long grass to the river, pausing briefly to unhobble Jankyn so the beast could better seek his own breakfast in the greenery. The long nose turned at once to nip her elbow in payment for the night spent without fresh straw and stable, baring his foul-smelling, yellow teeth when she gave him a sharp tap on the nose in return. Rowley was already untethered and he snickered a gentle good morning as she passed. "*Not a word*," she whispered, giving him a wide berth. "Just teach your friend here some manners, please."

The sun was already warm, promising another beautiful day, but at the crisp water's edge she nearly had second thoughts. Still, there was no telling when the next opportunity would come, so she rolled down her stockings, gritted her teeth and gathered up her skirts, wading slowly into the clear cool waters and pushing her bare toes into the shifting silt of the river bed for purchase against a gentle current. The water climbed and as she eased herself in, higher, until it began to lap at her knees. Small silvery minnow darted between her legs and the sunlight played on the surface, dancing in her reflection.

Her feet were soon numbed as her legs grew used to the water. Cold but exhilarating, shallow and safe. She scooped handfuls awkwardly onto her thighs, carefully avoiding her skirts. It was bad enough perched on Gabriel's chestnut mare to head into London, but plodding along on Jankyn, who might frankly be riding her, required the use of muscles she didn't know she had. Perhaps she was doing it wrong. Gabriel showed no sign of stiffness but she strongly suspected it would be a cold day in Hell before he displayed weakness in anything.

It would have to be colder still before she asked him for instruction.

Her fingers prodded tentatively at the top of her thighs. There was some relief in the touch but not enough and she frowned, feeling that she would be paying for the constant bumping in the saddle for weeks yet. She had to massage the flesh deeper. A gentle wash of current made to unbalance her so she curled her toes deeper into the mud. It was surely not worth the risk of getting her clothes wet; they would take hours to dry and the last thing she needed was chaffing on the surface of the skin to match the muscular burning under it. Still her fingers hesitated and she rolled her eyes in impatience. Puritan conventions of cover and shame were deep rooted; even in this place, even entirely alone.

A kingfisher darted past paying no heed, his mind focused on the search for breakfast to the exclusion of all else, as if to prove the irrelevance of her nervousness. She frowned. In a swift burst of will she set about tugging off the stays, peeling off the skirts over her head, and flinging them both to safety on the riverbank. A second later her linen shift followed and she slid to her knees, reaching under the water without hesitation, swallowing the shock and savouring the moment her naked body became sleek and weightless.

She held her breath, suspended momentarily in the silence, turning to float on her back. Her hair floated out gently about her and, for a second, she indulged in the fantasy she was a mermaid. The myth was appealing: a race of half-women with such power that they could compel the actions of men and lure them to destruction. A useful trick, she thought wryly, though the meaning of the parable was clear: never trust a woman. What about 'never trust a horse'? she wondered, staring up at the clear blue sky as she waited for the sting in her elbow to dull. There must be some parable on that message she hadn't read yet.

With a sigh, she shifted position to review what damage Jankyn's misshapen teeth had done, only a sudden disorientating drag of water spun her legs under and about and about, making her pirouette like a dancer. She tried to anchor her twisting body but found with a blind panic that her toes could no longer reach the sand. Towards its centre, the river had cut a far deeper channel. Her fingers flailed for the purchase on slippery reeds but they slinked away like eels. A strong under current tugged at her limbs and she kicked impotently against the increased flow until her legs, now lead-weighted with cold, felt entirely unbiddable.

At a distance, a family of ducks floated sedately against a receding riverbank, paying little attention to her fighting gasps for breath as they burst above the surface.

An almighty crash disturbed the water and the panic only increased as a strong arm slid around her waist, plucking her from the river. She tried to scream but took a mouthful of water instead, spluttering as she emerged into the cold air, her hair suddenly heavy against her neck and shoulders as she was dragged backwards up the muddy bank with all the grace of a gasping trout.

"God's teeth, what the Hell are you doing?"

She heard him before she could take a proper breath. His furious growl vibrated through his chest and he thudded back against the grass as Tara fell back against him, one of his arms around her waist, the other crossed over her chest, his fingers firm on her bare shoulder.

"What are you doing?" she squealed, panting, her chest heaving against the shock of his presence and the tightness of his hold. She struggled but he was unmovable, and after a moment she realised why, and stilled with an acute horror. They were at an impasse. If he let her go, she would be revealed to him. If he moved, his skin would drag along hers, already goose pimpled and almost painfully sensitive from the fresh air. Her nipples were so taut from the cold that they ached as his hot breath lapped at the nape of her neck.   She looked down at his tensed forearms. His shirt was water-logged and it clung to his skin, hugging the thick contours. An involuntary shudder rippled through her and the goose bumps spread across her whole body.

"I was swimming," she said, closing her eyes to focus quietly on stabilising her breathing, a mechanical in, out, in, out. His legs were naked, he must have yanked off boots and breeches before diving in.

"That wasn't swimming." Her hair was already drying in the sun and his words made auburn strands dance in the corner of his eye. "Last night… you said… I thought…"

"*Jesus Christ!*" Tara choked, finally understanding his fear. "You think that I would literally rather drown myself than spend another moment in agonised resistance?!"

He ignored the liberal coasting of sarcasm and took a breath to still his heart from racing. The hammering tattoo was not exertion, or anger, it was fear. He'd clearly mistaken a moment of stupidity for something darker. He wasn't thinking straight. "I think you're a bloody fool. Another couple of feet and you'd have been pulled further in and dragged beneath the surface by the undertow. I might not have been able to reach you."

"You shouldn't have bothered! Were you not listening last night? I bloody hate you. My head is not turned by your attention, you're not some kind of novelty -" The words spilled out as she fought to tear her mind from the feel of his hard body around her. There was a faded silver scar on his right thigh, just visible beneath the dark hair brushed there. Something, someone, had once embedded a jagged blade in the muscle, looking for vulnerability. A futile task, she thought. "You know I was well-versed in coupling when you took me from Jack…"

She swallowed at Jack's name and he interrupted: "I had to do that: we both needed witnesses to our consummation. But I think you can't swim to save your life and you were flapping around in a deep and treacherous bend in the river. Even a strong swimmer would struggle there. Jesus, Tara, never do that again."

"Do not tell me what I mustn't do."

"You were completely out of your depth. Again," he replied evenly. "Two days ago, I swore before God to protect you with my life. It'd be considerably easier to fulfil that vow if I don't have to save you from yourself as well as your unsuitable suitors."

"*Hpmfh*," she snorted, but he was right. Crumpled sheets and blood were evidence that might just stop Tollemache challenging the union. Plus, she couldn't swim. "You needn't pretend on my account that those vows meant anything. What you mean is do what you say or you'll beat me."

"I owe you an explanation," he said quietly against her shoulder, taking a deep breath and reaching out carefully for her skirts, tugging them over to bunch them about her front, willing her body to relax against him but unable to find a way to answer her unspoken question. "That sideshow was for Wortley's benefit."

"*Wortley?* You beat me to please your man servant?" Her voice rose and, incredulous, she half turned as she drew the fabric across her body, for a glimpse of his seriousness.

"He's not my servant. He's a spy. A God-awful one truth be told, but I'm grateful that the Government's purse doesn't currently consider me worthy of a better specimen. Now I'm back from Ireland, Wortley's reports on my loyalty are the price I pay for my latitude." She felt the shrug against her back. "There's a Wortley in every great house in the country. Cromwell sees traitors in every corner. Backstage. Front of house. In the box and the cheap seats."

"No wonder he closed the playhouses."

He laughed. "It's human nature to believe better what is whispered than what is witnessed.... Latimer knew it too – you remember he sent Wortley on an errand? He wanted space to discuss the prospect of military support for his blasted fifth monarchy… It's all a game, Tara. God, you're cold."

"Then why-" she started quietly, unable to protest as he tugged her cloak over her, wrapping his arms around her, over the fabric. "Why did you let him touch me?"

Gabriel froze. It had made sense at the time. The moment Tollemache cursed his name in Whitehall, Thurloe would have expected intelligence. If he married a troublesome, wilful daughter of a traitor to save her from Cromwell's own design, his work would be in tatters. But if the lobcock Wortley told a more *enthusiastic* tale of her… He stared down at the soft pale skin of her shoulder. "Wortley is a simple creature. I had to know he'd tell Thurloe that I was driven by some dark desire… and that I was determined to set you on a path of righteous wifely obedience. Then-"

"Then you are a selfish. self-righteous bastard, but no traitor," she whispered, in a tone he couldn't read. She stared sightlessly at the river ahead, peacefully lapping the edges of the bank, all ripples of the disturbance long since stilled. But she was still there, still within his arms.

"Tara, I'd never harm you. Nothing will harm you while I'm here… I've just worked too hard and too long to have my loyalty questioned. If they must, better they think me a slave to my cock than a traitor." His torso rippled with an involuntary shudder as he felt himself harden.

"That doesn't sound very Godly," she said tartly.

"The Lord Protector values my sword, not my soul," he answered wryly, shifting slightly, wondering if she could feel his growing arousal. He should be grateful that the picture was such an easy one to sketch he thought, as he fought every urge in his body not to bury his head in the long pale neck before him. The stubborn child he could conjure so vividly in his mind a week ago was a long way from the woman in his arms. "Besides," he added quietly, the whisper in her ear carrying the grin returning to his lips: "I didn't exactly beat you."

"You…" she started, but she bit her tongue and changed the subject. "So, Wortley is firmly embedded. But is there also good reason to keep your vicious old triptaker of a housekeeper? She thinks I engineered this insanity. Can she not disappear?"

He tilted his head to one side with a raised dark eyebrow and she rolled her eyes: "I didn't mean you should kill her."

"Just as well," he laughed. "Ann makes excellent coffee."

She made a frustrated groan and his body ached in response but a heavy thud, a crash in the trees distracted them both. An unearthly scream shook the silence and he jerked upright, her nakedness instantly forgotten.

"Stay down," he hissed, swiping his sword from the riverbank where he'd thrown it minutes earlier, before sprinting towards the wood covered only by the wet shirt.

Heart pounding, she grabbed at her clothes and her fumbling fingers pulled first shift and then stays over her cold, wet hair and skin as fast as they could, tugged up the skirt. She hovered, sinking down behind a willow and listening, breath held, until Gabriel stormed back into the clearing and shouted towards her. "You unhobbled your mount! What the Hell were you playing at?"

She peered around the tree and stumbled back a step as he approached; his jaw firm under the loose hair, made blacker than crow's wings by the water. He considered his sword a moment before swinging it heavily into the tree trunk with a frustrated grunt. The thwack made her gasp but it gave way to a heavy silence. With gritted teeth he quickly yanked on his breeches, picked up his pistol and powder cask and paced back into the wood.

"Where are you going?" she called after him, unnecessarily.

"Stay there," he ordered, without looking back, and a few seconds later, the echo of a single shot reverberated in the calm morning air. For a heartbeat, the birds stopping singing, but breathing heavily, she ran towards the sound, afraid of what she knew she'd find. Gabriel was walking towards her as she approached. He caught her waist and pulled her firmly in front of him, blocking her view with his breadth: "Don't."

"Let go."

At first glance, Jankyn actually looked peaceful. His large eyes were closed as if in rest, wisps of long grass were still poking between bared yellowed teeth. Only stepping onto a springy carpet of dead leaves, she realised that he was lying at an awkward angle. His front leg was still caught in the vicious trap, its iron teeth digging deep into pink flesh and shards of bone glinting white in the sun.

He looked otherwise intact, but he wasn't entirely. Gabriel had shot the horse directly through the brain, and at close range the exit wound was dramatic. The sweet smell of blood seeped from the carcass and fat bluebottles were already gorging. Soon all the forest's teeming insects would arrive at the feast, thousands of little teeth devouring the flesh… like the flesh of the rufflers. She stopped, transfixed, until could feel them on her too, their indiscriminate hunger, mouths that chewed and gnawed at bodies that would freeze and thaw and putrefy with the passing hours and years. An intense wave of nausea rose without warning and she stumbled back a few feet into the clearing before vomiting into a fern bush.

Gabriel turned away, clicking his tongue to summon Rowley. "You didn't have to see that," he said without watching as she rinsed away the acrid taste with a swig from her water flask.

"I did. It was my fault," she replied simply, wiping her sleeve across her mouth, but meaning more than Jankyn's untimely demise.

Rowley waited patiently as his master retrieved his saddle from a low branch and swung it onto his back, the very model of perfect behaviour. Unwilling to give her any quarter just yet, Gabriel gave the horse's velvet nose a gentle rub in return for a self-satisfied whinny. He pulled on his leather jerkin, folded both their cloaks behind the saddle and tightened the girth strap around Rowley's belly, before stripping the saddlebags from her now redundant tack.

"I'm sorry," she whispered.

He saw her then, standing awkwardly out of his way, and cursed his temper. This wasn't about the damn horse; he was angry at himself. He had to regain his head and recover mastery over arms that ached for the loss of her slick body. He shook away the thought impatiently, his voice softening: "It wasn't your fault. Those traps are evil. That one was covered in rust. It'd clearly lain hidden for years, probably since the war. Rather a demon than a man."

She shook her head a moment and looked at him, refocusing, feeling the need to say something valedictory: "He was a, erm, a good horse."

"He was a horrible horse; God rest his soul." His lips quirked and Tara turned away, swallowing an unwarranted rush of entirely inappropriate giggles. He gathered up the bridle and pushed it over Rowley's twitching ears, checking the buckles. "Still, we must keep moving if Thurloe is behind us. A couple of hours and we'll be in Salisbury. From there we can cross country to the Dorset coast this afternoon."

"Odd's fish!" Her brows furrowed as she calculated the distance ahead. "You mean me to walk to Exeter?"

"You'd prefer to fly?"

"I'd sooner swim," she retorted, glowering at his smug mount. Rowley sidestepped, anxious to get moving, his impatient snorts sounding too much like laughter. "Oh, stop being such a high horse. I know you never liked Jankyn but you needn't look so pleased with yourself."

Jankyn? Gabriel laughed outright at the nickname; the Wife of Bath never did achieve mastery over her husband. "Rowley's strong, he can take us both."

He mounted, slipping a boot out of its stirrup to give her own foot purchase. In one swift move he pulled her up to settle behind him. Rowley crabbed sideward as she tried awkwardly to rearrange her skirts, and slipped a tight arm around Gabriel's waist so that she didn't fall.

"I'll need to breath if I'm to ride," he observed gently and she immediately loosened her grip but her legs were splayed and the shape of the saddle made it difficult to keep distance between them. Every time she tried to pull back it slid her closer, opening her legs wider and pressing the intimate flesh of her thighs against his buttocks.

"Ready?"

She looked down and struggled to keep from sudden laughter: "Is now a good time to mention that you've put your breeches on inside out? You know, if we're to have good luck, you'll have to keep them like that for the rest of the day."

18. ON ÞINUM WORDE SNOTTOR

It was market day in Salisbury and the heaving streets were a riot of noise and colour. Stalls funnelled the commotion towards the main square, flanked on one side by an imposing Cathedral and the other by myriad miniature shrines to commerce. Women bustled and jostled with good-humoured purpose, filling their baskets with wrapped parcels of fish or meat, while men clapped the shoulders of old friends, loaded with quarts of ale.

Rowley made slow progress through the throng of tranters dragging wagons and cattle traffic, weaving through the baskets of cooked seafood on Fish Street to dismount at an inn there. Emboldened by the carnival atmosphere and the distraction of their parents, ragged children tugged at Tara's skirts before she had even slid down, offering a penny's worth of fruit for her lunch, imploring for two pennies to pay for theirs. She glanced sideways at Gabriel and he grinned in response, whistling the latest pack over and agreeing a generous sum with a stable lad to see to Rowley and manage the others in making spurious collections for their onward journey.

"So, your best friend has his limits," she murmured as Rowley's long nose nudged them out of the stable yard, as if impatient to be left to the peace and quiet a while.

"Gift shopping is not exactly the preferred activity of a red-blooded war horse," he laughed. "But we can't arrive at Treguddick empty handed. It won't take long, and we'll make up the time."

They meandered past stalls heaped with food or textiles, making way for pickpockets and prostitutes. Street vendors wove around them selling everything from matches and scissor grinding to oranges, hot gingerbread and love songs. Above good-natured catcalls and excited chatter, a sudden roar pronounced a victor in the cockfight concentrating attention in front of the Cathedral's main gates. She was briefly distracted by a bawdy puppet show prompting loud laughter from children and their parents alike, and when she turned Gabriel was inspecting a stall of curiosities.

"What are you looking for exactly?" she asked, a little impatiently, as she joined him to scan a table-top overlaid with a greasy cloth of bald velvet.

"Uncle Henry is something of an antiquarian... he has a particular fondness for Roman artefacts." He held a rough looking vase up to the light and grinned surreptitiously at her while appearing to examine its cracked patina.

"A fascinating piece of history, my Lord," said the stallholder, approaching gingerly as he assessed the fine stitching of Gabriel's clothing.

A non-committal hmmm was sufficient encouragement for the man to continue. He flipped back the brim of his felted Monmouth cap to make better eye contact. It was edged raffishly in the remnants of a red squirrel and Tara frowned, marvelling that the man would choose to adorn himself in the pelt of his fallen brothers. He held his hands together before him as if gripping nuts and his prominent nose sniffed the air for the treasure in his customer's purse. "It's sixth century. Roman. You can virtually smell the blood and sweat of the slave who formed its sensuous curves."

"The delft mark on the base is original?"

The stallholder laughed at that, displaying large yellow and misshapen front teeth. He shrugged, a good-natured gesture of having been fairly beaten by the better player. He thought for a moment: "I see you are a connoisseur. Perhaps you would be more interested in this..."

With a flourish he produced a small, leather-bound book from a box beneath the table. Tara leant forward and opened the embossed cover, gasping at the delicate beauty of its heavily illuminated frontispiece. This time the stallholder's speech was less obsequious. He didn't need to sell an item like this; it was more than capable of selling itself. "Eighth Century. Not Roman."

"It's beautiful," mused Tara, turning the pages gently. "The miniature illumination… It's painstaking work. I've never seen anything like it."

"What's its providence?" asked Gabriel mildly.

"It's monastic; from the marginalia and the style of the figures, it was likely produced in a sophisticated scriptorium, Jarrow perhaps or Lindisfarne… But it's a compendium of stories and poems, some secular, some profane. And look, can you read the text?"

"No," said Gabriel, brow furrowed as he traced a line of the impenetrable black letters. "It's clearly not Latin or Greek, Germanic?"

"Old English. The language of our ancestors," replied the man, pointing to a sentence at random with slightly less dense script and reading it aloud in a peculiar guttural accent: "…*nunc Stigiae fibrae te vorare malunt, tibi quoque aestivi Acherontis voragines horrendis faucibus hiscunt.* Ah, perhaps not the best extract; this is a vision recounted in Felix's Life of Saint Guthlac…"

"*Now the bowels of… Styx?... long to devour you and the hot gulfs of Acheron gape for you with fearful throat,*" mused Tara with a rueful smile. "Our ancestors were a melodramatic bunch."

Gabriel frowned in surprise, but the stallholder glanced at her with a grin as he turned the pages hurriedly, his enthusiasm warming: "Perhaps you will like this one better, milady: *Eala Gabrihel, hu þu eart gleaw ond scearp, milde ond gemyndig ond monþwære, wis on þinum gewitte ond on þinum worde snottor.*"

"Bloody hilarious," Tara murmured, pulling back her hand and folding her arms with a frown. The stallholder's face flushed with confusion and his eyes flicked between them, panicked to have somehow inadvertently lost the sale.

"What does that mean?" asked Gabriel, still amused by the transformation of cynical merchant into impassioned literary enthusiast.

"It's from a speech of exaltation by St John the Baptist, milord. He-"

"He says *Oh Gabriel!*" interrupted Tara sarcastically: "*How wise and keen you are, merciful and mindful and mild, wise in your wits and perceptive in your words!*"

"Ignore my wife," said Gabriel with a burst of laughter, putting an arm about her shoulders in a half-serious attempt to prevent her walking away.

"She's prone to irrational tantrums. I do believe it must be right to deny the weaker vessels access to books, see what price I pay for her learned mind?"

The stallholder nodded understandingly and tried to ignore the fact the over-educated woman had dug his most promising customer of the day sharply in the ribs. He spread his hands, appealing for calm, concerned that his patter would lose momentum faced with a physical brawl. The tall man had slipped his arm lower, encasing her body as he pulled her back against his chest and she was visibly fuming as she stamped her heel down onto his boot.

"Sir, I know my trade," said the stallholder, tugging back on Gabriel's attention. "Old Latin texts are ten a penny on the continent, but many examples in our mother tongue were destroyed when the old King Henry dissolved the monasteries. I bought this example in a house clearance in York, sir. Royalists…"

Gabriel tilted his head in polite concentration even as he held Tara's squirming body firm, elbows tight against her sides, so the patter continued: "The man in question was concerned to ensure that it came to rest in the collection of one who could appreciate its worth, and derive some joy from it."

"I know just the person." Decided, Gabriel gave a smile that lightened his features and the stallholder grinned back with evident relief. He nodded to a small boy waiting nearby who jumped up from the cobbles to wrap the book up in a square of linen before Gabriel could change his mind. Soon after, the boy was shaking out a second sheet to wrap a small marble bust of the Emperor Augustus and a generous sum of money changed hands, emboldening the salesman as soon as it reached the safety of his inner pocket.

"A trinket for the lady, sir?" he asked hopefully, holding up a pair of jade earbobs. "Green to match the clear calm depths of her beautiful eyes?"

"Calm pools to you maybe; I see nothing but stormy, turbulent seas. I am quite sure she doesn't deserve them," Gabriel said, shaking his head with an air of mock seriousness.

He shifted his hold and stepped back, neatly lifting her over a pile of cattle dung recently deposited on the ground behind them, before taking her hand firmly in his. He tipped the bust in his hand at the stallholder and led Tara back to Fish Street.

As he had promised, they kept a brisk pace all afternoon, tracking cross-country down to pick up the coastal path to the West Country. At first their silence reasserted itself; punctuated by artificial conversation on the practicalities of travel. But along quiet paths, under warm sunshine, Rowley's regular hoof beats effortlessly swallowed the miles beneath them. And slowly, imperceptibly, the riders held themselves a little less erect.

"You were right about the shrimp," he said, glancing back at her, with an offer of his water bottle. "They were delicious."

"I told you," she said simply, taking it gratefully and swigging deeply, brushing the remnants of several shells from her skirts. "I can't believe you've not eaten them before. You owe me."

"I owe you?" he mused with a short laugh and Tara tensed, unable to see his face for a tell-tale crease of humour. A moment passed while he took a bite of bread and then asked without warning: "Do you remember when everyone thought Charlie was dying of a mysterious bellyache?"

"I do…" she said hesitantly, unsure of the connection. "The illness defied diagnosis but the chaplain Hewitt found divine providence in it and prescribed a most humble devotional manner to be adopted by those closest to him. I spent hours on my knees."

"Then somebody discovered he'd just eaten a bad prawn…"

"That you stole from Kingston market…" she jumped on a memory, before tailing off with a sudden stab of guilt.

"That I stole?" he teased. "That may have been the tale we told, but as I remember it, the offending shellfish was liberated by another hand."

"Oh God." She'd been the one to sneak out of the Palace, to meet the traders' boats in Kingston. Within the landlocked walls of Hampton Court, the salt water delicacy was hard to come by, but it was her favourite. Worth the risk. "I'd completely forgotten that day. You took the blame. You told everyone you'd left the Palace alone and smuggled them back in the pockets of your breeches."

"Yes, it was very noble of me," mused Gabriel.

"Noble? You were supposed to be minding me! You just weren't prepared to admit that I'd given you the slip."

He grimaced. "And it cost me. Charlie purged his guts but I barely sat down for a week after my whipping. Can you blame me for being suspicious of the waterlogged maggots all this time?"

It was early evening when they reached the coast and Gabriel slid from the saddle by the cliff edge, standing for a moment silhouetted against a deep blue while he took in the view. He gave a relaxed smile when he turned back, the sea breeze playing on his loose hair, and he lifted her down, taking Rowley's reins forward over his ears and leading down a steep track into Lulworth Cove. Tara picked her path behind them, skirts hitched up and marram grass whipping her ankles as she followed the swaying haunches cautiously, pausing every now and then to look out at the vast ocean.

They left Rowley hobbled by a promising grassy crop to walk over deserted dunes, heading instinctively towards the water. The sand was soft and deep and without thought she grabbed at his arm for support when the footing was unsteady. Without a word he laced long fingers into hers and tugged her closer, supporting her weight. Once the dunes gave way to a flat expanse of beach, he shrugged off his jerkin and sat down. She eyed him suspiciously as he pulled off his boots, nodding to the wide expanse of sea before them and pushing a strand of wind-whipped hair from his eyes.

"Coming?"

"After this morning? I think not," she snorted, looking firmly at the horizon.

"I could teach you to swim."

In one move, he pulled his shirt over his head and from the corner of her eye, she saw the muscular plains of his chest ripple as he moved, the sun-kissed skin brushed with dark hair. She coloured, remembering the solid feel of it hot against her back and stood, turning abruptly away: "I'll build a fire and see to your horse. Bring back some dinner."

"Yes, milady," he grinned, tugging his forelock, laughing as she headed back across the dunes, refusing to watch him strip his inside-out breeches.

When it came, the night was black, moonless, and they sat close by each other to crack open the shell of a crab, picking out the flesh with the tip of his dagger once it had cooked in the flames of a low fire. They'd made camp in the dunes, in hollow out of the cool sea breeze, but she shivered violently and he shifted to gather her before him, wrapping his arms and cloak around her, sharing the warmth radiating from his body.

"I didn't know you had family so close to Exeter," she said conversationally after a while, enjoying the clean smell of saltwater from his skin as it mingled with the wood smoke.

"My father felt his own siblings were far more illustrious connections to claim at court," he shrugged. "But we were close. Aunt Margaret was my mother's sister. The Godolphins are Welsh... They used to live near Hay on Wye, their family seat not twenty miles across the Marches from Hellens Manor. For a time, I thought of Tretower Castle as home and my cousin Tom as a brother."

"Why did they move?"

"The war. Tretower was destroyed. Tenants stopped paying rent, the cattle were driven away, the sheep plundered. Henry took what they could salvage and invested in the tin trade almost accidentally. It was a sound move. They've made enough over the last decade to build a fine new home on the edge of Dartmoor. I've been promising to visit for years."

"And Tom?"

"Tom joined the army, fighting for the King before you ask, but he never had the stomach for soldiering. He's settled with them to manage the estate. He has a younger brother, Rupert, who is now in Europe. France I think. He was born just before my father had me join the royal household. I can only see him as a chubby babe in clouts, all pink skin and white blonde curls."

"When did you last see them?"

"Seven years ago, give or take. They write constantly, but I last visited after Worcester, to tell them about Lucius." He shrugged away a memory a took a deep breath. "They're good people; they take everything in their stride. I could tell Aunt Margaret you were one of the Pendle Witches come complete with demonic familiars to suckle and she'd still ask what you'd like for supper."

She smiled, relaxing against the heat of his chest without thinking: "You must miss them terribly. And your father. I'm sorry."

She felt him stiffen slightly but he didn't say anything and she flinched, remembering herself. She pulled forward ready to move away but his hand found hers. In the distance behind them, waves rolled over the beach and he spun Ralph's ring slowly on her finger, rubbing the thin silver until it gleamed in the firelight.

"I miss him so much," she whispered, almost just to herself.

"He is lucky to have had your love," he said, remembering his childish jealousy of Ralph, the boy clearly worshipped by his fearsome and fearless sister.

"It's been years but still it's like a physical pain to think of him at times. But the things I remember… there's nothing of consequence. I can hear him laugh and see him run, but I cannot tell a whole tale with him in it… Nothing that means anything, nothing connected. Just half thoughts. I lose my brother afresh every time I hear his name."

"We don't remember those things, I think, they remember us." His low voice was soothing and she leaned back again into the solid comfort, feeling the security of his arms tighten around her. "This is how your brother will always be with you, as my father stays with me. You'll never be alone."

19. TREGUDDICK

Treguddick Manor was about four miles south on the main road from Exeter but they approached from the east, meandering along a winding route that seemed purposefully to slow time until there was no longer any sense of the hour or even the day. It ran through deep green trees, narrowing in places and widening in others to reveal beautiful sun-dappled clearings, all the while without any real promise that an industrious estate awaited them until, without warning, a small stable yard materialised. Within it a whole world quickly opened up as if startled from a dream, people milling about on cue.

"Try and remember there's a good chance that anything looking like a worthless pot is actually one of Uncle Henry's priceless antiques," Gabriel murmured under his breath as a servant ran to announce their approach. "So please don't break anything."

She nudged him in protest as a man with cropped blonde hair emerged from a walled courtyard behind the stable block and shouted as he saw them, dropping a metal bucket that clanged down on cobbles. "Good God!"

"You flatter me, Tom!" Gabriel shouted back, laughing as he kicked his leg over Rowley's head and slid down to run to him, falling headlong into the man's embrace while Tara grabbed at the reins to avoid being unseated by a startled sidestep. She watched them tumble affectionately like puppy dogs, failing to notice the arrival of Sir Henry from the main house. The older man stepped forward into the fray without hesitation and clasped his nephew's shoulders warmly: "I can't believe my eyes! How good it is to see you, Gabe. Thank God that you are at last safely returned from that sordid isle of papists and plague and, and potatoes!"

"You know damn well sir, that we have all those things on this sordid isle too," Gabriel replied with a grin, grabbing his uncle's hand and shaking it excitedly. "And I'll thank you not to upset my horse, he is a fine Irish fellow."

"Well he shalln't be allowed in the house!" The older man snorted good-naturedly and waved expansively towards the grand crenelated property behind him, beautifully proportioned and augmented at the front with a wide seven bay loggia. "What do you think, Gabe? It's Italian in design, informed by the works of Scamozzi-"

"For the love of God, Hen, let him take breath before you lecture him on classical architecture!" The lilting Welsh belonged to a woman safely into her fifties, who squealed excitedly as she jiggled down the path from the house and swept passed her menfolk, scooping Gabriel into an affectionate bear hug. "Is my angel real? Ah! But it's been too long, my lovely boy!"

She held him tightly until Gabriel squirmed, making exaggerated gasping noises, "Aunt, please, I can't breathe!"

"Nonsense, big strapping lad like you can handle the love of a real woman," Margaret chided. "And if I remember anything correctly, you can also handle real food. Come in!" she released his body but held his hand firmly clasped in hers and he was led away like a child. "Hush now as we enter, mind, Leo is asleep."

"*Leonie Morgan?*" Gabriel's eyebrows raised over his shoulder.

Tom's chest puffed imperceptibly with his grin. "Leonie Godolphin now. And my wife is seven months pregnant."

"Oh Tom, it was written in the stars," Gabriel mouthed, grinning.

"Ru is here too!" Sir Henry called as he trotted after them. "He arrived this morning from France but is already in Exeter, gone shopping with his new wife to make sure they are ready for this evening. Did you see him?"

"*His* wife?" asked Gabriel, dark brows raised in surprise. "Rupert's wed?!"

"Yes, well, it was news to us too and it will certainly take some getting used to. My, you have arrived at an interesting time, let me tell you..."

"Gabriel..." started Tara, struggling to control Rowley's steps. Without his master as anchor, the horse rocked and swayed like a rowboat on the high seas and her knuckles were already white from clinging to the saddle.

"And what's happening this evening?" Gabriel asked, oblivious.

"The Whitsun dance, my boy," said Henry, rolling his eyes. "it's a tradition in these parts. A flagrant breach of curfew but it'll take more than an edict from Westminster to put a stop to-"

"Odd's fish, Gabriel!" Tara finally exclaimed as he disappeared into the entrance, his arm still held by Margaret.

Tom spun round and jogged back towards her. He was smiling, his handsome features alight with joy: "I'll beg forgiveness for my cousin, my Lady. I see he hasn't changed – he has as many manners as his horse but lacks the benefit of rein."

"Reins are pretty irrelevant on this beast as well," she said, smiling anxiously from Rowley's high back. "I'm Tara Villiers... Moore, I mean."

"I don't believe it." Tom paused for a split second at her name before smiling broadly and reaching out a hand to steady Rowley's bridle. She scrambled down and he passed control of the horse to a ready stable lad.

"You're Tom?"

He nodded and slipped an arm through hers with an air of easy familiarity. Clearly if Gabriel had deemed her worthy, that was good enough recommendation. "Please forgive us all our manners, Mrs Moore. We love Gabe dearly and it's been too long... We have much to learn."

"I've heard much about you," she said, instinctively warming to him.

"While I was growing, Gabe was more brother than cousin. We were inseparable for years, before his father got more involved in court," Tom shook away an uncomfortable thought. "Someone had to keep the stubborn, reckless oaf on the straight and narrow."

"Stubborn and reckless?" Tara raised an eyebrow with a gentle grin. "I couldn't begin to imagine."

Tom laughed, guiding her in through a wide entrance door. "I've been reading, in preparation for the birth of my child. Some say personality is formed in the womb. Gabe arrived into the world charming his wet nurse and fighting his father and not a lot ever changed."

She smiled at that, imagining a cloud of dark curls and strong limbs whirling throughout the corridors of Hellens Manor, coming to rest in the safety of his nurse's lap. That summer of 1641, Hampton Court thrummed with talk that Gabriel had inherited his mother's easy charm. Lady Hannah Moore had been a renowned society beauty and from the portraits in Ham House there were clear echoes of her high cheekbones, dark brown eyes and faintly olive skin in her only son. It was here too in Tom, she realised; that same bone structure beneath his fairer colouring.

"Tom," she said, squeezing his arm. "It's been a long journey and I need to clean up... Is there somewhere I could wash and maybe even sleep a short while?"

"Of course! You and Gabe shall have our finest guest rooms. Have you any bags?" He laughed as she shrugged, wondering abstractly where the inadequate contents of their saddle bags had likely ended up. "Not to worry, we have everything you need. You'll both be very comfortable here, for as long as we can convince you to stay."

Not long, she thought, permitting herself to be lost herself in his good-natured barrage of questions until she closed the heavy door of their allotted suite. She drank the fresh milk that Tom had insisted was fetched, washed as best she could with the ready jug and bowl and laid for a moment on the deep wool filled mattress, enjoying the warmth of a late afternoon sun. She would go to Exeter first thing in the morning. Search Eddie's possessions. Find the path to his men. *Five days.* There was time.

The house was quiet. Most of the servants were still occupied with work out-of-doors and she walked slowly along the corridors, running her fingers over a couple of tactile artefacts balanced precariously on the tall tables placed about for their display. The Roman bust from Salisbury had somehow already found a home on a plinth at the top of the staircase, jostling for prominence among other miniaturised conquerors and classical warriors.

Henry Godolphin was evidently proud of his interest and she didn't wonder that it was sometimes preferable to live in the past, where present pains could not reach you. How romantic the wars and intrigues of history could seem, when you weren't wholly preoccupied with the mundane challenge of living through them, the endless anticipation of action punctuated haphazardly by terror. To read reports in the Mercurius Politicus over the last few years, the brutal excesses of Cromwell's enemies were no more civilised than the court of Nero.

She followed the sound of voices, low but animated, and paused at the door of a sitting room, momentarily unsure. The warm family homecoming was Gabriel's prize, for... Still, she couldn't interrupt. She'd lasted a couple of hours, but had been driven downstairs partly by boredom and partly by a gnawing hunger. Still, it wasn't fair. Without intending to eavesdrop, she reasoned it would be worth getting a measure of the conversation before announcing her presence.

"So it's true then, Gabe." There was Margaret's inimitable singsong Welsh. "We do not get much news here, but Edward Villiers is in the Tower awaiting a second trial?"

Tara stiffened and exhaled with Gabriel's silent confirmation,

"Curse, catch me," said Margaret.

"I hear the Sealed Knot was never broken after Penruddock," mused Tom. "Whispers are that men remain loyal to Villiers and await orders for revolution all along the south coast."

"Then let us hope they aren't holding their breath," said Gabriel wryly. "No-one has the faintest idea how he communicated with them, yet, but there's no chance of an acquittal this time. Cromwell will not leave loose ends as he prepares for the succession."

Tara held her breath, waiting for someone to challenge him and explain how, in fact, given the lack of evidence her uncle would be a free man. Instead, Gabriel continued: "John Thurloe has been tasked with the investigation."

"He's a busy man," said Henry, his deep voice clearly audible. "We were expecting the Secretary of State in Exeter for a meeting on Friday as apparently he has concerns about the operation of the Stannary Parliament governing our little tin community. And then I receive word this morning that he's been delayed at least a week in the Capital."

Tara took a breath of relief. The Lasham landlady's intelligence was clearly not as relevant as they'd feared. Faintly, she heard Gabriel mutter: "Well, that's something."

"Cromwell must be desperate," said Margaret. "Even here we've whispers of invasion in the ports. They say the Prince of Wales is poised to return with Spanish ships."

"There won't be an invasion, Aunt. Charlie's fleet has been destroyed and he's racking up unsupportable debts on the continent. Every bit of meat and drop of drink, every candle is acquired on credit."

"One would expect a little more support from his siblings," muttered Margaret

"What of his sister?" This was a lighter voice, which still carried a hint of Welsh: Leonie must have joined them. "Will the Dowager Princess of Orange not send money from the Netherlands?"

"She can't," said Gabriel. "Mary lost her influence. In truth, she's entirely reliant on her in-laws after William's death. She's fighting internal discord in her states as the Arminians would limit the power of her son when he becomes stadholder. And frankly, as soon as she builds one bridge in Europe for Charlie, she burns another with the Dutch over her sympathies for him."

"Prince James?" suggested Tom.

"Engaged in the Spanish army," said Gabriel dismissively. "As is their youngest brother Henry,"

"I thought Henry was Cromwell's prisoner?" started Sir Henry. "Forgive us, Gabe, news is sparse."

"He was released some time ago, but had the audacity to return to his mother a vociferous protestant. Henrietta Marie had him expelled from the exiled court and so he joined the Spanish. The truth of the matter is that Charlie's wholly reliant on support from within our borders."

"Little wonder then that Cromwell's best men would focus on breaking Villiers' network while he lives." mused Tom.

"Is that why his niece is travelling with you?" asked Leonie suddenly.

"They're not just travelling together, Leo," said Margaret softly, with an unwarranted lilt of enthusiasm.

She heard a controlled exhale but lost Gabriel's quiet response in a rustle of silk gown and footsteps just the other side of the door where she hovered, obscured, breath held.

"…close to her brother?" Sir Henry asked thoughtfully.

"Yes," Gabriel replied quietly. "I had thought to install her quietly in Ham House while the Villiers trial played out. I had hoped she would… we have a delicate truce, but… but she blames me for Ralph's death. We both fought at Worcester."

"You killed him?" asked Tom bluntly.

"No," replied Gabriel, his voice firm but still quiet. "But he was hit, because of me. If I hadn't…"

"You're such a fool Gabe," chided Leonie gently, steering the conversation away and, silently, Tara thanked her sensitivity. "My father brought home tales from court before the war. He told me of the lot of you and well, from what I heard, I cannot imagine Tamara Villiers falling gratefully under any man's protection, even at the best of times."

"She was a hell cat then, and as a grown woman, well…" Gabriel had taken her cue and his voice was more relaxed. "I can command whole regiments to march two miles behind enemy lines in the driving rain before I might suggest she brush her hair."

"Well, that'll be where you are going wrong," Leonie laughed, and Tara's hand went instinctively to pat any unruly strands into place. Like he'd ever had the nerve to try-

"Cheer up, Gabe," added Tom. "I'm sure those persuasive charms are still in there somewhere."

She caught Gabriel's dismissive snort while Sir Henry brokered an uncomfortable question: "But why marry the girl, my dear boy?"

"I had to." There was a practical shrug in his voice. "She promised herself to one of Cromwell's more impressive henchman in return for his Highness' personal interest in Villiers' case. I gather he had been planning to use her as payment for loyalty since Penruddock."

"Well, you have to hand it to Cromwell," said Tom. "He's still as sharp as ever. He can settle old debts by handing her over to his cronies and more besides. If she's effectively within his control he could convincingly blackmail Villiers for intelligence."

Tara cringed at the plain summary and felt the shame burn in her cheeks. She had walked straight into Cromwell's design and it seemed any casual bystander could portend calamity coming a mile off. Tom was right, at best, all she would have achieved was putting Eddie in an impossible position of choosing between herself and his men. She hadn't thought of it like that.

"It was Silus Tollemache," said Gabriel quietly.

"Christ," hissed Sir Henry. "Tollemache was Major General here until recently... But Gabe, you may have thwarted Cromwell for now but parliament is full of over-reaching factions vying for power or position in the new world we have coming. Thurloe for instance, he'll apply pressure in whatever way he can to get what he needs from Edward Villiers. You're now exposed."

No one spoke for a moment, then Gabriel started: "It was my fault, Henry. I took her to Whitehall to plead and cry with the masses, play the part demanded of any dutiful niece. She'd be seen publicly in my protection to dissuade any attempts on her... Instead she tried to trade her life for Villiers' freedom. I should have known about Tollemache."

Margaret sighed: "There's no denying she's a brave woman..."

"But any blasted fool could have foreseen the risk of sending her in there. I shouldn't... Not ten minutes after clapping eyes on her in Petersham I knew that she was stubborn, proud..."

"None so bold as a blind mare," interrupted Sir Henry. "But I can think of a few more adjectives... But do not to get attached, my boy. She's a fine-looking creature-"

"She cares considerably less for me than you assume. She wants this to end as quickly as I need it to," said Gabriel curtly and she heard the sound of a glass being refilled. "And before you even think it, she's utterly indifferent to my wealth."

"The Villiers estates are highly unlikely to be restored," Henry continued thoughtfully. "Mind you. at your age, I should have been pleased to have taken her in a smock."

"How gallant of you, husband!" Margaret's light-hearted exclamation reverberated with her giggle: "Lucky for me that at your age the chance would be a fine thing!"

When the amusement died, Henry's voice could be heard again but its tone was more measured. "But seriously Gabe, how can this end?"

Tara shifted awkwardly, and lost the start of his response in a sharp intake of breath, She caught "arrange for a more permanent disappearance," and put her hand to the wall for support as she strained for more, but trod on the edge of her skirts and lost her balance, scrabbling for a grip on the wooden door as she fell forward. It slammed it heavily into the room and bounced back against the wall as she landed with a thump on the flagstones

Gabriel was at the doorway in a heartbeat, flanked by Tom, both men with their hands on the hilts of their swords. He looked down at her, a lop-sided grin breaking across his lips. His expression betrayed nothing of the seriousness of the conversation she had overheard and a dark eyebrow raised with humour.

Tara's eyes were wary as she scrabbled to her feet, taking in Tom's amused grin and behind him the soft form of Leonie, whose features flashed with kindness and concern. She folded her arms, more to conceal trembling hands than to appear defiant.

"I…"

"Leo, have you something that my wife could wear this evening? With any luck this dress is entirely beyond the botcher."

"It's fine," she frowned. "I only bought it a week ago, it was new for-"

"There's a dance."

He voice was incredulous. "I can't go dancing-"

"Don't worry-"

"I'm not worried-"

"You'll pick it up, I'm sure," said Gabriel agreeably. "And Leo was once nearer your size-"

This time he was interrupted by a snort when his cousin's wife prodded him in the back, eyebrows raised in mock outrage. He turned back with an innocent glance at her belly, barrel-like under her loose blonde hair, and her smile spread as she conceded a dress with a nod.

"Come then, Lady Denby," he concluded with a bow and a flourish. "You shall go to the ball."

20. TO THE GREENWOOD GONE

At the end of the barn, the gypsy troupe were in situ, perched on a boarded stage that balanced on straw bales. Two men with recorders squatted on wobbling milking stools, next to a viola player and two more violins. Another man sat on an upturned box with a bass violin between his legs, and all of the string players inclined their heads towards him, tuning their instruments in the candlelight. A final man, the front man, grinned as he teased anticipation with a steady beat from his tambourine.

Tara glanced over the shadowy space. There were near two hundred hot bodies squashed into the unassuming structure, lit by just a couple of wall sconces and the occasional grease-filled cresset, borrowed from the church opposite and balanced on poles that had been rammed into the compacted earth floor. A grand-looking candelabra stood by the stage to illuminate the players, dragged into the space especially for the event and weighed down with heavy stones.

Conversations dried up briefly as the crowd parted before them with a little ripple of silence. The local women were watching Gabriel. She was getting used to that. In many ways, he was no different to the squires and farmers around them. He carried his sword at his waist, too fine a weapon for most, and being so tall, he stood head and shoulders above the majority. But it was the way he moved that marked him out. He was sleek and strong, with an unselfconscious confidence that was mesmerising. *Was that it?*

"Gabriel..." She tugged on his shirtsleeve and leant in briefly to make sure she was heard, smelling soap mingled with leather and a hint of citrus. Henry's oils, no doubt. With the mud and dust of the road rinsed clean, she wondered abstractly how much of the journey had been a dream, sure only that the stares and whispers around her now were real. "Gabriel, they're staring at you. You're Cromwell's man... They're afraid, you don't belong here. We should go."

Everyone in the room risked fines, maybe even imprisonment as a traitor for attending the illegal gathering. Perhaps the danger added something to the heady air. Men and women, at ease, talking, moving, laughing, touching as their bodies swayed freely to the beat. Tara's chest tattooed with the percussion.

"Don't worry," he whispered into her hair. "I'm not known here; tonight, we're simply guests of Lady Margaret Godolphin." He touched her forehead briefly with the backs of his fingers, as if to smooth away the line of worry, his expression inscrutable: "Besides, they are not staring at me."

He led them towards a table at the back, past an open area cleared for dancing, and she watched as he shrugged uncomfortably in his jerkin. He didn't have a change of outfit but his simple breeches and shirt had been freshly laundered and pressed by a Treguddick housemaid with miraculous speed. His hair was tied neatly back. The silk dress Leonie had enthusiastically produced was deep red meanwhile, voluminous, with shortened sleeves. Under Margaret's excited direction, the stays were laced far tighter than she was used to, clinching in her waist and punishing her rib cage so that if she didn't focus on breathing steadily she had to snatch air into the top of her lungs.

Henry had stayed at home, ostensibly to re-catalogue his library although that had fooled no one and Tom had patted his arm with a grin as he passed him at the front door: "Sleep well, old man." Margaret needed no excuse; she emerged from Treguddick quacking loudly like a mother duck ahead of Leonie, who obligingly waddled for effect. She'd insisted on coming, since the dance was the most exciting thing to happen in the county for a year, but Tom was unconvinced. He'd finally conceded to indulge foot tapping on the proviso that she kept the beat sitting sedately on the side. Dutifully, then, she allowed her doting husband and his beaming mother to lead her to a comfortable looking hay bale, rolling her eyes at Tara with good humoured as she passed. She would sit down for now, the wide flashes of blue said, but not for long.

There was barely time to retrieve drinks from a barrel in the corner before a young man, handsome with the flush of youth and ale and dressed in an unusually fashionable ruff bounded over. His limbs were askance with enthusiasm and his long legs tripped over a stool leg so that he fell headlong into Gabriel's chest, the shock of his white blonde curls momentarily stark against the black leather.

"Gabriel Moore, I'll be damned! 'Tis wonderful to see you cousin!" He recovered himself with a broad grin. "Has Tom warned you? Be sure to look to your liberty; tomorrow is Whitsun and the ladies here will pick up the scent of fresh blood!"

"Rupert." Gabriel grinned into wide, clear blue eyes and he clasped the righted man warmly. "My God, you must be, what, nineteen now? You were barely breeched when I last laid eyes on you. And now look, a grown man!"

"Someone has finally noticed!" Rupert pulled himself up to his full height for inspection. Again, there were echoes of Lady Hannah in the cheekbones, also in the straight nose, and the riot of curls that topped his six feet. "I have finished my education in Paris and eloped with my French mistress and still I am treated like a child!"

As if shocked to uncover the truth afresh, Rupert waved behind him, where a pretty, petit lady hovered uncertainly. Clearly relieved, she smiled at his acknowledgement and walked forward to be introduced, the tightly fashioned curls in her blonde hair bobbing as she moved.

"Gabriel Moore, Earl of Denby, let me present ma mariee, Marie Gainsbourg, la fils de ma tutor Francais. She found me pouring over a tatty copy of some bawdy text and took upon herself a different kind of tutelage when-"

"*Enchanté*, Madam," said Gabriel, cutting Rupert off before he could incriminate himself further, offering a polite bow and a relaxed smile as he kissed her fingers.

She accepted the kiss graciously and dipped a curtsey in response before spinning back and poking her husband in the ribs with a hiss of barely controlled frustration. "*Mon Dieu Rupert! Cette est ta familie! Est-ce que tu non peut pas penser de quelconque description plus flatteureuse?*"

"*Je suis vraiment désolé, Cherie, mais…* I've told you a hundred times. No one here cares if you're papa is the King of France - Mama, you made it!" His expressive face, utterly impervious to her chastisement, became ever more childlike. As she passed by to talk with some locals, he swept Margaret into one of the bear hugs clearly favoured by the Godolphins, earning a gentle cuff over the ear before letting her go on and turning his attention back to the group. "Marie, my family would know two things.

Firstly, do you make me happy? And you make me extremely happy… and secondly will your father track us relentlessly, armed with a thousand rapiers to fetch my head on a platter? Even if that does happen, mon petit cochon, I am still a lucky man for I shall at least die happy."

She snorted a French sound and stamped her foot, curls quivering with the aftershocks. "Rupert, I have told you a thousand times. Call me your little piglet again and I will cut off your balls."

"Oh mon Dieu, je t'adore," he started, eyes wide with genuine astonishment as if he had been struck afresh with the realisation. "*Tu es trop belle quand tu es furieuxeuse.*" He cut off further argument with a sound kiss and after a moment she relaxed against him, her arms winding up around his neck.

"I have to ask, Ru," said Tom, ignoring the embrace as he joined the group. "What are the chances of a French invasion to recapture Helen of Troy here?"

"None whatsoever, as far as her father is concerned," Rupert whispered above her head in between kisses. "Elopement with bona fide English gentry was a God send for her family. Marie faisant le trottoir in Paris."

"Je parle francais! Quel idiot!" Marie snorted and stamped soundly on his toe, then disappeared unto the crowd.

"Oh. She's a little upset," said Rupert unnecessarily. Gabriel turned away in a bid to compose his features but caught Tara's eye. His lips quivered and it was all she needed to collapse into laughter. When Tom frowned and raised an eyebrow, they only laughed harder. Rupert shrugged, non-plussed, his gaze firmly where she had disappeared. Excuse me, while I see if I can't convince her to forgive me. She's no longer whoring, of course. She gave up that life for me," he added, puffing his chest proudly.

"You utter maggot-pate," Leonie laughed indulgently as she drew up to her feet beside them, "You may now have the body of a man, but this contains all the sense of a gatepost." An arm rested protectively over her stomach as she leant up with a free hand to ruffle then rearrange Rupert's unkempt curls, in the unlikely event that he had more chance of winning over his wife with a neater head of hair.

"You knew?" said Tom, his face torn between shock at finally understanding the cause of Marie's distress and anxiety that his pregnant wife was on her feet. Again.

"You didn't?" she replied, laughing as he slipped his arm protectively around her back.

Rupert submitted to her efforts but looked about him, nodding towards Tara as he noticed her properly for the first time. "Go shoe the goose! Gabe, are you going to introduce your girl? I'm so sorry madam, you must think me terribly rude. And there I was assuming he was here for sport."

"I'm not his…" Tara started, but stopped, and Gabriel steered her gently forward for his cousin to lift her fingers to his lips, adding simply: "She's not my girl, Rupert, Tara is my wife."

His eyes widened and he finally tugged his head away from Leonie's reach. "Enchanted, truly. Hell's teeth Gabe, you're actually married? By God, after everything Tom's told me… 'tis a day I thought never to see!"

Margaret was back, neatly interrupting her younger son's gaping astonishment by slipping an affectionate arm around his waist and closing his lower jaw firmly. "My angel," she started, eyes on Gabriel and glistening with excitement. "The players are keen to collect new music. I thought perhaps you'd picked up something on your travels?"

She stepped aside as a gypsy thrust his violin forward, giving an encouraging nod, a single gold tooth glinting in the gloom. Gabriel thought for a moment before taking the proffered instrument. He stroked the wooden body briefly and ran his thumb across the bridge to listen to the tuning before raising it to sit comfortably under his chin and taking hold of the bow, bouncing it along the four strings to get a feel for the weight and tone of the instrument.

"Dave Collins' Jig," he announced grandly for his little audience, before adding: "It's been a while; there's a reasonable chance this will squeal like a departing pig."

His foot tapped as he played and, after a bar or two, conversation around them stopped, a circle forming around the soloist and his impromptu concert. People clapped their hands, itching to begin the dancing, and there was a general exhalation of disappointment when the melody came to an end. Gabriel laughed and took a bow, handing back the instrument and shaking the gypsy's grateful hand.

"I didn't know you had so many strings to your bow," Tara muttered, eyebrow raised.

"The benefit of a courtly education. Something to thank Charlie for."

An excited anticipation descended on the room. The gypsy had returned to the stage and raised his violin. He picked out a plaintiff melody in a minor key that told of longing and love, and a few onlookers began slowly to clap along with the rhythm as the pace gradually increased and the musicians prepared to layer the tune with their own parts.

"Gabe, why don't you show our ramshackle court how it's done?" Margaret called across Tara's shoulders, ignoring a pretty blonde girl who had sidled towards him and who took advantage of the acknowledgement to hold out her hand in introduction.

Tara's eyes widened as Gabriel's smile relaxed. His eyes sparkled and her stomach gave an unreasonably jealous kick as he leaned down to speak to the girl. Unable to watch, she backed away to sit down beside Leo. "Thank you again for the dress. It's very kind of you."

Leonie shrugged good naturedly: "It looks better on you than it ever did on me. Keep it."

"No! I don't need... I mean I don't go to these kind of events... Not that I think... I'm not..." Tara stumbled, anxious to avoid sounding ungrateful or, worse, prudish, but Leo just laughed and squeezed her hand. "I get the impression that Whitsun means something different here..."

The edges of Leo's wide mouth creased as Tara's brows furrowed. With the music, the noise had increased and she bent to shout into her ear. "It's an old tradition in these parts. For this one night, those who've yet to make a marriage have a chance to, erm, explore their sweetheart before taking their vows."

Tara snorted on her ale, causing the girl to laugh out loud. "It's all perfectly innocent, for the most part, allegedly, but I thought you were from Exeter, didn't you know?"

She shook her head, laughing. "No! When I lived here, I was..." Tara looked up for inspiration to find Gabriel holding out his hand, beckoning her to join him.

"I can't dance," she mouthed dismissively, shaking her head.

"I know you to be a fast learner," he chided, soundlessly, and a gasp of laughter escaped her. Only the reminder of the sword-fighting lesson brought memories of the kiss that prompted it and her eyes narrowed.

"Come," he persisted, "just follow my lead."

Strong fingers closed over hers and tugged her to standing, then with his free hand on the base of her spine, he led her past the awkward looking blonde to the centre of the barn, where five other couples had gathered. Gabriel joined the end of the line and stood her opposite. A number of the dancers were tapping to the rhythm, counting the beats to judge their entrance and on cue, they began to move, myriad limbs controlled by one mind.

The dance told a simple tale and it only took a couple of repetitions to understand its cues and patterns. The couple at the head of the line spun first with each other and then their neighbours, working down the line to be re-joined together as the melody found resolution. Love denied, tested and finally fulfilled. As the music progressed, the tempo sped and, at some point, it transposed into a major chord; there was now faith in the tale, expectation in the coupling. Spectators along the edges clapped a faster beat. And the dancers responded with enthusiasm, the beat and the atmosphere demanding ever more.

Tara could not remember having felt so exhilarated. Her falling hair whipped around her face and she panted as she kept pace. In the heat of the moment, it was as if they had been locked in this dance her entire life. The final notes were played and he smiled, offering a bow. She laughed as she dipped a quick curtsy in return: "I must catch my breath."

They meandered back through the crowd to the rear of the barn, but as she went to take the empty stool next to Margaret, he caught her by the hips and pulled her back. She turned and steadied herself with a hand on his chest, feeling a possessive arm move about her waist as she panted. He moved his fingers to her face, softly brushing aside the filigree hair on her hot cheek.

"I…" She started, looking up to meet his gaze and freezing as their eyes locked. For the briefest moment, Gabriel read arousal in her body. Her green eyes widened, the pupils dilated, and he marvelled at their intensity. Her lips were full and wet, her pale skin flushed. Then without warning her confession spilled out: "I heard you, earlier."

"What do you mean?" His dark brows furrowed, the smile lingering uncertainly on the corners of his mouth.

"I'm not the fool you take me for."

He stiffened, imperceptibly, and his hands slid slowly from her face, her waist. He kept his features bland as he asked again evenly, "What do you mean?"

"You'd have me disappear." She glared at him, defiant. "Would you kill me?"

"Rumour has it our Gabe's seen to la petit mort of many a fine maiden, Tara!" Rupert called over drunkenly, interrupting with a suggestive waggle of his eyebrows. Gabriel shot him a sharp stare before realising that Tara had backed away a couple of steps, into Margaret's ample bosom. A line of revellers passed between them and she twisted suddenly, weaving neatly between the bodies as she made for the wide barn doors.

"God's blood, Rupert," he snapped before making after her, trying not to break stride as he manoeuvred through the same tide of sweaty, drunken obstacles .

The chill night air blew a sobering wind and as Tara emerged from the barn she picked up her pace, walking blindly in what she hoped was the direction of the city. They were seven, maybe eight miles outside Exeter and she walked with purpose through strobing moonlight, along the roadway flanked by dry stone walls. A cornfield fell away into a valley on her left and there was a church meadow on the right. She would go straight on. With any luck a tavern would have a free room for the night. If not, well, she would cross that bridge when she came to it.

There was always Eddie's house. That was the reason she was here after all. Eddie. Destroying whatever link she could find to his men, stopping the uprising. Not a bloody barn dance.

Five days.

"Just let me go!" She cried without turning as she heard his footsteps close behind her in the darkness. "Goddammit, Gabriel, this is hard enough, but I won't wait for you to tire of me. I don't need your protection, your name, or your bloody dance lessons. You'd literally fiddle while Rome burns-"

"I don't need another lecture." Once free of the barn his long strides had easily collapsed the distance between them and she felt the lumped hardness of the dry-stone wall against her back as he pulled her round to face him. "Ignore Rupert, his blasted tongue runs on wheels. Why on earth would I save you from Tollemache only to kill you myself?"

"Then what does 'arrange for a more permanent disappearance' mean?"

He started, unable for a moment to formulate an answer.

"Let me go," she said simply, eyes narrowing. "Let's bloody end this now. If you won't kill me, then divorce me."

"On what grounds?" he laughed aloud at that, throwing his head back.

"Adultery."

"You would rather be hanged as a bedswerver than live as my wife?"

"Actually, I meant you as the guilty party, not me," she retorted. "But fine. Incompatibility."

"Another excellent idea," he replied dryly. "Only if the mighty John Milton was ridiculed for that suggestion, I don't suppose I'd find a more receptive audience in court."

"Then how exactly do you propose to end it? If I'm to be born dutifully until the law changes, I would know it-"

"Do not sully my feelings for you with talk of damned duty."

"Feelings?" She pushed hard against his chest. "You mean pity? Expectation of riches? Is that it? You're waiting for a dowry? You're the worst kind of hired thug biding your time until, what, Cromwell sees fit to reward your service and grant you the Villiers' estates he would offer Tollemache?"

"Strong words from someone prepared to sell a more feminine brand of favour!" He braced himself against the wall a moment. When he turned, his voice was measured again but it held the promise that she was walking on dangerous ground. "Do not talk of divorce again."

Tara faced down his glare. "Divorce, annulment, voiding. Call it what you will. I'll get what I came for at my uncle's house, then I'll make my own way back to London to support him. I'll not be a moment's more trouble to you."

"You have no blasted idea how much trouble you are."

Movement flickered at the corner of her vision and Tara dragged her eyes from his. In the distance, silhouetted against the moonlight, six horses pounded along the ridge of a field towards them, towards the barn. They were coming from the direction of Exeter and their pace and gait did not suggest that they were intending to join the party.

"Dragoons," she gasped, the argument forgotten in an instant. Instinctively she reached out and under her fingers the muscles of his forearms hardened to iron.

He manoeuvred her back behind him: "Go and end the party, Tara. Tell everyone to get out and then run. Don't rely on sanctuary in the church meadow, just run. I'll delay them."

Heart beating fast she hesitated, but seeing the firm set of his jaw, turned and ran back towards the barn. Without taking his eyes from the approaching soldiers, Gabriel walked further down the driveway to meet them, his sword hanging from his waist and his demeanour one of calm control even as the horses clattered to a stop around him.

21. DRAGOONS

"We've reason to believe there's an illegal assembly here tonight, harbouring criminals... traitors."

The sergeant started almost apologetically as soon as he was within Gabriel's earshot. He couldn't be entirely sure who was amongst the bodies in the barn, but these people were his neighbours, potentially his friends, and his heart was heavy. He didn't join the New Model Army all those years ago to enforce laws like this one. If only the Lord Protector's London men hadn't chosen today to arrive in Exeter for an inspection. If only he hadn't received the petty intelligence of the dance within the earshot of his former Major General. And if only that bastard didn't enjoy this all so damn much.

"Tell the crowd to disperse."

A heavier figure nudged his horse forward into the moonlight, looking about him almost as if he were a little bored by having to police the frivolous immorality of the insignificant. "Obviously," he drawled, "when the goodly sergeant here says have the crowd disperse, he means put it on its knees for processing. The magistrates will require the names–"

"Tollemache," Gabriel growled without acknowledging the uneasy sergeant. "I told you to leave us be."

The brute looked even more enormous on horseback. Travelling in his official capacity, he wore the battlefield costume of the harquebusier cavalry. An iron cuirass encased his torso with a breast and backplate and underneath it he wore a buff coat. His right hand, covered in a protective metal gauntlet, held the reins loosely; the left was heavily bandaged and rested limply across his lap.

"*Well.*" His lips curled into a mocking smile. "Please God this truly is a remarkable coincidence. I knew my fiancé would turn up in Exeter at some point, but providence obviously blesses my promised union to deliver you both so neatly into my arms." He turned to bark at the soldiers around him: "This blaggard is known to me as an enemy of the state. Hold him fast. Now."

Two of his men swung from their saddles and pulled Gabriel's arms back. His eyes hardened and he struggled, just enough to keep their attention on him.

"I sent you home once already with your tail between your legs," he spat as Tollemache landed heavily from his own horse and unsheathed a stout, straight–bladed sword. "Now fuck off."

"You're in no position to be issuing orders."

He stepped forward leisurely, letting the sharp point of his blade push slowly into Gabriel's chest. A small circle of red bloomed above his heart but he swallowed the pain, saying nothing as Tollemache laughed and cast his eyes towards the barn with an imperious air of victory.

"Where's my bitch, Moore?"

He gave a short moment for his captive to reply before lifting his sword. He considered it briefly, before dragging the razor-sharp edge slowly down his face without warning. Blood pooled along the line instantly, tracing the path from temple to jaw as Gabriel gritted his teeth in silence, his arms clenching within the grasp of the two soldiers. One of them grunted in surprise, awkwardly shifting his hold, but Tollemache just glanced thoughtfully at his damaged hand, hanging at his side in its grubby bandages, then raised his left elbow and swung it sharply into the other side of Gabriel's face.

"I owed you a mark," he hissed as Gabriel gasped for air. "Just a little something, to remind you to keep your tongue from my quim, although I doubt you'll live long enough to learn the lesson. Illegal gatherings, conspiracies. I'll see you hang at the next assizes, Moore. Unless you'd rather we end this sooner? I'm not averse to a widow. I've a strong stomach for well chew'd meat."

Gabriel's threat was chillingly calm: "I'm going to kill you."

Tollemache thought a moment, giving a hollow laugh. Then he drew his face up close, his breath stale: "I hear you showed her how to chew after a beating. She's fun to play with, eh?"

"Sir!"

Another soldier still on horseback dragged Tollemache's attention away to the barn doors briefly where, in the distance, movement flickered black and white in the moonlight. People were pouring out of the large doors and scattering silently in all directions, clambering over the path's stone walls to escape into the church meadow or, opposite, into corn-planted fields. No-one took the road; all avoided the armed horsemen without so much as glance in at them.

"Bastard," hissed Silus under his breath, suddenly understanding the tactical delay in Gabriel's performance. He exploded at his men: "Get to work! Do you want to be arraigned for treasonous enablement while you sat idly by and watched them go?"

It was enough to have the sergeant sliding from his horse and jogging towards the barn with his hands up, appealing for order.

"You!" Silus grunted back at a younger man struggling to control his own skittish mount. "Burn the barn."

The horse stopped moving but so did the soldier. Any sane man would know the idiocy of the order. Fire spread rapidly and with so many people about it would take a miracle to avoid casualties. Scare some troublemakers, the sergeant had declared before they left Exeter, not burn them alive.

"Sir?" he started.

Silus' eyebrow raised with his voice. "Are you deaf or stupid? Burn it. The barn is an obscenity. It stands as a testament to the weakness of the sinners inside. We'll smoke out every last one."

Gabriel jerked about for sight of Tara. In the distance, he could see Tom and Rupert helping Leo over the low wall. Margaret was in the cornfield already, nearly clear, but she looked desperate, fretting impotently, staring back at the barn and wringing her hands. He followed her gaze with a fearful sickness rising in the pit of his stomach. Flames were already licking the side of the barn and there were screams, people running sightless with panic. The soldiers were slowly corralling the bulk of the escaped crowd onto a courtyard area, pushing them onto their knees with hands behind their heads.

There. Tara stood stock-still, dark hair whirling and bare skin bleached white by the moon as her eyes scanned the crowd. She was looking for him. He spun back to Tollemache. Hell. Silus had noticed his breath hitch and turned his head slowly towards Tara, savouring the moment of discovery. He heard her angry scream above the cries of strangers and he struggled roughly against the soldiers holding him. She'd seen him.

Gabriel heard her footsteps above the chaos as she skidded panting to a halt: "For God's sake, Tara, I told you to run."

"How touching," Silus mused with a sour grin. "Knowing your bloodthirsty temper, my warm-hearted fiancé runs to us with fears for my safety."

The fear in her eyes, when she caught sight of the blood on his chest and face, told him instinctively she was not listening to a word he said. He struggled harder and she paled but jutted her chin towards Silus and looked him directly in the eye. She pulled a sword from behind her back and pointed it towards him, the blade wavering as she shook. "Let him go."

"I think not," Tollemache snorted dismissively. "Say goodbye to your boy, wench, from this night I'll fill you as a man."

She stepped forward, undeterred, her voice alive with anger and fear. "I was unarmed and unconscious in Southwark, you bloody coward; will you risk now that I don't know how to use this?" She nodded at his damaged hand and swiped the blade so that it made a sharp whooshing sound in the air. "Who knows what else I could cut off? If not tonight, then another night? I would never stop fighting you. You wouldn't dare sleep. But this is between us... Stand your men down, let him go, let everyone go, and I'll come with you willingly."

Gabriel closed his eyes. "Hell's teeth, Tara!" he shouted again, struggling to keep his voice steady as self-loathing sliced through him. So much for blasted sword play, what had he done? "Get gone now or so help me God I'll-"

A heavy-footed soldier crashed into the group from behind, impervious to the confrontation he was interrupting, his breath coming in pants. "Mick, it's your sister, she's in the barn!"

"Aggie? What the Devil? She's still a child!" Mick's grip loosened slightly and Gabriel felt the familiar tremor of turmoil as the solder battled between discipline and desertion. He steeled himself to break free, forcing his arms to relax ready for his moment, giving his captor space to follow his heart.

"Jed said he went in with her earlier. They were at the back, by the stage. But he hasn't been able to find her since the flames started and she's not been rounded up." The deep concern in his eyes was real and the corporal hesitated just a split second more before he let go entirely and backed towards the barn, twisting as he moved to run straight towards the flaming entrance.

"Worthless ballers!" Silus raged at them, hollering an order towards another soldier as he lifted his sword to focus on his captive: "Get her!"

The soldier began to move but Gabriel was quicker. He twisted loose of his second captor and disabled him with an elbow to the nose. Pulling Tara's hand, they ran hard towards the stone wall, to the spot where he had seen Tom. Barely breaking step, he swung her up and lifted her clear of the wall, dropping her without ceremony into the cornfield on the other side.

He could hear himself shouting for his cousin, but he was strangely focused as he turned back to the barn: "Get her clear, Tom, you hear me? Run!"

"Gabriel!" Tara's scream rose clear above the night as he ran away from them past another soldier, slashing warningly in the air with the sword she had carried, the sword she hadn't noticed him take from her trembling hand.

Damnable fool, Gabriel muttered to himself as he reached the barn entrance and drew up to hurriedly peel off his jerkin and shirt. He dunked the linen in a watering trough, balling it against his mouth as protection from the heat of the flames. A shock of stinging smoke made his eyes water and the building creaked under the onslaught of the fire but he could just see the corporal Mick, still in heavy guardsman's metal armour, hovering uncertainly just beyond the entrance, screaming impotently for his sister.

"You'll boil alive - take your blasted breastplate off man!" Gabriel shouted, before taking a deep breath and bolting past him into the darkness, his naked skin already covered with a gleam of sweat.

Time was running out. The groans of the tinderbox structure around him were like the chimes of a clock, counting down to oblivion. Greedy flames were eating effortlessly into the dried beams and from above there came an ominous creaking before a heavy lump of oak crashed down a warning just next to Gabriel. He glanced up at the damage; there were perhaps just a few minutes before the rest of the roof fell and Mick's cries behind him became even more desperate.

If anyone still breathed in that place they would have been forced to the back, past the straw bale stage where the band had stood, but it was impossible to see more than a few feet ahead. The flames lit a disorientating scene but the heat seared his eyeballs. He squinted, eyes streaming, running along the path his memory dictated, narrowly avoiding the structural supports that smouldered red-hot, stumbling on cups, shawls, stools, all the detritus abandoned on the barn floor as people fled.

He was moving more slowly now, drawn like a moth to the white-hot funeral pyre in the distance. He wove between obstacles, whispering a prayer as he grasped the backs of chairs, felt around the hard edges of tables. There, at the board they had settled upon earlier, Tara's cloak still lay abandoned. He picked it up and swung it around him for protection, faintly noticing as he did so that there was a small body on the floor underneath, curled up tight.

The girl didn't even flinch as he bent down and croaked a scream at her. Her slight limbs were heavy with unconsciousness as he dragged her out from the shelter and into his arms, stumbling sightlessly back towards the mouth of this Hell.

Mick ran towards him as they emerged, his hand raised to protect his head from falling debris and his cries chocked with relief. "Aggie! Thanks be to God. Does she breathe?"

Gabriel opened his mouth to speak but no sound came out. He pushed the girl into Mick's arms before his knees buckled and he fell to the floor, doubled over to gasp painfully at the clean air as he watched the man run clear of the danger with his sister in his grasp.

"As you like it, Moore, we'll avoid the hanging and you'll burn for your treason." A brutal kick at the side of Gabriel's chest sent him sprawling and his already heaving lungs constricted in shock and pain.

He rolled instinctively to escape Tollemache's second kick, back towards the barn. He squinted up through watering eyes to see its entrance now starkly skeletal against the sky, and scrambled to get to his feet, tripping on the corner of Tara's cloak as the brute relentlessly advanced. A fist made contact with his rising ribcage and he fell forward again, flattened by the winding. Another kick, this time into his thigh, the boot thudding heavily into the soft tissue of his muscle, threatening serious damage to his knee. If he couldn't get up, if the man broke a bone, it, this, would be over.

He twisted away again, rolling further this time, finding all fours and somehow standing. Tollemache was coming back around and he felt down desperately for his sword, pulling it from the sheath just in time to meet Tollemache's blade as it swung towards him. The weapons locked heavily and Gabriel stumbled backwards, trying to brace himself against the sheer weight of the man but finding no purchase on the compacted earth. Tollemache grunted as he shoved him back towards the barn, back into the flames.

Gabriel twisted awkwardly to see a smouldering roof support coming up quickly behind him and he was slammed back into it hard, feeling a red shock of heat through Tara's cloak. Tollemache laughed as he yelled in pain and pushed him away with a spurt of desperate strength, yanking the burning fabric from his flesh and throwing it aside. Then, eyes fixed on Tollemache, he pulled a short dagger from his boot.

With little space between them they circled each other slowly, moving like wolves, teeth bared, panting in air thick with scorching smoke, their blackened skin glistening with sweat that evaporated as quickly as it rose. They took turns to slash heavy weapons in the direction of the other, stabbing with shorter blades into empty air. As swordsmen they were well matched, but it was increasing difficult to read the other's feints and tell tales, eyes streaming with burning tears.

Chunks of wood fell from the disintegrating roof struts above, thudding haphazardly to the ground around them, barely audible amid the roar. Then the flames momentarily hushed with a rush of cool air, an unearthly groan coming from the building as it seemed to bow suddenly inwards, straining as if a giant man outside leant against the walls to push it over. As quickly as it had exhaled, the barn breathed in again, new flurries of wood fell and Gabriel spun around to break the stalemate, taking advantage of a thick new cover of smoke to feel his way back around the wobbling roof support.

He grunted as his sword found purchase in Tollemache's side, feeling the spongy resistance to his metal with a fleeting sense of victory. The man bellowed in surprise and swung heavily sideways with his elbow, meeting Gabriel's stomach with a crunch of ribs that forced him to the floor. But he twisted as he fell, using his weight to plunge his dagger into Tollemache's boot.

He felt the scream as a release of breath when the man came down heavily on top of him, but he couldn't hear anything except the pounding of blood in his ears. They rolled over and over, each struggling slowly, desperately, for the advantage. Blades long lost, they lay punches where they could, until one hand finally reached out for the candelabra still somehow standing next to the stage. Unsettled, the elaborate metal crashed down harmlessly away from the bodies. But the rock that had weighed it down was still there, fingers curled around the weapon.

A heavy grunt and a dull thud, and the pursuit was over.

22. THE PRESENT

Hidden from view behind bushy horse chestnut trees, in the corner of the sloping cornfield, Tara paced the edges of an imaginary square, hugging her chest. The sounds of the scene on the ridge above came straight from Hell: screams and thuds and the clashing of metal, punctuated by the hisses and crackles of serpents' tongues, spitting flames towards Heaven. Against the fiery backdrop, soldiers and weapons were silhouetted. Every so often, hot wind gusted from the barn bringing ash that swarmed like a whisper of moths and her mouth filled with the taste of acrid smoke. Gabriel was in there. She'd watched, incredulous, as he ran towards its destruction. How could he breath-

"Oh my sweet girl, we should never have brought you!" Next to her, Margaret knelt next to Leonie, her low voice cooing comforting sounds to slow the girl's frantic breathing. "*Breath*. In and out. In your condition! *Breathe*, two, three."

"I'm fine," Leonie gasped unconvincingly.

Tom stood stock still, a few feet from the women, his wide eyes reflecting the flames as they devoured the barn, reaching higher and higher into the black sky. He too had watched Gabriel emerge once only for the bulk of Tollemache to push them both back, inexplicably, into the inferno. Torn between sense and frustration, he had hovered indeterminate minutes, scanning the skyline for sight of him but seeing nothing.

Tara's desperation increased by the second: "I won't just sit here, Tom; I have to do something! I know that bastard, it's me he wants, not Gabriel. He will kill him!"

She gave a cry of determination, striding out across the uneven grass towards the barn, but getting no further than a few feet before Tom pulled her down to the hard ground, his sinewy body stronger than it looked.

"You can't go near there!" he hissed, pinning her shoulders down. "Jesus, think of Leo if nothing else, be quiet for her sake! I have to get her clear, they'll be scouring the land soon enough."

Her pummelling fists finally muffled her mouth, turning cries into sobs that racked her whole body. Sensing her defeat, Tom shifted his weight to release her and hung his head, preparing to say into the darkness what he knew the women couldn't. "Gabe's gone."

"No, no... *No...*"

"Curse catch me, child," said Margaret simply, her voice barely audible over the cacophony. "You do love him."

She stared blankly back at Margaret's ruddy face as it looked up momentarily from Leonie.

"I..." she started.

"My God!"

Silhouetted against dull-red smoke, a man's blackened figure emerged from the flames and stumbled across the courtyard. Tara leapt up to run, and he rolled across the stone wall, falling heavily to the ground just before she could reach him. Tom was just a second behind and between them they managed to right him and drag him to cower down for safety behind an outcrop of gorse.

"We need to split up," said Tom practically, hunching down over the body of his cousin. "We're too large a group to go unnoticed. Gabe, can you move?"

Gabriel nodded, prevented from speech by the need to drag at cold air.

Tara looked up at Tom: "Rupert should have found the carriage by now. He'll be coming back to the crossroads to collect you. Take Leonie and Margaret back to Treguddick. The soldiers know him, and besides you can always claim you are out looking for a midwife."

She eyed the gentle slope of the cornfield as it ran down towards the bottom of a valley. "I'll stay with him. If we can slip into the woods down there unnoticed, I can easily track the brook along to where it meets with Godolphin lands. We'll be a couple of hours behind you, more if I tire of carrying him," she added, eyeing up his exhausted bulk.

"Ta- N- I wo-" The staccato words were inaudible but his stern glare left little chance they would be lost in translation. She paused a moment then shrugged, and Tom agreed to ignore his cousin's protests. "Are you sure?"

"Yes. Go, for God's sake."

She watched as Tom took a moment to assess his cousin, before gathering Leonie and Margaret to skirt the edge of the field and re-join the road beyond the church. Then she took a deep breath and attempted a small smile: "Can you make it down the hill or must I roll you?"

She'd looked away before he could answer but, in any case, it was lost. The soldiers' shouts were harsh above the creaking crackle of the barn as it finally toppled inwards, heaving and groaning towards its fiery oblivion. "What's that? I can't hear you. Perhaps I may thank Heaven for small mercies."

She lifted his arm and took it around her shoulders, shaking with the effort of helping to hoist him to standing alone. He wobbled gently before finding his feet but soon they were picking their way through the furrows and ridges of corn, zig-zagging a path behind the haphazard cover of bushes until they reached the tall hedgerow marking the bottom perimeter.

With a grunt of exertion Gabriel hoisted Tara over, before falling awkwardly across it himself, and in a moment's pause to breathe their eyes met. With a barely perceptible nod they continued, across a second, darker field at the bottom of the valley, to where the trees would close around them. Before long they had picked up the Wray Brook and Gabriel fell to his knees, scooping handfuls of water over his face and torso, dragging mouthfuls down over his scorched throat. It was stagnant and he gagged before flopping painfully back onto the bank while she scanned the trees for company.

Without a word, she helped him again to his feet and they stumbled along the still, silent path of the brook for an hour until, finally confident that they were beyond any rational search radius, she sunk down against the trunk of a fallen tree, breathing heavily as he slid down beside her.

"I thought..." she panted, turning to look properly at him and tailing off when she saw the state of him up close. His head was tipped back against the rough bark and his chest rose and fell dramatically with the effort of breath. Where it wasn't blackened from the smoke, his skin was bruised or torn. Under the monochrome moonlight, gashes of blood ran along the ridges like black lava and impulsively she traced one. His skin rippled in response to her touch and he winced, but his eyes stayed closed.

"I thought women were the gentler sex." Coming from smoke-filled lungs, his rasping voice didn't sound like it normally did but the gently ironic tone was familiar.

She stood purposefully and yanked down a petticoat, ripping it swiftly apart into strips. Then she knelt down on the brook bank a few yards away and leant forward toward to disturb her reflection, wringing out the makeshift cotton bandages in cold water. When she returned, he was leaning forward, wordlessly flexing his left hand, the long fingers stretching before they balled again, still ready for the fight.

"Let me see," she started, crouching down beside him. She offered a small encouraging smile and raised an eyebrow at another momentary wince as she took his right hand in hers. On examination, the smallest digit bent from the knuckle at a slightly unusual angle. This was a good start, she thought ironically, something she could actually help with: "Your little finger is twisted. I need to drop it back in the socket."

A small wry smile formed through a grimace at her diagnosis. "I know," he hissed. "Just don't- ah!"

Without ceremony she lifted and dropped the digit back into its correct position and his posture visibly relaxed, shoulders less taught as the muscles of his back unclenched.

"Thank you," he whispered, flexing the right hand as he had the left. "The bastard was made of stone."

"Maybe that explains why you look as if you've fallen off a cliff... Keep still," she shifted onto her knees and her fingers felt more purposefully over his torso this time, seeking out injury. Her brows furrowed as she wrapped the wet cloth over a shining burn on his elbow, securing it with a knot.

"What happened here?"

"The entrance was blocked, I had to find another way out," he replied matter-of-factly, swallowing the memory of rising panic as he hammered against the back wall of the barn for a weak point to escape.

"Tollemache?"

"Dead."

Tara stilled, hearing the quiet satisfaction in his voice, her stomach clenching. Was he really gone? There was still evidence of the man's existence on Gabriel's skin: spatters of his dark blood clung to the hair on his arm, bruises evidencing his force bloomed on his chest. She touched one and he flinched again, momentarily, but he withstood the feel of her fingers and let her pose his limbs as she needed to better assess the severity of damage.

"Does anything else hurt?"

He gave a small shake of his head.

"You're lying...," she murmured, eyes narrowing.

"Everything hurts," he replied with a cough and an imperceptible hiss as the air tickled his lungs "But everything will mend soon enough."

"I need to tie your hair back, to wash your cheek," she said, pulling a length of cord from a helpful pocket in Leonie's skirt and slipping quickly behind him to gather the dark waves.

She was too slow to hide the gasp at the sight of his back. Picked out by the moonlight, white scars striped his skin at steady, controlled intervals. He hung his head and his broad shoulders tensed again in a rigid line. Prince Charlie's whipping boy. The phrase had meant nothing to her before. Every boy was thrashed at some point, some more regularly than others, but few, surely, with the brutality needed to create damage that would last a lifetime. Everyone knew Charlie to be a poor student, recklessly fond of practical jokes, but this... it felt personal. Whoever inflicted these marks had done so in cold blood, far removed from any red-hot surge of anger or impatience.

Elsewhere, his flesh carried the myriad tattoos of a soldier's experience. His right shoulder was grazed with a ragged scar that might have been caused by the spinning drag of a bullet. His thigh had been pierced by a point that looked as if it had been thrust up into him while on horseback. His cheek, she realised with the clarity of guilt, would now be marked forever by Tollemache's vengeance. But, until this moment, he'd managed to keep his back hidden and she wondered with a surge of tenderness what other scars remained buried.

Awkwardly, she forced her fingers to reach over the welts and gather his hair. She avoided tugging at the knots, but extracted a couple of larger objects deposited by the fire or swept up from the barn floor and quickly braided the loose waves, securing the cord at the nape of his neck and noticing a redness marking out his spine.

"Stay still a moment," she murmured, finding her feet and heading a few paces back along the brook in the darkness, peering for the spiky silhouettes of the burdock heads she thought she'd seen as they passed.

"What's that?" He glanced over his shoulder as she dropped to her knees again behind him.

"Beggar's Buttons," she said, struggling to hide the hitch in her voice as she rubbed the stem of the plant between her hands to free its juice and rub a sticky cover down across the burn with a gentle fingertip. "A blacksmith once… I'm told it can help."

Then she ducked back around him and lent down to the water with a practical air to wet a fresh pad. He didn't make eye contact when she settled to attend his face and she watched his inscrutable mask with unexpected rawness, as if it were her own aching heart she was trying to read. The water slowly revealed his features as it took away the dried blood, leaving an angry red gash where Tollemache had traced a line with his blade from cheekbone to jaw. She felt at the wound tentatively, reluctant to tear inadvertently apart the layers of skin that had already started to knit cautiously together.

"It's not deep. But it could do with a couple of stitches."

"Shame you're not one to carry needlework to a dance."

"How do you know what I like to do?" She cocked her head to one side. "Would you prefer a wife content with sewing?"

"Wife," he said softly. "Thank you."

"I thought..." she started again, taking his right hand in hers and turning it over as if examining it intently a second time, searching for something she might have missed. On impulse she lifted it to her lips and pressed a kiss on the rough skin. "I thought you weren't going to get out."

"I told you," he whispered, voice rasping, with a small smile. He curled his fingers around to stroke her face gently and his gaze glistened with moisture that might still have been the effects of the smoke. "I'll find a way or I will make one."

She closed her eyes then, afraid to look directly at the dark intensity in his, and her lips brushed along his palm as she felt the darkness thrum around them. "Gabriel, it wasn't your fault. What happened to Ralph... any of it... it's not your fault. I..."

His head bowed to hers, foreheads touching. There was a tremor within him and a salty tear rolled over her lips. "Tara, please... I swear on my life, I will keep you safe. Nothing will hurt you while I am breathing... But I can never give you my heart and you would never take it. There's too much history between us and, God knows, too much future."

She tilted his head to look directly into his eyes and threaded her fingers into his hair, feeling the hard shape of his skull and afraid to let go in case she lost her nerve. "But now, husband," she replied after a moment, in a voice she hardly recognised as her own, "right now... I am only interested in the present."

The confession stole any shred of reason that remained and he leant forward, snatching her breath with a deep, demanding kiss. His mouth was hard at first, his tongue tasting faintly of ale but mostly of smoke. With a momentarily wince at the pain in his ribs he rose, holding her to him and kissing her hungrily, walking her backwards until he could lay her down on a patch of soft grass and cover her with his warm body. She tangled her arms around his neck, feeling nothing but the most luxurious mattress as she pulled the unyielding strangeness of him heavier onto her and breathed in the wood smoke and sweat on his skin.

He tested for limits in her kiss as he had once before, giving her a last chance to regain her senses, before pulling back to give just enough space for his fingers to tug slowly at the ribbons threading her stays, watching the ends flicked and dragged along her skin, sending ripples of shivers across her throat and dragging whimpers from her mouth. He unwrapped her slowly, reverentially, before tugging off his breeches to lay alongside her.

Their skin touched along the lengths of their bodies but his limbs tensed suddenly; a last effort of denial for a promise of redemption within his grasp but maybe never further away. The night had robbed all colour but left behind myriad greys in which it was just possible to believe that there was more to the world than the stark contrasts of black and white, duty and order. More to him than the binary brutality of the past and more to what might come than an empty darkness.

"Jesus, Tara," he whispered, pausing to gaze down at her breasts, pale to the point of luminescence in the moonlight. Unable to stop himself, he leant to kiss the mounds slowly, his tongue gently teasing the peaks until the dark nipples bunched and she panted at the ache building within. Then he lay kisses upwards along the delicate skin of her neck, finding the pulse beating strong and fast. "I don't deserve you."

"No, I doubt very much that you do," she laughed, pushing back the loose waves of his hair that had fallen from her poor attempt at a braid.

He grinned then and kissed her mouth again, hungry for its sweetness. She felt his warm insistence hard against her belly, responding to her body as it arched up to meet his with an elemental demand, the throbbing ache in the pit of her pelvis now an urgent need, an emptiness. Her arms tightened around his neck and her legs wrapped around his waist, revealing a slick, ready invitation. He gave one hard thrust with an impatience he didn't recognise and broke the slender barrier. In a split second of surprise he stilled, before covering her cry of pain at the sharp rupture with a deep, tender kiss and giving her time to stretch around him, to feel him possess her.

She smiled as the burning and shock subsided: "I'm fine."

"You're beautiful," he murmured back, nuzzling for the sensitive lobe of her ear as her nails dug fresh demands into the muscular curve of his shoulders and his body began slowly to move against hers.

Above her, within her, he laid claim to her body, his hands marking the completeness of his possession with teasing strokes along her skin. Her arms, breasts, belly, thighs, all his for the bidding, his to command, and she closed her eyes, feeling nothing but his touch and a blissful heat pooling in the pit of her stomach. She stiffened as his fingers closed on the nape of her neck.

"Tara, open your eyes. Look at me," he whispered. "You're beautiful.

And you're mine."

There were no shadows in his dark eyes, no possibility of pretending that this longing could be sated and they could ever part politely as friends. She shuddered, realising her soul was laid as vulnerable and exposed as her flesh and the visceral tremor pulled him swiftly under to release. It was unexpected, sooner than he'd wanted or planned, and he cried out, a groan of ecstasy and frustration, withdrawing as quickly as he could to waste his seed in the grass before collapsing down on her legs.

"Are you alright?" he asked after a moment, looking up at her through fallen hair, his chin resting on her belly. His voice sounded husky still, his brows slanted in what might have been apology.

"Yes," she said simply and smiled, content to enjoy the weight of him upon her and the knowledge that he'd found a heavy satisfaction. A nightjar called loudly and she stared up at the rustle of leaves, gathering the fragments of her heart back together as tidily as she could.

He thought a moment and moved up to lie alongside her, raising her hand absent-mindedly and kissing the tips of her fingers, one at a time, observing matter-of-factly. "Your fingers are really very long. I know men with smaller paws."

She nudged him playfully to his back at that, and stretched gently onto his chest, one hand stroking over warm slope of his belly, the other smoothing back his hair so she could lean forward and press her lips to his forehead. Careful of the sword wound she lay kisses along the delicate skin of his eyelids, past long, dark lashes, soft and almost childlike against the hardness of his body, and down his straight nose. At his lips she paused briefly while his fingers entwined with hers, gently pulling her arms either side of his shoulders and fixing her across him, to give him better access to her mouth.

"You lied to me," he said without rancour, pushing her gently up so he could watch her reaction. "I'm your first."

She frowned. "I had to. I thought you wouldn't... that you wouldn't want to... if I'd known another. Besides," she added carefully, "you lied to me; Eddie didn't tell you to stop my wedding."

"I had to," he echoed quietly. "I couldn't let you marry him."

"Jack…"

She pulled away from him to lie alongside, heavy with the sudden realisation that she'd given the man she'd been prepared to swear her life to no thought these last few days. She tried experimentally to coax a guilt to life, to feed it with news of the reckless deal with Cromwell, the speed of her marriage to the Earl of Denby and, now, its willing consummation. But the simple truth was that she felt nothing barring an urgent need to mould her body to Gabriel's, to dissolve her aching flesh into his. It was inconceivable there was ever a time before him.

She across glanced at him, staring inscrutably up into the night sky, the moonlight making clean, uncompromising lines of his nose and jawline, the softness of his hair fallen back against the grass. He rolled over to return her gaze and leant in to gently kiss her mouth, whether to spare her the pain of speaking her unfaithfulness aloud or him the pain of hearing it, she wasn't sure. Still, the firmness in his voice brokered no room for argument or regret. "I mean it, Tara Moore. Here, now: you are mine."

Without warning he flipped her onto her back, taking his weight astride her. Slowly he gathered both of her hands in one of his, pinning her arms above her head and freeing his fingers to trace a slow line all the way down from the centre of her forehead to between her rising and excruciatingly sensitive breasts, where he paused to circle each erect nipple, rolling them gently between thumb and forefinger. She arched her back and he moved on lower, past her belly button.

"I'm sorry," she said sweetly, giggling with the ticklish shiver, trying to distract him, "what did you say?"

He kissed her neck, tasting the salty, earthy sweat of exertion and she caught the dangerous grin as he moved up to take her mouth. "Listen carefully, while I tell you again."

She moaned at his touch then, tugging her arms to find she was caught firm and her heated skin prickled in anticipation as his thumb pressed on, drawing the line deep between her legs. She gasped at the intrusion and he smiled as he swallowed the sound, his tongue mimicking the demands of his fingers on her engorged flesh. The shock of an exquisite tension began to build.

"*Mine.*"

23. THE INSOLENCIES OF THE LIBERTY OF SOLDIERS

From the outside, in the stillness of dawn, the little town house looked relatively intact. There was no immediately discernible damage save for a broken pane of glass, but on closer inspection the lock had been forced and a singular board nailed roughly across the entrance. It was a feeble attempt to deter entry and Gabriel wrenched it away without effort. With a galvanising breath, she pushed at the door, shoving it over a lump in the flagstones where it habitually dragged. Eddie Villiers may be a high-minded man, she thought wryly, but he was never a practical one.

It was difficult to say whether the chaos inside was the result of heavy-handed collection by the authorities, or the too-strong temptation of looting since its occupant's arrest. Tara flicked her eyes over the simple front room, trying quickly to make a mental inventory from memory. She frowned, righting a settle, scanning the bookshelf anxiously until a silver candlestick glinted from the top. The former then. No thief would have missed what little treasure her Quaker uncle had or displayed.

Six days.

Gabriel followed her in and pushed the door to behind them, before letting the doorframe take his weight. He said nothing, not wanting to interrupt. When they'd woken early under the scant protection of Leonie's damaged dress they'd walked straight here, silently acknowledging the need to fulfil the task before Tollemache's death became common knowledge.

In the small adjoining study, drawers had been pulled from the desk and upturned on the floor. It was no more than a cursory gathering of evidence by the local militia, acting on remote orders from the capital. On her knees, Tara ran her fingers absent-mindedly over the scattered paperwork, pausing briefly to tug on the corner of a letter from George Fox on behalf of the Religious Society of Friends, clear evidence of Eddie's non-conformist heresy. She put it aside.

From a haphazard pile of invoices, a bill of sale for a night's stay in The White Horse Inn at Mortenhampstead caught her eye briefly, beneath a receipted order for shoes. A couple of yellowed pamphlets about the evils of the Commonwealth lay in a second crusted pile. Once common enough on the streets, these had been banned three years ago, after the failed uprising by Penruddock. Thurloe would see these as clear evidence of revolutionary zeal. She edged them out carefully.

The first vindicated a high and mighty Christmas Ale that formerly would knock down Hercules and she smiled at its harmless reminiscences, until her finger traced the text of the second pamphlet. This one revealed the evils of the Protestants in Ireland, where Gabriel had not just fought but commanded the Pigges of the English Sowes. The crude images were disturbing enough, but just in case the reader was not entirely sure, the author hammered home his disgust of Cromwell's troops, engaged to a man in stripping and spit roasting children in front of their parents or simply dashing out their braines. She shuddered. It was barely believable such vitriol had been kept.

She collected them up with the bill of sale from Mortenhampstead and moved them to the grate. No need to add fuel to the fire, she thought ironically, her shaking fingers sparking a flame with the steel and flint on the hearth. She watched the pamphlets burn. The brittle pages crackled and disintegrated in a heartbeat but the acrid smell lingered, making the task familiar: she lit similar fires when her father was arrested.

The authorities had been complacent then, too. The trial started and Gregory Villiers, unfazed by the impenetrable Latin proceedings, demanded to see evidence against him, the proof that he commanded a Sealed Knot network. It was a game of impossibly high stakes. He wasn't permitted to compel his own witnesses, but no one standing for the Protector could place him in the same town, let alone the same room, as the other men on trial. No letters, no messengers. No witnesses. Days passed. It took an improbable and illogical last-minute testimony from a broken wreck they claimed was a co-conspirator to justify his death.

And all the time, no one thought to ask his daughter.

"Tara?"

She jumped, startled by the soft word, and gasped as she spun around. In that split second, she saw only the anonymous figure of a warrior. His jerkin and shirt had long since disappeared, consumed by the flames; the flesh on his naked chest was bruised black. His hair was loose, swirling about his head like a nest of vipers and the angry red line running the length of his face evidence of cruel violence. He looked wild, like he could do anything, in any godforsaken place. Dashing out their braines?

"Are you alright?"

She caught his eyes then, a glimmer of softness, edged with the tenderness of concern. The flames were nearly out and a gust of wind from the broken window caused a spluttering in the grate that shook her firmly. No. "I'm fine. It's just, I need some time alone."

"I'll wait for you outside."

"I want you to go," she said, surprising herself. Painful memories and doubts were being dragged unwilling to the surface of her thoughts like slippery eels from the deep sea. He didn't need to see this. "It's going to take a while... to go through everything."

He paused. Instinct warned him to keep close, made him nervous that every darkened corner held a danger. But, logically, Tollemache was dead; he'd felt the last breath leave his bulk with a disturbing shudder. And Henry's news was clear: Thurloe's arrival was delayed. If she found any messages from Villiers to the Sealed Knot, she would bring them out of the house, so the spymaster wouldn't find them. She would bring them out to send word to the men of the destruction of the Royalist fleet. And out of this chaos, he would find them. "I'll come back for you in an hour."

She raised her chin and one eyebrow.

"Fine," he finally conceded, swallowing the nagging unease. "I'd better find Tom and check everyone is safe and well. Besides, I'm getting hungry; I need to spit roast some children."

The eyebrow went higher in an expression of sardonic impatience and he laughed, hands spreading in defeat. "Last and final offer. I'll send

Henry's carriage for you at three. But Tara, if you're not back at Treguddick by four, I will find you."

"I know." She paused a moment. "Though in the meantime, there's no need to terrify the good people of Exeter witless. Take one of Eddie's shirts. There should be a clothes chest in the bedroom."

She hung her head and listened as he left, waiting for the house to settle back into its silence. It was filled with the residue and warm debris of lived-in years and she moved between the few rooms gathering small armfuls of items, depositing them back before the fireplace like offerings. More pamphlets; more Quaker literature; a spare cloak; the silver candlestick, uglier than she remembered. A small, carved box of letters. She hesitated here; these had to be personal. Eddie would not leave any truly incriminating notes so obvious. But what if he had?

She jiggled the lid loose. Ever the romantic, Eddie had kept two faded love letters, each, she noticed wryly, from a different woman. Beneath them, an enjoinment to join James Nayler to preach holy, holy, holy and tremble in the way of the Lord, and a prosaic reference from his school master to an Oxford tutor that made her breath hitch. But then, at the bottom, two letters addressed to Gregory Villiers, care of the King's army. The elaborate script on the wrapper was faded but her mother's hand was immediately recognisable. Angela Villiers' pen was as clear, beautiful and rounded as the woman that held it.

The first was marked June 1645 and Tara took a deep breath, sinking down onto a wooden chair. Her father had been with the royalist army for over two years by this point, leaving the family home in Dorset to be defended by his wife, his teenage son and his little girl. Together, to begin with, they martialled a small garrison of aged men who had been on the estate all their lives and had no-where else to go in the chaos of war. And these men were enough, to begin with. Weycroft Hall was a castellated fortress; walls six feet thick surrounded by a wide moat six feet deep.

Angela Villiers was not a woman to wallow in indecision or self-pity when parliamentary forces arrived and made camp a few hundred yards from those walls. Tara smiled, remembering her mother storming about, ordering for the lead to be stripped from the roof for the casting of bullets or for the rallying of ancient defences, the old Tudor cannons previously only retained for some quaint historical aesthetic. Before they became useful. Before the war.

THE SEALED KNOT

Darling Gregory,

These are dog days. The heat makes us all weary and we list like Ships on sandbanks, waiting for the frothy tide of action to draw us up from our stupor.

Ralph is frustrated. He is fifteen in three weeks; strong and bored rigid here playing nursemaid to his Mama, a role he assumes only as a personal affront to his Gallantry. Watch your sword arm, old man, I would wager that one of these nights the allure of King and Country will prove too strong and he will sneak out to join you before the crack of Dawn, as if avoiding a request for rent.

Little Tammy finds endless tasks for him, as if she understands the need to make him feel Useful. She told him at breakfast today that while he is already a fine Swordsman, t'would be worth his while to practice a little more Enthusiastically with our eight-legged lodgers. (The Spiders do seem uncommonly large this Summer.)

Our other unwelcome Visitors are poor company. They continue to bombard us with poisonous words, dismal 'news' and prophesies of our doom. They play loud music daily, even on the Sabbath. An infernal racket of drums and pipes; Heaven only knows what your dear brother Edward would make of it. They even stole the Church Bells for the weight of iron and you will be sad to know that some of our Venetian glass was shattered when shots were fired from the empty Church Steeple. Perhaps you will laugh to learn that during a period of particularly noisome "music" we moved the gun carriages to teach them a Lesson and some of Cromwell's good subjects went to Old Nick for their sacrilege. You would be Proud.

We are mightily well Stocked. and we have plenty of fresh water from the Well. Would that Stephen Steward's whey-faced wit ran so deep.

Your loving wife,
Angela

Tara spun Ralph's ring on her finger and unconsciously took a deep breath as she unfolded the second letter. They would have to keep up such games for another three long years, and by spring 1648, the siege was no longer a laughing matter. Gregory Villiers fighting in Maidstone and, as predicted, Ralph had long since fled Weycroft to join him under the King's banner.

She pined for his company in the mired stasis Weycroft Hall had become. Their small garrison had been somehow augmented during lulls in the siege by the wives, daughters and mothers of absent soldiers, all seeking shelter from the threat of roundhead pacification in the countryside. To a woman, they were restless, testy, bitter and scared, and when she couldn't hide in the library, she found herself used alternately as plaything or proxy for settling their grievances when the lady of the house was absent. She was absent a fair amount, Tara remembered with a wry smile. Angela Villiers spent obsessive hours avoiding the lot of them on the premise that tending her tiny rooftop herb garden would one day supplement their meagre meals.

My Darling Gregory,

Shortly after lunch today a Drum sounded to announce a Parley and so Stephen Steward lowered a rope ladder for the Commander of the Parliamentary Regiment. This man told me that so far they have hesitated to press, discharging their respects to my sex and honour. And yet soon, he added by way of threat, my obstinacies will throw me upon all the insolencies of the liberty of his Soldiers and his Sergeant.

I told him that I cannot be sure it is your Pleasure that I should entertain so many men in your house and he laughed, not unkindly at first. But Weycroft is important to Cromwell. He spent a long hour trying to talk me into waving a white linen aloft but he left red-faced with the air of one who has Tried to reason but has found reason Wanting. Nonetheless I count his grudging admiration of my Fidelity and Courage a victory.

Would that you could tell me you were to come soon!

I know you cannot and I know now my life is sought after. I write because I want you to know that I'm not afraid. I have not one drop of disloyal Blood within me and I welcome the chance to give my life for our God, our King and our Country.

Protect my boy. Keep him safe. Tammy is grown a Strong and resourceful girl; whatever is to happen now, she will be safe with Robert Farrier. Find her, when this is over.

All my love,
Angela

She stiffened, her fingers busy smoothing and pleating and smoothing and re-pleating folds into her skirt. The blood red silk rustled, whispering a steady incantation. *He's dead. He can't hurt you. Gabriel killed him.*

The insolencies of the liberty of soldiers.

A poetic phrase to describe the actions of the besiegers who finally took the stronghold by force at the end of October 1648. They stripped the women and paraded them shamefully about the great hall before pushing them naked and shivering onto the road outside. Then the hefty bulk of his sergeant held her mother face down on the table, skirts hiked up around her waist. Silus Tollemache had smacked the lady of the house until tears streamed silently from her closed eyes and sweat ran rivulets from his forehead, through the encrusted dirt of his sun-reddened face.

He'd seen her then, only half obscured behind the doorframe, frozen in fear. His lips curled into a nasty smile and he held her horrified gaze the whole time as he kneed her mother's legs apart and forced himself deep within her. There was no sound but the animal grunts of his exertion and Angela's strangled, smothered cries until he finished with a groaning shudder.

"You're next," he mouthed, laughing, drawing her mother's vacant gaze in her direction.

Angela read the threat and turned to swipe at him, but he caught her arm and twisted it until she cried out. He let her slide unthreateningly to the floor but she launched herself at his leg, sinking a small quill-sharpening knife into his bare calf. He screamed, his features freezing into shock, and Tara ran, sliding unseen into the ancient priest hole behind the kitchen. Looking back, that small, brutal act of defiance was her mother's undoing. Without it, she was just another spoil of war, but that split second told the victor she would not be vanquished.

While Tollemache ravished her body, the troops invaded her home. They laid waste to the wine cellar and swarmed from room to room, smashing and slashing, until two men stumbled on the anteroom to the kitchen containing racks of dried and drying herbs. She heard them emerge drunkenly triumphant, waving a bundle of rosemary Tara had plaited into a doll out of boredom, holding it aloft as clear evidence of sorcery. She remembered gripping the rough floorboards in her hiding place so hard that splinters pierced her skin.

The blanket of inebriation gave Tara the chance to escape and slide unseen past befuddled soldiers who had quickly given up on finding a missing girl child. She barely remembered running through the darkness to the local village as her mother had once instructed and virtually no recollection of the local blacksmith taking her in, but the ball of impotent rage and guilt still rolled through her hollow stomach.

She heard later that one of the soldiers died on the third day. Possibly it was the natural inevitability of some disease or wound he carried with him; more likely it was alcohol poisoning. Tollemache's pronouncement was murder, but in the absence of an armed enemy, attention quickly turned to other means of retribution from the royalist household. The clerical authorities were urgently called to investigate witchcraft and Lady Villiers dragged from the bowels of Weycroft Hall for interrogation. In a makeshift court they denied leniency for her dogged refusal to admit the hex and she knew now that for Tollemache, it must have been a relief, to know that the woman he failed to frighten was, quite literally, unnatural. Angela Villiers was hanged from the portcullis gate five days after he had walked in beneath it.

Her father never spoke about the siege. He permitted a cursory hug when Robert Farrier's apprentice pushed his unrecognisable child into his arms three years later, but on the subject of her mother, and Ralph, he remained silent. For Gregory Villiers, the only peace to be had was in prolonging the war. Unthinkably, the King was beheaded in January 1649 but while Cromwell consolidated his power, Villiers worked on the organisation of resistance. He established the Sealed Knot in Devon and Cornwall, vowing to ready the path for his exiled boy King to return.

It was no world for a child and so Tara stopped being one. Todd Pengelly, Robert Farrier and Mad Michael Evelyn saw to the men on the ground, the steady supply of foot soldiers along the south coast to harry regiments of the New Model Army, uncover intelligence and plan for Penruddock's uprising. She was their messenger. She devised a code for her father's orders and intelligence and moved freely, an unseen go-between.

She blinked and looked about the room again. Her old needlework bag was shoved down behind the desk. Its contents were a tangled mess; half-finished patterns and colourful woollen threads knotted and intermingled together in no particular order and little hope of purposeful resurrection. Her fingers tugged through the contents in a futile attempt to separate the stands, cursing when an uncased needle lurking in the chaos pricked her finger. She pulled out her hand to assess the damage and with a jolt of surprise, found that she had inadvertently dragged a familiar-looking square of muslin into the light.

The pattern was not in any way remarkable or even particularly well executed. A decorative border in speedy crewel stitch wove approximations of purple tulips for royalty with Star of David for hope, wisteria for steadfastness and a single stem of violet as the signature of Villiers. In the centre, a bible passage selected from Romans in dark blue thread:

"Tribulation worketh patience; And patience, experience; and experience, hope." Her father's favourite.

Perhaps he enjoyed the thrill of goading Cromwell's men, mocking them for failing to see what was directly before them. Perhaps he simply thought to be better hidden by appearing in plain sight. Either way, it had worked for years. When he was charged, she panicked that she'd made a mistake somehow, but the code breakers remained ignorant. And if she needed any more proof the code was unbroken it was here: by copying her template, Eddie had simply, literally, picked up the thread of his brother's treason.

She could pick it up now. Send word to the men; stop the uprising. She knew what she had to do.

The sound of the door scraping over the stone interrupted her thoughts and she let out an irritated hiss, drawing the sleeve back across her eyes: "I thought we had an agreement."

"The Lord Protector thought so too."

24. SPEAKING BLUNTLY

Tara stood immediately, heart pounding and back to the fireplace, scanning the room for weapons. The candlestick was out of a reach but she could do some serious damage with the poker lying on the floor by her feet. Her right hand flexed, ready to grab at it as a man with a prominent forehead and dark blonde, shoulder length hair appeared in the doorway.

"John Thurloe."

Tara's jaw tightened imperceptibly but she kept her eyes firmly on him. "I know."

He tilted his head in question as he closed in, taking her hand and raising her fingers to his lips, all the time maintaining a cool contact under heavily lidded eyes. He offered a smile that lingered like a slimy residue of a snail. "You are bewitching Madam; little wonder the Lord Protector took such a close interest in your plight."

Tara's overwhelming thought, from the recesses of her brain which still noticed such things, was that he was short, no taller than herself. But he carried his status as though it more than made up for any lack of stature and, to a large extent, he was right. Secretary of State and spymaster; one of the most powerful men in England and barely forty. His unblinking features somehow conveyed simultaneously a power of threat and an indifference to her fate.

"I have expected you here, sir, in Exeter. My uncle's case is an important one." She spoke politely, struggling to suppress a shudder at his beady gaze and her own callous reference to Eddie's life. "There's little else filling the pamphlets here and I thought you might take a personal interest sooner or later. Your fame precedes you."

He sniffed at the air like a bloodhound, as if to demonstrate the well-founded nature of his reputation. "You have lit a fire."

"I was cold," she replied evenly.

He shrugged and his empty smile fell away as he scratched busily at a spot of dry skin on his left hand. "Why are you here, so early in the morning, Miss Villiers? Oh apologies, Lady... Denby now, isn't it?"

She ignored the question and nodded to the candlestick. "My uncle has few possessions, but I would keep them from thieves."

"You know you may not remove anything from this house without my express authority? I issued strict instructions to the local militia to secure the entrance and exits."

"Did you? The house was open." She smiled as she lied and nodded towards the bookcases with a feminine fluster of words: "My husband has brought me to Devon to meet his family, I had to be introduced you see, we had a passionate and fast engagement and I had not met them. I knew his family well as a child of course, but not the extended members, as it happened. We never expected to see each other again, you see. The war... but of course you know about that."

Thurloe nodded encouragingly as his eyes followed hers but he frowned at the irrelevance of empty shelves to the tale of her courtship. "And?"

"And since we were in the area... Forgive me, sir, I am sentimental, I wanted to secure a couple of personal items belonging to my family: some old letters from my mother sent years ago, before, during the war. I also have my uncle's spare cloak and of course this candlestick. It was presented to my parents on their wedding day. These can surely be of no interest to the authorities?"

Thurloe frowned, "I am quite sure, my Lady, that these items seem to you quite harmless."

He patted along the cloak for hidden plackets and then carefully picked up one of the folded letters from the side table to skim read its contents. He seemed to have made his assessment when he folded over the page and replaced the letter on the top. "Forgive me my Lady, I do not of course presume to question your motives."

"Thank you, sir," she whispered.

"What's this?" Thurloe nodded at the needle and thread still dangling from her left hand and the embroidery draped over the arm of the chair. He started scratching again.

"A self-indulgence," she shrugged. "My husband considers embroidery a tiresome habit, but it helps me relax and I had thought I might have to wait some hours for him to escort me back to the family estate. He has to carry out some business today. I am not sure what, I must admit I have no real understanding."

"But you are not a normal woman, Lady Denby. I'd be highly surprised if there are many subjects on which you have no real understanding." He came closer and dragged a leisurely finger over the pulse spot beneath her ear, smiling indulgently as she flinched and fought to control her breathing. "You're afraid, though. And why is that? Your heart is racing and your skin, it's shining with a fine sweat.

"You may relax, I am not about to attack your person," he added laconically, glancing pointedly at the metal poker on the floor before turning his back and walking slowly about the room, taking in its contents with the cool assessment of a professional. "Violence is not really my forte."

"You have other strengths," she said carefully, lips pulled into a tight line as their conversation was stripped bare of the trappings of civility.

"Torture has long been outlawed," he shrugged, a little resentfully. "So of course I am not what you would call an avid student of the continental instruments some use to break and twist the body of a suspect until he, or she, relents and reveals his, or her, truth..."

"And yet you're here for something that will break my uncle. He preaches with Fox. That is his only enthusiasm and it is not a crime."

Thurloe nodded a concession but continued conversationally as his fingers dragged over the desk and its tumbled detritus, sliding papers into and out of his view with no more than a mild interest. "It takes a sharp tongue to speak so bluntly my dear, but you really needn't be so challenging. Just think of me, sent here, simply doing my best to break the silence in such a way that does not involving breaking anything else..."

"It's an unpleasant task. Priests and pigeons make foul houses after all," he waved airily at the room. "To be honest, I didn't even want your uncle arrested, now, but he was named in front of His Highness and my hands were tied. I had rather hoped simply to watch him for a little longer. We have long known, of course, that he has some incredibly interesting connections…"

He paused then, and was watching her closely. "Perhaps it surprises you but Edward Villiers does not rely for recreation solely on reading almanacs and preaching holy-"

"Reckless gossip-"

"He has been organising a series of uprisings,"

"Allegedly. Why are you telling me this?"

"My, my, you really are direct! I have to say it's rather refreshing - at court no one says what they mean. As the Lord Protector grows ever older, anyone would think we all hide behind piglet tails, twisting and turning into good little republicans." His thin lips twisted into a wry smile. "Interesting, is it not, that your uncle was betrayed in the traditional sense? Denounced by a co-conspirator from the dregs of his royalist organisation. Shameful lack of loyalty. Frustratingly however our informant had not actually witnessed Edward Villiers of Exeter, he had just heard mention of his name."

"What of the man who named him?" she asked, practically, as if she didn't know the answer.

"Dead. Or as good as by now." He tilted his head and gave her a sidelong look, waiting.

"Then all you have is hearsay. Even if the court is somehow compelled to convict, it would never apply the maximum sentence on the basis of that alone."

"Hmmm," Thurloe assessed her coolly. "Ordinarily, maybe you would be right. But you underestimate the temperature of the Capital. Cromwell is ailing. The judiciary in London is a conservative beast, reaching to protect the status quo, anxious to crush the seeds of revolution."

He ran his finger along a dusty shelf, tilting his head to read the book spines. "His best chance, of course, were your uncle found guilty of high treason, would be a deal to spare his life. Just in case. He need only give us a few names, a few details, and I could save him from the scaffold…"

"But," she said carefully, "hypothetically speaking, even if he knew the names of others, Eddie would never betray them."

"You're right, of course. I have met with him once already. Edward Villiers is a rare man of conscience, fortified by his particular brand of heresy. He will not give the names of his underlings or his masters, and I strongly suspect his infirmity would render any attempt at those more persuasive methods we discussed entirely wasted.

"His body would likely collapse into heart failure before we extracted any intelligence," he added pragmatically, before turning, as if the thought had only just occurred to him: "Of course, another person might make that deal on his behalf. For instance, and just hypothetically you understand, it could even be you."

"What-"

"Think, Lady Denby. You might be able yet to save your uncle's life. Were messages conveyed by note or by whisper? Who does he command? Is there an extensive network of traitors or a few selected bodies? Does your uncle speak directly to the Stuarts?"

"What would the sentence be commuted to?" she asked quietly.

He thought a moment: "Imprisonment, or deportation to the colonies."

"But you said yourself," she replied, drawing herself up. "He's over seventy and in what can hardly be described as rude health. He would survive neither."

Thurloe shrugged again as if that were irrelevant and frowned, distracting by scratching again at the spot of dry skin. "Neither is infinitely preferably to the alternative, Lady Denby. Have you ever seen a man hanged close to asphyxiation, cut from the gallows and sliced opened by a butcher? It takes considerable skill to keep a man alive against his will to marvel at the spectacle-"

"But still you have no actual evidence of his having issued orders or received them," Tara interrupted, ignoring his attempts to unsettle her.

Thurloe moved slowly around her and goose bumps rose on her neck with a warm breath. "I am not a fool, Lady Denby, I doubt very much I will be able to find anything amid this chaos but I will find some leverage. Every man has his weakness. Even your husband, for example."

"What do you mean?"

"He is one of the greatest parliamentary commanders in the land. I have heard tall tales of his recent exploits in Ireland, all in the restless service of the Protectorate. Fearsome in battle, respected in court... He fights hard enough for Cromwell; but I wonder that he would do near anything to protect his most treasured possessions."

Tara bit her tongue and an interminable pause dragged out until his tone changed: "On another note, one of fascinating coincidence, I understand that what remains of Silus Tollemache's charred body was dragged from a burned-out tithe barn outside the city this morning. One can only speculate as to what convinced him to visit such a desolate place in the middle of the night."

"The countryside is teaming with rustlers, my Lord. They are army-beggared, and-"

"You're right of course, there are many men with an axe to grind."

She spun around to catch Thurloe's cold eyes. He was still smiling politely but the words carried an unmistakable threat. She pursed her lips and replied non-committedly, picking up the letters and the needlework, slipping it into the pockets of the cloak. "I'm hungry and must find some lunch. My husband is awaiting my return."

"But of course, I have detained you long enough. Please send my regards to your husband. I do hope he is well, and that nothing is keeping him up all night. Apart from your good self, of course."

She nodded politely as she reached the door.

"And my Lady? Don't forget your candlestick."

25. MINERVA

Tara stepped out into the street, weighed down by the knotted ball of lead in her stomach and the candlestick in her hand. Almost immediately, she found herself flattened back against the front door to avoid a barrow crashing along the uneven cobbles. Its driver gave a leery, toothless smile and the smells of rancid meat left a wave of nausea bobbing in his wake. She stumbled along a short distance, rounding the corner on to Bartholomew Street where she could slide unobtrusively to the ground, back against a whitewashed wall. *Breathe.*

While her heart calmed, she turned the candlestick over in her hands. Odd's fish, it was ugly. In a hopeless imitation of fussy French styles, poor workmanship left lumpy, clunky ivy leaves coiled like fattened snakes around the stem. But as well as an appreciable lack of aesthetic value, it also suffered by virtue of being a wedding gift from a spurned suitor of her mother, carrying a remembrance of scorned fury that left it unused and, ironically, as pristine as the day it was presented. It was a rather blunt instrument.

Which is not to say it was worthless. There must be at least six precious pounds of silver between her fingers, portable and easy to melt down. Tara felt a sudden pang of gratitude towards the unknown suitor behind the gift. Perhaps it had been his intention to establish in the marital home both a jarring reminder of his existence and the means for Angela to find her way back to him should life with Gregory Villiers prove lacking. Perhaps he would approve of it supporting her daughter.

Six days until the uprising.

The thought of leaving him tumbled through her empty body like a rock, but it didn't matter; she couldn't stay close to Gabriel only to indulge childish fantasy. She let her head fall back against the wall, blinking away the threat of frustrated tears. Tollemache was dead but would Cromwell try again? Thurloe was right, there were other ways to put pressure on Eddie. Other threats, other exacted retributions. She had to… how did Gabriel put it? She had to arrange for a more permanent disappearance.

This, this thing, this so-called marriage… it had to end. He knew it. His family knew it. He wouldn't love her. He couldn't.

Enough. She was sick and tired of being positioned like some blasted ornament on other men's mantels. She had to plan properly for her own future. The candlestick was too unwieldy to keep secret. She had to sell it, now, count the funds to support Eddie and herself. Alone, as master of her own fate. There was almost certainly still a silversmith or pawnbroker on the quay who would take the item, no questions asked, and turn it into liquid coins. Judging from the last ring of the cathedral's bells, it was still some way off noon. There was time.

The docks in the West Quarter teamed with life, tongues wagging freely, a chaffering multitude above the bangs and slams of industry. With the candlestick safely tucked under Eddie's cape, she relaxed a little, dodging the bustle of pigs and people, relaxing into a bliss of anonymity. Amongst all the comings and goings, no one knew her as Gregory Villiers' daughter here three years ago, and no-one knew her now. She wove through bodies almost heady with freedom, scanning the buildings for the familiar three golden balls indicating a pawnbroker's store.

"*Mussels! Lily white mussels!*"

"*New mackerel!*"

The cobbles were still spread thick with netted fish from the morning's haul, but other commerce took place in the narrow alleys leading from the waterfront. She turned down Racke Lane, briefly distracted by the scent of hot food. Not far in, the smell intensified before a kitchen offering meat pasties. A stable-style door was half open, and a small boy sat back against the crumbling wall next to it. Maybe nine or ten, his pallid face was expressionless to the point of seeming drugged, and as he watched her approach, he shook his head slowly. From inside, shrewish female voices hissed rancour. She wasn't welcome here.

Slightly unnerved, Tara stepped back over the open channel of dirty water in the middle of the alley and found herself caught suddenly in a swell of drunken, listing bodies, vain-glorious with boasts and free with their hands. The men thinned as quickly as they had swamped her and she was alone again, breathing heavily. She turned a sharp corner after a tatty barber's pole. The buildings squeezed in tighter together now, a rabbit warren of lodgings no longer capable of classification into distinguishable alleys or passageways.

She peered up in the gloom, unable to see the sky as the jetties of first and second floors lent in overhead with increasing ambition, only to be shoved forcibly against the wall by the back of a large man. She yelped but he didn't notice her, squashed awkwardly behind his bulk, his attention firmly on his own bloodied hands as they came away from his stomach. She could feel the shock shuddering through his torso, then the last rattling gasp of his lungs before he fell to his knees, exposing her to the short, knife-wielding killer.

"God's wounds, Son-of-a-bitch!" hissed his taller, hooded colleague. "Where the bloody hell did she come from? You'll have to kill 'er! Cap'n said no-no witnesses."

"If the cap'n wants her dead, he can do it hisself," replied the short man, pushing back his dirty blonde strands and calmly wiping the stained blade against his breeches.

"I didn't see anything," said Tara hurriedly. "Nothing."

The tall man thought about it. "Fine. We'll take her back. Besides, 'e's not left the stock since we docked; he must be b-backed up from balls to brain. 'e'll know what to do."

None of them moved for a moment while she took several large breaths but then she bolted and the killer launched himself at her, knife still in hand. She squealed as everything went black as he yanked the hood of Eddie's too-large cloak forward over her face and spun her about. "Hush girl. Can you feel my knife? Nothin' doin', you'll need to see Cap'n Blakelock. Struggle though and I will slip this between your shoulder blades and save him the bother."

They jostled her sightlessly between the tight maze of walls, one hand on her shoulder for guidance. Her heart pounded but she counted. Right, twelve steps then left. Ten steps. Left again. She felt the heat of the sun and realised they'd been disgorged from the warren. Did anyone notice? The tip of a blade made a succinct point against her spine. A few more footsteps back on the lumpy cobbles of the dockside and they entered a cool and cavernous transit shed, footsteps echoing on the wooden floor as they crossed the empty space towards a seemingly deserted corner.

"Open it."

Tara peered gently under her hood as the taller man flicked a look back over his shoulder. He hesitated a moment, eyebrow raised at the man behind her, before reaching for the iron ring on a trapdoor in the floor. Then her hood was yanked back entirely and Son-of-a-bitch's knife motioned towards the ancient stair treads.

It was a small, gloomy space. The captain perched awkwardly on a barrel in the one pool of candlelight, pouring over a small, upturned crate spread thick with blank import receipts. He didn't raise his eyes to acknowledge them. Short fuzzy hair covered his scalp and chin in patches, scattered between angry red welts, the brutal effect at odds with the overtly gracious style of his dress. He wore a threadbare red velvet doublet, from which his ruddy neck emerged too thickly set for the stock to be tied properly. Dirty lace cuffs dragged from the edges of his wrists, catching on the rough splinters of his makeshift desktop so that he cursed periodically with irritation.

"Come then, Son-of-a-bitch, tell me, did you adequately express my disappointment to the customs official?"

Tara realised then that only the shorter man had followed her down. The knife-wielder. Son-of-a-bitch. She felt him flinch as he clasped her upper arm, clearly unsure for a brief moment if he had entirely misunderstood the nature of the task he'd been set. "I.. I stuck 'im, Captain Blakelock sir, he's dead."

The captain snorted and licked a stubby finger to count slowly through a pile of parchment sheets. "Very well," he said, murmuring to himself as if this was a surprising but not unwelcome turn of events. "If he will renege on our deal, he must expect the consequences. My port seal is in two halves and I need two customs men to sign and seal each blank receipt... Why the hell else would I drag this bounteous hoard all the way along the canal to Exeter? He would've cost me dear, to say nothing of our friend the controller. Never matter, I'm sure we'll soon find another of his over-worked, under-paid colleagues with whom to share the cut-"

"Cap'n, sir… " interrupted Son-of-a-bitch, hesitantly.

Blakelock sighed and shifted uncomfortably on his barrel to re-count. Something was missing and he frowned, his attention still on the paper. "For Christ's own sake, Son-of-a-bitch, leave me be, I'm sure the controller will raise a toast to your continued good health tonight, provided of course you also handed over the crate of sherry with my compliments?"

"I did, but there's a problem, Cap'n," He gave a shove in the small of her back then, pushing Tara forward to stumble a little before she regained her balance. "This one saw us."

"You bloody groutnoll! Must you make a pig's ear out of every damn-" Blakelock looked up with a red-faced frown and she stared him resolutely in the eye. The cogs turned as he thought for a moment.

"Do you have a name, my dear girl?"

He cocked his head to one side with a sudden air of graciousness that did nothing to dissipate the menace. The man was clearly not born to such airs but he had certainly collected them on his travels and had the wherewithal to rehash them into something approximating breeding when occasion demanded. For his collective of seafaring criminals, the parody was no doubt sufficiently close to the real thing as to be indistinguishable.

"Yes." *Not Villiers or Moore. No connection with Godolphin.* Suddenly aware of the expensive red silk beneath Eddie's cloak, she could see that the opportunity for ransom or blackmail would be too tempting if the Captain decided that Son-of-a-bitch had happened upon a silk purse after all, and she was in no mood to add kidnap to his collection of capital offences. With murder and smuggling already scrabbling for space under his tightly pulled belt, it was likely he had nothing to lose.

"Nosy wench came upon us in…" started Son-of-a-bitch deferentially, but Blakelock waved him dismissively to silence.

"So, you have a name, but you won't tell me what it is. No matter. A rose by any other name still smells as sweet." He looked for a moment as though he would enjoy the game, walking slowly over to remove the cloak, impervious to her hissed objection. He cast his eyes down the curves of Leonie's dress appreciatively, settling on the candlestick still clasped within her fist. "Well, you're undoubtedly a goddess and you come to me bearing a truly unique artefact. We shall call you Minerva."

"Call me what you will but be quick about it," she snapped impatiently, faking the bravado her stomach couldn't muster. "And give me back my cloak. I have business elsewhere."

Unfazed, Blakelock inclined his head towards a man materialising from the shadows, cropped black hair plastered onto his scalp like a helmet. She startled, she hadn't seen him lurking silently in the shadows and quickly surveyed the room for more hidden crewmen. Wasn't that one of Gabriel's rules: know your enemy? What else might he do, she wondered frantically, taking in the weapons hanging casually at each man's side. The captain must have seen her flinch: "Oh, you mustn't mind the reek of him, Minerva. He's no great shifter, admittedly, and once a year his clothing is ready to revolt, but he is an excellent judge of character... Finch, what do you think of our new driggle-draggle, eh?"

Finch moved tall and wiry into the meagre pool of light, his beady eyes glaring at Son-of-a-bitch until he backed off, enabling him to strut a nonchalant circle around her, taking his time to form an assessment, his scrutiny unhampered by the patch slung over one eye. "The dress was fine once, but she doesn't care to keep it. Perhaps she has fine dresses to spare, but perhaps she just thinks she has more important things to think of. She has not seen a looking glass for some time," he paused as the captain smirked and despite herself Tara's hand went to her hair, to pat down unruly curls.

Finch gestured towards the candlestick. "My reckon, sir, is that she stole it," he surmised. "She's a maid from one of them big houses at the top of the High Street. Had enough of domestic servitude and wants to see the world. Took the dress too. A thief. She's on the run from the noose."

Tara felt her pride pique at his unflattering inventory. "How dare you!"

"I like it, Finch! Wants to see the world! Yes, that will do. Thank you."

With that the game was over and Blakelock returned to business with a rattled list of commands: "Drag the men from the Trew's Weir whores. We sail at 2pm or we'll miss the tides; we still need to transfer the cargo to the Albatross at Topsham. First though, both of you, scout about outside a moment and see if anyone looks as though they are missing our Minerva here. If they are, tell them she was last seen heading to the Cathedral to absolve her sins. She's coming with us."

"No. There's no way in Hell I am going anywhere with you." Tara started, turning to follow behind Finch and Son-of-a-bitch, who had obediently mounted the cellar stairs without hesitation.

Blakelock crossed the room quickly and blocked her way. He was shorter than she had first thought, by the sound of it wearing block heels in his boots, but the hulking assessment had been correct. His muscles were clearly bulked from the physical labour of seafaring and his neck flexed as he leaned towards her. "You understand my predicament, Minerva, I'm sure. You're the only witness to a very problematic *event*."

"I won't tell a soul." She took an instinctive step back and shook her head forcefully.

"Of course, you wouldn't *mean* to. But, if you *did* you'd bring the entire corps of customs officers down about my ears, and you'll no doubt have realised by now why I'm not mighty keen on their connecting me to that man's unfortunate demise. My entire operation," he waved an airy hand towards the close walls of the cellar, only she could see now that they weren't walls, they were crates, piled floor to ceiling with imported liquor. Rows upon rows of stacked contraband. "Not to mention the snivelling lives of my men and my own worthless neck, depend on the utmost discretion."

"But I have to go. I said I won't tell," she countered, exasperated and shaking with a rising panic. He made another move towards her and she took another step away until she felt hard crates against her back.

"And *I* said you'll come with us, despite what *you* said and you'll soon learn that on the Albatross *my* word is law, etcetera, etcetera." He smiled and caught the hand she'd raised to push him back, closing thick fingers around her wrist. Her skin rippled as he leant in with a whisper. "Welcome to my watery world, Minerva. And remember it'd pay to be grateful I haven't had Son-of-a-bitch slit your pretty throat. Play nice though, I could always change my mind. Good job you brought me treasure."

The candlestick. When she bought the metal weight suddenly down on his head, the exposed, patchy pate took the full force. He stumbled back with a hissed curse, frowning beneath a stream of blood that flowed freely from the broad gash. Briefly disorientated, he tripped back over his makeshift desktop, scattering the pile of receipts and, in slow motion, his head caught the corner of a poorly stacked crate behind him with a sickening crack. For a time he was still, suspended momentarily in her horror. Then his body thumped heavily back to the ground, scraps of parchment fluttering peacefully around him until the crate he had dislodged wobbled and fell with a resounding crash on his body, glass bottles shattering and the reek of brandy filling the confines of the cellar.

Son-of-a-bitch and Finch can't have got far. She barely had time to register what had happened before they burst back into the cellar at the noise, pistols drawn and brows furrowed as they clattered down the stairs and looked about for their captain. The barrels of their weapons turned quickly towards her, black chasms gaping open like their mouths. They were speaking, shouting even, but she couldn't hear them. She could hear nothing but the pounding of her heart.

Her voice started softly, conversationally, of its own accord, as she motioned in the direction of a pair of boots, protruding from the barrel. "Gentlemen, it would seem there's a vacancy at the head of whatever enterprise you're running here."

The men's eyes widened and she took deep steadying breaths while they took turns to peer quickly behind the fallen crates and register what was left of Blakelock's empty eyes, glazed with the shock of mortality amid shattered glass. Blood was pooling, spreading calmly out across the flagstones. One of the men grunted in questioning surprise but, ever professional, both their pistols remained trained on her head without wavering.

She forced bile back down as a sweetness filled her nostrils. "You'll no doubt be thinking that great responsibility comes with great power, and you'll be feeling the pressure of those ebbing tides.

"Of course, the new captain wouldn't be entirely without assistance. There must be six pounds of pure silver in this, *singular* candlestick." She grimaced theatrically at its ugliness and placed it, still tinged with Blakelock's blood, heavily down on a barrel top before looking slowly from one man to the other: "Although there are currently *two* of you."

Understanding flickered in the men's faces and, slowly, each pistol arched through the air towards the other.

"I'll leave you to work out the finer details."

Carefully, gently, she moved out of their way, stepping quickly up the stone steps and out of the trapdoor, breaking into a run as soon as it slammed down behind her. Seconds later another loud bang echoed through the warehouse, suggesting that the matter had been settled.

* * *

Gabriel was mounting Rowley as she walked steadily through Treguddick's stable yard on her way to the main house, and slid immediately down: "Jesus, Tara, thanks God! I nearly missed you! I was coming to find you – we agreed a time, why did you leave Villiers' house early? The carriage said it was empty. You're deathly pale. What happened?"

"Not now."

She passed him but with long strides he caught her up easily and took her by the elbow, steering her swiftly up the stairs and into a panelled withdrawing room arranged to connect to their bedchamber. The space was well appointed with tapestries, upholstered chairs and a writing desk but she barely registered the decor. The window faced west, and late afternoon sun set the room aflame, its burnt orange light spreading behind her. The maid had only just shuffled out and soon warmth from the low fire in the grate would spread as generously as the fading sunlight. For now, though, she looked down and was surprised to see her hands were still shaking.

"Talk to me," he urged as soon as the door closed behind them. "What happened, Tara?"

She took a deep breath. "You mean besides my uncle being locked in the Tower, my forced marriage to an insufferable bully and then being forced to watch the same intolerable husband nearly burn alive?"

"Yes, besides all those things," he said, treading carefully, the shadow of a lop-sided grin on his damaged cheek as he sought her eyes. He took her hands in his, blowing between his fingers to warm them up. "What happened?"

Tara hesitated, still that flicker of doubt at the edges of her need for him. Last night, blinded by fear and relief, she could have sworn... but it had taken Thurloe to bring her to her senses. *One of the greatest parliamentary commanders in the land.* She pulled back and flexed her fingers into reluctant life. "John Thurloe happened. He came to Eddie's house. He sends his regards."

He made a frustrated grunt as she turned away and moved between two high-backed chairs to stand before the fire. *Blasted fool.* He'd swallowed the tale of Thurloe's delay without question when it came presented unwittingly by his uncle. *Idiot. How was he getting it so wrong?* He couldn't afford to make mistakes like these. He'd compromised evidence of the communications network. He'd walked her straight into Thurloe's net.

He hung his head: "I'm sorry. I should've taken you straight to Villier's house last night. I heard Thurloe was still in London, but it was a lie."

She shrugged, non-committal, staring at the small flames picking up in the grate. "He knows Tollemache is dead and believes you involved. But I don't think he has any evidence... The local militia must've agreed not to mention the dance; he didn't seem to know about it... I suppose if they admitted the gathering, they'd have to give the names of their families and friends."

"The people here will protect their own when they can." More softly then: "Did he touch you?"

"No." She gave a hollow laugh, taking in the state of Leonie's silk dress and realising why he'd asked the question. Even Blakelock's men could see it. And if a dance, a fight, a flight, impromptu first aid and a restless night on the grass had not taken sufficient toll, the walk back through city muck and country mud had been the last straw. She scanned the rips and stains and picked at a loose thread. "He was looking for leverage against Eddie."

Whatever adrenaline or self-preservation that had propelled her legs towards Treguddick was finally depleted. It was as if she couldn't summon the will to move, and she stared at the unravelling silk flower on the stomacher as if it contained all the secrets of the universe.

"Against you too." she added in a whisper, "He thought you'd do anything to protect me."

"Then the man's not a complete fool."

He came up behind her then, pulling her gently back against his chest and bringing his arms around her reassuringly. Surrounded by his visceral heat and solidity she was freshly surprised to realise that it wasn't just her hands, her whole body was shaking. Slowly, he lay a gentle kiss on the top of her head and waited.

"I went through a lifetime's papers and there was nothing to implicate Eddie or to help him," she said, watching the flames and feeling the needlework tucked inside her placket burn. "Thurloe talked about the case. He has nothing besides hearsay from the king's old chaplain Hewitt. It's exactly as it was for my father; the link cannot be made conclusively. Not that Thurlow will let a lack of evidence affect the outcome of the trial… He let me take a few personal items… a silver candlestick, some letters, my old needlework bag…"

She paused, before anticipating his next question. "I left Eddie's house before noon and walked to the dock to sell the silver. I need to pay for his board in the Tower."

There was something in her voice that made him swallow the admonishment that of course he'd give her all the money she needed, and he turned her gently about to face him, so he could tell her Villiers' keep was already, indefinitely, paid for. Her eyes were wide, glazed with the horror of fresh memory, and he frowned with the hammering realisation that the dirty brown splatters across the front of her bodice were not mud. "Tara, who's blood is this?"

She hesitated a moment before the events of the afternoon, the knifing and the smugglers and the cellar, slipped out in clipped, detached tones. When she got to the part about Blakelock's insistence that she join their motley crew he pulled her impulsively against his chest, fingers spreading tight across her back. "The smuggling crews are dangerous men."

"Do you think I don't know that?" she snapped, finding energy in an anger that had her twisting out of his grasp. "Jesus, Gabriel, every bloody man I meet is dangerous. You have no idea what it is to walk abroad and know that every single lobcock I come across is stronger and larger and, as if that wasn't enough advantage, he also has the weight of the law on his side. He might attack or ravish or kill, without even waiting for the darkness of night to cover his crimes. For they're not crimes, not really! Ravish me and I'm wanton and we'll be married; beat me and I was a deserving shrew. Kill me and they'll say *well, she was a witch anyway, since the farrier's old geese came over all peculiar last week so good riddance…*"

He raised a dark eyebrow. "How did you get away? Did anyone follow you?"

"It's possible," she shrugged helplessly, the flare of anger spent, "but I doubt they'll come for me."

"I won't take that chance." Gabriel turned away and crossed the room to open the top draw of the desk, pulling out a pistol and laying it flat on the writing surface. "You're still the only witness to the murder of a customs official. Tom will stay by your side-"

"Where are you going now?" she demanded with more than a hint of exasperation.

"Topsham," he said simply, sliding a mean-looking knife into his right boot. "The Albatross. I have business with the captain."

"Stop being a blasted hero!" Her whisper was barely audible and she sunk down onto a chair. "I've already killed him. Jesus, Gabriel, the captain, Blakelock, I killed him."

The rest of the story gushed out of her without any chance to edit the narrative, but she had barely finished when an uncharacteristically shrill voice screamed her name, cutting through the tension. She jumped and Gabriel stood, his right hand instinctively on his sword.

"Oh, thank the Lord, you're back!" Margaret swept into the room without knocking, her arms full of clean linens from the washhouse. She frowned momentarily, raising an eyebrow at Gabriel until he sheathed his weapon. "I haven't time to ask. The babe's on its way. Leo's fallen into a great travail. Her time's come too soon. Tom's gone out nidgeting for the midwife but we're needing you upstairs, my love. Come along!"

"Of course," Tara replied, pulling herself together as she pulled herself up.

Gabriel paused a moment as she followed Margaret's retreating form. "Tara, you said you brought letters from your uncle's house, what were they about?"

"They're personal," she replied quickly, tensing again at his inquisitiveness. The impassive query was impossible to read. It might have been mere curiosity, but it might have been more. *One of the greatest parliamentary commanders in the land.* Her heart hollowed with the sudden certainty that he too was looking for a way to the rebels. "None of your business."

Gabriel cursed his impatience as he watched her disappear through the door. *Minerva*. Heavenly sponsor of the arts, yes, but not such a docile creature. She was an armed warrior goddess, skilled in strategy and fiercely loyal. Captain Blakelock had underestimated her to his cost. He had, too, when he took her to Whitehall expecting her to beg contritely. And again, when he thought she'd lead him to the rebels without a fight.

He was losing control, making errors of judgement; blindly stumbling about and reacting to threats when he should be managing them. Falling for Thurloe's easy deceit, clearing his path to Tara with the rumour that he was still in London, was just one more mistake in a spiralling descent. He was slashing impotently at shadows as he fell, unable to focus on anything clearly except her face. *Think, you blasted idiot.*

He leant forward onto the desk with a deep breath. *Think like a soldier, follow your damned orders.* Obviously, she was looking for something more than a paper to magically exonerate Edward Villiers, but what? What had the man sent her to retrieve? What had he sent her to destroy, to communicate? How would she pass on his intelligence about the destruction of Charlie's forces and the impossibility of invasion? There were no clues in the items she'd recovered from the house: a few personal letters and some blasted needlework. It made him sick to think about how tenuous his grasp was on her thoughts, her actions. Her safety.

And marrying her in defiance of Cromwell's plans had brought other complications. He pulled the parchment wrapper out of his breeches pocket and unfolded it, re-reading the elaborate black script as if there was a chance that the scrawls might have transposed into something less like cold-blooded vengeance.

Postscript. Whitehall, 1 June 1658

Sir, I would loathe to Trouble you with anything so hard upon your service in Ireland, which I hear you did Effectively, to our great benefit and the Commonwealth's. But I have further Instructions concerning your future Employment. I would call you my Strategic Adviser and bid you repair to our French ally Marshall Turenne to be used at his Discretion.

I do not doubt that your fulsome abilities will be ever improved in the faithful discharging of such trust as shall be imposed on you, for the good of the Commonwealth.

So this appointment is proper for outward Form, in compliance with custom, I will write a common Reference to the Lord Deputy Fleetwood. But be assured I mean a great deal more by it than mere suggestion: I mean it shall be Done, without debate or consideration.

I have not that particular shining bauble for crowds to gaze at or kneel to, but - to be short - I know how to deny Petitions and how to refer: I therefore know that my reference shall be looked upon as an indication of my will and pleasure to have the thing Done.

I desire you do not concern to answer my expectation herein and I rest,
Your assured friend
Oliver P

A sentence of banishment, nothing less. He grunted in frustration and crumped the paper to a ball, throwing in into the fireplace and watching it curl in the flames. The years in Ireland, the blood… they counted for nothing. The only question was how much time he had left.

26. A SEALED KNOT

Margaret ran up the carpeted treads ahead of Tara, and together they followed the sound of low, long moans to enter a large bedroom. It took a short while for her eyes to become accustomed to the gloom, but the wave of heat was immediate. Heavy curtains were drawn across the windows and someone had even pushed a rag into the keyhole. The floorboards were strewn with straw, giving the impression of a humid stable, and swaddling rags were laid out on the bed.

Covered by a loose shift, Leonie was on all fours, rocking before a roaring heath as she issued deep, guttural groans. Tara froze but Margaret fell immediately to the floor beside her, pushing her loose blonde hair back behind her ears, stroking her spine and making gentle cooing sounds. Marie was already settled on a high-backed chair next to them, legs drawn up and needlework spread across her lap. Her large needle passed backwards and forwards through the fabric with minimal assistance, while other faceless female bodies wove through the shadows behind and before her, finding ceaseless industry in lighting candles or patting pillows, spreading fresh straw or folding sheets.

"Look at the state of you!" Marie whispered conspiratorially, indicating for Tara to sit at her feet. "You had a good time in the end, non?"

Before Tara could reply, a new woman entered the room, brandishing a covered basket and a busy air of authority. "Evening ladies, I'm Joan, the midwife."

She rolled up her sleeves, nodding enthusiastically at the proffered introductions and Margaret's brief summary of the labour pains. No mention of the events last night, Tara glanced at Marie's impassive features. No one was ready to tell the whole truth just yet.

"So, babe's eager to make an appearance!" Joan eyed Leonie impassively, before turning to calmly extract a crotchet hook from her bag, impervious to the pained cries and pants. One of the maids set to ripping a sheet into strips and dunking them in cold water for Margaret to hold against Leo's forehead. "Well good news is you gossips have a while yet to natter."

"Gossips?" Tara asked, distracted by the brutal looking hook.

"God's siblings... Have ye never been in a birthing room before?" Tara shook her head, ashamed suddenly, and Joan paused briefly to look bemused before pulling out the rest of her needlework project and putting it neatly to one side. Then she knelt down before Leonie and ran a practised hand over her distended belly, eliciting a long low groan. "Don't fret love..." She raised her eyes back to Tara: "We will support the lass and pray for the good Lord's mercy. It's a long and thorny path but there is felicity indeed in these torments. Nothing could be more natural."

"What can I do?" Tara asked quietly.

"Well, you can start by ladling out the caudle; I imagine we are all thirsty in this heat. And one more important thing," Joan said, grinning suddenly, "Relax."

Tara found the warmed, spiced wine and watched distractedly as Joan and Margaret hoisted Leonie onto the birthing stool, to sit upright before the fire. It was a simple-looking contraption, with a hole rather than a seat, and it brought home the practical inevitability of the birth. She handed the cups around, downing one herself without tasting it and sinking back down by Marie's feet, resting her head back on the hard arm of the chair.

Hours passed, and lost in an exhausted fug, Tara lost all markers on time. The sky outside the curtained window turned from orange to deep blue to dark black. Without cue, someone sang a low, soothing melody, but it was at odds with the violence of the contractions racking Leonie' body and served only to lull Tara's eyes closed for a second until they sprung open again with the next scream.

"The pains are getting longer, Leo," nodded Joan, encouragingly, one eye on her pocket watch, the other on rebalancing the crochet on her lap.

"'Tis a good thing, my darling, the longer they get, the closer you are to coming."

"It is possible that Tom told her something similar, non?" whispered Marie laconically, nudging Tara suggestively with her toe and nearly setting her off balance. She shrugged as Tara shot her a look. "Pah - it is true! These men will never understand that we value speed above all things."

In the dreamlike darkness of the room, it struck her that the birthing stool might as well be an island, a tiny sandbank on which Leonie alone was marooned. Even if they wished it, and they surely did, the gossips could no sooner control the waves of pain as command a rising tide back to the ocean. When the contractions took hold, Leonie clung to her mother-in-law's hand but Margaret didn't notice the half-moons on her skin where fingernails were digging in; she took exaggerated breaths, in and out, trying to keep the girl focused on the rise and fall of her own chest to the exclusion of all else. But then every time her wide-eyed screams became too unbearable to hear any longer, the pain seemed to momentarily ease and Leonie remembered the women around her.

"I must be delivered soon," Leonie pleaded with a grim smile, eyes closed and sweat plastering her hair to her forehead. She gripped Margaret's hand. "I'm so tired, I must sleep. I cannot do this any longer."

Joan thought a moment, then wiped away the anxiety on her brow to crouch in front of her patient and placed both hands on her large belly, pulling downwards with surprising strength until Leonie screamed and clawed at her arms. The midwife murmured apologies, catching Margaret's eye. Something unspoken passed between the women and she reached for her large basket. She rummaged briefly and Tara released her held breath when she pulled out an innocuous package, wrapped brown in paper. The relief was short-lived however, evaporating when Joan explained to Leonie with forced enthusiasm that ergot of rye might help make the pains more productive and speed the birth.

"Do you understand, my darling? We need to help your baby along..."

Her tiredness was burnt clean by fear as Tara saw Margaret's eyes fill with tears that she hid behind her daughter-in-law, wiping the back of her hand across her face as soon as the opportunity presented. In the brief gap after the next punishing contraction, Margaret kissed Leonie's forehead and slipped the purple herb into her mouth, washing it down with caudle and whispering of her pride and of the future.

The atmosphere changed as the women waited, paused like statues, sweat running rivulets down. Margaret's soft promises were the only sound. The child would live, with strength and love to enjoy. They would all live to enjoy together. Leo was to be a wonderful mother. But even Marie's grin had faded, her face blanched white in the gloom. She caught Tara's confused eye and gave a hurried sotto voce explanation with the whisper of a prayer. "I have seen girls use this poison to purge the womb. The dose must be exact or... mon Dieu."

"Mother Margaret," Leonie panted urgently. "I'm to die, I know it. Tell Tom I am sorry. I love him so much. I have written to our child. Tell him! Keep my words and..."

"Hush!" beseeched her mother-in-law, hiding the deep concern in her eyes with practical efficiency and mopping Leonie's brow again with a fresh strip of linen. "You mustn't talk such nonsense my darling, or what will the babe think when the first words it hears sound like a goodbye from the most important person in the world?"

"Tell him!" Leonie screamed. "Tell him about the letter!"

Another wave engulfed the girl and Tara gripped the leg of Marie's chair, watching in horror as the next contraction worked its brutal, urgent way through Leonie's exhausted body. Her shift had long since been tugged open as the girl sought relief from heat and her full breasts swung heavily against her belly. It was elemental, this fight between life and death, and the ripple passed violently downwards over her abdomen, forcing Leonie to brace herself hard.

Tara found her knees and slid across the floor impulsively, taking Leonie's hand in hers and bearing a bone-crunching squeeze. "Your voice will be heard," she promised, her voice cracking and no more than a whisper but the vow was loud enough. "Every day. Your baby will hear you every day. I promise."

Leonie closed her eyes and nodded, panting, as she waited for the next battering. It felt like an eternity but no more than half an hour more could have passed before the midwife felt with her fingertips along the ridge of Leonie's swollen belly and the softer valley of her perineum, under the patchy cover of her shift. She turned to Margaret, relief etched on her face: "It's working! The rye is working!"

As if on cue the girl let out an unholy scream and Joan grabbed her hand: "The babe's coming Leo! Finally, it's really coming! You've nearly done it my girl, one more push!"

"I'm breaking… in half..," she cried, groaning long and deep as the dark head crowned, impossibly large. Seconds later the glistening body of a baby boy slipped into the midwife's waiting hands. Well-practised, she caught the bloody bundle with lifted it smoothly to Leonie's chest before plucking a clean linen to wipe gently at its nose and gaping mouth. She was rewarded with a high cry of surprise and the women in the room exhaled tears of relief, clasping each other in celebration while Joan kneaded Leo's belly to express the placenta.

"What will you call him, darling?" Margaret asked once she was settled on the bed, clutching the precious bundle to her chest with exhausted wonderment.

Leonie's attention came momentarily back to the room. "I agreed with Tom that if it was a boy, we'd call him Henry."

"Oh, Leo!" Margaret clasped her hands together and fresh tears fell freely as she gazed at the lusty new face, screwed up in astonishment and preparing to howl his indignation at being born. "Hen'll be mighty proud of that. You've done so well, my darling, all this long night."

"This good morning," corrected Joan, sweeping the curtain aside to show the faint glow of dawn on the horizon. A new day, and a new life.

* * *

Tara hesitated, her hand on the latch to the withdrawing room, renewed waves of exhaustion lapping at her limbs. Did it really matter where he was? She could barely think straight. *I cannot give you my heart, Tara.* She had the answer before she'd asked the question. Once her work was finished, she could submit to the oblivion of the large, rope-strung mattress. She pushed open the door and startled to see Gabriel sitting by the fireplace, deep in consideration of a square of thick card in his hand.

"You're not asleep," she said needlessly.

"I couldn't sleep," he said, rising without hesitation to pull her into his arms. The solid wall of his warmth melted the stiffness in her limbs and, despite every intention, she thawed as she leaned boneless against him. *You mean something to him,* whispered the dizzying demons of fatigue and caudel. *But what? What was he really here for?* He kissed the top of her head. "I sat with Tom. The babe, and Leo?"

She nodded and felt some of the tension leave his chest. "A boy."

She could sense rather than see the smile forming above her head as she leant further into his embrace, unable to resist as he took her weight. "You women were making an infernal racket."

Tara snorted into the clean smelling cotton of his shirt: "I can only begin to imagine what sounds you might make if you had to do that."

He laughed and held her a little tighter for a while, raising a hand to stroke her cheek gently. "You're exhausted. Have you even eaten? There's bread and cheese on the table. Come to bed; I'll bring it with us."

"No." Tara shook her head, casting her eyes about for the food. She was starving, she realised, she hadn't eaten all day. There hadn't been time. "I'm wound too tightly to sleep."

"I'll sit with you," he offered.

"No, please. I need to clear my mind. The birthing... it was... brutal. Perhaps a little needlework..."

"*Seriously?*" He frowned but nodded, stifling a yawn. "Well first see what Ann has forwarded; Rupert picked it up as the stage passed yesterday afternoon." He glanced down at the invitation he'd been twirling between his fingers and Tara retrieved it from the side table. Black ink swirled in shaky, flamboyant fashion: "*Earl and Lady Denby are cordially invited to the wedding of Mary Cromwell and Thomas Belasyse, the Viscount Fauconberg at Hampton Court Palace on 14 June 1658.*"

"A party invitation?" She snorted: "We're summoned to show contrite faces at Cromwell's court in less than a week?"

"I do rather suspect our invitations were an afterthought. Perhaps he wants to draw a line under-"

"Ha! The bastard can-"

"*Careful...*" He warned, before shrugging a sudden smile: "Though I can't see how we can turn him down unless fortune smiles and we're killed in some tragic accident on the way back to London."

"If fate can't manage it, I'm sure Cromwell will happily lend a hand..." she tailed off, biting back the sudden fear. *How closely had Thurloe watched Eddie? Had they broken the code after all?* No, surely not. She took a deep breath. Of course, Gabriel was invited and she... she was, for now at least, his wife. "If we must go, you could be a bit more positive about it."

"I'm positive it will be interminable," he yawned finally, a hint of a grin playing again around the corner of his lips. "But Cromwell is a consummate professional. He won't mar a fine occasion with pique at your marrying the wrong man. And, of course, he has access to some very fine wines."

He turned then to pick up the glass of whisky he had been nursing, downing it. "On the other hand, the court is like a duck pond, frothing with scum and heaving with toadies, all croaking their congratulations for his illustrious dynasty, watching their backs with one eye on his son, Richard. Only now, through his daughter, His Highness has made a match with Belasyse, and the Viscount Fauconberg is Yorkshire's finest parliamentarian. What better way to grandstand your power and permanence than by marrying into one of the most prominent old families in England?"

Better than marrying the troublesome offspring of a disgraced traitor, no doubt. She paused a moment, phrasing the question carefully: "Will it not please you to be part of court life again?"

He laughed at that, shaking his head. "Court is far more dangerous than battle. The only thing that pleases me is the prospect of warm oblivion, ideally with my wife in my arms. Don't be long," he smiled another yawn, planting another kiss on the top of her head as she picked up a lump of cheese.

Tara waited, watching him disappear through the double doors to their chamber before retrieving her old needlework bag. She dragged her attention back to Eddie's men. When she'd finished, a steady series of geometric shapes would form a border around the bible verse. The squares and rectangles would be neat, but scattered with errors: crossed stitches with the top bars running at the wrong angle, underlapping where they should do overlapping, or even missing entirely. Only a trained eye would find them, count them and read the words emerging from the pattern.

And once it was done, it was only an hours' walk back to The White Horse Inn at Mortenhampstead. She smiled wryly at having found the tell-tale receipt in his house. Eddie had been passionate but entirely uninventive in the three years she'd been away. The code, the inn… nothing had changed.

Everyone at Treguddick would be sleeping late today. She could, surely, slip out early and make her way to the crossroads without notice. She would leave the message to be displayed by the publican and read by the network; told to Todd Pengelly, Robert Farrier and Mad Mike Evelyn. It bore her family's mark and it would carry enough authority to warn and direct the rebels, to stop them fighting and dying.

There was limited space on the fabric. She quickly calculated the minimum letters needed and began to work rhythmically along the row. "*Coalition fleet destroyed. No uprising.*" The wool was decrepit; it snapped more than once. She cursed and rubbed her face, holding the needle to the window to draw the dark blue line back through its eye against the spreading dawn, trying hard to recapture some of the peace she used to feel at work.

As an afterthought, unable to resist, she added: "*Love to Lucy.*" Mad Mike would appreciate that.

Five days.

Enough time for the message to get out. A random man from each unit always used to convene in the tavern every third night to receive direction from her father and, later, from Eddie. Chances are they would be keeping an even tighter vigil now, waiting for news, for someone else to take control. Waiting for her, not that they knew it yet.

Her eyes moved to the small legend beneath the bible verse and the seemingly innocuous initials "*RV*" - a momento mori of her family's sacrifice for the King. With a few small stitches, she added the date: "*5 VI*".

She leaned back in the chair a second then rose to scoop a handful of cold water from the pitcher on the sideboard over her face and neck. Then she ran her eyes over the fabric, double checking the mistakes, counting and recounting until her freshened gaze lost its focus. Finally, content, she picked up the needle and thread a last time and pulled it through the fabric after the initials.

THE SEALED KNOT

It was done, and at the end, a tight knot sealed the message.

27. THE PROTECTOR WAS INEXORABLE

Report of proceedings of the High Court of Justice on Monday 5th June 1658

A formidable Sanhedrim of above a Hundred-and-thirty heads, consisting all the judges and chief Law Officials (and others necessary names according to the Act of Parliament), sat in Westminster Hall, at Nine in the morning, for the Trial of John Hewitt Doctor of Divinity, Sir Henry Slingsby, and three others whom we may forget. The court sat day after day till all were judged.

Poor Sir Henry, on the first day, was condemned to die. He pleaded what he could, a very constant Royalist all along; but evidence of Sealed Knot business in Hull was too palpable.

Reverend Dr Hewitt, once chaplain to the late King Charles, refused to plead at all, refused even to take off his hat until an officer of the court came to do it for him. He conducted himself unwisely and likewise received the sentence of death.

The others narrowly escaped, by good luck or the Protector's mercy, and suffered nothing.

As to Slingsby and Hewitt, the Protector was inexorable, stating: "Hewitt has taken a very high line; let him persevere in it!"

It is well known that Slingsby is uncle by marriage to Lord Fauconberg, who shall soon wed His Highness' daughter Mary, but that fact could not help him.

The Protector said: "Royalist Plots, the deliveries of garrisons to Charles Stuart, and the reckless usherings of us into blood shall end!"

Hewitt and Slingsby suffered on Tower Hill on Monday 5th June; amid the manifold rumour and emotion of men.

28 CARNAGE

Tara woke with a start from the violence of her dream and the sickly-sweet smell of blood in her nostrils. She was alone and a dull ache throbbed in her temples. She reached up to dig her fingertips into her scalp, seeking relief. Blakelock had died a dozen deaths since she had lain down awkwardly on the bed next to Gabriel and succumbed to a restless sleep within his unconscious embrace. Each death was more gruesome than the last, and each by her own hand; she'd brandished hard-edged weapons with a curious vacillation between chilly indifference and heart pounding terror. But still he kept rising for her to strike down.

Just a dream. She turned her head to the leaded panes, trying to convince her body what her mind had already grasped. The scene outside was bucolic, Godolphin's flower-filled garden bathed in the bright light of morning. Leonie was already up, sitting on rugs in the sunshine nursing her baby son. She couldn't see her face but Tom sat close by, laughing as he leant over tenderly to touch her cheek, or adjust the linen at her shoulder. Tara lay back against the pillow, feeling too much like she was intruding on the intimate newness of their family, threatening their safety with her violence. It wasn't entirely a dream.

Dead. Blakelock, Tollemache... Just like before, blood trailed behind her like the tail of a comet. Mama, Papa, Ralph, now Eddie. Whatever came of this hopeless marriage and her attempts to communicate with the Sealed Knot, more blood would certainly flow. It would stick to her hands. She could *smell* it.

She rolled reluctantly to rise and let out a groan of practical irritation that temporarily banished the ghosts. Her courses were starting, typically haphazard and predictably inconvenient. As if on cue, her belly twisted painfully and she reached for a linen hand towel on the bedside stool, feeling down under the cover to stem the flow. This was the last thing she needed when contemplating a long journey back to London by horseback-

"Oh, you're awake, my love?" Margaret poked her head cheerfully around the door, impervious to the normal restraints of privacy. "You look peaky! Are you well?"

"I'm fine, a headache that's all," she mumbled with the nearest thing to a relaxed smile as she could muster, tugging the blankets up for cover. "My courses…" she added, with an unreasonable flinch of shame.

"Say no more, duck, I'll have one of the girls bring you something to deal with both," said Margaret companionably, taking the confession as an invitation to come into the room and plant herself without ceremony at the foot of the bed. "I don't know what you're used to, but the women here use sheepskin strips. Very effective, with a belt, and comfy to boot. We've plenty to spare."

She patted Tara's foot through the sheets, stretching out her own short legs into the air a moment, flexing her toes in her slippers, clearly mulling over the right words for whatever she'd actually come to say.

Tara smiled; she'd never lived amongst people with such a compulsion for sharing. A sudden rush of affection washed over her. "Thank you," she said, meaning it.

"I'm thinking you'll consider the curse something of a blessing after last night," Margaret's eyes crinkled and she nudged Tara's foot as it tensed. She hadn't even considered the possibility that the night with Gabriel might result in the same labour, let alone a new life. Fool. It was one thing to be married to the man, another to carry his child, risk her life to be bound to him forever… She was nothing to him; he'd told her as much, but she couldn't imagine him giving up a child so easily.

"I'm not in any hurry to do that," she murmured, with half a rueful laugh.

"Gabe will be a wonderful father…" Margaret started carefully. "I wish he'd known my poor sister, God rest her soul, so he could have faith there's goodness in him. When Hannah married, we all of us wept but she kept saying: 'It's true love!' At first at least, I suppose it was."

Tara frowned. The tale felt too intimate for an outsider. "Margaret, I-"

"Lucius Moore was a vicious bully. He harried my poor sister til the day she died. Gabe carries the scars of that man's drinking on his heart as well as his skin, but the apple has fallen a long way from that twisted tree. He is not so hard as he thinks he needs to be."

"The scars on his back... his own father?" They lapsed into silence. She'd assumed that the blistering lines were born in Charlie's poor penmanship or irregular Latin grammar... but Lucius Moore? Careful, measured Lucius, laying careful, measured stripes across his only son's back? Hearing, willing, him cry. She gathered up her knees under the blankets.

"Hannah was not so lucky as Leo on the birthing bed and Lucius blamed his boy from the start. Said he murdered his mother on his passage into the world, as if original sin were not enough of a burden... It might have started with grief, but it ended with old-fashioned spite." She tailed off until, finally, she could bring herself to finish: "I just wanted to tell you, I've watched the both of you, and it would break my heart if..."

"Margaret, please," Tara interrupted softly, compelled to her own truth. "This isn't a marriage of love; I think you know that."

"I've gathered there's little by way of convenience in it."

"I think..."

"No, wait, lovely. For years now, there's been not a house in the land not riven by bitterness. First the politics, then the blood. The revenge... There's not a man alive who knows the secret to come to terms with what's passed, or how to build a world when its forgotten. Still, I've seen it with my own eyes; you are stronger together."

"Then we'd need to fight for the same thing." Tara murmured, biting her tongue against a political diatribe, but Margaret ignored her.

"He's fiercely loyal, Tara. I have to tell you, you have, he..."

"He what, ladies?" Gabriel's shoulders filled the doorway and he glanced between the women. In his presence, Tara felt her chest relax a little and she smiled at his uncharacteristic self-consciousness. "On second thoughts,

I think I'd rather not know."

"Good Lord, Gabe," exclaimed Margaret after a heartbeat. "Look at the size of you and you're a cat on the floorboards!"

He smiled and bent to plant an affectionate kiss on his aunt's head. "The babe's beautiful, Aunt. Has Rupert stirred?"

"No, my angel," chuckled Margaret. "Your cousin's like the marigold. His wit opens slowly with the sun. I wouldn't expect to see him until well past ten."

Gabriel rolled his eyes, bright from the morning air that tinted his cheeks. He looked younger. "Uncle Henry is gone back to Mortenhampstead to help with the tidy up. With Tom and Rupert indisposed I would see what assistance I can be. Tara, do you mind if we stay another day? There's time before the wedding, just."

"No... but... I mean of course I don't mind. But I want to come with you, to Mortenhampstead. You'll wait for me to get ready?"

"You look pale," he started with a frown but tailed off when he caught her raised eyebrow. "Fine, I'll have the stable boy saddle Leo's mare-"

"Whyever don't you both walk, Gabe?" Margaret interrupted, standing and patting his arm gently to stop him from leaving a moment. "It's a beautiful morning. Enjoy the air. The bacon's reasty but cook can wrap some rolls and cheese for your breakfast. If Tara feels poorly when you arrive, Hen can introduce you both to his doctor."

"Tara?" He waited for her nod, eyes ringed with concern, before disappearing in defeat.

"Thank you, Margaret."

"Nonsense. If it's as troublesome as I remember, the last thing you'll be wanting this morning is a pony ride and besides, the walk will ease your cramps," She gave a broad grin before following her nephew out. "Mind Dr Milgate though, Hen is mighty impressed by the young quack but he has no understanding of our trials. He'll pronounce an excess of black bile and slap a leech on your belly as soon as look at you."

* * *

"I could throttle him," said Gabriel with a sideways grin at her frown. Margaret was right; it was a beautiful morning and, after some precious sleep, he felt a blessed lightness for the first time he could remember as they traced their route, through the fields and along the brook to Mortenhampstead. The songbirds were the only noise above the sweetness of her sudden laughter.

"Because he's married une prostituée? I hadn't thought you so averse to *experience*."

"You would call me wanton, wench?" Gabriel grabbed suddenly for her waist, swinging her proud over the edge of the bank until she squealed with more laughter, scattering an indignant family of coots from the surface of the water below.

"I would call you scoundrel, gargell-face! Make-bate!" she screamed until he pulled her back, revelling in the feel of her hammering heartbeat relaxing against his chest.

"And incorrigible," she added quietly.

He raised an amused eyebrow and bent impulsively to kiss her upturned face. It was the first kiss since the fire, when he had lain with her, and he stretched it out self-indulgently, remembering as he explored the softness of her mouth the exquisite sounds it could make. The whimpers and cries that were his undoing.

"You don't really mind though, about Rupert?" she started again with typical candour when he reluctantly released his grasp, and they began to walk again.

"I'm not exactly thrilled about it," he conceded. "But he's too much the romantic to concern himself with practicality. In his mind he is simply Abelard, liberating Heloise."

"Well let's hope for a happier ending," she laughed. "Wasn't Abelard's cockstand lopped off when Heloise's father caught wind of their elopement?"

"That's what worries me," he grimaced. "Only it's not her father he has to worry about, it's her *soutener*, her pimp. Marie isn't just any whore, the bawdy house she belonged to is owned by the self-styled Marquis de

Clapiers and he is not a man to relinquish his property with a Gallic shrug. He's a violent bastard and, since he has all their dirty little secrets in his pocket, he enjoys the protection of every great man in Paris."

She raised an eyebrow and glanced across at him: "How do you know that?"

"The real question is how Rupert did not know," he said, rolling his eyes. "God knows I love him but he's a blasted dalcop. He's leading Clapiers straight to Treguddick, straight to Tom and Leo and the babe. Henry and Margaret are comfortable, but they haven't the resources to pay him off. Clapiers operates in a different league."

"Bring them back to Surrey then," said Tara simply. "To Ham House."

"And lead him to you?"

"What's one more murderous brute in pursuit? Attract the Marquis' attention and when he comes, settle the debt."

He frowned. It sounded straightforward but she'd enough experience of politics and men to know leading Clapiers into their life now was a very real risk. He took her hand without saying anything and watched as their long shadows kept step alongside them; two black figures fused, bending and curling around stones and branches and tussocks as one. On uneven grass, she didn't lean on him physically, although he would gladly have taken her weight, but still he could feel it; she took a quiet strength from him. A strength to do what she must. He knew it because he took the same from her. He swallowed dryly and something seemed to dislocate in his chest with a real physical pain.

This dream would end with Edward Villiers' trial. Somewhere, somehow, in the last week he'd forgotten but this desire, this *need*... it was a weakness; he was a bastard for letting her see it. But he was a damn fool for failing to realise that he couldn't harbour her body from the storm without throwing his own soul to the sharks.

* * *

The villagers were out in force when they reached Mortenhampstead, criss-crossing the main road with purpose, and Gabriel was swiftly requisitioned by a gang of bulky farm hands to heft aside the beams of the burnt barn, clearing the site.

"Tara!" Henry waved excitedly as she watched him go. "Gabe's heading to the barn already? Good, good - no sense in waiting to rebuild while the weather is fine; harvest is due in a matter of weeks and will demand shelter. But how good of you to come! Are you looking for a job? I wonder if you could please help my good friend, the doctor? He is too busy today-"

"Of course," she smiled, and with the embroidered message burning inside her placket, she followed him towards a makeshift tent at the crossroads, which boasted a hand-painted "Astrologer and Physician" sign

Young and enthusiastic, Doctor Jago Milgate was earnestly engaged in a variety of visible, fee-earning actions. A long queue of patients snaked around the tent, nodding appreciatively as he rubbed in salves of bee's wax and butter, applied cantharide plasters to raise blisters for popping, "*to rebalance bilious humours*" he whispered enigmatically to Tara, or inserted clyster emetics behind a canvas modesty sheet. His bag contained a limited number of remedies, she soon realised, but he selected from amongst them with a considered air of gravitas, depending on whether his customer ailed with minor burns, smoke damage, costive bowels or outbursts of hysteria. Amid the industry, Tara smiled politely and counted the coin, biding her time.

"Might I buy you a drink for your trouble?" Jago asked at length, with a nod towards the White Horse Inn. He ran stained fingers back through dark blonde hair and replaced his hat. He then re-plugged a large jar of foul-smelling ointment and slipped it safely into his medical bag, patting the leather with the self-satisfaction of a job done well.

"You may even pick my brains at no cost if you will; I have a large number of recipes for beauty lotions in here." He tapped his temple smugly before panicking: "Not that I meant to imply you need any assistance! Your beauty is ample. I mean…"

"A drink?" She's have preferred to venture to the inn alone; Jago's patronising manner was hard to stomach while her belly throbbed with renewed vigour.

She looked towards the inn and a slight breeze ruffled the banner on its ale-stake. it displayed a crudely painted songbird and with a flash of understanding and a loud snort of relief she saw this was the right place. *Sing to the sparrow*. This was the place Eddie was trying to lead her to. Suddenly unable to control herself, giggles spilled out. She'd been wrong-footed by his clue because she'd always thought the White Horse's painted sparrow sign to be a decidedly less fanciful pigeon. Jago's pained expression only made matters worse and she clutched her sides, recovering slowly, taking his hand to lead him playfully to the alehouse: "I'm sorry, honestly, I'm light-headed with the success of the afternoon. I meant yes, that would be lovely."

She selected a booth at the dingy back of the bar room and the doctor's spirits revived with the promise of a little privacy. Jago was an interminable bore but after two jugs of ale he slipped out for a comfort trip to the house of office, if there was one. Without hesitation then, she lifted down the frame from the wall next to her and laid it on her lap. With trembling fingers, she prised open the back and tugged aside the existing embroidery, sliding in the replacement message from her pocket and hanging it back onto the hook.

The near identical verse of Romans now between her fingers was dated 10 May, surely Eddie's last instruction, before his arrest. She scanned the border for its mistakes: "*Rise 10 June. Ready port for King.*" It was tempting to unthread the border as she would habitually have done. leaving the template ready for reuse. But she slipped out of the booth and dropped it onto the fire, watching to make sure the flames ran along warp and weft.

"Miss!" A hiss from behind the bar made her jump, but the ruddy publican paid no mind to the burning needlework as he beckoned her over with a furtive glance around the near empty bar room. He frowned, uncertain if he recognised her face. "The old man sent you?"

Tara nodded, the pounding in her heart increasing as she accepted a small fold of paper between her fingers, slipping it into the top of her bodice without looking. "They left a message for him two weeks back. Said it's important. They've been betrayed. It has to get to another fella with a funny name. God's blood, I can't remember it. Lord of Misrule something, I think. No, wait, it was *carnage*, Lord Carnage-. What can I get for you, sir, another glass?"

"You look guilty," said Jago, placing an overly familiar hand on her upper arm as they eventually emerged from the gloomy tavern into the early evening sunshine. Jago had approached his third ale with as much enthusiasm as if it were one of his own foul concoctions and time had dragged. "I hope not on my account. I didn't mean to lead you astray, my Lady."

She gave him a sharp look of impatience as Gabriel approached, glowering at the pair of them. "When Henry said you were helping the doctor, Tara, this is not quite what I imagined."

"A lady deserves the company of a gentleman, sir," Jago sniffed and stepped awkwardly in front of her, straightening his doublet with as much dignity as he could muster. He took in his rival's tumbling hair and crumpled, sweaty shirt, his filthy breeches and the angry red line on his face, evidence of very recent violence. "She arrived with Sir Henry Godolphin and I cannot allow that she is demoralised by you, lord of carnage, or whatever you would call yourself. You'll address the lady through me; she is tired and not in the mood for nonsense."

Tara stiffened. Jago had heard the tail end of the meandering instruction after all. She cursed the innkeeper. She cursed the damnable ache in her belly and the pounding that had returned to her head. She cursed the fact that Eddie had never revealed the true identity of the man at the head of the Sealed Knot; the fight with Tollemache that had left her pass to the Tower revoked so she had no hope of asking. She cursed the pretentious doctor and her surprisingly possessive husband, both sharing an unnecessary talent for turning up at precisely the wrong moment. She glared as Gabriel pointedly ignored Jago, holding out his hand.

"Come. We'll walk back."

An inspired rush of professional instinct made Jago step further forward. "That really is a nasty wound… Come back tomorrow and I'll gladly prescribe some sympathetical powder. It's marvellous stuff, very modern; apply it directly to the offending weapon and 'tis guaranteed to cure all green wounds that come within compass of a remedy. It is made with moss from the skull of an unburied man. I'm pleased to say I have secured a private supply… for there is a *great* quantity of it in Ireland-"

Without warning, Gabriel stepped forward and swung a punch directly onto the man's nose. Jago doubled forward, falling to his knees, spluttering as red blood began pouring from his nostrils.

"What the Hell, Gabriel?" she screamed, and his jaw tightened as he controlled his breathing, shaking out his damaged fingers.

"Tara, come with me. Now."

"*No*," she snapped back, heart pounding as it recovered from the shock of his sudden violence. She spun on her heels to leave both men slack-jawed and empty-handed, striding across the village square to Henry for a carriage ride back to Treguddick.

But she smiled. It was done. She'd done what she came to do.

29. THE DAWNING OF THE DAY

Gabriel squeezed his heels in Rowley's side with a grunt of frustration and lurched forward a few hundred yards until he was forced to rein up again and wait for the others to catch up. The horse snorted weary disdain. Nearly three days on the road, he thought ruefully, and he was still chivvying like a demented sheep dog. He looked back at them ambling slowly towards him, three abreast, and wished for a moment that he could simply rope their beasts together and physically drag them along the main roads to Surrey.

Not that they were at all concerned by the possibility. Marie was leaning forward in the saddle to make herself heard around Rupert's bulk. The lightness in her voice, the slightness of her frame and the stubborn, bouncing curls in her hair made her seem young, but not quite as young as he thought she wanted to be. At times, caught off guard, her eyes seemed full of weariness. Tara understood, she'd described Marie's past as a loose thread she'd snip out whole if she could, stitching the story seamlessly together again with the same efficiently as Tara approached her tapestry. Gabriel looked away a moment, sightlessly scanning the road ahead. He knew how hard it was to leave some things behind.

Whatever the Frenchwoman's observation had been, Tara laughed aloud and he turned back to hear Rupert's wordless exclamation in return. The riders had reached a fork in the road, and, without any warning, his cousin reined abruptly away, breaking into a gallop. Marie gave a cry of excitement and spurred her own mount after him. *All well and good*, he thought with a frustrated grunt, *if only they weren't riding pell–mell in the wrong bloody direction*. He shifted his weight and cantered back towards Tara, voice raised in exasperation.

"What the Hell? I see they can move fast enough when they want to – what now?"

"Do you not see where we are?" Tara raised an eyebrow with evident amusement and realisation dawned even as he started to shake his head. Stonehenge. The undulation in the landscape was unmistakable. The stone circle was still obscured by trees but it was there, just north of the main road, and they had only to veer off and head through the woods a little way to find it. "Rupert has an interesting theory on the stones and we decided to make camp here tonight to hear it. Mr and Mrs Godolphin have just taken a short detour to Salisbury for supplies."

Gabriel grinned, despite himself. He'd mentioned a fascination with the ancient circle over dinner in Treguddick and it was surely close to solstice now, when they were reported to align the sun, channelling the fates. Latest learned thought suggested it was a Roman temple, dedicated to the sky-god Caelus, but Rupert's theories were always amusing even if they were reliably wide of the mark. It would be a welcome distraction.

Tara had already reined off the road and he started hesitantly as their horses fell into step alongside each other through the trees: "Tara, the past few days, you've seemed a little, I suppose distracted. If there is anything I could do?"

Tara frowned momentarily but said nothing, her head to one side, waiting as the trees thinned for a glimpse of the stones. "What do you mean?"

Awkwardly, Gabriel started again. "I don't know… it may be nothing more than your courses…"

He had the good sense to look uncomfortable at the direction his line of questioning had inadvertently taken but Tara stared at him, open mouthed, her mind for once as clear and empty as Caelus' realm above them. "Did you seriously just say that out loud? For Christ's sake, I-"

"Donn?" Gabriel exclaimed, cutting her off abruptly: "Something must have happened. Ho! Well met, man!"

He squeezed Rowley to pick up the pace towards the red-headed figure leaning back against the heel stone, positioned just outside the main circular structure. Donn must have heard him. His fingers worried the brim of his hat, scrunched against his belly, but his form remained inert while Gabriel slid from his saddle to approach on foot. Something didn't look right; Donn held himself too poised, tense.

"I'll feckin' kill ye, ye worthless prick!" Tara could sense him springing from the stone before he launched, knocking Gabriel flat on the grass with a right hook to the side of his jaw.

"Donnacha!" she screamed, fogged with confusion as she kicked her leg over the saddle and ran towards where the men were struggling on the ground.

Donn had fallen on him, red cheeked and hard eyed, bringing a hail of blows to his chest and head, reopening the wound on his cheek and covering them both in his blood. In his frenzy, the Irishman was impervious to Tara tugging back on his arm and she cast about in desperation for a weapon. No decent size branches but there were apples fallen from the nearby trees, the windfall of an early crop. She scoped them up in her skirts, lobbing them randomly at the bodies until finally Gabriel's instinct for self-protection reared its head and he twisted, using his weight to flip Donn onto his back so he could sit astride his chest, pinning his arms helplessly to his sides.

"What. The. Hell?" He raised his fist in warning, an apple catching him square on the temple with heavy thud. "And you! Stop it!"

Tara stepped back, admonished as she read the pain in Donn's face. "How did ye do it?" he was croaking, panting. "Did ye put a knife to her throat like yeez bastard puss-faced savages in camp or just smooth yer path with feckin' cream-skinned la-di-da?"

Gabriel lowered his arm slowly, pushing himself off and stepping back as Donn rolled onto his side. He sunk to his haunches and waited as the younger man gasped for control. "How could ye?"

"How could he what?" Tara cried into taut silence, hearing nothing in return but the sound of both men dragging in lungfuls of breath and Rowley sidestepping awkwardly, his hooves dampened by the grass.

"Ye should be getting' away so, Milady," said Donn after a while, springing suddenly to his feet and turning his back to retrieve his battered hat and kick twice, three times, at the towering heel stone in agonised frustration. "Ye dinna want to be hearin' this."

"No," said Gabriel quietly, glancing up at her, his eyes so black that fear rose from the pit of her stomach, violently unseating the confusion. "Tara should know."

"You're scaring me," she started, looking from one man to the other, recognising the pain of grief as well as the hollowness of guilt. "Gabriel, what in God's name did you do?"

"Yer gentleman here ravished my sister. N-Neala. He's feckin' killed her."

"She's dead?" Gabriel hung his head, winded by the news.

"Aul Paddy Kielty says as how its yer scrawny bastard what's killed her." Voice breaking, Donn pulled a thin fold of parchment from his breast pocket, still tight in its wrapper, and threw it at Gabriel's feet.

"She was with child?" Gabriel froze a moment, his features hollowed by shock, then spring up without warning, moving to clasp Donn to him. His firm hand wrapped around the nape of the younger man and he held tight and silent until Donn relinquished control and let large sobs rack his frame.

"My sister..." Donn's rasping voice cracked against Gabriel's shoulder. "She was all that was feckin' good in that Hell."

With shaking fingers, Tara picked up the folded letter and scanned its contents with a frown, waiting impatiently for the words to form themselves into something she could understand. She couldn't get further than the date in the dense hieroglyphics. "This was written in February, four months ago. It's followed you to England, Gabriel. It looks to have been forwarded by the barracks in Galway..."

His voice was no more than a whisper: "What does it say of the child, Donn?"

Donn sniffed audibly, stepping back out of Gabriel's hold. "It's weak. Paddy's me da's brother. He says he'll tek it in with Mairie, but it's not a chance of livin'. Says he hopes not, for the lot of 'em are bound for feckin' Connacht."

"But..." Tara started, stopping when she saw the haunted look on Gabriel's face.

"We need a fire."

He backed away from them then, turning towards a nearby crop of trees, the lines of his body stiff. Tara hesitated, torn between going after him and letting him face his demons alone, but the choice was made for her as Donn slid back to the ground. She sunk down beside him, wrapping her arms about his slim frame to offer what silent comfort she could until Rupert rode up with a bellowed "Ho!" that startled them into standing. His blonde hair glowed luminescent in the early evening sun and his arms were full with a lumpy looking sack. Marie trotted up behind him, her cloak still tight around her petit shoulders and barely a curl out of place.

"Tara! What have you done to Gabe's hair?" he started, with amused eyes.

"Rupert, Marie, this is Donn," Tara withdrew her arms and folded them awkwardly. "He's come from Ham House to meet us."

"What good fortune we found you! Tara, I told you these stones were lucky!" Rupert started enthusiastically. "Good to meet you, Donn. You look timber-pounded man, what the Hell happened?"

"Luck o' the Irish," shrugged Donn, wiping an arm across his face. "Damn site luckier than t'other fella…"

Rupert frowned a second, before shrugging off his uncertainty and shaking Donn's hand, introducing his wife.

Together, they cleared ground for camp within the protection of the stones and below the buzzing sounds of Rupert's conversation. He was on fine form, seemingly entirely impervious to the tension in the air. When Gabriel finally reappeared, arms full of firewood, Tara watched him build up a large fire with a hollow cavity in her chest. She hugged her knees and stared at the catching flames while Marie shared out their Salisbury haul: bread, rabbit pie, cherries and local cider. And they ate while Rupert whittered on about the giant race of golden-bearded Vikings who'd dragged the monoliths around them to standing a millennium before.

It was late, it must be, but the sun was reluctant to relinquish its hold on the springtime world. The longest day of the year, Marie explained as she patted an almanac purchased in Salisbury. That was something to be grateful for, thought Tara abstractly; no long, dark night in which to lose his soul. Solstice was a time of light and fire; the seeds planted in pale earth would erupt now with the heavy promise of harvest bounty. The stones stood out around them like blackened, broken ribs against the blue twilight and, from within the carcass, they sat as if waiting, too, to be born.

Rupert was insistent he would wait out the short hours of darkness to know the energy of the changing season. *Was it possible that there was magic in this place?* She offered up a silent prayer to whatever Swedish behemoth Rupert had deemed responsible for it. Let the sunrise spread light and hope and renewal further than the fields. Let Donn find a peace. Let Eddie be saved and the Sealed Knot men find her message and stay safe. Let Lord Carnage reveal himself… let her tell of the betrayal in the organisation before more lives were destroyed.

Let her love as she would. And, for now at least, let it be enough for him. If she was ever going to be able to drag him towards the light, it had to be.

She sniffed and refocused on the company. Rupert's meandering thoughts had moved south, to the French barbarian hunting his wife, and Tara stilled, keen to learn as much as possible about the man she had suggesting luring into their lives.

"The Marquis François de Clapiers speaks in endless riddles." Marie's voice was calm but full of an abstraction that suggested she'd worked hard to distance herself emotionally as well as literally. "He thinks dispensing borrowed wisdom makes him sound clever."

"As if being barrell'd up with learning makes him less brutal," snorted Rupert bitterly.

"He took your finger?" asked Gabriel quietly, looking up towards Marie.

Tara shot him a confused glance but Marie just lifted her left hand to hold it objectively against the firelight and, for the first time, Tara noticed that the ring finger was missing entirely, just above the knuckle.

"*Oui*," said Marie with an uncharacteristic sangfroid that belied the horror of the act, as if he had simply made off with the ribbons from her hair. "I would not love him, not how he wanted to be loved. He said that if he could not have the whole of me, no other man would." She glanced at Rupert and was rewarded with a humourless grunt.

"Others fared worse." Marie shrugged with a practiced air of indifference, but Rupert picked up her left hand and Tara's eyes moistened as she watched him kiss the damaged knuckle.

Then, with his customary ability to change his thoughts on the turn of a sixpence, he announced without preamble: "I need to piss," and leapt up to leave the stones. Marie laughed and there was a freshness in the sound, as if Rupert could literally chase away the nightmare into the shadows ahead of him.

Darkness had finally descended. and Gabriel caught sight of a shiver along Tara's spine. He hesitated, about to slip off his cloak to lay it about her shoulders, but she glanced up and for a moment their eyes met. Something in the look made him move to sit down behind her and pull her gently back to rest against him as he leaned against a stone. With immeasurable gratitude he felt her body relax against his, until she was gathered wholly between his arms, his cloak wrapped about the two of them.

"I know you," she said softly, eventually, interrupting his heavy thoughts. "I know you wouldn't hurt… Donn knows it too. I'm so sorry, about your child and, and Neala."

He leaned forward and let his head fall against her shoulder, surprised to feel wetness on her hair and realising with some shock that the moisture was from his own tears. They rippled through his muscles and he could feel suddenly how violently they ached, his whole body tense with the effort of control, so she wouldn't know the pain that threatened to devour him. Tortuous images raced across his brain of Neala Kielty. Pregnant, half-starved and pale to the point of translucence, destroyed by the seeds he'd planted, not just last summer but years before, when he followed Lucius…

He refocused mentally, as he always had, on his orders. He rehearsed his report to Hyde. The White Horse Inn was clearly the key to Villiers' Sealed Knot men. Mortenhampstead was virtually equidistance from the major West Country ports, it made sense that orders were given there to Lyme Regis, Plymouth, even Falmouth… Whatever she'd done in that gloomy bar room, it wasn't for the sake of that quack's company, it was for the rebels. She had surely stood down the planned uprisings. It was done. Quietly, effectively, bravely, *alone*, she'd done it.

Only somehow, thank God, Milgate had stumbled on the name *Lord Carnage*. She must have a return missive to deliver to the prominent traitor.

But he'd seen it in her eyes, when she stepped blinking into the sunlight with the quack clinging as tight to her arm as a cocklebur. She was uncertain… afraid even. Not of the doctor, nor of him, but of a responsibility. The fear was of failure. *She didn't know the real identity of Carnage.* And that, he knew with a sickness in his stomach, could only mean she'd soon be stepping along the slippery, snaking loyalties of court, casting recklessly about in an adder's nest for clues to identify the ultimate Sealed Knot leaders. The names of those who directed her uncle.

The wedding at Hampton Court. Tara would have seen the opportunity. She'd already be turning a roomful of senior parliamentarian guests into a hunting ground, without realising that on the turn of a penny, the hunter would become the hunted. Instinctively, his arms tightened further around the vulnerable softness of her body, even as his heart filled with self-loathing. Soon, they would both face a choice: she would have to choose to trust him, and he would have to choose to betray her. The aching in his balls, his brain, his heart was the same petty, selfish distraction that had caused tragedy once already.

Whatever it took…

"You knew me as a child, Tara," he whispered, sounding distant, "you've no idea what I'm capable of. Of everything I am now… everything that I'll do."

"I'm not afraid of you."

"You should be-"

"Then why is it that it's only when I'm with you…" she replied, laying her head back against his chest, "only with you that I feel safe."

Safe.

He remembered when she first came to him. *Neala, you're safe.* He'd given his word then and he'd broken it. In Ireland, he'd thought he'd given his all for service: his sword, his honour, even his damned humanity. He'd been convinced, then, that there was nothing more to give. But the sacrifice demanded now was greater than he'd thought possible. His arms drew closer around her, pulling together tightly the fragments of his chest. An owl hooted somewhere in the trees behind them and, heavy with resolution, he drew aside her fallen hair and tenderly kissed the exposed skin along the back ridge of her shoulder.

"Tara," he whispered. "Whatever happens, I swear I'll always-"

She half-turned, frowning at the intensity of his words, and kissed his mouth gently, before pulling back with a small smile.

"What's funny?" he asked.

"You smell of apples. Nice to know I've decent aim."

Gabriel frowned, with mock seriousness. "I'd assumed you weren't actually aiming at me… Although if you *were*…" He squeezed her then, his hands on her belly threatening tortuous tickles as punishment. It felt halfhearted but she indulged the distraction, burying her face in his shirt to muffle her giggles.

"Look what I found lyin' amongst the baggage." Donn had taken a turn out in the darkness. He paused, giving a faint, sad smile as he thrust a violin towards Gabriel, an awkward olive branch that made Tara's heart break.

She half-turned back: "I didn't know you'd brought that."

"I didn't," Gabriel replied, confusion registering in a small shrug against her shoulders. He took the instrument from Donn's outstretched arm and turned it round in her lap to strum the strings with an objective detachment. The habit was deep rooted. He listened to the open notes reverberate in the cool night air and gently adjusted the bone pegs until he was content with the tuning, before stilling the strings' vibration, "I don't know-"

"Ah! I completely forgot to say!" Rupert called over, tugging Marie along to settle closer by their side. "Pa told me to give it to you. A farmer in Mortenhampstead found it abandoned in the church meadow and the gypsies were long gone. He sent it to Treguddick after the clear up; he thought you might like it. Between us, I gather it's as much thanks for ridding the county of that Major General brute as for hefting the burnt beams about."

Rupert gave a relaxed grin, pulling his knees up to rest his arms, and raised a bottle of cider to his lips before offering it to his wife. "*Merci*," she yawned, her fingers running absent-mindedly along his thigh. Rupert kissed the top of her head.

"Play something for us," Tara said softly, placing her hand over his, and after a moment's hesitation he laid the instrument flat against her lap, braced against her belly as if it were tucked under his chin. He curled his left hand around the neck and in the low fire light he began plucking the notes of a simple series of chords, a pizzicato so unusual it might have been made by slow, melancholic voices.

Donn sighed in recognition: "*Fáinne Gael an Lae*. Neala's favourite." He stretched back on the ground by the fire, tipping his hat forward over his eyes. After a couple of beats, he took up the melody and began to sing softly in Gaelic: "*Maidin moch do ghabhas amach, Ar bruach Locha Léin…*"

She didn't understand the lyrics but the gentle yearning in the Irishman's voice, soft and tender above the simple rhythmic repetitions, sent a shiver of goose bumps along her spine. She watched the steady movement of Gabriel's fingers; there was a question in the depression of strings and yet he plucked so softly that a lump formed in her throat. By the end of the second stanza, Donn had stopped singing, lulled finally asleep, but there was a throbbing in her heart.

"Tell me, tell me what it's about," she whispered, compelled by a painful force she didn't understand to know the depth of his grief for Neala.

Gabriel leaned in and started the arpeggios again, his hair falling to graze the line of her jaw as he sang softly in English, his voice so low and vulnerable she heard it more as a vibration through his chest.

"*On a mossy bank I sat me down with the maiden by my side
With gentle words I courted her and asked her to be my bride
She turned and said, "Please go away," Then went on down the way
And the morning light was shining bright at the dawning of the day.*"

As if on cue, a shaft of sunlight spread from directly above the heel stone, bathing them in pale yellow fire. *Dawn*. The night was over, and another day begun.

"Shall we wake them?" she whispered, nodding gently in the direction of Rupert and Marie, wound closely around each other and comatose under his cloak.

"No," he said softly, his eyes caught by a flash of silver as she spun the band on her middle finger. "Let's keep this for ourselves, an ending… or a beginning."

"A revolution."

He gently turned her face to his and kissed her thoroughly, his lips demanding and yet tender, his body incapable of lying to her. And she kissed him back, closing her eyes to the sun.

30. THE GOODNESS AND LOVING KINDNESS OF THE LORD

To General Robert Blake, Admiral of our Naval Forces, at Sea.
Whitehall, 12th June, 1658.

SIR,

I have received your letter of the 20th April and its account of the good success it hath pleased God to give us in the Canaries, especially in your destruction of the King of Spain's Ships in the Bay of Santa Cruz.

The Lord's mercy, to us and this Commonwealth, is very signal; in our Spanish Enemy's loss of galleons and treasure, but also in the preservation of our own ships and men. It was indeed very wonderful, and according to the goodness and loving kindness of the Lord. it doth demand That we should fear Him, and hope in His mercy.

We notice how eminently it hath pleased God to make use of you in this service; granting you wisdom in the conduct and courage in the execution. We have sent you a small Jewel, as a testimony of our own and the Parliament's good acceptance of your carriage in this Action.

We are also informed that the Officers of the Fleet, and the Seamen, carried themselves with much honesty and courage against the Spanish. We desire you to communicate our hearty thanks and acknowledgments to them.

Thus, beseeching the Lord to continue His presence with you, I remain,
Your very affectionate friend,
OLIVER P.

31. MASKS

"My little brother Henry has reported volumes on your husband's courage, Madam, and now I see he must be an exceptionally brave man to abandon you in this steaming marketplace. Does he not realize that every man meanders a wedding party with love on his mind? Mrs Moore, if I am right?"

Tara nodded politely and looked up into clear blue, intelligent eyes. Richard Cromwell was blonde and fine boned, with a general air of delicacy not, reputedly, shared by his sisters. She silently cursed Gabriel for vanishing after the service had finished; this was certainly a treacherous sea to be bobbing about in alone, and Richard had the neat, pointed lines of a dogfish. "I have not yet given up Mr Moore for lost."

"From what I hear, he would never allow himself to be at such a disadvantage. Quite the will for survival. But you look lost, if you don't mind my saying." He took a swig from his champagne glass and gave a sudden grin, still sharky but utterly devoid of lewd flirtation. "I haven't seen you at court before, my Lady. Do you know many in this cream of English, nay, European society?"

Tara relaxed a little at that, letting her eyes dart over the gaudy crowds, grateful to talk about something other than her errant husband. The wedding of Mary Cromwell and the Viscount Fauconberg had attracted over 500 guests to the palace, all broiling like cuts of pink meat in the heat of the orangery; honey glazed in the golden light of early evening. Large porticoed doors had been opened onto the formal gardens but even those guests spilling slowly out into the gravel found no cooling relief. The sky was heavy with a darkness portending more thunderous downpours and the gravel was scattered with damaged rose petals,

Richard was right about one thing though: despite, perhaps, rather than because of the spectacle of love fulfilled, the atmosphere sizzled. Men strutted about like peacocks, gazing languidly at the trussed peahens around them. A nearby group of decaying gentlewomen peered superciliously at a younger company of girls, wrapped tightly in fine silks and flattery, frantically fanning themselves between giggles.

"No, Mr Cromwell, I don't know anyone. Perhaps you would point out a few notable guests?"

"With pleasure… There, for instance, you're looking at the most eligible and idle ladies of quality in the room, but I would recommend giving them a wide berth unless you have kind words for their war paint. They swallow only sycophants for sweetings." Richard rolled his eyes, long lashes sweeping dramatically as he took a deep breath and ran a finger under his modest ruff to let the heat escape his embroidered velvet doublet.

"To the left is Lady Hampton; her only virtue is the hedge modesty, which stops a man climbing over only to land in her faults… On her right is Lady Somerley, her own face hung with toys and devices like the signs of a tavern to draw strangers. You'll surely agree that her clothes sit like a saddle on a sow's back… And there, at the centre of that storm of feminine charm, is the self-styled Lady Rich, otherwise known as my baby sister, Frances. She was widowed in February when her first husband died after only three months of marriage."

Tara peered towards the girl, trying not to smile at his waspish summaries. "How sad."

"Oh, don't be sad, Mrs Moore! You must have heard the rumours of his vicious temperament. One might well ask why on earth father pressed on with the match but, in his limited defence, negotiations took so long that Rich was already ailing of consumption by the time of their nuptials and the settlement for dear Frances was substantial. She really couldn't have done better."

"I've heard rumours that one of your sisters is to marry Charles Stuart," Tara said bluntly.

Richard snorted at the provocation. "My dear sisters will make worthy matches for any youth of ambition, but you'll be waiting for hens to make holy water before father blesses a Stuart union."

Unfazed, he scanned the crowds again and steered her gaze towards a short, uncomfortable-looking man with a surreptitious nod. "Look, there, John Russell will likely prove Frances' second husband. He doesn't look like much, does he? He's said to be fantastically melancholic. Apparently he distinguished himself in Ireland. I have my doubts that a person of such small stature could contain a keen courage, but I'm no expert in military matters… Perhaps your husband would vouch for him?"

Tara shrugged; it was a wonder any man could distinguish himself amongst the reported brutality. Abstractly the question tugged again as to what exactly Gabriel had done to return so noteworthy, but she stamped on it, turning her attention back to the girl in question. Frances Rich looked too young to have had any husbands, let alone to be contemplating a second. Marriage was a fast-moving market.

"Is your own wife here?"

"Dorothy?" he asked unnecessarily, sipping at his champagne with an air of infinite weariness. "Somewhere… probably with one of the children. She is remarkably fecund, it must be said although, truth be told, her chief commendation is that she brings a man to repentance."

Tara choked for a moment on the bubbles of her drink and cast her eyes about for a tactful change of subject. She nodded across the room in the direction of the Secretary of State, standing with the bride and her father. "There, I do recognise John Thurloe. Have you spoken with him yet?"

"Speak to Thurloe? Good God, no. Ten parish constables are not so tedious."

Mary had one hand on Cromwell's arm as she looked intently at the spymaster. No, it was not on the sleeve of his black doublet, Tara realised with a shock. Her pale arm was entwined under his; she was holding him up. The Lord Protector seemed smaller than she remembered, as if he had folded in on himself since she'd stood before him in Whitehall and they watched him a moment, each alone in their thoughts.

"I would say my sister has the patience of a saint," muttered Richard dryly, "but just look at father: such is the root; such is the fruit. They both seem genuinely to like the man, even despite his championing this hopeless match with Yorkshire."

"This wedding was Thurloe's idea? I didn't have him for a fairy godmother."

Richard tilted his head, the corners of his eyes crinkling: "I'll wager that when the clock strikes midnight you'll not have Thomas Belasyse for a convincing Prince Charming either."

"She doesn't love him?" she asked, conscious of the naivety of the question when he smirked.

"We are not all so lucky as to marry for enduring passion, Mrs Moore." Richard clinked her champagne glass in toast before continuing: "I believe your own match is quite unique in that regard. To hear father and his Major General raving not four weeks back, one could be left in no doubt as to the size of your husband's balls."

"I am extremely lucky," she shrugged, eyes on Mary.

Richard snorted, looking back to the bride. "Anyway, enduring passion is not her concern. It is an enduring shame for Mary that she is neither masculine enough to be considered for succession nor feminine enough to pass for my oldest sister. That nose, poor thing; she never stood a chance. The exemplar, unparalleled Elizabeth is the apple of father's eye. Such a shame she is too ill to be gazed upon with wondrous amazement this evening. Still, we must each of us accept our fates, I suppose, even when we are less than convincing."

A cloud passed briefly over his brows until he took another generous gulp of champagne and rubbed his naked chin in renewed contemplation of the assembly, ready to resume the game. "Now then, who else is worthy of note? You're basically looking at a rag-tag bunch now: those with enough ambition to keep up the glory of their own greatness, those with enough sense to be prominent *ex* royalists and those with enough debt to be avoiding the city streets at night."

"Happen as I'd hoped his stock at court would've dwindled by now," interrupted Viscount Fauconberg, gathering up Tara's fingers for a moist but disinterested kiss as he shook his broad face in incredulity at Richard. "That sorner lost an entire fortune at the tables a week ago and took out his frustration beating on my good friend Danvers in a bawdy house. And now look at him, nothing but a shipwrack, boldly supping at my feast like a fly!"

"Oh Thomas, come aloft! *Relax!*" Richard gave a patient smile, holding his glass out for a refill as an impassive page passed by with an embossed bottle. "Have some compassion on your special day, man: gambling is an enchanting, itching disease. Besides, Danvers can look after himself and I'm quite sure that once Carlton's devotion to profligacy is brought to father's attention his days in the sun will be numbered. And 'til then, well in court, as they say, every woman will have her wanton fit."

"Or every dog his day," corrected Tara primly.

A burst of laughter erupted behind her and the blushing groom started, turning to see Gabriel. At the sight, Fauconberg's red face immediately transformed and he wiped a sweating palm on the seams of his breeches to clasp him, plump, rosy cheeks wobbling in anticipation of intimacy.

"At last! I am right pleased to meet you finally Lord Denby! You know of course there's not a dinner party in polite society at which tales of your daring do are not whispered scandalously? And I suspect from the rugged look of you that you are equally revered amongst the sweaty, hardened hordes of men in your command."

"I know little of polite society, Viscount Fauconberg" said Gabriel mildly, with a gracious nod to Richard. "I'm only recently returned."

"But of course, fresh off the boat!" The Viscount's jowls jiggled with his growing excitement, oblivious to his new brother-in-law taking eye-rolling leave. His gaze moistened as he took in the stature of his newly returned champion, and a pink tongue ran wet over his fat lips. "You are doubly welcome, sir! But my! Now I see you up close you truly bear the scars of a warrior. May I say sir that the scratch on your cheek rather suits your countenance? I am given to understand that the fighting was most terribly brutal?"

"Skirmishes and sieges," replied Gabriel. His face was masked with polite blandness but Tara wondered that others always seemed so entirely impervious to the waves of tension that radiated from his body at the mention of Ireland. From his look of static awe, Fauconberg had never so much half-raised a sword in anger, let alone seen a battle.

"Happen you have a stomach of steel, sir, to seek the dastards out one by one." Belasyse' blank face split into a smile as the threads of his brain anchored him back to safer ground. "But you are not just a hero; you are a hunting man! How right marvellous! We are a man short for our trip to my father's estate in Yorkshire next week. It'll be a bloody event, mind; strong, powerful hunters satisfying their most base urges for flesh. You must bring your talents to bear on our little party! I trust I can count upon your company?"

"My Lord," Gabriel demurred, pulling Tara into his arms without warning. In the sudden movement, she tripped on the hem of her skirts and twisted to grasp at the front of his jerkin, exclaiming as his hands ran possessively down her back and over her bottom. He laughed, eyes sparkling at her frowning glare and kissed her nose lightly, glancing back at Belasyse with an apologetic shrug. "We are newlyweds, my Lord. As tempting as the offer is, I fear my wife would be heartbroken if I abandoned her so soon and for so long to skewer wild northern beasts."

"Nonsense, sir!" countered Belasye, pausing to wink suggestively if unconvincingly in Tara's direction. "As I explained to Mary, we have a lifetime left to do duty by our women."

As if finally remembering the reason for the current gathering, Belasye scanned the crowd until his gaze alighted on Mary Cromwell, now Mary Belasyse. She was still stuck firmly to the right-hand side of her father, now nodding seriously at a conversation with a sober and ancient puritan. The sparkle fell slightly from Belasye's eyes.

He turned back to Gabriel and tried a different tack: "What say we move the party to the Weald? His Highness will indulge me, I'm sure. The hunting's sublime and it's a considerably shorter journey. No more than three nights away. It was the mad King Henry's personal playground, you know. Some say his rabid ghost stomps through the night still, giant thighs and red beard quivering with excitement for the chase. On moonless nights one can still right hear the royal rechate, calling the hounds!"

"A few days in the Weald?" Gabriel released Tara without ceremony and bowed to their host, smiling graciously. "That I cannot refuse."

The blush deepened in Belasyse's cheeks and he returned a deep bow in acknowledgement. "I look forward to it."

"Are you going to tell me what the Hell that was about?" Tara demanded as the wide Yorkshireman moved away with surprising agility through the listing crowd. "If we weren't at that man's wedding…"

"Don't say it," whispered Gabriel with a shudder, glancing over the bodies floating past and pulling her tightly towards him.

"I don't know how you can be so flippant about it," she started, noting out of the corner of her eye the tray of champagne glasses passing precariously close behind her back, on the arm of a distracted page. "You've just agreed to go and make camp with him in the middle of nowhere. It doesn't sound as though he expects to hunt stags."

"Needs must." He shrugged and his eyes narrowed when her frown remained, the hint of a pout on her lips. "Wait, can my loving wife be jealous?"

"No! I just think-" He cut off her flustered denial with a deep kiss, satisfied only when her body relaxed boneless into his arms. He pulled back reluctantly, his fingers spreading out across the nape of her neck as he nudged her head gently sideways to give him better access to her throat, and the spot under her ear that raised goose bumps across her chest, even in this heat.

"I would give all at this moment to attend to my duty with increased vigour," he whispered, smiling as he watched a bright green light play on her pale skin, refracted from the emerald drops he'd found in Hannah Moore's box.

"Not where I must witness it, I beg you."

"My Lord Thurloe," Gabriel's voice above her shoulder recovered quicker than her wits, and Tara turned, willing solidity back into her legs and feeling back into her lips, which tingled pleasantly from the force of his attention.

"My Lord Denby, a pleasure to meet you finally. And might I say it is a joy to see you again, my Lady, and so soon upon our jaunt to the West Country. Might I also say that the green silk is extremely becoming on you. It is perhaps for the best that my Lord Denby here stakes such a public claim to your favours; your engagement was so hurried it would be easy to forget entirely that you are spoken for."

His lips curled into something resembling a smile as his beady eyes ran along the bodice of her dress and up into Gabriel's warning stare. Thurloe lifted his hand as though to run his fingers along the high curve of her breasts and Gabriel tensed. She sensed his muscles coiling as though he would strike like a snake the moment the Secretary of State tried to touch her, but after a moment Thurloe just shrugged and lowered his hand, scratching the persistent sore on the back of the other.

Someone cleared their throat, and she looked up almost gratefully at the interruption. "My Lord Latimer."

Cloaked in his formal robes of office, the churchman landed like a black crow, complete with his customary air of self-importance and an utter indifference to the awkwardness. John Clifford was trotting dutifully behind but had been distracted by a passing plate of fancies. Latimer nodded at Gabriel and Tara, an action hampered somewhat by the stiff white ruff about his neck, but he addressed Thurloe directly. "What a pleasant surprise it is to find you here among the great and good. It has been a while since we last saw one another."

"Since I last saw *you*, my Lord Latimer, or since you last saw *me*?" Thurloe asked with a polite tilt of his head.

It occurred to Tara, not for the first time, that for a spymaster, Thurloe was hampered by features that gave away everything of his internal monologue. Perhaps this explained his directness; there was little damage to be done in giving voice to the tale that everyone had already read plain as day on his face. His smile was little more than a thin lined grimace at the sight of Titus Latimer; he might as well have declaimed sonnets of distaste and mistrust aloud.

"A friendly eye only of course, my Lord." Latimer smiled, waving in airy dismissal of the import of spying on colleagues and the implicit threat in the Secretary of State's personal interest.

"Of course," replied Thurloe. "As is mine."

"But speaking of which, Thurloe, I must tell you with regret that I am unable to keep the servant boy you recommended."

"Did he disappoint?" Thurloe enquired with an air of sickening sweetness, and Tara thought of Bulstrode Wortley back at Ham House, sending in his prurient reports on their own lives. She felt Gabriel's fingers tighten on her elbow but he seemed distracted by a scene across the room.

"His head was full of Mercury," started Latimer with an exaggerated shrug. "but he was as lazy as Saturn."

A steward clapped officiously, denying Thurloe a response as he called order to the room. Red-faced and shiny with sweat, Clifford pulled up behind his master and the other guests reluctantly gathered back inside the orangery, out of the first cooling drops of rain. They sidled around one another, either for a better view of the stage at one end of the room or for the psychological safety of being near trusted companions. Tara peered fruitlessly towards whatever had caught Gabriel's attention and when she looked back Thurloe was gone.

A hush descended and, path cleared, Cromwell himself took to a raised dais and tapped his fork against his glass, clearing his throat noisily: "Family, friends. Thank you for coming today in this intolerable heat, to bear witness as my daughter Mary becomes Lady Thomas Belasyse, Vicountess Fauconberg."

The Lord Protector paused and looked around the silent room a moment before a ripple of polite applause encouraged him to continue and he drew a sleeve across the beads of sweat on his forehead. Watching his awkwardness, Tara wondered if he would feel his replacement in Mary's life. She may not be his favourite child, but by the look of it she was his most devoted. Father for husband; it was every sensible woman's destiny to trade one kind of protection and provision for another.

"Wait here," Gabriel whispered into her ear and the hairs on the back of her neck bristled, feeling his departure with the tickling movement of air behind her.

In front, Cromwell continued with his prepared speech: "...And while you all are granting liberties, surely you will not deny me this, it being not only a Liberty but a Duty. I must bear my testimony to England, as I have done and do still, so long as God lets me live in this world."

There was a sudden commotion at the rear of the orangery, a shuffling confusion and a muffled shout as a man was led bodily away through the grand entrance doors by two armed guards, one on either side. Tara started, heart pounding, but no one else seemed to move. Around her, every man and woman kept their eyes firmly forward on the Lord Protector as the doors clicked closed behind them.

"...Every man is to give an account to God of his actions, therefore he must in some measure be able to prove his own work. I have had a great deal of experience of Providence. I now present to you my testimony."

Behind him, long curtains fell aside to reveal a large bucolic backdrop; the English countryside painted green and lush. From a small gallery overhead, a group of musicians began to play and from makeshift wings four players emerged to take centre stage. Clearly representing the seasons, they were implacably masked like the chorus of a Greek tragedy, save that their costumes were too bright and gaudy. They walked a formation of tight geometrical shapes and intricate patterns, each shimmering as they moved with silken leaves of greens and gold, save for Winter, who was draped in a sparkling cape of frost. Spring was giving an introductory verse and Tara shifted anxiously, unable to discern any sign of Gabriel. She lifted her chin a little higher, peering about an appreciative audience.

After the lengthy oratory of the opening set, the action brought about a shift of the elaborate scene. Green and pleasant England gave way to an apocalyptic wasteland of red fire and black stone, the painted trees now standing as stark as crucifixes. The players had also shed their leaves and returned as evil cavaliers, blue sashes about their breastplates to denote the royal allegiance. They were grotesquely comical with large noses and larger cocks, which bumped haphazardly into the scenery and lewdly into each other. The crowd welcomed the relief, shouting 'boo!' and tittering with self-congratulation at having ended the war on the right side.

The music picked up pace as the Lord of Misrule arrived, bacchanalian in his costume of wine flasks, and the cavaliers danced revels to their satanic deity. In the intense heat, their makeup slid slowly down their faces, an additional visual trick of decay no less effective for the fact it was unintended.

"Subtle," murmured Tara sardonically, earning a sideways glance from Latimer. She stared back unabashed, a tickling tear of sweat dribbling down between her breasts. Gabriel, with his furnace-like torso encased in formal velvet, would surely be suffering. She felt a small, uncharitable sense of satisfaction. Leaving her alone with the churchman was hardly evidence of an enduring passion.

There was still no sign of him, but the mysterious Lord Carnage was surely somewhere here. Her father had made occasional reference to a senior Lord, someone close to Cromwell, who directed the rebels. Blurred features hovered at the furthest edges of her memory. It was as good a place to start as any, although discounting the Cromwells, Thurloe and Latimer, taking away the women and the youths, there must be around two hundred potential male options amongst the assembly.

She took a deep breath. Lord Carnage had directed her father and Eddie; he must know who she was. She had to stay visible, be accessible, invite his attention. She scanned the heads, hoping for some glimmer of recognition, some clue or signal among the blank faces. A field sign, she thought, remembering Gabriel's frustrated dismissal of the leaves his men had carried to battle. With a burst of determination, she began to move slowly through the stifling heat of closely packed bodies.

Back at the front of the hall, the players had been re-cast as simple puritan folk stumbling with honest joy upon the safe haven of Cromwell's court. A rather exalted concept of parliamentary order, she thought bitterly. The reality involved fixing at least one eye permanently over your shoulder. Then the bleak backdrops rolled entirely away to reveal Cromwell himself sitting on a raised throne.

"We are delivered from evil!" The puritans fell to their knees with gratitude and he delivered the epilogue as honouree and hero. The bodies closed in tighter to hear the Protector's valedictory resolutions and she had to raise a hand to create space so that she could pass between the doublets and sleeves. The other hand went instinctively to the inside of her placket, to close protectively over the scrap of parchment she would deliver to Lord Carnage when she found him.

Nothing.

She patted along the inside of the silken folds of her skirt; stopping to explore the further regions. The blasted message wasn't there. No holes in the seams. It can't have disappeared into thin air. She took a deep gulp of air and shoved her hand back into the placket, offering under her breath a last chance for it to materialise without recrimination. Nausea swelled as her fingers swept again through the slippery fabric. *Nothing.* It was gone. She pushed more forcefully back through the crowd; the small wrapper must have fallen out. Frantically, she scanned the floor, but the bodies closed in tight and the path was blocked.

The saddlebags. *Please God, let it be in the saddlebags.* Did she actually remember placing the message inside her placket? Maybe not. It was hard to tell with the room spinning. There was still a chance that she'd left it with her horse and Rowley in the stables. *Fool.*

She turned to leave, brows furrowing slightly when she caught sudden sight of Gabriel through the mass of bodies, all applauding, exhaling, ebbing and flowing again with the end of the masque. He was ordinarily head and shoulders above a crowd, but his dark head was inclined towards a short blonde woman, slight and expensively dressed, with shiny ringlets neatly curled in the modern fashion. The woman laid a proprietary hand on his chest and he absent-mindedly spun a small signet ring sitting on her little finger. An unexpected seed of jealousy took root in her stomach as he smiled in response to something she said, laughter lines creasing the corners of his eyes.

"Well, that is unfortunate, my Lady. I see your husband has a fondness for low company." A familiar voice whispered over her shoulder: "The Duchess of Albemarle is nothing if not vulgar. A proud, mincing peat and yet a washerwoman of low extraction. Heaven only knows how she lured General Monck away from his wife and family, but she clearly has a talent for it... Perhaps his attachment to her explains why he insisted on taking up the Scottish Commander in Chief position, all that way into the boorish north. She is *quite* unfit for a civilised puritan court."

Tara looked directly at Richard as he swayed drunkenly, his now blood-shot eyes rolling about like a ship at storm trying to remember where she left her anchor. Her stomach lurched. "She's not the only one."

32. FOUR'S A CROWD

Robert Waterman surveyed the fast-moving flow with a whistle. "The River's in spate my Lord. The rains've been heavy on and off all day. I'll pull no further than Ham, and I'll need an extra thrupence for that."

"*Din djävul!*"

The gruff exclamation betrayed well enough the universal heat of irritation and incredulity, but the object of its ire merely shrugged. "Aye, well, if you'd like to fashion yerself a longboat you can go all the way down the Thames and out to sea. But you'll not get me on board."

"I'll have your licence man, by order of the Lord Protector, and the waterman's guild will ensure you never set oar in the water again!"

The ferryman paled at that, his mumbled apologies failing flat against the Viking's broad face, and Gabriel called out as they approached: "My Lord Ambassador, my Lady Hedric. Is there a problem?"

"Ja, there is a problem sir, my wife and I must get to our beds in Chiswick! This horunge took our coin happily enough to bring us here this morning, but he is now refusing to take us back!" Handsome brows lifted beneath loose blond hair, above red cheeks flushed with wine. "Whoever heard of a sailor afraid of a little water?"

Gabriel smiled diplomatically. "You'll go as far as Petersham?"

"Aye, sir. But like I explained to the Lord here it's too dangerous to go further with the spring tide as is. I know what I'm doing sir, my father and his father before him rowed this stretch and... You've come from Ham House, haven't you?"

Gabriel gave a cursory nod, before turning to the couple and bowing graciously. "Gabriel Moore, Earl of Denby. May I present my wife, Lady Tara? The Thames can be a treacherous mistress my Lord. If you are agreeable, I think the best idea is that you come back to my home this evening. You will be comfortable and we can see to your onward journey as soon as you are ready to rise in the morning."

"Alexander... please, a thousand times, ja. Here is our knight in shining armour!" Lady Hedric laid a jewelled hand on her husband's arm. She smiled with relief and something intimate passed between the couple.

"Then it's settled," Gabriel smiled, taking the ambassador's hand in a firm grasp, as the waterman rushed forward to assist his wife. She held up her full skirts to pick her way gingerly down the jetty stairs, settling on a padded passenger bench at the stern, her hem safely out of the filthy bilge. Gabriel stepped down onto the vessel, bracing himself against the violent rocking as the Viking sat down heavily beside his wife. He reached back to take Tara's hand: "A moonlit river cruise, my Lady? Donn can collect the horses tomorrow."

"No, I-" Tara started from the riverbank, but bit her tongue when he raised dark eyebrows. There would be no opportunity to riffle through the saddlebags now, and no way to suggest a reluctance to be parted from her horse when ordinarily she'd take any opportunity to avoid the saddle. She frowned and stepped down into the wherry unaided. "I can manage."

Fanned by the cooling river breeze, soothed by the gentle strokes of the oars, the Ambassador's large, flat face relaxed by increments until his blue eyes crinkled and his belly rocked with laughter at Gabriel's tall tales of the evening. He gave a passable impression of the groom and Lady Hedric clutched her sides, tears sliding between the giggles. No mention of the blonde, husband?

Tara turned her face to the black riverbank. What now? There must be something else to do, some way to find this Lord Carnage, or the treachery might never be uncovered. Plans and names in the Sealed Knot were being passed to Thurloe with devastating consequences. Ann had brought back news to Ham House just two days ago of the beheadings of Sir Henry Slingsby and Dr John Hewitt on Tower Hill. How many more lives would be lost now because of her clumsy, damnable ineptitude?

"What say you, Lady Moore?"

Lady Hedric was sat between the men like a delicate pamphlet between two solid bookends, grinning wildly and touching both freely. Gabriel's right hand lay obligingly limp in her lap, but his attention was firmly on the Ambassador and the terms of the Treaty of Roeskilda between Sweden and Denmark, which effectively balanced access to trade routes at the entrance to the Baltic. Apparently indifferent to the fact that conversation had become more serious, she was asking something politely irrelevant about Gabriel's home.

"I don't know…"

Tara watched her husband dispassionately a moment, looking for a telltale sign of discomfort. Lady Hedric was perhaps ten or even fifteen years older but she was still an attractive woman. Her complexion was smoothed with ceruse and her lips tinted red with cochineal. She stretched out his fingers one at a time with a suggestive playfulness while Alexander gave animated insistence that the Commonwealth should work harder to prove itself worthy of the trading opportunities with Scandinavia. There. Gabriel's wry riposte did not break step, but his free hand rumpled through his hair. It wasn't much, the man was a consummate professional, but it was enough to loosen the grip in her chest.

She looked away before their eyes met. With the benefit of Lucius' schooling, Gabriel understood the nuances, the relationships, the rules of court life. She had felt a grudging admiration for the ease with which he'd traversed the room at the wedding. He seemed to know everyone there. He knew what to say and how to say it to charm them; when to challenge, and when to keep his opinions shuttered behind a mask of bland politeness.

He knew everyone there.

When she glanced up and he was looking directly at her. She met his eyes head on, caught for a heartbeat in their intensity. The hunger snatched her breath and she could feel her body already responding to his demand. But could she trust him with this? Was there another choice?

She was the first out of the wherry when it pulled up alongside the Ham House mooring, and she tripped ahead to rouse Abigail with apologies and the promise of time off in compensation for readying a guest room. As it happened, the maid trotted quickly out from the kitchen to meet her in the hall, bobbing a distracted curtsey, her fingers fluttering against her skirts as she pointed in the direction of the stairs: "You'll want a pail from the icehouse, Milady?"

Tara frowned a moment, seeing red rimmed eyes focusing too hard on the black and white tiles, sensing a nervousness born of guilt. Abigail's face was flushed pink, her hair fluffed loose from her cap. Ned must be with her in the kitchen. She could imagine what Ann would make of that impropriety, carried on under the master's roof, and the thought made her smile. She nodded: "Please. It feels like the temperature is rising."

When Abigail arrived awkwardly into the first-floor sitting room, brandishing glasses filled to the brim with small chunks of ice, she received a round of applause for her trouble.

"What an angel," murmured Alexander. He took a sharp intake of breath as a cold cube rolled around behind his teeth. "You are surrounded by heavenly creatures, Lord Denby. You are indeed a blessed creature."

"We are both blessed, my Lord," Gabriel smiled, tipping his glass in salute. "Skål!"

Hedric gave a gracious nod as she fanned herself languidly: "It is too hot for formal gowns."

"I can't wait to get out of these stays." Tara scooped the ice from her own whisky. Abigail had opened the windows wide but there was no movement of air to ripple the curtains and the room was still intolerably close. Lifting strands of damp hair from her shoulders, she dragged it over the skin with a groan. From the corner of her eye she sensed Lady Hedric nod and then from nowhere the Viking was behind her.

"Is it that kind of evening, my Lord?" he asked Gabriel, gently kissing the exposed nape of her neck. "Spirits and flesh?"

Tara squeaked at the unexpected sensation, shifting quickly out of his reach as she took in the calmness of Gabriel's polite smile and the reluctant shake of his head. He had her hand and was pulling her firmly towards him as he addressed Alexander over her head. "No, my Lord. I won't share my wife with another man. Or even, regrettably, such a beautiful woman."

She could feel, rather than see the ambassador's amicable shrug. "Then forgive me, sir. English hospitality has changed considerably since we first came to meet your King."

"The prevailing puritan wind finds such activity distasteful."

"Have we offended you?" Alexander's question was blunt but not confrontational; overlaid with a peculiarly Scandinavian ability to defuse awkwardness with straightforward efficiency.

"Not at all. It was a generous offer of a feast, were it not for my very particular appetite." To prove the point, his fingers ran possessively up Tara's chilled neck and he gently turned her face to his, seeking permission in her wide, green eyes. When it came, he moved without hesitation, bringing his mouth down on hers, demanding a deep response, drawing out a groan from the depths of her belly.

The Ambassador and his wife exchanged heated glances and, in perfect understanding, they headed for the door without the need of niceties. "Älskling, do you remember when we first married and you looked at me like that?" whispered Hedric as they left. "You said you would crawl to Valhalla on hot coals for me."

Alexander's response drifted in low tones from the hall. "I believe I said Stockholm, *mitt hjärta.*"

Tara burst at that, shaking with silent giggles and causing an awkward clashing of teeth. Gabriel pulled back and kissed her forehead by way of compromise, his own chest vibrating with the effort of not exploding while his guests were still within earshot.

"Would you, you know...?" she asked hesitantly, as the laughter subsided. She hadn't meant to start here, but-.

"Alexander is a fine looking man," he laughed.

"That night, after the fire. You were disappointed I was a virgin. Would you-?"

"No, Good God, no-"

"I wanted you, Gabriel. It was new to me but I knew what I was doing."

He pushed a heat-curled tendril of hair back behind her ear, picked up her hand and kissed her fingers tenderly. He picked up her scent on her wrist and put his lips on the delicate pulse point, feeling the hammering tattoo of her heart. It wasn't enough, but he couldn't trust himself to stop if he moved further, if he traced the vein towards the sensitive crook of her elbow. He pulled back, stiffening as he released her hand: "This is new to me, too. But I can't-"

"Can't what?" she interrupted, hoping her voice was not wavering as her chest heaved. It had come from nowhere but it was here, that nagging memory of denial she had so recklessly dismissed. The words came back to her. *I can't give you my heart, Tara.* Could she trust him with this message, with her treason, if he felt nothing for her? The second the words escaped her lips she prayed to swallow them back whole: "You looked like you could with that blonde."

"*What?*" he started, genuinely confused until his eyes narrowed and the remnants of laughter evaporated as swiftly as the ice in warm whisky.

"Why the Hell did you marry me, Gabriel?" she demanded. "There were other options. I could have slipped away. I could have taken my chances with Jack. Tollemache is dead, there is no reason to keep me a moment longer."

He paused a second, placing his cup on the board before turning to her. "Tara, I didn't-"

"You didn't *want* to marry me," she finished, the storm in her eyes abating as quickly as it sprung up, leaving nothing but a curious, empty calm. "I *know*... I didn't want to marry you either for the record. But I'll not spend my whole life atoning to a husband who'd rather have hitched his carriage to another brood mare."

He stared at her for an inscrutable moment and she looked away, shame blossoming at the allusion to his life in Ireland: the baby who'd perished before he even knew of its existence; the mother who's died for his love. He dragged his fingers back through his hair. "It's late and we've drunk too much. We'll talk tomorrow, but not now. Go to bed, Tara. Use the blue room."

As the door closed behind him, Tara stood by the window, utterly bereft. Tears threatened to prick her eyes and she knocked back her glass, giving an involuntary shake as the liquid slid along her throat, burning a fiery brand of resolve to the pit of her stomach. There's no time for this, she knew. Besides, it wasn't just the message at stake anymore, she was damned if after everything she would wait patiently until he was ready to release her. What happened to the man who had staked his reputation, his life… after everything, was she no more to him than Ralph's little sister?

She followed his path, taking the stairs two at a time and flinging open the door to his chamber. Gabriel sat at the foot of his bed, shirtless but still wearing his breeches. He might have been bending to remove his boots but something had stopped him, his head was in his hands. He started and his back straightened as she swept the door closed and marched across the floorboards to stand before him, forcing herself to swallow the rising fear of foolishness and to calm her chest, heaving from the exertion of will and exercise. His brows furrowed in question, but he didn't speak and slowly she straddled his lap, her eyes wide, searching his for a sign.

She bent her head to his, slowly tasting the whisky on his lips, gently teasing a groan from somewhere deep inside his throat. She could feel his body tense under her fingers. There was a warring in his chest but with every light touch along his jawline she could feel his intellect losing the battle with his need. With growing confidence, she shifted her weight and smiled to feel the straining fabric of his breeches against her thigh. "You don't find me completely repulsive then?"

He pulled back a moment, frowning. "Can you be serious? Hell's teeth Tara, I want you so damn much that it hurts to look at you."

There was a muffled bang from outside the door and Tara flinched, frowning at the noise. The servants might have finished seeing to the Ambassador and Hedric. *Weren't they all asleep yet?*

He pulled back her attention. "When I'm alone, this is so simple, I know who I am, but whenever I'm with you, I…"

Moved unexpectedly to tenderness, she made to stroke down his damaged back but he grabbed her hand, holding her still as his eyes darkened. "Touch me there again and I will restrain you."

His voice held a hard edge of warning but the champagne and whisky were working through her system alongside the blossom of relief and she couldn't prick the bubble of laughter as she reached out her free hand: "Here, you mean?"

He stood quickly with her legs still wrapped around his hips. Turning about, he lowered her back down softly onto the bed and pushed her hands up above her head, pinning them there while he swiftly loosened his belt.

"I... Gabriel, I was joking-" She stammered as he swiftly wrapped the leather around her gathered wrists, his actions gentle but firm as he ran a finger under the bind to satisfy himself it wasn't too tight; that it would hold her fast without chaffing the delicate skin.

"I warned you," he said with a grin, hooking the leather strap over a candle holder screwed tight onto the edge of the bed frame and tugging on her legs so that her arms stretched out straight and her body was captive.

She twisted frantically as he slowly unthreaded her stays and stood to pull her skirts down over her feet, finally he pushed her linen shift up to gather over her head at her wrists, exposing her entirely. A sobering embarrassment washed over her and she put renewed effort into trying to turn herself away from his gaze, but there was nothing she could do. She couldn't stop him.

"Do you trust me?" His words sent shivers down her spine. He didn't wait for her answer but left the question hanging, before leaning down to kiss her lips, gently at first but slowly more demanding, until they felt swollen.

"Gabriel, please-" Her lips tingled and her breath was coming fast and shallow, making the protest sound unconvincing even to her own ears. He moved over her slowly, pausing to blow cool air gently over her breasts, smiling as the nipples stood erect and then taking each one into his mouth, sucking and teasing the tips until they felt heavy, aching with need. He pulled back again, letting her heated skin chill and she moaned softly, a low groan of pleasure that made his groin throb almost painfully.

"Trust me," he whispered, quickly pushing off his boots and breeches with a hiss of relief and when she raised her eyes to his, she caught his dangerous grin. "If you want me to stop, say Cromwell."

She laughed aloud at that and then there was no more shame or embarrassment. He bent his head to kiss her breasts again. His mouth closed tight and hot around a nipple and she squirmed at first to free herself, but he could feel her surrender as the panic turned to need and she arched towards him.

"No!" she squealed, tensing afresh as he buried himself between her legs, his hands pinning her thighs apart gently but firmly. "You can't!"

"I can," he murmured, inhaling her scent with a groan of satisfaction. "Trust me."

The deep vibration in his throat reverberated against sensitive skin as he deftly licked and nipped at her sex, coaxing a different tension into life, manipulating it with confident strokes until her pants came quicker and quicker. Her back arched and she screamed as the spasm rolled violently in waves along her spine, breaking against her emptied head.

He blew cool air over the shuddering nub of flesh and slid upwards to cover her skin, slick with sweat and rashed with goosebumps. He flicked the leather strap loose as he entered her, and her hands immediately found his shoulders, tensed with the effort of control. She wrapped her arms around his neck, holding him in place within her until they rolled together and she straddled him. His hands tightened on her hips and she gasped at the depth of his possession. Then, as their rhythm began, she marvelled at the possibilities of control. The slightest shift of her weight, squeeze of her muscles, arch of her back, and she could draw growls and groans from within him that made her lightheaded with power. But there was a cost. Without warning, her body surrendered again to its own demand and she bucked above him. A second later he lifted her forward and climaxed violently under her.

"It scares me, how much I want you," he murmured as he lay down beside her.

"Then it's the only thing that does scare you."

He snorted dismissively, rolling on to his back, staring blankly at the ceiling: "You think that I am fearless? It's easier to be fearless when you have nothing to lose."

The statement was unreadable and she twisted onto her belly, smoothing the linen of the pillow as a distraction. Trust me. It was time, she couldn't do this alone. She started softly, working loose a feather from the bedding with her fingernail. "Gabriel, I need your help."

"Tamara Villiers needs my help?" He turned to look at her, eyes narrowed in amusement, and ran a finger gently along her brow, pushing damp hair back behind her ear. "I'm your slave, yours to command. What is it?"

She frowned and looked away, feeling the deep breath and hearing her shaking words before she could agonise further over the sense in speaking them aloud. "I want you to help me deliver an important message to a senior member of the Sealed Knot."

"The royalist organisation? What do you know of that?"

"I think you know."

He laughed suddenly, raising an eyebrow. "Is this a trick?"

"No," she replied testily, unwilling to be distracted. "Gabriel, please... you know who I was when my father was alive."

"And you know who I am now."

Their eyes met and she took a breath. "Eddie's arrest is not without cause. He has bands of men along the south coast. They were to rise up and support Charlie's invasion but I stopped them, in my uncle's name, when you told me his fleet was destroyed."

"How?"

She shook her head. "That doesn't matter. But in the process, I discovered that the organisation has been betrayed. Charlie's men have been betrayed at a senior level, someone with a national view of the organisation. Maybe it was the reason the Yarmouth plot was foiled. All across the country, letters are being intercepted, names revealed as we lie here."

She watched as he rolled away to sit on the edge of the bed, waiting until he finally looked up to face her: "What do you need from me?"

"I had a coded note containing the name of the spy feeding information direct to Thurloe. It's meant for the man at the very top of the Sealed Knot. He'll know what to do. You seem to know everyone at court, I thought perhaps you might have heard whispers-"

"Which man?" he interrupted gently.

"Lord Carnage." He raised an eyebrow and she shrugged, adding dryly. "Let's work on the basis that's not his real name."

"What is his real name?"

"If I knew that I would have found him myself!" she snapped, putting her head in her hands and taking a deep breath. "I don't know. He directed Eddie for years, my father before him. But I can't get into the Tower to ask since Cromwell revoked my pass. I believe he's high ranking in parliament-"

"Why not ask Villiers' men?"

"There's no point. At best they'll know a Lord Carnage exists, but they won't know how to reach him. Regional and local cells are kept independent, in case one is infiltrated. True identities are hidden. It's safer that way." She paused for a moment. The implication was clear enough but there was no harm now in laying bare what she was asking. "In case anyone is captured..."

Gabriel nodded, then ran a distracted hand back through his hair: "Tara, what do you mean you had a message for this Lord Carnage?"

"I... I took it to the wedding. I hoped, I don't know, to recognise him maybe, or find a sign. But I lost it," she said, feeling a queasy lurch at the admission. "I just need you to find me a name. That's all. I will do the rest."

"That's all? I'm sure Thurloe has been trying to find your Lord Carnage for years without success."

"I'm desperate, Gabriel. I wouldn't ask if I wasn't."

He was quiet for an inscrutable time and she waited patiently for him to assess the risks against any meagre benefit. Finally, he turned back: "I'm a soldier Tara, I stay clear of the whispers and gossip of court, but that doesn't mean I don't hear it. I have some contacts. I'll find him. I'll make arrangements to meet your Lord Carnage in London this week and pass on your message."

A deep recess in her mind prompted memory of the hunting trip to the Weald he had agreed to attend with Thomas Belasyse. "But..."

"My only condition is that you stay clear," he interrupted. "I won't have you involved in this treason a moment longer. It's too dangerous."

"But-"

"I mean it Tara." His voice was firm. "You must swear you'll leave the entire exercise to me. I won't have you caught up in it. You leave the Sealed Knot behind."

There was no choice. She nodded, and her frown was cut off by his sudden kiss. The corners of his mouth were twitching as he pulled back. "Although before servicing your traitorous inclinations, I must see to my stomach. I'm going to the kitchen. Are you hungry?"

She nodded abstractly, surprised at the ease with which his plan was formulated yet unwilling to quibble over the details. She knew what she was asking; any sane man would avoid the task completely, let alone a decorated commander of the New Model Army. She watched as he pushed himself off the bed, facing her as he pulled his shirt on over his head. *So I don't see his back*, she realised, and an uncomfortable tenderness returned in her chest, at odds with the vital warrior before her.

The shirt barely conformed to the dictates of modesty, covering him in opaque fabric to mid-thigh, falling open at the neck. If she was the one padding about the dark corridors, Ann would be traumatised. Powerful legs were visible and there were shadows where the gentle curve of muscle began at the top of his chest. Unbidden, a restless heat pulled her to stand without speaking and trace the lines of his body with her fingertips, no more able to keep from touching him than stop herself breathing.

He dropped back on the bed, taking her astride his lap. She was conscious of the mattress depressing and then little else as he kissed her deeply, his long fingers sliding back the loose hair behind her ears. He pulled back an instant to hold her gaze with a darkened intensity. "Tara, whatever happens now, know that I-"

"Sssh," she whispered, nipping at his bottom lip with a grin. "I'm starving."

33. THE MESSAGE

"Get up, sweet slug-a-bed, and see
The dew bespangling herb and tree!
Each flower has wept and bow'd toward the east
Above an hour since, yet you not drest…"

Gabriel opened one eye warily as Tara clambered onto the bed and swung her leg over to sit astride him in her shift. She carried halved plums in each hand and the juices splattered on his bare chest as she declaimed with a smile. He regarded her for a thoughtful moment before snapping to wakefulness and flipping her over on to her back, provoking the yelp of astonishment he'd come to enjoy.

"*Nay! Not so much as out of bed?*" he picked up the thread of Herrick's poem, a mischievous grin spreading across his features as she laughed. "*When all the birds have matins said, And sung their thankful hymns, 'tis sin…*" He bowed his dark head and kissed her then, tasting the ripe fruit still sweet upon her lips. Her hands still held aloft his breakfast and the juices were running down her outstretched arms. "*…Nay, profanation…*" he licked at the drops as they meandered across her pale skin and smiled at the rash of goose bumps rising in the wake of his tongue, "*…to keep in…*"

He nuzzled her neck until her head tilted back to give him better access to the delicate skin on her throat. Her legs hugged around his waist, thighs tightened in anticipation of his entering. "*Whereas a thousand virgins on this day…* Hell's teeth, what's next?" His eyebrows furrowed as she giggled. "I've forgotten the damned line! What do the virgins do?"

"Cousin!" A fist hammered on the door to the bedchamber, with sufficient vigour to threaten the small collection of miniatures hanging on the walls. "Gabe!"

"*Now?*" Gabriel barked in response. Poised above her, he hung his head and she laughed, running her sticky fingers back through his hair, the plums long since dropped onto the floorboards. He raised an eyebrow: "Dear God, man, really?"

The disembodied voice started more apologetically: "I know you've guests still asleep but Ann said Tara was up already. He's blasted found us, cousin! I don't know how! He writes for settlement. I must show you now."

"Remember this was your idea." Gabriel muttered wryly to Tara, rolling his eyes before pushing himself reluctantly off the bed with a grumpy grunt and swiping his breeches from the floor.

To his intense frustration, Gabriel spent considerably longer calming his anxious cousin than Rupert took to convey the details of the Marquis de Clapiers' demands in the first place. By the time he returned, Tara was still on the bed, her shift still loosely covering her body, but she was now wholly absorbed by a piece of parchment on the mattress before her. She'd balanced a jar of ink between the pillows and found a quill pen from somewhere, one sufficiently sharp to begin writing, and she scribbled industriously.

She looked up at the depression of the mattress, her eyes bright: "Is everything alright?"

He nodded and kissed her forehead as he moved the inkpot to a more secure spot on the bedside table: "Your dastardly plans are coming to fruition, 'tis all. I'll tell you later. What's all this?"

"Look." She held out the parchment to him. On it, she'd scribbled workings and crossings out in the margins of a careful transcription:

αLCαcmpαbmarepnαagvpwcαlycαfcdvyiibαewαryαxfevjyiαφ

He frowned: "Your missing message? How?"

"I made a copy, before the wedding. I'm not a complete novice remember." She shrugged a small smile and the open neck of her shift slid off her shoulder, the skin still flushed pink as if it retained his heat.

He shifted uncomfortably and reluctantly dragged his gaze to the letters for a while, scanning dutifully for reason or pattern. "It's a cipher."

"Oh, really? I had no idea," she remarked dryly. He raised an eyebrow before looking back at the figures. "Can you read it?"

"No. We use them to communicate in the army. It's a common enough trick to write a message like this, but a damn site harder to read one without the tabular key."

She frowned and he fought an urge to smooth away the furrows in her brow. Instead, he pulled across a fresh sheet of parchment and took the quill gently from her fingers, quickly sketching out a table containing two sets of the letters of the alphabet.

"Look. In its simplest form, assuming it's a Caesar Cipher, it's very easy to crack." He wrote out "RNWO" by way of demonstration and she flicked her eyes between the letters in the columns.

"PLUM," she laughed.

"That's right. You simply move along the same number of letters each time. The key was two."

She pulled forward her own message again for a comparison and frowned. "But this one?"

"The good news for your rebels is this one looks impossible. Even on the dance floor of Hampton Court, your message is safe. The writer has dragged the message through any number of tables, different alphabets even, probably using different keys for vowels and consonants. This was written for only one reader: Lord Carnage has the key." He considered it again and smiled a moment: "But I can top and tail it for you. My first guess would be that "LC" stands for our mystery man."

"What about the Greek, these figures are Greek aren't they?"

Gabriel tipped his head to the side: "Are you seriously telling me you can understand Old English but not Greek?"

"We had a limited library at Weycroft," she started defensively: "And I preferred the adventures of Beowulf to the dirges of Linus."

"Ha, you always were a would-be warrior. Well, it looks more complicated but that's actually the easy bit." His head bent forward over the paper. "You see the sigma?"

She nodded, folding her arms to prevent herself pushing back his hair and burying her face into his neck, inhaling the scent of him.

"It's just a Greek 'S'. I'd wager that stands for a 'space' between words. The message starts with an alpha, an 'A', to make it clear that it is the beginning and ends with a zeta, 'Z'. That way, our Lord Carnage can be sure he's got the whole thing." He paused a moment, before adding: "I suspect that the writer tagged on the phi for good measure just because it looks sufficiently like-"

"Like a sealed knot," she finished quietly.

* * *

"I'm beginning to wonder if this was a good idea," said Tara quietly to herself, eyes narrowing as Gabriel finally loaded the pair of pistols on the kitchen table.

The ritual had been painstaking and time consuming. After near enough five full days in the Weald with Belayse's hunt, the weapons needed careful cleaning. So had the man who bore them. She watched the muscles in his forearms tense as he checked the weight of the pistols in his hands and warmth flooded her chest as she remembered the slippery, oiled feel of his limbs when he finally returned late last night.

There were advantages to living amongst the modern conveniences of Ham House. The bathroom was one of these and she'd led him there by low candlelight without speech, stripping him almost immediately, demanding heavy proof in her hands that he was still hers. At first amused, his eyebrow raised wryly at her careful inventory of new scrapes and bruises. But as she washed his hair clean, he was soothed by her attention. She made him sit still in the barrel-like bath while she took a self-indulgently long time to draw the steam over his skin, filthy from camping and exertion, until finally, driven beyond any possibility for patience or control, he rendered her fastidious attempts to erase all physical traces of the hunter futile. With a primal demand he lifted her astride him in the water, devouring her flesh as if she were one of the beasts on the hunt.

Later, in the candlelight of his chamber, his possession had felt different again. He kissed her deeply, stealing her warm breath for his own life, as if he was trying to claim her very soul for spoils. She ached in places she hadn't thought possible, but his touch was shot through with exquisite tenderness and care, as if every second might be their last. And here he was again preparing to fight. Impulsively she moved behind him, laying a spontaneous kiss on the top of his head and inhaling the scent of tea tree oil released by her lips.

"*My whore*." Across the table, Rupert's long fingers teased the edges of a well-thumbed note. He re-read aloud the clear demand, written by a deliberate hand: "'*The Waterman's Arms, 19 June, 9 p.m. My whore owes me.*' He actually dares say that: *my whore*. Marie is my *wife*."

He stretched back, his dishevelled mop of blonde curls as thick as Gabriel's and loose about his shoulders. Ann bustled past collecting empty coffee mugs and tssked loudly at the improper use of the furniture for weapons cleaning, muttering under her breath about reckless invitations to bad luck and the unsurprising loss of the silver candlesticks from the dining room with all the comings and goings. Rupert was impervious; he lifted large feet onto an empty chair and yawned, the smooth naked skin on his chest patterned with the late afternoon sunshine that poured in through the kitchen door.

"Am I boring you, Rupert?" asked Gabriel, his attention unwaveringly on the matchlock mechanism of his primed pistol. Check, recheck and check again. He strapped a short length of match to the barrel, so one end reached the pan, and Tara frowned momentarily. This was all suddenly very real.

"I'm sorry," Rupert replied blankly. "Stress makes me sleepy."

"Perhaps if Marie had spent more time *asleep*." Gabriel muttered sardonically, catching sight of the pained expression crossing his cousin's childlike face and feeling a pang of remorse. Love could be found in all manner of strange places, perhaps it was not so unlikely in a bawdy house. Besides, he knew enough of soldiering to know that fear affected men in as many different ways as there were men to start with. The consternation in his features relented: "Forgive me, that was uncalled for."

The younger man shrugged without rancour and rubbed a weary hand over his face. It looked older in the half-light, trace worry lines ruling his forehead. "I'm sorry to drag you into this, Gabe. We'll pay you back, every last penny."

"God's blood, as if I care about the money, Rupert. But the Marquis de Clapiers is a violent man. I'll go to Putney and pay off the debt but if you insist on coming with me, you must be prepared to fight. You would fight, cousin?"

Rupert's response barely skipped a beat. His smooth skin rippled and he stood up suddenly alert, leaning forward onto the table, his eyes fixed on Gabriel's to impress the extent of his commitment. "For Marie, I would die."

Gabriel nodded seriously. "Then for God's sake, get dressed and fetch Donn. We leave in an hour."

* * *

The swarthy publican put a bulky arm across the bottom of the staircase, looking them up and down with barely veiled suspicion: "They'll 'ave my licence at the next quarter sessions if there's one more garboil within these walls. I'll not be 'aving trouble, tonight, sirs."

"The Marquis' thoughts exactement." A large, bald Frenchman behind descended past the gatekeeper, a hand out for swords and pistols. Gabriel held his snapsack aloft, the canvas heavy with the demanded payment, as he was patted down for hidden weapons in the folds of his breeches or doublet. Rupert sustained the same manhandling, raising a querying look that his cousin pointedly ignored as the last small blade was spotted and extracted from the top of his boot.

"Be careful with that. It's sharp," said Gabriel, earning a snort from the Frenchman before he nodded at the publican in dismissal and ushered them up the stairs to a private second floor dining room.

In the darkness of the panelled room, the Marquis was waiting for his settlement at a small table, dimly lit by candlelight that diffused above his head in a plume of tobacco smoke. Under controlled waves of brown hair, his dark features were long and neat, and his eyebrow arched as they entered. Five heavyset guards posed, brooding, about the room and Gabriel motioned to Rupert to stay back as he approached the table and removed his hat, carefully placing it with the snapsack in front of the Marquis, taking in the primed pistol laid casually on the board, the barrel pointing straight at him.

"*Je suis Gabriel Moore, Earl of Denby. Cet homme est mon cousin, Rupert Godolphin.*"

Slowly, Gabriel loosening the drawstring neck of the canvas bag and pulled out a bound wad of notes, placing it down on the table and spreading his fingers in the international language of supplication: "*Parlez vous Anglais?*"

Clapiers took a leisurely drag on his tobacco pipe and emitted smoke from his nostrils. He met Gabriel's eye in cool challenge. "*Non.*"

"No matter. We will speak the same language, for now," replied Gabriel mildly in French. "There are notes to the value of five pounds sterling in each bundle. And here," he went on, pulling out a small purse of coins, placing it carefully down next to the paper, "are bags of counted coins, two pounds sterling to a bag-"

"I know you by reputation, sir. I can trust the Earl of Denby not to shortchange me."

It was Gabriel's turn to shrug while the acrid smoke swirled around his head: "You're a businessman and this is a simple transaction. I don't take offence in counting. The stakes are high; let us be straight with one another."

The Marquis nodded and flicked back an errant lock of hair over his shoulder: "Then there is no harm in it. Go ahead."

"Can I trust you, monsieur?" Gabriel was slowly creating neat piles from the small bags of clinking cash. He paused a moment and cocked his eyebrow: "When I leave you to this bounty, can I be sure that you won't threaten my family again?"

Clapiers thought for a moment, rubbing his naked chin and smoothing down a moustache along his top lip. He exhaled a heavy white cloud and leant forward to speak quietly: "This sum secures release from her contract. But, since we will be straight with one another, Marie was extremely popular amongst my more important associates. At first they simply couldn't resist the tightness of youth but by the time that gave way she had more than enough tricks to keep them coming."

Gabriel's features remained impassive but there was sufficient lewd insinuation on the Frenchman's face that Rupert started forward, swearing.

One of Clapiers' man immediately grabbed at his arms from behind and the Marquis waited until the grip tightened before letting loose a loud stream of French disdain: "Can you smell them on her, boy? Pah! I can barely look at you, boy, knowing the men she has fucked before you. How does it feel to know you cannot hope to satisfy her? How would it feel if I told the world her dirty little secrets?"

"Fucking lobcock, I'll kill him," Rupert hissed at Gabriel's back in English.

"Oh, I should say there is more chance of your wife rediscovering her virginity," Clapiers laughed, clearly understanding the tenor of the threat. "Never mind. Two dogs will never agree about one bone. Earl of Denby: put a leash on your pup."

Gabriel threw a brief warning glare over his shoulder so that Rupert reluctantly stilled, and then, returning to the task in hand, resumed his steady withdrawal of the jangling money bags. "Monsieur, I do not see what relevance there can be in her past clientele."

Clapiers put his head on one side and eyed Gabriel thoughtfully. "It means that she knows a little of the indelicacies around my business."

"Is not your entire business indelicate?" asked Gabriel with a good-natured shrug.

The Frenchman snorted. His eyes narrowed as he considered his pistol on the table, before shaking his head with a regretful grin. "I hear you're worth more to Cromwell than your fortune, sir. And I suspect you understand well enough already that some certain parts of my activities are even more indelicate than others. In fact, I am thrilled to finally meet you, Earl of Denby. I have always thought that we could come to a mutually beneficial arrangement, you and I…"

"Forgive me," interrupted Gabriel mildly. "But just so I've lost nothing in translation: Marie Godolphin will never be truly free of you?"

Clapiers taped his pipe on the table with a frustrated hiss. The smouldering fire had extinguished and Gabriel lifted the candle to offer fresh flame to the tobacco. The Marquis grunted as he manoeuvred his pipe to be relit and sucked quick puffs to drag the heat through the dried leaves, until the smoke began again. "You have terminated her contract. But I may need periodically to remind her to hold her tongue… or to ask her assistance in loosening another's. I will not ask her to spread her legs, unless of course she wants to-"

"And when that time comes," Gabriel's features hardened and the candle poised mid-air. "What of my cousin?"

The Frenchman stroked his chin again, confident as he surveyed Rupert's tense form, still held firm by a bodyguard: "*Qui vole un oeuf, vole un boeuf.*" Once a thief, always a thief.

"I did not steal her from you, you blasted-" cried Rupert, struggling momentarily but tailing off when he caught Gabriel's dark stare.

Clapiers shrugged placidly and turned his attention to the growing mound of cash in front of him. He spoke in English: "Earl of Denby, as every good Frenchman knows: a strong thief deserves a strong halter. *A gros larron grosse corde.* I have the right to satisfaction. One of these nights I will castrate your pup."

A loud shot echoed around the room as Gabriel fired the pistol lying primed and hidden at the bottom of the snapsack. A small hole in the Marquis's forehead began, after a frozen heartbeat, to dribble a thin line of red downwards over the man's straight nose. It barely seemed more than a scratch at first but as he slumped heavily forward to the desk it was obvious that the bullet's exit had torn open a gaping chasm at the back of his head.

Shock momentarily disabled the man holding him and Rupert flipped up an elbow to jab his nose, once and then a second time as he faltered backwards. With a parting frown of confusion, the Frenchman crumpled to the floor and his colleagues backed up, hands raised as Gabriel grabbed the Marquis' weapon and swept it around the room.

"Rupert. Window."

There were muffled sounds of shouts from the bar below as Rupert darted to open the leaded casement, tentatively stretching a long leg out onto the roof tiles as heavy footsteps hammered on the stairs. The door flung open as Gabriel followed him out and the publican burst red faced into the room brandishing a cudgel.

"I fucking warned you lot this is a peaceful establishment!" he bellowed without irony. He swung instinctively as Gabriel leaned back in and threw a bag of coins towards him, the weapon bursting the bag and creating a heavy shower of gold pattering against the walls and furniture. The Frenchmen and the two locals, arriving into the room behind the publican, fell to their knees immediately, scrabbling to catch the glinting raindrops, as Gabriel and Rupert scrambled up and over the ridge of the building to its rear side, propelled along loose and shifting tiles by momentum and adrenalin. A terracotta slice slid away, and a distant smash echoed in the stable yard below.

"Jesus," hissed Rupert through gritted teeth as he sought to gain his balance on all fours, trying to peer over the edge of the roof. Donn was already mounted below, his red head luminescent in the light of the torches as he led Rowley and Rupert's horse towards the street. He cast his eyes up and nodded imperceptibly towards them. "There must be thirty airy feet of nothing beneath us. Gabe, I can't face heights!"

"Then don't look down," muttered Gabriel with a hint of exasperation before nudging away Rupert's knee with his boot. His cousin lost his balance entirely, dropping down with a terrified scream, blonde hair streaming above him like a halo, to land on the roof of a ground floor lean-to.

Gabriel cast his eyes down and frowned momentarily. The roof had succeeded in breaking his fall but Rupert's right foot had punched straight through the hatched covering. An escape would be more challenging if he was hurt and Donn clearly entertained the same concern as he reined in the skittish lurch of his horse. No. *Thank God.* Rupert's voice rose, cursing loudly with irritation rather than pain as he yanked out his heel from the thatch and slid down to the cobbles unharmed.

Satisfied, Gabriel quickly pulled himself back up to peer over the ridge. He grimaced as the publican marched out through the front porch, accompanied by a few of the more motley-looking regulars. The man's cudgel was restored, pale wood picking up a shaft of moonlight as it swung urgently between his hands. Two others trained their pistols on the roof and Gabriel ducked, feeling the whistle of a musket ball disturb the air by his ear, too close for comfort. He flattened himself onto the tiles.

"*Go!*" He hissed back down at Donn, who obeyed the order without hesitation, kicking his heels into his mount and yanking Rowley's head into line. Rupert shot an uncertain glance towards the roof but his horse had started and he followed hard on Donn as they escaped the yard with a clattering that faded as they turned the corner into the street outside.

There was a moment's silence to breath before the ultimatum: "Come, whoreson! You've killed the Louis Baboon under my roof. You'll answer to the law, or we'll shoot you down!"

34. SPRINGING SOONER THAN THE LARK

It was well past midnight when she heard the dogs barking in welcome and felt the tentacle squeezing her chest loosen its irascible grip. Hooves clattered into the stable yard. *He's home.* She glanced at Marie with a grin and stood to leave the kitchen, where they had kept vigil together since dark, buoyed by Ann's hot coffee if not her frosty manner.

The Frenchwoman paused by the door and put a light hand on her arm: "Rupert and I will find some way of thanking your husband. He has made it possible for us to be together without looking over our shoulders. Tonight, I am hoping that you will find some way of showing him how important that is."

"I will," Tara promised quietly, the lead weight in her stomach lurching as her mind raced to the hours of darkness ahead, when she would mould her flesh safely to his.

The night air was humid and she smiled as she crunched along the gravel path towards the stables. Rupert was already coming towards her. A slight limp perhaps, but nothing more; it might have been tiredness alone. She picked up her pace though the archway to the vegetable garden and caught glimpse of Donn in the yard, heaving the saddle off Rowley. Rupert caught her elbow as she moved to pass around him.

"Come inside," he said, breathing heavily.

"Why?" she started, uneasy, but Rupert had embraced Marie, who relaxed against him only a second before realising that something was wrong.

"*Quel est le problème?*" she muttered as Rupert quickly took her hand and led back to the kitchen, urging back over his shoulder: "Please, Tara, come inside, I'll explain."

Donn caught up with them as they entered, still panting hard. He stood awkwardly beside Rupert, their backs to the empty kitchen grate and heads hanging low like cowed schoolboys waiting for a beating. She turned on them both before the door closed: "Where's Gabriel?"

"We left him on the roof of The Waterman's Arms," started Rupert clumsily.

Tara almost laughed at the ridiculousness of the confession. "The roof? And there isn't a ladder between Putney and Ham? Why did you leave him on the bloody roof?"

"Oh Milord wouldna have had much difficulty overcomin' that inconvenience," said Donn hurriedly, "Notwithstanding the pistols."

"*Pistols?* So, notwithstanding your blind faith in his ability to fly, someone was also shooting at him?"

Rupert nodded, shifting his weight. "Yes, but only until they decided to have him arrested for breach of the peace. No-one could find the night watchman, so the publican sent men with word to Colonel Huson's company quartering at Putney for a sergeant. Donn and I waited to find out whether they'd take him back to the barracks or let him go, since Huson's is an Irish regiment and we thought there was a good chance someone there would know him and smooth things over-"

"Smooth *what* over?" She demanded, briefly distracted by a nagging strand of narrative, but she batted it away. "No, tell me later. Where the Hell is he?"

"Milady, he came down when the carriage arrived to fetch him, so he did, but it wasna sent by Huson. It belonged to John Thurloe-"

"They've taken him to the Tower," Rupert finished and Marie exhaled with a French expletive.

"*Oh God.*" The air was too close. Tara dragged in a couple of deep breaths as she spun slowly around, trying to think, but her lungs were forced tight against the constraints of her stays and her limbs were slow to do her bidding. In the low light, the colours faded before her eyes and she had the strange sensation of sinking underwater. The kitchen was a claustrophobic ship's cabin then, submerged beneath the turmoil of the waves, a metallic shine from cook's pans glinting like treasure through the gloom. Her legs felt rubbery. She was a mermaid after all. *Thurloe knew*. The spymaster wouldn't involve himself in petty blackmail and brawling. He knew what she'd asked. She'd sung to Gabriel and lured him to his death.

"Milady!" Donn caught her as she fell forward, reaching blindly for the edge of the table, and he took her weight until he could awkwardly let her sink to her knees. He dipped onto his haunches beside her, brows furrowed in concern at the sight of her face, deathly pale in the shadows. "Mr Godolphin, sir, will ye you help me take Milady up to her chamber?"

"Of course," Rupert said, jumping to the task and winding her arm around his neck.

"I'll have Ann fetch smelling salts," offered Marie, leaving the kitchen ahead of them.

"No." Tara appealed directly to Donn. "I'm going to the Tower."

"Absolutely not!" Rupert laughed suddenly, bracing his good leg to take her weight. "It's a misunderstanding, nothing more... don't worry. Clapiers was a vicious brute, but Gabe didn't look overly concerned. He'll be out by morning and Thurloe will be wondering what all the fuss was about."

"Ye canna be doing such," agreed Donn. "Milord told me, before we found the Frenchman: whatever happens I'm to keep ye close."

"Oh God, he told you that too, didn't he?" she flashed at Rupert, finally seeing through his and Marie's relentless and enthusiastic company while Gabriel was away hunting. "He told you to nursemaid me while he went to the Weald?"

Donn interrupted to save Rupert from embarrassment. "He fair ordered that ye stay put here, so he did."

"*Ordered?*" she replied, raising an eyebrow. Her strength came slowly back and she batted off Rupert's well-meaning hold, pulling herself up with the table. "Rupert, you've clearly damaged your leg, you need to rest. Donn, short of tying me to the kitchen board here you can't stop me leaving. And if you can't beat me?"

Donn grimaced, shaking his head as he contemplated his options. "I'll join ye. Although Himself'll be havin' my guts to string that wretched fiddle."

* * *

Tara paced impatiently while Donn watered the horses. She selected three sharp-looking rapiers from the sword chest in the chequered hall and, virtually as an afterthought, packed some bread and cheese for the ride. She filled three water bottles and forced in the wooden stoppers. The practicalities sustained her for a half hour or so, before she stormed out into the freshness before dawn.

It took three hours to get to the Tower, only to be informed by a supercilious guard that the prisoner had already been transported on to Whitehall. She left with some reluctance after trying again, pointlessly, to see Eddie. The pass to see her uncle had been revoked almost as soon as it was granted. Lunchtime crowds made traversing Thames Street difficult and they inched towards the centre of government lost in their own thoughts. When they made it to the main gate, all Tara could think of was the woman on her knees outside Cromwell's office, in the rain, a month ago, when it all began.

"State your business, Ma'am, if you would." For all the crisp smartness of his uniform, this new guard had a kindly, gossipy air.

"I'm looking for Gabriel Moore."

"Commander Moore?"

"You know him?"

"You'll not find a soldier in London who doesn't, Ma'am. He's a hero-"

"He's here?" she interrupted testily. "Have you seen him today?"

The guard's eyes narrowed: "Who wants to know?"

"I do!"

"Was he supposed to meet you here?"

She glared at him.

"Ah, I see." The man shifted uncomfortably, casting his eyes towards a corner of Horse Guards Yard opposite, where a handful of women wore gaudy silks with a listless air of hopelessness. He looked around him to find his colleague waving some lewd sign language at one of the women.

"What? What do you see?"

"Look I don't mean to get a man trouble with his... mistress, Heaven forfend, what with you being a nice-looking lady and all, but I'm thinking that you fair slipped his mind. He's an important man and it'd be fair to say he was in the manner of being... preoccupied."

Tara's patience finally snapped. She felt it twang like an overwound string and her fists trembled: "God's wounds, have you seen him or not? Is he here?"

"The Commander was here for a while this morning but he left on foot about two hours ago. He wasn't armed, which struck me fair odd it did, as to be honest with you he looked a bit worse for wear. No doublet. Bit of blood. But he walked out all casual, like, chatty even. Said he was off home, said he had to say goodbye to his wife."

Tara was barely conscious of sinking to her knees. Donn's arm came about her waist, hoisting her awkwardly back to standing and the horses as he joked to the guard about the futility of empty-headed romance.

* * *

From the riverside, it was still a surprise, this house. You came across it without warning, sitting placidly amongst tall trees in overgrown fields. Walking distance from London, just, and yet a million miles from the chaos and clutter of the city's streets. Further still from the underground labyrinth of the Tower. He took a deep breath.

Donn. He nodded to the man in acknowledgement as he approached, his eyes narrowing as a second figure chased him along the curled gravelled entrance.

Tara? Wordlessly, he buried his face in her neck and lifted her free of the tall grass as Donn doubled back. She was shaking and he tightened his arms around her. Feeling her body relax against him, he laid a gentle kiss on her hair and carried her silently home, savouring the feel of her weight safe in his arms while he could.

"Rupert?" He asked over her dark head as they came into the entrance hall to find Donn and Ann waiting.

"Last seen headin' out a few hours back," said Donn, carefully. "Took the Lady Godolphin with him an' no doubt now sittin' exactly where ye told him to."

"Good." Gabriel nodded at Donn's frown and the groom left to head to the stables. "Wortley?"

"Gone, sir." Ann smiled with relief as he turned to her. "He took his things and went in the night. Good riddance, if you ask me, snarling little weasel of a man, wretched hobnailed chuff, good for nothing raggabrash..."

Tara wriggled reluctantly out of his arms as Ann went to set the kettle on. She lifted a hand to brush back his hair and stroke his damaged cheek, breath hitching as she saw the fresh blood on the collar of his shirt. His hazel eyes were creased at the corners from the housekeeper's vitriol but she bit her tongue; there were more important things to discuss than the disappearance of Bulstrode Wortley.

"Bastard has been driving me wild all day," he muttered, sitting down heavily and pulling off his right boot with a distracted hiss. A small sharp stone fell with a ping into the tiles and she waited impatiently to see if he was talking about the stone or the spymaster.

"I came to London, to find you—"

"I told Donn to keep you here," he frowned.

She raised an eyebrow: "You thought he'd be able to? Thurloe... what—"

He took her hand and kissed it thoughtfully, before leading her upstairs into the sitting room and pouring a large measure of whiskey from the sideboard. Ann arrived with a raised eyebrow and a hot coffee to deposit by its side, and he watched her leave before motioning to Tara to sit and recounting the interrogation.

Thurloe had cells set aside on the first floor of the Tower but when the bone-rattling carriage arrived in the middle of the night, two burly guards bundled the prisoner straight down into its black underworld. He was jostled roughly along from behind, his hands shackled behind his back. The Norman builders who had dug out the cellars had been no respecters of stature, but it occurred obliquely to Gabriel, as he ducked to follow the same passage Tara had trodden not two months earlier, that Thurloe's preference for rooms above ground had nothing to do with ceiling height. The chilling walls beneath had soaked up the pain and fear of five hundred years and ghosts seemed to cling to the shadows.

He shivered involuntarily as they came to an empty cell and pushed him inside, with a controlled shove in the small of his back. One of the guards dissolved immediately but the other lit the single sconce before slamming the heavy door shut. There was no turning key though; it remained unlocked. Not yet under arrest, then. He paced a while, waiting, then finally took a seat on a stool beside a small wooden bench, his back to the door, and sat alone in the gloom for some inordinate time until it opened again.

"Good morning." Thurloe moved around the table to face him with a grim, almost apologetic smile: "Do forgive the manner of my fetching you. I wanted to talk to you alone, and in private. Firstly, I must pass on the Lord Protector's personal gratitude for the delivery of the French spy. The Marquis de Clapiers has been known to me for some time, of course, but I must admit I was impressed that you found him holed up in Putney."

"He was not exactly discreet," said Gabriel coolly.

"Hmpfh! Well His Highness is pleased to have him removed without the need for some elaborate assassination. The French are trying his patience; we are losing faith in the alliance. It's been a hard-enough sell to a country schooled in suspicion and mistrust. Very resourceful of you to make it look like a common or garden brawl..."

"He threatened my family," said Gabriel quietly.

"Still, quite the body count considering you are no longer at war, assuming we add Tollemache's bulk to your little peacetime pile." Thurloe scratched vigorously at the back of his hand and gave Gabriel a second to confirm his guess, shrugging at the silence. "Our Major General is a little too old fashioned for this modern world. After that unpleasantness with your wife, it would be completely understandable were you to have helped him shuffle off his mortal coil."

The spymaster linked his hands behind his back and paced the limited width of the dark room uneasily, his large forehead picking up flickers of the candlelight. He almost seemed nervous.

"Do you mean to charge me with murder, Thurloe?"

"No." Thurloe shook his head. "I mean to give you a chance. Cromwell has some residual faith in your loyalty and while treason is most despicable in the hearts of those closest to him, I know that you loved him once and may love him yet. You have one chance to be useful before I tell him exactly who you are."

"You'll have to elaborate," said Gabriel calmly.

"Your wife is a traitor."

"Nonsense." He snorted dismissively.

"She was schooled at the knee of Gregory Villiers and his zealous brother... Even under your roof she now makes violent plans for Charles Stuart and uses her wiles to goad men to action."

"My wife is tender-hearted. She still grieves for her brother and her parents and is preparing now to mourn her uncle. She is understandably melancholic at present. Nothing more." His head tipped slightly as he added with a small smile: "And as to her wiles, they are a matter solely between husband and wife."

"Liar!" Thurloe's temper flared without warning and he slammed his fist on the table, the rush of air from his sudden petulant outburst playing on his captive's hair. "Careful, Commander. I know you have been loyal on the field of battle but remember a fish breathes destruction if out of his element. You're in my world now... in His Highness' world."

With the slightest movement of air across the candle flame, Gabriel was aware of the door opening quietly behind him. Heavy boots stopped just inside the cell and Gabriel remained stock-still, resisting the urge to turn and face the man directly. Thurloe looked up with the shadow of a deferential nod but there was no overt acknowledgement that Oliver Cromwell had stepped wordlessly inside. Still the atmosphere changed, heightened with the stakes at play before the most important spectator in the country.

After a long moment of silence, Gabriel raised an eyebrow and eyed the spymaster with a bland stare. "Is not His Highness a key proponent of habeas corpus? If there are to be charges against me or my wife, I would hear them."

"She has sent messages to members of the Sealed Knot, she stopped an uprising," Thurloe's small black eyes flicked over his captive's face, scanning for evidence of guilt.

Gabriel looked him unblinkingly in the eye but the corner of his mouth twitched suddenly and he couldn't resist pointing out the obvious. "I thought you said she was guilty of inciting violence."

"This is not a laughing matter," snapped Thurloe, spinning about and turning away in frustration. "Is that what you think of me? That I trade in jokes and fancies?"

"Truth be told, I don't think of you at all," said Gabriel coolly. "But fine, let us pretend for a moment this is not as ridiculous as it sounds. Come then man, what exactly am I to have done at her bidding?"

"You met with a man at the top of the Sealed Knot in London this week, to pass on a message. Beneath my very nose! Did you think the stench of your betrayal would not reach me?" Gabriel made a contemptuous snorting sound but said nothing, waiting for Thurloe to reveal his whole hand. "I want his real name, this Lord Carnage. Who is he? I want all their names."

"I imagine you do." Gabriel nodded, indicating that the demand sounded entirely reasonable.

"So, tell me," said Thurloe impatiently.

"I *can't*."

"You know the pretender's invasion depends on securing the passage for ships. With access to this Lord Carnage, I can flush out the rabble-rousers in every port in the country. We've destroyed his fleet but cannot suppress news of the destruction any longer. The Spanish always re-group. I'll find the remnants of the Sealed Knot traitors now before they go to ground. With or without you. And when I find them…" Thurloe scratched again at his neck and drew a weary hand over his face. He raised an eyebrow as he contemplated Gabriel, ready to try a new tack. "One way or another the Sealed Knot will be brought down; would you burn with it? This is your chance. Are you comfortable, sitting there and telling me Tamara Villiers is some innocent ingénue?"

"I wouldn't say comfortable, exactly," replied Gabriel dryly, rattling his hands still behind his back, so the chains clunked in the darkness.

The spymaster thought for a moment, flicking his eyes towards the Lord Protector before unlocking the manacles, flinching momentarily when Gabriel bought his arms forward and massaged tingling life back into his wrists and fingers.

"I appreciate that. But I can't help you."

"Perhaps you don't understand. This is not a negotiation." Thurloe brought his face down level to miss nothing of Gabriel's response. He was so close it would take no effort to reach out and capture the man's scrawny neck between firm fingers and squeeze. Gabriel forced his hands to lie loose on the table, unclenched. No good would come of attacking the man save providing a momentary salve to his anger. God's blood but it was tempting.

Thurloe glanced about the gloom and let his eyes settle on some old chains drilled into a wall. He moved towards them suddenly and ran long thin fingers across the iron manacles for good measure. "Of course, if I can't get what I want from you, I will have a discrete word with your lovely wife."

"You have a talent for the melodramatic, Thurloe, you must really miss the theatre. And I had thought you an enlightened man," Gabriel replied carefully.

"You'd prefer we discuss this in your own language? Guards!"

The door slammed open then with a heavy thud as two men strode in. One pulled back his arms and held him firm while the other punched hard, three, four, five times with impunity across his head and chest. He felt the scar on his cheek reopen and tasted the metallic tang of blood. His legs buckled when the air was forced up from his lungs and they stepped back, panting heavily, to leave him gasping on his knees.

"I want the names. I want the coded message your wife would deliver and I want the cipher." Thurloe's face was bent down into his, his stale breath teasing at the edges of the ragged wound on his cheekbone as he drew painfully at a lungful of sordid air.

One of the guards stepped forward at an unseen prompting to rifle roughly through his clothing. He pulled a wrapper out from Gabriel's breeches pocket and presented it to Thurloe with smug satisfaction, like a cat laying a disembowelled mouse at the feet of its mistress in anticipation of a saucer of cream. "Here, my Lord!"

"That is private," hissed Gabriel, spitting red saliva onto the floor before him as the guards dragged him to sit heavily back onto the stool.

Thurloe's face split into a cruel smile and he glanced up to catch Cromwell's eye before slowly unfolding the paper, savouring the moment. Nodding dismissal at the guards, he set it flat on the table between them. On it, Tara's neat hand declaimed, *"Whereas a thousand virgins on this day… spring sooner than the lark"* and Gabriel's chest lurched seeing it again. She'd slipped it inside his saddlebag before Thomas Belasyse's hunt, a lover's playful promise of fulfilment. It also couldn't be closer to the truth and Thurloe saw it too. He paled with the realisation that he had shot his bolt too soon and for a second there was silence.

"*Enough.*" Gabriel's voice had lowered to a growl and he looked up as the spymaster's triumphant grin faded. "Whatever intelligence you think you have is flawed. I have signed my loyalty to this regime and to the Lord Protector in blood, such that you, drawing your strands of whisper and accusation with quills, from the comfort of your desk, could not hope to understand. I will not tolerate this a moment longer."

He stood up suddenly, the action sending his stool clattering loudly to the floor. Standing, he towered above the Secretary of State and felt the twisting power balance in front of their silent, brooding audience: "I have spent the entire of the last week hunting in the Weald with the Lord Protector's new son-in-law. *Your* recommendation for the hand of his daughter, I believe."

He lent forward over the board, resting on his fingers. "I'm a reasonable man, for a soldier; I understand your fear might on some level justify this insult and inconvenience. But Thurloe, lay a finger on my wife, even so much as threaten her again and I will kill you."

* * *

"You seriously mean to tell me that you threatened to kill one of the most powerful men in England, within earshot of Cromwell, and then you just walked out of the Tower?"

Gabriel nodded. "In fact, Cromwell gave me his personal apology for Thurloe's behaviour and insisted I accompany him back to Whitehall for lunch."

"But Thurloe was right."

"I know."

"Someone was listening." She paused as she remembered her distraction. "But what if Thurloe finds some evidence of your passing my message to Lord Carnage?"

"That's not possible." His voice lowered as he turned to face the window. The screaming in his bones to pull her back against him would be nothing but a fleeting reassurance for either of them; there could be no safety tonight in his arms.

"Even you make mistakes Gabriel," she frowned. "You could have been followed, overheard... Whoever was watching us, that night, they may be biding their time to profit from it."

"No, Tara, it's genuinely not possible. Thomas Belasyse was also in Whitehall for lunch today. He vouched to Cromwell that I made no contact with anyone outside his very intimate gathering in the last week."

"Then Thurloe looks a complete fool..." She stared carefully. "But then how on earth did you deliver my message in London?"

"Do you remember at the wedding, when guards removed an elderly man while Cromwell spoke, during the masque?"

"Yes..." she said quietly, frowning. "Was *he* Lord Carnage?"

"No. He was Lieutenant-Colonel Edmund Stacy and he was hanged and quartered at Cornhill last Thursday." He paused while she sank down onto a chair, winded by the news of more executions. "Thurloe's men were watching you that day, Tara. If you'd cast about asking questions or passing notes, you'd have been arrested too. I wasn't prepared to take the risk. I took the message from your pocket, during the reception."

"Why on earth didn't you tell me this before?" she asked quietly, starting to feel as if a door had been left open to intruders. "And how did you even know I had the message then?"

"You've forgotten who I am." His usually taciturn features betrayed an inner struggle and he took a step back, dragging his fingers through his loose hair. "I knew Edward Villiers was planning uprisings in the West Country. I took you to Exeter to learn how you communicate with the rebels. When the Mortenhampstead quack mentioned Lord Carnage... I've heard the name before in connection with the Sealed Knot. I guessed you had found something to give him."

"*Oh God...*" She stood and backed away from him, heart pounding as if she had woken into a bad dream. She wrapped her arms tightly around her chest as her mind raced ahead.

"We were getting close," he said quietly. "I thought you'd be forced to trust me sooner or later."

"And you wanted Thurloe to think he had something on you. Oh God, that night..."

He nodded.

"You *knew* someone was listening," she continued, shaking. "Wortley? You'd already stolen my message, so you knew that I was desperate... and when you could be sure I trusted you... you counted on me asking for help there and then so you could set the trap for Thurloe."

She took in his silent confirmation with a step further away from him, spinning around and breathing deeply to control her response.

"Tara, you need to calm down."

"Don't you dare-"

"Thurloe was a serious threat, to both of us," he interrupted. "He's been itching to pull me in for years. He knows that you're the key to Villiers' men. This was too good an opportunity to force his hand, but the intelligence had to be convincing. Killing that French spy-"

"The pimp Clapiers was a spy?"

"Yes. It gave him the chance to take the gamble hoisting me in. He couldn't keep his powder dry. Now Wortley's gone and Thurloe can't put doubt into Belasyse's words without putting doubt in his own judgement."

"A neat sleight of hand," she gave a hollow laugh, "focusing Thurloe's attention on the one week you have a watertight alibi."

"He'll leave us be for a while, at least until Villers' trial."

She flinched at the callousness of his summary. "There's no *us*."

Every single sinew and fibre in her wanted to scream. It wasn't just a minor card trick; it made smoke and mirrors of everything. That night... it was no more than an empty honeypot, designed purely to hold the prurient, sweaty attention of Bulstrode Wortley, to make sure he waited long enough to hear the words he was always supposed to take straight to Thurloe. Head turned by his attention, she'd spoken her script like a pathetic, lovelorn girl.

And worse, *a thousand times worse*, the lives of countless men depended on news of the double agent reaching the top of the Sealed Knot. Her uncle's men. *Her men*. She'd failed them, left them utterly exposed. It was only a matter of time until all their names were handed to Cromwell on a platter.

"Where is my message now?" she demanded, turning back to him. "Give it to me."

"It's over Tara. You need to let this go."

She raised a shaking hand as if to slap him but he caught her wrist, holding it firm. "*You utter bastard*. Those men, all those lives! *How could you?* You could have let me find another way. How could you see only an opportunity to save your own hide, to play your own games?"

His jaw tightened but his voice remained impassive. "Those men are not my priority."

"Your only priority is yourself." She made a contemptuous snorting sound, twisting away: "I... I *trusted* you. Do you mean to help Cromwell build the case against Eddie? Do you know the stakes-"

"Do I know the stakes? Hell's teeth, Tara, this is treason! I can't keep you safe if you're determined to march to the gallows-"

"How long until you deliver me there yourself?"

"I did this to protect you! I told you nothing will hurt you while I am here and I meant it," Gabriel stiffened and made a faint attempt to recapture her arm but missed. "Forget the message."

"Who the Hell are you?"

He looked at her, his face set into an impassive mask. "I'm the dead carcass you're chained to, until death do us part, remember? The rest is unimportant."

"The rest is *everything*," she started, backing away, incredulous, waving airily at the room: "This, all of this! It's all a lie."

He shrugged, downing his whiskey. "I had to make a choice... I told you I wouldn't love you."

Her voice when it came was remarkably calm, despite the pounding of her chest. "I never asked you to love me, Gabriel... after Ireland, after Neala Kielty... But you let me think Thurloe had arrested you for treason *because of me*. I thought you'd stand on the gallows, like my father, like... *because of me*. Christ's blood I thought I'd killed you. Only now, knowing how callously you'd condemn good men... now I wish I had."

A deep male voice interrupted the tension, yelling for the Earl of Denby, heavy footsteps on the stairs falling hard upon the exclamation. She looked at him a moment longer, green eyes narrowed as she took in his unreadable features, before pulling her emotions as tidily within her as she could and backed from the room, neatly dodging the breathless man who'd crashed in unannounced. He was closely followed by Ann, terse with irritation, and Tara passed them both unhindered. She headed for the stairs. Tears blurred her vision by the time she reached the bottom tread, but she paced steadily over the checkerboard hall and out of the house without looking back. ☐

35. MISSION BELLS

Her purse still held her personal stash of coins and notes. There was one advantage to marrying the Earl of Denby after all, she thought, breath hitching: she still carried practically every farthing she'd left home with less than a month ago. Hazy evening light seeped through the fenestrals and she lit a candle. Her eyes swept her small, bare room, the simple cot bed, the linen chest and the small table, and her fingers felt reflexively along her neck. She still had the jewellery he had given her before the wedding at Hampton Court.

She pulled out an earbob and laid it on her left palm, torn briefly between pride and poverty as the exquisite emerald flashed in the candlelight. Pride won. She looked around for something to wrap the jewels in, to get them safely back to Ham House in her absence. The second earbob fell out of her shaking fingers and rolled across the compacted earth floor, disappearing under the linen chest.

With a curse, she lent precariously over the knee-high storage, patting amongst the dust and detritus of the obscured corner to retrieve it, careful in case she inadvertently touched one of the mice that had scampered away like chaff in the wind when she'd opened the door. Her fingers had just made it out when a shadow fell, obscuring the candlelight. A figure loomed suddenly large behind her and hands came about her waist, pulling her back.

"Get off me! Never, ever, touch me again," she screamed, shaking her head as fingers clawed at her mouth to gag the noise. She forced her elbows back and kicked wildly at shins as she became airborne, taking advantage of a pained grunt to quickly twist, swinging at where his head ought to be. Her fist, carried by its own momentum, made contact with Jack's left eye before she could stop it and he released her immediately, bending over to clutch protectively at his face.

"God's wounds, sweeting," he hissed. "Goodwife Cooper came and swore she'd just seen you head towards your old cottage... I just thought to greet you, or whatever thief she'd taken for you. I didn't mean to have you screaming blue murder."

"Oh God, Jack, I'm so sorry!" She fell to her knees before him and cautiously brushed aside the loose blonde hair to peel back his fingers and assess the damage. The hair was darkened at the temples by sweat. He'd run to her from Butcher's yard. She smiled apologetically, watching the bruise bloom across the eye socket, his shocked pale blue irises standing out ever more clearly against the rising purple. "I didn't know it was you."

Jack winced as he peered sideways at her, taking in the changes. She'd clearly been crying, but that wasn't it, and the red rims of her eyelids left him unmoved. She looked different. Less fragile and more solid perhaps; a little thicker around the middle? Likely decent meals at the manor after all, he thought, but still, she seemed stronger generally. Time was she wouldn't have lashed out so instinctively.

"Time was, my sweeting, it wouldn't have been no other man." He stood up, adding softly. "You have to come with me."

She moved silently away at that, apparently engrossed in finding a clean rag to dab at the bloodied edges of the bruise, where her thumbnail had ripped the skin a little.

"You screamed when I embraced you. What did he do to you?" Jack asked quietly as she returned and Tara shook her head, frowning at his notion that being grabbed from behind might constitute an embrace.

"Nothing."

"Don't laugh at me. This isn't funny," he replied testily, lifting her face to look at him. "You were to all intent and purpose my wife. Must I be forced to stand idly by as you scream to the entire village that the sanctimonious lobcock in the big house has ravished you?"

"I did no such thing. And nor did he-" she started, before abandoning that line of argument for lost. Jack's clear blue eyes narrowed slightly, and his fingers pushed through her hair to hold her head fast as he bent to kiss her.

"Jack, no," she whispered, her fingers coming up to block his lips as gently as she could.

"What's the matter? Why won't you kiss me, sweeting? It is just us here. You're acting as though the walls have ears."

"The bed curtains do," she murmured dryly to herself, trying to pull away.

His expression changed then but his hold on her did not. Silence fell heavily between them, and she felt the need to fill it. "It's too late, Jack. We can't. It's over. I'm married."

"Really? What marvellous news! Pray tell... and do forgive my surprise, it's just that you've literally not told me a thing about it!" The sarcastic lilt was incongruous with his frozen smile and his fingers closed tighter, catching on her hair until he could pull her head back a little. Her hands went immediately to his wrists. "Was it a beautiful service?"

"Stop it, Jack, you're hurting me... I know how you feel. I... I felt it too. Please, I didn't ask for any of this."

"No, of course you didn't. Tamara, isn't it, these days?"

"No-"

"No, you ambled into it as innocent as a lamb." He tightened his fingers until she gasped at the sparks of pain across her scalp: "It's just that from what I hear, you barely bleated."

"Well now, this here looks like mighty fine craich, but I would be suggestin' to ye, Mr Ludlow, that if ye know what's good fer ye, ye'll be takin' yer hands of Milord's wife, so ye will."

Startled by the brogue, Jack took in the figure in the doorway with cold blue eyes. Donn wasn't large but his limbs were taut and tensed, ready for a fight. The Irishman whistled in amazement, his level tone doing nothing to mask the threat. "Sweet Jesus, man, lookin' at yer wee eye there, I canna help but be guessin' Milady has already done some damage. Ye should be off now gettin' some cold water on that. I'd be more than willin' to assist yerself to a nice paddle in the Thames to cool off."

"This isn't over," Jack muttered quietly, looking Tara in the eyes to enunciate the promise. Then he turned his scowl to Donn and pushed awkwardly past him out of the door.

"What the bloody Hell are you doing here?" she snapped immediately. She was shaking, trying not to feel the enormous relief that washed across her as Jack left. Something had changed in him, this man she had been prepared to love, honour and obey for the rest of her life.

"Ah, tis fine to see ye Donnacha," he said with a grin, Jack dismissed instantly from his mind as he ducked under a beam and perched on the top of the chest. "Sure I've been missin' your handsome features something terrible these last three hours."

"Has it been three hours? I've missed the last coach to London then," she said blankly, sinking to the chest beside him.

"Ye have," he confirmed, matter-of-factly. "But all's well that ends well, mind. An' I'd go so far as to mention, Donnacha, that I canna be waitin' so to get back to Milord's country pile, where the livin's so easy on all those downy, rope-strung mattresses."

Tara folded the rag she had used on Jack, setting it neatly on a stool, curing the delay. Every day wasted was another day Cromwell's spy was reporting on the rebels, on their plans and activities, their names and their families....

"I'm not going back to Ham House, Donn, you've had a wasted trip, unless you'd kindly take a small parcel to the house for me... I'm surprised though, I thought this time he would let me go, as if sending your groom, no offence, constitutes a serious attempt to stop me."

"Beggin' your pardon, Milady, but he's not tryin' to stop ye. He was called away on business. It's me that's come on here, without needin' tellin' from himself."

Tara steadied her features and waved in the direction of the door. "Well, thanks for, you know, with Jack. But since I now need to catch the early stage, I must get some sleep."

Donn nodded in understanding: "That's a grand plan, Milady. Only now ye've all night with no supper… Come with me. I'll see to it as ye'll get a fine evenin' meal an' I'll take ye to the stage first light if yer still wantin' to go. It's just as how there's somethin' yer needin' to see before ye leave us fer good."

"What is it?" she demanded.

"Like I said, yer needin' to *see* it," he replied amicably, undeterred by the frustration in her tone.

She looked at him impatiently and was struck afresh by the kindness in his eyes. They were ringed with faint lines of worry, she noticed: Gabriel really didn't know he was here, then, and she couldn't shake the impression that he probably wouldn't approve of whatever object Donn was going to produce. That alone was just enough to tip the balance in favour of curiosity. That and her stomach's traitorous grumble at the mention of food.

"Fine," she said finally, "But this had better be good."

Outside in the fading light, he had tied two horses to a low branch. She raised an eyebrow as he unhooked the reins, stroking the nose of the chestnut roan affectionately as it whinnied in greeting.

"This is a little presumptive," she remarked, eyebrow raised. "You didn't know I'd come with you."

Donn just chuckled, cupping his fingers to give her a foothold and launch her up onto the beast's strong back. She gathered the reins, realising momentarily how natural it now felt, compared to the time she had first perched nervously on its back. If there was really nothing else to take away from the last few weeks, she had accidently become a competent horsewoman.

"Aye, yer grand, so ye are," Donn said with a grin, reading her thoughts as he swung himself up onto his own saddle and reined away.

"Where are we going?"

"To get some supper," he said simply, gently turning his horse's head towards the main road to Kingston.

Donn would not be drawn on what it was she had to see and eventually

Tara gave up asking. Their horses fell into step and they lapsed into a companionable silence, as Donn gave her space to consider her plans. To Mortenhampstead, to warn the men. *But then what?* The Sealed Knot was missing a link without her uncle but even if he were acquitted, would he still be able to take up his role? Her belly lurched and she swallowed the truth she'd been denying for too long. There was a permanent break in the chain. If she could only find Lord Carnage, she could bridge the gap, control the men herself. They crossed over the Clattern Bridge in the direction of Thames Ditton, and the lamp lights of Kingston soon faded behind them.

"Suit ye for supper?" Donn cocked his head towards the Bell Inn, standing proud amongst a haphazard assortment of tumbledown shacks. Mosely?

"I suppose so," she replied warily, almost faintly surprised that Donn was still pursuing it, they'd passed any number of options. Still, she was hungry and doubtless he'd realised that whatever artefact he was poised to produce would be better received on a full stomach. As it turned out, the inn produced a very passable line in beef stew, and Donn waited patiently as she cleaned her plate, and downed the remnants of her ale.

"We'll be off now," he said, standing suddenly and picking up the candle. He took her hand, leading her past the indifferent landlord at the empty bar, and shut them both into a small, windowless back store room, putting the candle down on the racking that held rows of wine casks.

Tara frowned, "Serious-" but Donn clamped his hand across her mouth. He mimed the imperative of silence before pushing aside a filthy rug in front of the racking to reveal a cellar hatch set into the flagstone floor.

"Donn," she hissed in a low voice, playing the game but starting to feel markedly uneasy. "This is wearing a little thin. Why did we ride miles for supper and why we are we now padding about so hugger-mugger? Tell me now."

He paused for a moment, listening for footsteps outside the door. Finally satisfied, his toes tapped a rhythm on the heavy trap top. Tara watched incredulous but he received a muffled "Ho!" to indicate admission was granted. He then proceeded to pull it open and step down, half turning to offer a hand down rickety treads into a dimly lit cellar. Two candles gave little by way of illumination and she waited anxiously for her eyes to accustom to the gloom, holding her own breath when she sensed the inhale and exhale of several other bodies.

"Sir." Donn nodded and stepped aside to reveal the gathering to her, and her to the gathering.

There was a small wooden table still bearing the remnants of a hasty supper. A trencher held a half-demolished loaf and some cheese. Cups of ale looked to be randomly distributed and three chairs were pulled close. The men that occupied them were obscured by heavy dark clothing but opposite the door sat the unmistakable form of her husband. Low light flickered across his features and his brows furrowed first in confusion and then in anger as he saw her. He turned a furious glare at Donn who merely shrugged, apparently impervious, although from behind she could see his hands fluttering with nervousness.

"What is the meaning of this?" Hushed, indistinct whispers turned to Gabriel. "Who is this woman?"

"This is my wife." He said softly, addressing his companions but looking directly at her. "She's no threat, you have my word."

"What the Hell kind of dinner party is this? What's going on? Donn?" Tara turned back but he was gone, the thin strip of pale light afforded by the trap door extinguished.

The larger of his two companions thought a moment, before rising and attempting to bow with a courtly flourish. Hampered by the tight space, his right hand unsettled the trencher, and the figure opposite issued a deep sigh, steadying the candle.

"Welcome, Mrs Moore. I am Edward Hyde, Lord Chancellor." Lifting back his hood he inclined a plump face towards her, his chin fuzzed with the beginnings of whiskers that twinkled pale red in the flicking candlelight. The man was considerably older than she had first thought. He looked like a genial grandfather and smiled at her polite curtsey, given instinctively from a lifetime's habit notwithstanding that her brow furrowed. "Charlie's Lord Chancellor. You know he keeps a determined court in Flanders."

"What's going on–"

"Tara," interrupted Gabriel gently. She felt, rather than saw his defeat as he drew shaking fingers through his loose hair. "This is Lord Carnage."

Tara stared blankly for a moment, waiting for the features of a man to emerge from the shadows opposite Hyde. Instead a small, bird like face materialised from a heavy hood, a grin tugging at feminine lips. It was the same blonde-haired woman from the wedding: "The Duchess of Albemarle?"

The Duchess nodded with an exaggerated roll of her eyes: "Excuse the nomme de guerre, sweetheart. Edward does love an anagram."

"NAN Monck nee CLARGES," Hyde said, emphasising the words conspiratorially, as if that explained it. "It's not perfect but it does sound rather fearsome, enough to put the bloodhounds from the scent of our good lady here. It was certainly the best I could do in the time available."

"Speaking of which…" prompted Gabriel at the distant sound of church bells from Mosely village, "Nan must be back within the half hour."

Hyde sighed, the expelled air tickling the edges of his moustache so that it glimmered: "You're right, Gabriel. If we must dance to the tune of fortune, at least let us study the keeping of time. But still, must we call carriages just when things were getting interesting? The organisation and the King are eternally grateful for the warning Nan. It certainly makes sense that someone in our organisation has been running to Thurloe. Sir Richard Willys though? Are you sure of the source?"

"Willys has been betraying our plans to Thurloe for at least three years… since Penruddock…" Nan flicked her eyes to Tara: "And we have the horse's mouth here, as it were, no offence darling. The message comes from Villier's men in Devon, via his niece."

She realised then that Gabriel had passed on her message at the wedding, before she had begged for his help, before… she nodded at Hyde and the Lord Chancellor received the certainty of the news with an air of infinite sadness. "We are factious and fickle, like spoilt children. Little wonder we must turn to the damned Presbyterians for alliance."

"Before you go, Nan, what news of Lady Claypole?" asked Gabriel, changing the subject. "She wasn't at the wedding. Have you been able to see her?"

Tara's heart quickened. It was no secret that Cromwell's favoured child had interceded on behalf of a number of royalist prisoners. "She would speak for my uncle?"

Nan shook her head, pulling up her hood. "Elizabeth's still extremely ill; she's all but retired from court."

"Is there hope of a timely recovery?" Gabriel asked, practically. "The trial is set for the second of September."

"I don't know. The truth of it is that the physicians don't understand her case. She lost a babe in June; some say it's an ulcerated womb."

A line of tension had formed across Gabriel's shoulders and Tara stilled, sensing the rawness in his remembrance of Neala Kielty and his lost child. Still Hyde continued, oblivious: "I did hear that she was mighty afflicted by Cromwell's insistence on Dr John Hewitt's beheading. It hit Charlie hard too, the chaplain was a favourite of his father. We had reports she beseeched His Highness to do away with the High Court of Justice altogether but judging by poor Hewitt's end, she is losing her touch."

There was a moment's silence. "Do not give up hope, my dear, the fox runs as long as he has feet, as they say. Your family has given much for the King's cause and the name Villiers is well-respected. Charlie's kept a close eye from the start, as you know, and he is now especially determined that your uncle is liberated and gathered safely into the royal bosom."

"From the start. Of course." She looked over at her husband, seeing clearly for the first time. It was Charlie; he'd told Gabriel to find her and keep her close... remove any potential leverage over Eddie, lessen the chance of him giving up the Sealed Knot men. And in the meantime, her husband would feed her just enough of what she needed to know, prime her to pass on news to Eddie's men to keep them safely hidden, until direct control of them moved to a worthy successor. Gabriel himself? Tom? Then she'd no longer be needed.

She might have expected to feel anger, or betrayal, but there was rather a curious emptiness. He'd warned her, after all. *I can never give you my heart. There is too much history between us, too much future.* And she'd played a scripted role, unable to do anything else, as he manipulated her with consummate professionalism to control the threats from Cromwell and Thurloe. The future was now. *The end, now.*

"Nan?" she asked softly. "What will you do about Sir Willys? Is there instruction for the men-"

"She's gone," said Gabriel quietly.

"Where?" Tara scanned the room but the blonde had disappeared like an extinguished candle.

Gabriel put his finger to his lips at the creaking of floor boards above their heads and Hyde bent towards her with a whisper: "Mosely arranges itself on the south of the Thames, but did you know that Hampton Court on the north side was built on the site of an old Templar manor? Its founding preceptor was a nervous fellow; he dug a tunnel under the river to evacuate his entire order in the event they outstayed their welcome... And Cardinal Wolsey was also a nervous man, justifiably so as it turned out. When his builders were working on the Coombe Conduit water channel, he had the tunnel reinforced and its entrance secreted within one of its myriad store rooms."

"But where is the exit?"

"Here, within this alehouse cellar." He nodded towards a dark corner, piled high with racks of wine. "Now you know one of the better kept secrets in the realm. Not many know of it. Certainly not Hampton Court's current incumbent. The old King Charles, the publican of course, who fought with Charlie at Worcester. Ourselves..."

"And General Monck?" said Tara, remembering that the Duchess of Albemarle's husband was the Scottish Commander in Chief. The Sealed Knot was slowly revealing itself, peeling back its layers to a core of distilled power.

Hyde shrugged. "Charlie insisted. Monck is a canny man, my Lady, he knows the scales will not always tip in Cromwell's favour. He insists upon regular visits to his great friend in Hampton Court, to restore balance to his humours, so his wife can spend time with me..."

"I know Monck for a man of eventual action," murmured Gabriel. "Let's just hope his plans accord with our own."

"Amen." Hyde pursed his lips. "Truly though Nan is an extraordinary specimen. She will keep him on the right path. I don't know many women prepared to traverse 500 yards of thirteenth century tunnel in the dead of night with just a candle and the company of rats, to see my pretty face and hear me sing" He paused to flutter his eyelashes like a courtesan and Tara smiled at the incongruity of the action in the dank cellar.

"Speaking of which, you were saying?" prompted Gabriel again, bluntly, one ear back on the church bells outside tolling the hour. *Ten o'clock.*

The older man grinned and nudged Tara: "I come a long way from the Continent to meet with your husband, my Lady, and hard on this interview I face an arduous trip back. I appreciate I am not able to give much by way of advance warning in order to arrange some entertainment but at very least, one might expect a little more by way of polite chitchat."

"You can have all the polite chitchat you want when we are all safely on the other side of that blasted tunnel," Gabriel said gruffly, but there was a hint of a crease about his eyes. "In the meantime, tell me what I am doing here with such urgent summons. What do you need?"

Hyde shrugged with good humour but his bearing shifted imperceptibly. A fierce intelligence suddenly intoned his voice, all hint of playfulness evaporated, and Tara wondered how many others had been fooled by the benign, gossipy air. "Cromwell is at war with Spain and calls France his friend. This has furnished us rather conveniently with a Spanish army which, initially at least, seemed the best chance of regaining the kingdom. However..."

There was a small pot of salt on the table and he pushed aside the trencher and cups before tipping it up, pouring a neat pile of white grains on the surface. With a long fingernail he drew an approximation of the south of England and next the east coast of Europe, before jabbing a short finger towards Flanders. "Since the parliamentary frigates laid waste to our naval capability, there has been disarray in the Spanish Netherlands. Our coalition troops are weakened and demoralised. Charlie is coming to terms with the fact that he cannot march into England at the head of a Spanish army..."

"No bad thing," suggested Gabriel, his eyes narrowed in focus. "Given the average Englishman's fear of popery a Spanish invasion might only have strengthened Cromwell's hand. It would have been more use for us if the Spaniards were already here at parliament's behest."

Hyde nodded and gave a grim smile: "You have a sharper notion of politics than our young prince, God Save His Soul. I've warned Charlie on more than one occasion not to give up his kingdom to the papists, nor his strength to the women for that matter, but if he could liberate his people from them..."

"You think Cromwell will sue the Spanish for peace? It would put him in direct contravention of the Anglo-France alliance he negotiated in March."

"That is exactly what it would do." Hyde poured a new pile of salt on the left of the table and drew a rough map of the West Indies, moving his digit around the islands as he explained: "There's no limit to the man's hubris. Look, Jamaica is new ours. Barbados, Antigua, Barbuda... Spain has meanwhile conquered Cuba, Puerto Rico, Trinidad, etcetera... But look at poor France: Chief Minister Manzini cared so little for her colonial affairs that he let the Compagnie des Îles de l'Amérique governing her interests languish."

"France has nothing more than a patchwork of privatised exploitation rights," Gabriel agreed. "But Cromwell's had a few victories in the New World of late. He could yet win the war with Spain."

"Perhaps," said Hyde. "But Nan tells me he hasn't the coffers to fund a prolonged campaign. Besides, he's too clever to sue for peace when he is losing. He expects decent terms after your fine New Model Army soldiers captured a foothold on Jamaica just five weeks ago. Now is a perfect opportunity."

"Seize the initiative; divvy up the sugar trade in the New World," muttered Tara.

"Control of the white gold is control of Europe; the profits and fortunes in sugar cane are truly vast. By joining together with Spain, England would render France..." He waved his hand in the air as if his fingertips were a bluebottle and clapped, squashing the irritation dead between his palms. "Just imagine what France would make of that."

Gabriel could imagine exactly what France would make of that, starting with the likely fate of the Commonwealth's Strategic Advisers still on French sovereign soil when the treachery was discovered and the declaration of war was made. *I mean it shall be Done*, Cromwell had written, without debate or consideration. He shook his head with a wry smile at the man's scheming. It was not banishment then; when it arrived, his order to repair behind allied lines on the continent was nothing short of a death sentence. Hell hath no fury.

"There will be fall out across Europe and we need to control it in order to profit from it," Hyde continued, "It's been nearly ten years, Gabriel.

Nearly a decade since King Charles was murdered and our cause is close to floundering. Too many princes are expelling our diplomats; they think the Commonwealth is a power to do business with. Few are ready to invest in our future. Speaking of which, how was our Viking friend?"

"Friendly enough, but the Treaty of Roeskilde is floundering and Cromwell won't be able to prosper through Baltic trade or unite the protestant powers in Europe if Sweden resumes its war against Denmark. I have my doubts that we'll be able to give them what they want in the short term," said Gabriel impassively and Tara blushed in the darkness, remembering the feel of the ambassador's fingers on her neck. "The entire region is… pre-occupied, facing its own troubles."

"Hmpfh." Hyde paused a minute to dismiss the potential of Scandinavian support. "Then it is even more important we show Cromwell for the hypocrite he is. To be prepared to break a solemn treaty for gold? This would indeed be a timely reminder for our royal neighbours that regicides do not play by the same rules."

"What do you need?" Tara got nothing from Gabriel's inscrutable features but she read the tension in his hands as they calmly gathered his hair back into a leather cord.

After a moment, Hyde grinned: "Cromwell will soon approach the Spanish King. A Whitehall secretary overheard the plan while pretending to be asleep in his office, can you believe? The offer letter will leave Portsmouth within the fortnight on a ship called the Althea. This ship is bound for Jamaica but we expect it will intersect discretely with a Spanish vessel out to sea, somewhere off the west coast of Ireland."

Gabriel nodded. "Then we have a limited window to expose this treachery to the French."

"And, as luck would have it, their flagship La Glorieuse is also currently bound for Portsmouth. She intends no more than a little grandstanding of Cromwell's current alliance, but she presents an opportunity. Our Prince hopes that you will find an opportunity to intercept the letter…" Hyde paused a moment, to fish a fold of parchment from inside his jerkin, "and replace it with this flattering nonsense. Then hand the original to the French. They will do with the information as they will, in their own time, but no doubt maximising the damage to Cromwell."

"I'll work alone?"

Edward shrugged apologetically: "There is a Sealed Knot band in Portsmouth, of course, but since Villiers' arrest I haven't been able to make direct contact with them -"

"I can do that." Tara's interjection received a sharp warning glare from Gabriel but she faced it down. Hyde paused but said nothing, judging the matter best settled between them. He swept the grains of salt from the table before raising his eyes for confirmation.

Gabriel took a deep breath. "You want me to stroll into the most heavily fortified naval port in England, find a secret note on a heavily guarded naval warship, replace it with something you've cobbled together in the back of a moving carriage after a bottle of port, and then undermine the Anglo-French alliance by delivering it straight into the custody of a passing French frigate?"

The Lord Chancellor smiled.

36. WHITE GOLD

Edward Hyde left the cellar in the traditional way once a heel tap from Donn confirmed the path was clear and watching his large rear ascend, Gabriel stilled, sensing her heartbeat.

"Why didn't you tell me?"

"I didn't want you to hear it like that," he said quietly, feeling the inadequacy of the apology.

He hadn't betrayed her, or her men; her message had been delivered, Willys uncovered. She might even believe he'd been trying to keep her away from the danger. But now, thanks to Hyde's tactless storytelling, every one of his actions was distorted by the hue of a tainted looking glass. *Charlie's orders.* His storming the wedding to blasted Jack Ludlow, his insistence they marry, the trek to Devon, his killing of Tollemache. All down to nothing more than a dutiful carrying out of orders. *His touch?* No, not everything. There was raw truth when they joined, when they kissed, even when their fingers only accidently brushed along the other's skin. That thrumming urgency was real; the only lie was in its denial.

He hazarded a look in her direction. Her eyes were wide and bright and her skin luminescent in the candlelight. It was all he could do not to fall to his knees and bury his head against her, as though by putting his mouth to her belly he could speak directly to her soul. To Hell with duty or orders or honour. A stabbing in his chest made him want to hit something, hard.

"You did what Charlie asked of you," she said eventually, turning away.

"That's all."

"I could kill Donn," he murmured, fighting every urge to turn her back and confess the longing within him. She had to leave him and she deserved to walk away unscathed.

"I know."

"I wanted you free of this infernal..."

"I know, Gabriel, I know, *I know*... Please, don't..." She tailed off awkwardly and glanced at him over her shoulder. "Just tell me, how long have you been working for Charlie?"

"Six years, give or take," he replied after a moment.

"Why?"

Gabriel startled slightly at the question, turning abruptly to collect his sword and his hat from an obscured corner where he had left them. "Ireland."

"What happened?" She put a tentative hand on his arm as he passed and removed it again hurriedly, feeling the tensed muscle beneath his doublet.

Gabriel frowned. Perhaps this was what he'd needed all along. He could purge the last remnants of tenderness in her eyes with one tale, burn them clean once she knew what he was really capable of. He lent forward on the back of a chair and focused on the table, hanging his head so that his features were hidden by escaped strands of his hair.

He started softly. "In Hampton Court, I introduced you to a man called Charles Fleetwood. He was my commander at Worcester and soon after he was offered the role of Lord Deputy of Ireland, charged with destroying all confederate resistance. There were men known as *tories*, allied to the Stuarts and fighting Cromwell's invasion." He gave a short, humourless laugh. "I told you how keen I was to fight a foreign enemy... Fleetwood made me captain and sent me on in 1652 while he married Cromwell's eldest daughter. I joined the forces sieging Galway, travelling through country as void as a wilderness, ravaged by plague and fighting and famine. Wholesale slaughter. I could cover twenty, thirty miles between garrisons without evidence of a living soul. Man, beast and bird, all dead. Before long I was even praying for it to be so. A hungry person is a fearsome thing... all thinking and all feeling starts with food. Twice, I came upon camps to find bodies like bottles in the smoke, huddled around stinking carrion, plucked black and rotten from ditches.

"Wolves thrived in the absence of men. Women and children perished and their bodies were left and preyed upon. Cromwell knew well enough what had become of the land. He put ten pounds a head on a bitch and had garrisons organise public hunts. There was no food to let men eat but plenty of imported deer toil for the hunts... So it was that on Sunday we armed the same men we'd hunt and kill as tories on the Monday."

He paused a moment, his eyes glazed. "When I got to Galway, there was plague and hunger within the city walls but still the Irish held out. They knew that opening the gates would unleash fates worse than anything God could deliver. After Drogheda and Wexford..." He glanced at Tara then for a glimpse of understanding and she hung her head; news of the brutal massacres of civilians had made it back then.

"The following May negotiations for surrender began with Galway's commander Thomas Preston. He was an Irishman and his wife was Flemish-foreign, so my immediate commander Charles Coote was doubly suspicious. We were also run ragged. We attacked well enough but the tories in the countryside were like the wolves, circling in small packs, picking off men at our rear.

"One day Coote summoned me. He had intelligence on a known tory leader who'd evaded capture for years, despite the bounty on his head. He was hunkered in a hovel beyond Ballymariscal, not twenty miles from Galway. I was to assist two majors being sent to fetch him: Miles Corbet and John Jones."

"*Fetch* him...?" Tara started.

"An example had to be made. Coote was desperate for a show of force, to claim the city for English soil. He wanted the parade ground awe of something dramatic. We all were. We wanted it over.

"We followed the intelligence warily, expecting a trap, but arrived at dawn at a tumbledown shack. It looked abandoned, but the sound of his snoring lifted the branches patching the roof... He sprang up quickly enough as we entered, but he was dream drowsed and I arrested him easily. Plus of course there were three of us, each armed to the eye teeth with hard weapons, while he was surrounded by the soft, starving bodies of his wife and children."

Tara slid down onto a stool at the table with a gentle inhaled hiss. From this angle she could see his face, dark eyes looking vacantly at the candle flame, the skin of his cheek bruised black by Thurloe's guards.

"There were five of them, the youngest a babe in arms. Boy toddler twins, not yet breeched and out of skirts. An older girl and a boy of nine or ten. It was hard to tell. He was half naked, emaciated, he looked exactly like a match with flaming hair. I had the bizarre notion that if he stood still, I could maybe count the age of him by checking off the ribs along his chest. The woman, his wife… she had long blonde hair and it was loose, flowing to her waist. Corbet grabbed her and wrapped it around his fist. He dragged her outside, screaming, behind the structure, to where the woods began."

"Didn't you stop him?"

"No," he said quietly at the horror in her question. "God help me I did not. My orders were to apprehend the man, not protect his woman's virtue. Corbet was my superior. He was a brutal bastard but I thought she wouldn't die of it."

The tory was a big man and he struggled against Gabriel's hold for all he was worth. Jones pulled one of the toddler boys close to his front as a warning and the tory stilled, seeing the emptiness of casual violence in his eyes, hollow and feverish with victory.

"Seems to me as the last thing we need is more tory fuckers," Jones sneered, and Gabriel watched in horror as Jones drew his blade along the boy's throat and blood poured peacefully out, drenching his dirty white smock. The tory fell to his knees as the child slumped, trying to crawl along the mud to his son's body. Jones looked at the blade and staggered back against a table where the other children were cowering, as if he couldn't quite believe he had done it.

"All Hell broke loose. The tory lept up and pushed me over easily, punching and kicking. I took the blows in shock until his wife outside began to scream, as if she knew what had been done to her boy. Jones snapped from his trance and ran to find Corbet. The tory followed and I came after, staggering from my beating.

"Corbet emerged from long grass covered in blood, his flaccid cock hanging loose. When I looked across the tory was carrying his babe, screaming at his other children to scatter as ran to where his wife's screams were becoming fainter. The older two ran into the trees. One, the girl I think, clutched the toddler twin.

"I felt nothing but fury. I drew my sword. Jones was loading his pistol, ripping the top off his powder flask with his teeth and pouring the gunpowder into the barrel, ramming down the shot. He raised it and closed his eye to pick off the children as they ran, but he was distracted by choking noises. He turned to look at me. I had buried my blade between Corbet's neck and shoulder and I yanked it out to run at him. He shot at me, but the pistol misfired. A flash in the pan blinded him and he was too slow to pull his own sword. I pushed my weapon up through his chest and held him impaled until he died."

"What happened to the tory?"

"He hadn't got far. I found him in the long grass, cradling his wife's head. There was blood everywhere, deep pools of it gathering on the ground. The babe was lying in it, splashing drops on grass heads as it kicked its skinny legs and wailed. She was patting the ground to feel for the little body. Her eyes were firmly on her husband." Gabriel swallowed: "Corbet had been at Drogheda and knew a thing or two about killing women. He'd sliced off her breasts. I gave the man my dagger and without hesitating he took it and drew it across her throat, his eyes steady on hers.

"When it was done, he looked at me, the blade bloody in his hand. I was surprised to find my own sword still raised, still red. We both knew what had to happen. I would take him back to Coote for execution or die trying."

The tory drew himself up: *Swear to me that my bairns'll be safe.* Then he calmly slid the blade along his own throat, keeping pale blue eyes on Gabriel while his blood arced bright red across his wife's body. He slumped forward onto her, covering up the hideous wounds on her chest.

"He killed himself," said Gabriel softly. "It was over."

"The children..." Tara's voice choked.

"I picked up the babe and scoured the woods for hours, but the older ones had the sense to hide or the legs to carry themselves far away. I couldn't find them... I went back to the cottage and dug graves to confound the wolves. The babe was hungry and I was helpless. I carried it to a local village... there was a nursing mother who had buried her own child the day before. An odd thing to be grateful for, isn't it? Then I went back to the woods. I'd sworn... But nothing, still, nothing. There was nothing..."

Tara gripped hold of Hyde's ladder-back chair but Gabriel shook his head as Donn tapped on the trap door to join them. Silently, he watched him descend the steps before concluding the tale. "I had to make report to Coote. I told him it was a trap as we feared, that I'd escaped after we were set upon."

"Did he believe you?"

"It didn't matter in the end - a higher power forced his hand. There was another outbreak of the plague in Galway... Preston negotiated passage to France then opened the gates. He left to join Charlie in Paris and took my offer with him." Gabriel dragged long fingers through his hair, strands escaping the cord as if he were in danger of literally coming undone before her. "I thought I'd be called to France, but Charlie bid me stay in Ireland with Cromwell's army."

"To fight the tory confederates who supported him?"

His eyes clouded with the horror of a thousand brutal encounters. "Only they weren't high-minded political rebels for the most part. They were men defending their land, their homes and their families, from brutal, inhuman bastards like me. The hunger... Cromwell would have me kill men for trying to feed their starving families."

"How could you...?"

"It's never so hard to fight men who want to kill you... Fleetwood had judged me to have a talent for violence and he's right. I was the *other*, the invading barbarian every man in his right mind would repel. I was sent to Dublin, to command a force clearing the remote areas of the Wicklow Mountains. The law prevented giving quarter to the Irish and we took no prisoners. We forced men from their homes in the name of the Protectorate so the sordid likes of Jones and Corbet could strip their wives, steal their land and call themselves master.

"Those we left standing had a choice: starvation in the old world wasteland of Connacht or exile to the New World."

"Resettlement?" The hope in her whisper was hollow.

"Slavery," he said grimly. "The wretches were rounded up for auction. Most of the men were already dead but their women, their children... Cromwell's army, *my* army... it found unfathomable numbers, trussed them like turkeys and crammed them into the holds of cargo ships. They were traded for white gold so Cromwell could sweeten his porridge and pay his bills. And all the time, for years, I killed and smiled and bowed and killed."

"How could Charlie leave you there?"

"He's no fool. It wasn't even punishment for following my father at Worcester, though it felt like it for a long time... By the time Henry Cromwell arrived as Major General, I was well trusted. I got close to him. I collected intelligence arriving direct and uncensored from our Lord Protector. and passed everything straight to Hyde."

They lapsed into silence a moment, until Tara asked quietly: "Why didn't you tell Hyde you're under house arrest thanks to the errand I tried to send you on?"

Gabriel flinched, wondering how Tara could know. She was right: Thurloe had played the only hand he had left and given him a five-mile radius of Ham House within which to conduct his business. Were he discovered further abroad, there would be an immediate assumption of desertion of duty, of treason.

"I'm right, aren't I? Thurloe had to do something to remind you he was in control-"

"It doesn't matter," he interrupted levelly. He picked up his sword and buckled the scabbard onto his belt. "Cromwell plans to send me to France as strategic adviser, whatever that means, to be at the disposal of the French commander Marshall Turenne."

"*Jesus.*" Tara started, calculating the consequences. "And so you either carry out Charlie's orders and face a court-martial in London or do as Cromwell directs and wait until Hyde's plan concludes, at which point war is declared and the French will certainly execute you as a spy."

He gave a rueful smile. It was a familiar tale: *damned if he did, damned if he didn't.* "You were supposed to go to London when you left me... Rupert and Marie are already there, waiting for you at Charing Cross. You should be with them by now. My name should be a protection until Villiers' trial."

"This is madness," she whispered.

"Tara, Find Rupert. I've sent him with enough coin to let an apartment. Be near Edward. You have to get clear of me *now*."

"Hell's teeth, Gabriel, you can't surely have expected that I'd just sit patiently in London for the next month, discussing continental fashion with your cousin all the time I thought my uncle's men were exposed? Hyde's plan is insanity. You can't possibly do it on your own, you'll be caught and then what-"

"*Look at me*." He met her eyes and his deep gaze held her fast. "It's time Tara... if Hyde's right, this letter could end it all. Support for the Protectorate will tumble. I'm not afraid."

"Ye damn well should be," murmured Donn suddenly. "Yer runnin' a fool's errand if ye go into Portsmouth harbour alone. Ye're more than fairly furnished with height an' hair, Milord. Ye hardly blend into a crowd as it is, an' the entire army knows yer name. Some bugger'll spot ye, 'specially if the word goes out yer wanted."

Gabriel ignored him. "Go to London, Tara, I'm serious."

"So am I. I can reach the rebels directly for support. I did it for years. And besides, I was going that way anyway... You don't have the monopoly on treason, Gabriel. I know these men. Hyde needs me. You... you need me."

Gabriel paused a moment then looked away, his shoulders tense as he moved towards the trap door to leave. "Tell me how to find them. I'm not taking you to Portsmouth."

"It's not your decision. You do not tell me-"

"I was eleven," Donn interrupted softly. "A skinny wretch but eleven still, give or take. Neala was fourteen."

Gabriel turned to him, dark brows furrowed: "You know?"

"Ye kent me when ye were stoppin' the English hangin' me for a thief, did ye not?" Underneath loose hair the Irishman's features were unreadable. "Neala too; I was thinkin' ye surely knew that she didna seek ye out in yer camp purely on account o' yer pretty face... We saw ye kill yer men... Ye took my baby sister Saoirse to safety. Me an' Neala got away with Padraig and for a while we lived safe in the woods, until the boy sickened. We came back to the village for help an' that's when I was picked up by the English. Neala followed behind the army camp to be near me, an' when they tired of me, ye found me an' saved my life again.

"Ye kept yer oath, man, best as ye could. The Lord knows it's about time I was returnin' the favour. I'm comin' with the both of ye."

37. HARDENED RESOLVE

"Todd!"

Todd Pengelly frowned, caught by surprise as a cloaked woman took his hand and pulled him in past the heavy church door, through the small north porch. Deep, muffled voices hushed momentary. Stepping forward into the nave, striped by moonlight and darkness, Todd acknowledged a few familiar nods before Tara turned back and threw her arms around his tall, sturdy frame. Regaining his wits, he enveloped her in a warm hug, his broad, flat face breaking into a beam over her shoulder.

"By God girl, I didn't think to see you again."

"Nor I you," she whispered into his unkempt beard.

She finally pulled back, only to gasp as Mad Mike Evelyn materialised from the warm night behind them. He slipped between them and scooped her into his own thin, hard arms.

The compact form of Robert Farrier grunted from the darkness, announcing his own presence with typical understatement: "Put the lass down Mike, she ain't a child no more."

"Too grown for my nonsense now eh, Tatty Angel?" Mike swung her into the air and she muffled a childish squeal as the years fell away.

"Too heavy for your decrepit back!"

"Too heavy by half," he laughed as he set her down, an incongruous sound in the serious atmosphere, and he winked before hobbling off in an exaggerated geriatric fashion, following Robert's short, angular shadow as it moved business-like towards the front pew. There would be time to catch up properly later.

She watched as they wove through the gathering of Portsmouth royalists, men who took their cue at Mike's arrival and started to fall slowly into loose formation behind him. There were only a few small pools of light, created by pungent oil-filled cressets, and even the tremulous flickers could not disguise the fact that Mike's black curls were touched with lightening shocks of white. Robert was completely bald, his hat removed now out of respect for the venue. There were more folds around all their necks, thicker middles under their simple tunics. But her uncle's men were still vital, still capable of being brought to rally for the sake of their King. Still committed to the Sealed Knot. To the name Edward Villiers.

She corrected herself mentally. It was her embroidered message to Mike Evelyn, her unbroken code that had summoned every one of these men to this meeting. It would be her instructions they followed tomorrow night. They were no longer Eddie's men; tonight, tomorrow, they were hers.

"How is he?" asked Todd quietly, still by her side, reading her mind.

"I'm scared, Todd." she started, with an honesty that startled her. She shrugged helplessly as he took her fingers in his large, rough hand and gave them a gentle squeeze.

"From the bottom of my heart I thank you for your message in Mortenhampstead, for standing down the uprisings. You're Gregory's daughter alright. Your courage saved a lot of lives, many of whom are here in this room. You're not on your own now, lass," he said, "so come on, let's hear what all this is about."

Tara left her hand in his a second longer to make the most of the comfort. Then she turned, taking a deep breath and pushing back the heavy hood on her cloak, ready to fold the fear back up neatly inside her pounding chest. She picked a path through the milling bodies of Mad Mike's rebels. There were a few glances of curiosity to see a female form, a few frowns of dismissal, but mostly the men parted without paying her any attention. When they reached the front, Todd sat heavily beside Mike.

She squatted down and put a hand on his sleeve: "You kept news of this meeting from Sir Richard Willys?"

"Aye, lass, not a word," he replied softly. "He believes me to be sourcing oak for a new dinghy commission. In fact, a most promising letter arrived at my workshop last week from a new supplier in Hampshire. Good quality timber, heavy discounts and fresh-baked cherry pie for substantial orders. It's almost like its author knew exactly how to lure me across three counties at speed."

Mike snorted and Tara smiled, sensing the famed Lucy Hallowell's gently ironic touch in the summons. So, she was still using her late husband's press. The advertisement was a clever way of getting attention, as long as they weren't creating a trail for Thurloe. "But-"

"No Tatty, Mrs Hallowell doesn't know you're here. She doesn't know any details," Mike confirmed quietly, pre-empting her concern about how widely knowledge had spread. Todd and Robert were discrete but there were thirty-four men due in the church. Some might have told their wives about the nocturnal meeting. Gabriel himself, currently outside with Donn to keep watch in the darkness for militia, brought with him a real risk that they were being watched. It was more dangerous if the printer's widow knew as well... She glanced at Mike and he looked directly back at her with unwavering eyes. Knowing would put Lucy Hallowell at risk as much as any man here. *He'd not told.*

She offered half an apologetic smile: "She is yet Mrs Hallowell? Still no luck in that quarter, Mike?"

He shrugged, no hard feelings, and wiggled his substantial black eyebrows. "She's near to having me, Tatty Angel. I know it. In recent months I've sensed a softening-"

"Well that's where you're going wrong then," muttered Robert dryly from his impatient perch on Mike's other side. "Lasses tend to prefer more hardened resolve."

Todd gave a snort of laughter, but Mike shrugged amicably. "Laugh it up, lads, laugh it up. Next time I ask you to attend this house of God, it will be to witness my nuptials."

"Next time? I should like to know what *this* time is about first," Robert replied gruffly. "When are you going to tell us what you're planning, Mike?"

"Hear, hear." Todd flicked his eyes back over the ragtaggle rebels. They were still hovering uncertainly in small groups of two or three along the aisle. Mike said nothing in reply but cocked his head towards Tara.

"You're here at my invitation, not Mike's," she said, taking a deep breath. "Is everyone here?"

Mike nodded and she stood to address the room, starting a hesitant welcome: "Gentlemen... please take a seat."

At the back of the church, the door opened and Gabriel slipped inside. He caught her eye and nodded: *all was well*. Donn would stay outside for now. He walked up the aisle towards her, moving confidently, ready to command, and the men made way before him, dissolving between dark pews. Robert gave her a mild, questioning frown, and there were whispers from the men as Gabriel passed to sit beside Todd at the front. They sensed it in him, the habit of command, but she felt her old resolve grow. *These were her men.*

"Gentlemen, I need your help."

A silence descended as her words sunk in, punctuated by a single gruff voice from the darkness: "Lost your cookery books, my lovely? I'm sure as there are many men here who'd happily show you what to do with hot sausage meat."

A few muffled snorts bounced around the bare walls and Tara shot Gabriel a warning glare as he moved instinctively to stand and bring order. Reluctantly he sank back down and she turned calmly back to the audience: "I've a more satisfying employment in mind, gentlemen. Perhaps I misjudged you, but I'd heard there are those amongst you here in Portsmouth whose manhood oft swells as big as a couple of dumplings."

Open laughter and cheers shook the pews and the tension that had radiated began slowly to dissolve. Confident that they would now listen, she started again: "I am Tamara Villiers. And you are here because I need your help."

The power of her name made the laughter stop immediately and the anonymous heckler stumbled on a speech of contrition: "Forgive me, Milady. Anything..."

She shook her head, cutting him off. "I need you to create a diversion in the dockyard tomorrow night."

"When do we engage?" asked Robert, with perfunctory efficiency.

"You don't engage," said Tara firmly, prompting a flurry of whispers. The men she'd watch file into this remote church on the outskirts of Portsmouth were farmers, shop keepers, carpenters, stable hands. They were fit men, strong and undoubtedly committed but she was certain most hadn't raised arms since the war ended and the briefest glance at Gabriel's stern features outside confirmed her suspicions. He'd seen it too, making his practical assessment with a cool military eye. A decade's distance from battle made a man rusty. Some rebels had bought their sons, young men who likely remembered the war from the side-lines if they were old enough to remember it at all. There was no time to train them.

"Listen to me," she said, trying to make eye contact with as many men as possible in the shadows. "The job is distraction, not engagement. You are not to fight unless you absolutely have to."

"We're not cowards Milady," insisted one of the younger voices. "You heard right! We've the stomach and the balls for it. We'll willingly die for Charles Stuart. Long live the King!"

Mad Mike stamped his feet as another muffled cheer went up, echoing in the nave, and Tara smiled, waiting for it to subside before continuing. "No one thinks you cowards. I know more than most what you risk just by being here... But I mean it. I will not have a single one of you exposed, injured or captured tomorrow.

"I need a distraction. There's a naval ship currently in the harbour called the Althea." She nodded in the direction of Gabriel and he stood again, prepared to lay out a strategy, but sensing they were all looking squarely at Tara for direction. "This man has to get aboard it, find something of vital importance to our struggle and remove it unseen."

"Rum and biscuits?" Another young voice rose and a few chuckles murmured in the darkness.

Gabriel gave a small smile and shrugged as Tara offered him the floor. His reply carried a gentle hint of humour and she sensed the men warming to him. "That's not the half of it. Having left the Althea, I must then smuggle my top-secret rum and biscuit haul onto La Glorieuse before getting off again."

"La Glorieuse…" mused Mike, rolling the words around on his tongue. "The three-masted French ship that anchored here last week, the one with all the bells and whistles?"

Gabriel nodded and Todd spat suddenly on the floor. "The Louis Baboons are a pampered bunch. Fucking tart, that frigate. Ah, excuse my French, Tatty."

Tara bowed her head demurely to one side to hide a smile.

"You're talking about two of the most heavily armed and guarded ships in all of England," someone pointed out reasonably. "This will need to be one Hell of a diversion."

"It will," she confirmed, and there was a moment's pause before the rebels mooted options.

"We haven't time to rouse a riot," said Mike. "We couldn't get the longshoremen agreed and organised."

"Fire?" Another voice offered hopefully.

"Explosion," said Tara. "Can you rig up enough gunpowder and keep everyone too busy to spot my friend here?"

"By tomorrow? We've four or five barrels, enough for one pretty serious explosion… Just one chance mind but still…" mused Mike. He balled a fist and threw it upwards letting his fingers flutter down like falling debris. "Kaboom!"

A couple of the younger lads at the front smirked and nudged each other, an air of restlessness building in the darkness. "The munitions! We'll hit the Square Tower armoury and teach Cromwell a lesson! We'll send his minions to the seabed!"

"No, you won't," said Tara firmly. "We need a soft target?"

"Milady" said Todd, "With respect, you're talking about setting off 250 pounds of gunpowder smack bang in the middle of the most heavily fortified military port in the county, if not the whole of Europe. Chock-a-block with the slimy French and Cromwell's bastard navies. You'll have to choose, which would you have us blow?"

"Neither."

"Your father weren't concerned with…"

"My father's not here. I'm telling you this organisation will not be responsible for unnecessary killing. We will not be able to maintain the support of the people by murdering their sailor sons as they sleep, and Charles Stuart can't be blamed for French deaths." Tara thought a moment. "The food… My guess is that the navy is even more obsessed with its belly than you lot. There will be a navy victuals store in the Port, right? We'll hit the food, not the men."

"Actually, that's not a bad idea," said Mike. "It's a fair distance from the ships. It's been a while since I had a proper look but from memory it's a flimsy structure. It'll give our gunpowder maximum impact. Besides, it's not ten yards from the rope and pitch store… even if they ain't worried about smoking their bacon, the whole port'll want to stopping fire spreading. Once the rope and the pitch take, the whole place'll blow."

A general murmur of approval spread throughout the church as the finer logistical details were fixed. A drayman volunteered to smuggle the gunpowder into the port with the ale he delivered to the tavern. Three men with experience in explosives would be waiting to rig the charge. Others were allotted tasks ranging from lookouts to hiding the buckets that would be needed to fight the fire. Timing was everything. Gabriel would board the Althea alone but when he was ready, the explosion would cover his leaving it. The shock and the fire should create enough chaos for him to row across the harbour and board La Glorieuse unseen.

"But, Milady, what if we have to fight…?" asked one of the younger voices in the back, his eyes flashing in the flickering light.

Gabriel looked to Tara for leave to speak before addressing the question: "We have the advantage of surprise, but it would be suicide to engage large numbers of soldiers and sailors. They're highly trained, remember, and very well-armed. Given half a chance they will move like a pack of dogs. They will surround you and take you down, to Hell or worse."

Todd nodded with an air of polite deference to Gabriel's evident military experience. "Sir, if any of the men are discovered in the port without papers but with armed with pistols, I assume there'll be an automatic assumption of treachery?"

"Yes." Gabriel nodded. "Leave your pistols behind. Any necessary fighting will be at close quarters in any case, fists and blades. You are working men; every working man reasonably carries a blade."

A pale hand rose from a younger man who had not yet spoken. "We've daggers, and no doubt a few dirks between us. Some will have chaff knives from the fields. Which blades would be best?"

"All of them." Tara raised her chin before Gabriel could answer. "You take all of them."

38. SON OF A BITCH

She tripped quickly from the heaving tavern and swung her legs over a low wall by the water's edge, staring out into the blackness of sea and night sky and hearing nothing but her shallow snatches of breath. The last in a line of ships, the Althea was moored calmly alongside the port wall, its creaking gangplank empty, its crew torn between the lure of hammocks or ale. Behind it, maybe a mile out into the deeper water, the French frigate La Glorieuse had dropped anchor, holding itself proudly apart from its reluctant allies.

She stretched out her hands and curled them over the edge of the wall, ten digits spread wide against the stone. From his position leaning cross-armed against a barrel on the other side of the dockyard, Donn nodded imperceptibly. He turned and walked slowly back towards the tavern, barely flinching when, a second later, the storeroom behind him exploded, walls and roof ripped clear, wood shot spiralling and fiery by the blast.

Tara flinched.

Ten.

Ears ringing, she spun about, her pounding heart and ad hoc pistol fire the only markers of time in the sudden chaos of bodies racing haphazardly across her vision. Soldiers massed swiftly from nowhere, ducking to avoid falling debris. They were shouting, she could tell that from the open mouths and gesticulations and hastily drawn weapons, but it was as if she were looking at them from the bottom of the ocean, moving slowly against the heavy drag of water.

Nine.

"Mind the Louis Baboons!"

Mike's Portsmouth men had done it; the small structure was destroyed and attention was truly focused away from the ships. They celebrated with a volley of fireworks, startling the port with a playful display of yellow tailed rockets in the night sky. Proving that it was no accident. All eyes lifted from the victuals store, or what remained of it, breathing in air tinged with acrid gunpowder and a faintly tantalising smell of roasting meat.

Eight.

"Where are the French bastards? They'll pay for this!"

Another explosion came from the collapsed store and sent more rubble shooting violently out. She froze as seamen hit the decks before her. The fire was spreading close to the corner of the rope and pitch store. Screams rose out and the bells of St Thomas' peeled backwards to raise the alarm.

"Get water! Quickly!"

"Where are the buckets?!"

"S'Blood! Shift the pitch! Coil the rope! See to the armoury! Shift the powder!"

Seven.

The plan was clear enough but somewhere in the shock of its execution she was losing faith. Before he slipped silently along the gangway and dissolved behind the Althea's rail, Gabriel had been insistent they should light the fuse on his signal. Under its cover, he would come back onshore with the message, hidden by the confusion, within the count of ten.

Six.

She'd already spent an anxious infinity in the first-floor dining room of the tavern, eyes darting between the window of the Althea's aft cabin for his agreed sign and the ponderous progress of the ship's captain along the deck above, as he discussed matters with the armed men on lookout. But that was nothing compared to the agony of counting a few seconds now.

Five.

Even from this distance, her eyes were watering with the heat of the flames. She peered for the clock face on Customs House, behind smoke from the exploding gunpowder that billowed ghostlike across the damp docks. Squinting, she took in the formal defensive positions being adopted by the sailors on the Althea as the gangplank was retracted.

Four.

Then, across the water, below the deck of the La Glorieuse, its hatches opened and the French cannons were run out, aimed at the dock side, warding off attack.

Three.

"*Ah!*" He arrived silently behind her, cap pulled down over his face, features blackened with spent gun powder and shirt barely covered by a too-small naval jacket. It pulled tight across his back and he struggled to shrug it off, his arms constrained by the woolen fabric bunching beneath his shoulders.

"You can't do it," she hissed. "You can't board La Glorieuse. Look at its gunports: the French've trained their cannons and their eyes on the harbour. You'll never get across the water on a rowboat unseen."

"I know. It's alright."

"You'll never get on it–"

"Look at me," he ordered, bringing her back to him, then cursed, momentarily distracted by the straining doublet before the seams finally gave way and it fell free, fluttering into the sea below them. "It's *alright*."

Her eyes widened in surprise as he stepped onto the wall beside her, put a tight tube of papers between his teeth and dived into the darkness. Above her heartbeat and the tumult of the port, she barely heard the splash.

The water was cold.

In the first shock, his lungs constricted and it was a moment before his limbs would move. The sharp ache near his abdomen deadened almost immediately; he was conscious of the damage only as a dragging hollowness as his head broke the surface and he twisted about to get his bearings. It was harder than he expected, forcing back the heavy water until he was moving, but he took measured breaths around his precious cargo. The letter was bound tightly in oilskin but it wouldn't stay waterproof for long.

The sea was calm at least and with a couple more strokes he found a strong, silent rhythm. Course set towards the French hull, he glanced back at the dock. The fire was not yet under control but the initial panic of shouting and hollering had given way to well-practised drill. The seaman were engrossed by duty and passed leather buckets sloshing with water along chains of men towards the flames. Then the wind changed, and dark smoke spilled across the stage like a curtain at the end of a play, obscuring his view.

It was thirty minutes, maybe more, before he reached the stern of La Glorieuse and looked up at its towering castle above him; three storeys of officer cabins perched high above the deck. He grasped the pilot's ladder, slippery with weed, taking the roll of parchment in his hands and dragging in breath for a moment. He stifled a cough with some difficulty. Thick, disorientating smoke had found the ship before him. *Keep moving.* He reached up for a hand hold and slowly climbed towards the quarter galleries and the cabin's cabin, moving along rails when the ladder stopped.

Finally, he was on a level with the squared porthole he was looking for, opened mercifully wider than he had dared hope. He swung across to be level with the sill and crouched down ready to enter, pausing to check the cabin was empty. There was only the faintest trace of moonlight through the clearing smoke but it took only a glance to confirm there was no one inside. Someone had been there though, very recently, he picked up the faintest smell of candlewax and cologne. And by the door; a familiar pair of women's boots. *What the Hell?* He leant forward, shock momentarily outweighing sense and nearly slid from the narrow ledge. Grabbing at the slippery frame, he regained his precarious balance with some difficulty before twisting his weight, swinging in through the opening.

One job at a time. He forced himself to start by swiftly unrolling the parchments. He peeled off the bottom letter, laying it flat on the captain's table, securing it at each corner with whatever heavy items he found to hand. For good measure, with a rueful smile at the unnecessarily dramatic flourish, he stabbed a small knife meant for sharpening quills through the centre of the message, planting it into the oak below.

A second later muffled voices approached the cabin door. *No-where to hide.* He slipped out of the window, keeping a low profile against the rail. The flames were out now, smoke dissipating in the fresh night breeze, leaving him dangerously exposed to view from the dock where seamen were moving about more slowly, silhouetted against lantern light and braziers, content to leave the destruction for the morning light. A wave of dizziness rolled over him and he rumpled his hair. He scanned the figures for a glimpse of Tara, any flash of pale silk in the moonlight. *No sign.* Donn was loitering alone. *Damn it, has he lost her? Was she on the blasted French ship? Why-*

He'd thought it'd be easier to leave the frigate than climb aboard it, but his heart pounded heavily and for the briefest of moments his vision doubled. He shook his head firmly, drawing a cold hand across his face. A group of sailors were waiting for the Althea gangplank to extend again. They'd see him, across the water, as soon as they turned to board. He saw the slightest incline of Donn's fiery red head before the Irishman lurched drunkenly across the slippery cobbles towards them. *Cover to leave unseen.* He hesitated, his mind screaming irrational fears. But if she was somehow on board La Glorieuse, Donn surely wouldn't let him leave it. *The boots.* He must have been mistaken. She had to be somewhere in the port…

Gabriel's eyes narrowed as he watched Donn recoil when a man's fist made unannounced contact with his nose. He fell back theatrically, staggering into a line of barrels by the water's edge, flame tinged salvage from the store. There were loud shouts of irritation and dismay when the last barrel was nudged into rolling on its base, a rapid shallow spin that left it teetering dangerously close to the edge of the dock wall. No longer the centre of attention, Donn swiftly retreated into the darkness and Gabriel took his cue. He stood and dived, hitting the water at the same time as the Althea's bonus haul of rum.

It wasn't cold this time. Out of the chilling air he was aware of nothing but the silkiness of the water against his skin. Like being wrapped in warm, comfortable blankets. He closed his eyes, swimming mechanically across to the far side of the harbour, to the agreed point where Donn would be waiting. He was getting slower. His arms felt numb, his legs long and heavy, dragging like spring ropes on his torso. He realised he was smiling, ready after every stroke to surrender to the caress of the waves. He could feel her smooth skin against his as a mermaid floating alongside him, the currents in the water rolling into and out of limb-like forms between his legs, under his chest.

Was this how she felt, that day? That day, outside Mottisfont Abbey? She was falling under, when he'd dragged her, naked, slick-limbed and prickled with goose bumps onto the riverbank. *No, she was fighting.* And what if Donn had lost her? *She might be fighting now.*

The boots. He opened his eyes and stopped to tread water for a moment, slowly orientating himself by the bobbing lights of the dock's braziers with a supreme effort of will. Then, somehow, with as deep a breath as he could gasp, he took long, increasingly powerful strokes until his fingers found a seaweed-slippery rung of a ladder drilled against the dock wall. Then he stretched with difficulty, dragging himself laboriously upwards to clasp Donn's outstretched hand and haul himself heavily over the edge. He landed with a squelch onto the cobbles and twisted onto all fours, dropping the parchment roll and shaking his head vigorously, loose hair sending splatters of cold saltwater flying.

"Ye've been gone in the water fer over an hour, Milord. I was startin' to worry."

The hot air before him misted as he panted hard: "Ta-?"

"I'm here." She slipped silently alongside them and he saw her bare feet as she bent to retrieve the tightly rolled parchment, his shoulders falling until he rolled over onto his back, knees in the air, dragging the cold air into his lungs.

"What's this? There was nothing to bring off…" Tara dropped down beside him and picked up the oilskin-covered prize, carefully unravelling the wad of parchment flat against the stones. It was wet, smeared in places, but still legible. A neat ledger of names.

"The Althea… is… a slave ship," he gasped grimly. "On her way to the Indies… Bound for… Cork… Donn… she'll pick up your people…"

Donn frowned and reached for the papers. He flicked his eyes at Gabriel as he did so: "Paddy wrote they'd head for Connact. Not feckin' Hell."

He took a few steps along the harbour wall to pick up some lantern light from the headland on the sheet before him and read falteringly aloud, squinting at the flourished lettering: "*FACSIMILIE: A List of Names of Passengers formerly of Ardrahan & divers other settlements in the county of Galway headed for Barbados on Board the ALTHEA, July 6th, 1658, in alphabetical order. Nota Bene: The names which compose this list are generally respectable, but as labourers they possess a want of order, neatness and economy. All are quite unable to bear the expenses of the passage & provide for their subsistence on arriving at their destination & are therefore unsettling themselves under the notion of the British Government furnishing a conveyance to the colonies."*

"It means-"

"I know what it means, Milord. Cromwell plans to fetch them in Cork and sell them into slavery in the West Indies… There're well over 100 souls here… *Aheren, Dougal – 53… Cormac, Patrick – 46… o'Donnell, Wm – 31…o'Donnell, Wm – 54… o'Donnell…*" He paused and looked up, his face a deathly white as he carefully peeled off the second sheet and skimmed the list until he reached 'K'. "*Kelly, Malachy – 12…* he's here… *Kielty, Patrick – 63… Kielty, Maire – 59… Kielty, A…* I canna make it out. A-? God's blood, it's a babe. Six months. What if it's yers?"

Donn tailed off with a sharp intake of breath and, gently, Tara took the soggy parchment from his fingers. When she looked up, understanding had already passed between the two men. Gabriel was back on all fours. His chest no longer heaved with the effort of breath and he seemed impervious to the drips of water running along his long nose. He looked up, his skin reflecting a pale moon and the effect was one of marble-like hardness. His voice carried a matching line of steel. "I'll get them off, Donn; I'll get them. I'll… I'll…"

Her brow furrowed at the blooming of black across the lower back of his wet shirt and she sank to her knees by his head: "Gabriel?"

"Catch him!" Donn was moving towards them in slow motion as Gabriel's limbs suddenly quaked, his body collapsing onto the cobbles. Tara just managed to slide a hand between the hard stone and his chin and his head landed heavily on her upturned palm as Donn thudded down by his side, yanking the shirt out of his breeches to see the damage. Rope wound around his waist, holding a pad of ripped cotton, soaked through with sea water and blood.

"Oh God." Tara swallowed dryly and hissed into his ear: "Gabriel! Wake up! You have to wake up, we need to get you somewhere safe. *Please.*"

"Ye need to be keepin' his head a moment." Donn pulled the wadded fabric aside to reveal a ragged wound, about the size of a penny piece, just above his hip. "He's been hit, must've been shot in the panic after yer explosion. Stubborn feck just laced hisself up. Please Jesus there's an exit wound an' whatever went in has come straight back out."

With practiced hands he hefted Gabriel onto his side and ran his fingers under the waistline of his breeches, along the underside of his belly. Tara held her breath until Donn sighed with relief: "It's here, here. It's gone straight through; it canna have hit anythin' important given he's got this far. Let's be rousin' him."

With some effort they righted his upper body and pushed it back against the dock wall, where Gabriel rewarded them with a rueful grimace. "Hoist with our own petard, eh?"

"Ye'll be hoist by the hangman's rope if we don't get ye outta here quickly," Donn prodded the edges of the wound until Gabriel's eyelids fluttered open with a hiss. Tara yanked down a petticoat for a new bandage and held it tight against around his waist while Donn re-wound the rope, passing it behind his slumping back. "Milord, ye'll be stayin' conscious for a wee bit yet, if ye don't mind."

"Go," he murmured dreamily, eyes closed again. "I need to sleep this off. Take her, away. I'll be fine… in the morning."

"Wake up, God damn you!" Heart pounding, she slapped his cheek as his head nodded forward, scanning the harbour and counting the listing masts along the harbour wall. "We need to stay with the Althea, right? Donn, when we arrived there was a sloop on the other side of the harbour that I think we might be able to use. I've no better ideas for getting to Ireland… Come on."

They made haphazard progress across the dock, keeping low by the wall, dragging their charge along with a combination of encouragement and threat. Through blurring vision, Gabriel forced his focus on compiling a mental list of the ships they passed. All impressive naval vessels built for war, until a smaller, three masted lugger that had seen better days creaked against the moving tide.

"There's no… Hell I'll let you… step -" He stopped hard as the Albatross materialised before him and with the sudden loss of momentum, Donn stumbled and Tara was spun forward.

Ignoring Gabriel entirely, Donn nodded towards a heavyset man ambling down the Albatross' gangplank towards the port tavern, back open for business now the threat of spreading fire was over. "Milady, mind yer fella there…"

"When will you bloody learn Gabriel, you don't *let* me do anything," she hissed, quickly extricating herself from his shocked grip in order to run up alongside the large sailor: "Sir! Take me to your captain. It's urgent."

The man considered her a moment before sighing deeply and turning back with a wistful glance at the tavern. She followed close behind his long gait back up the short gangplank onto the Albatross, mouthing over her retreating shoulder: "Trust me."

"Cap'n, sir, there's a woman as wants to see you. Says it's urgent." The sailor stood aside to reveal her figure in the doorway and instinctively she re-arranged her dress, trying without success to seem a little more self-possessed than she felt stepping into the claustrophobic cabin.

"God's blood! Is that you, Minerva?"

Tara breathed a sigh of relief she didn't realise she'd held as she eyed him, sitting behind the large mahogany writing desk, dressed shamelessly in Blakelock's ramshackle finery. So, Son-of-a-bitch had emerged victorious from the cellar in Exeter. She'd seen this man commit murder, but the cold eyes of Finch might have been a harder sell. "I must congratulate you, Captain-"

"Calderditch… Captain Calderditch, my Lady," he started, recovering his shock with a wry grin as he dismissed the crewman with a nod. "You see you did me a fine turn."

She nodded curtly; there would be enough time to exchange pleasantries once they were safely out on the Irish Sea. "And I left you a considerable amount of silver. It's time to repay the debt."

* * *

The frenzy of on-deck activity necessary to leave the port gradually subsided when, approaching the headland, the breeze picked up its cue and the slack in the lugsails, cracking them to attention. From there, Calderditch explained, they would drift into the wide channel of the Solent, where they'd hug the length of the south coast at a safe distance before starting out across the Irish Sea. The Althea could easily outpace them side by side, but with a decent head start and a fair wind, they had a chance.

Hoping for some distraction from the queasy lurch of her stomach, Tara picked her way unsteadily to the helm and stood next to the captain. Calderditch wore the mantel well. He remained impressively still as his dozen or so men scurried about checking, winching, securing, utterly impervious to the rolling of the deck from side to side as their calls settled down to the practical business of making the deck shipshape for voyage.

"Secure the halyard! Mind the spar, Miss!"

She dodged a dangling rope and grabbed tightly to the rail, focusing on keeping her voice even and her brain stable: "Tell me, Captain Calderditch. You are master of all you survey, but do you not dream of trading in this life for a more peaceful existence on land?"

"I think not." He watched the bobbing lights of Portsmouth recede beyond sparkling black waves and hung his head for a moment that might have been regret. The ragged lace at his throat picked up the breeze and fluttered rakishly for a moment. "Why wake a losing gamester from a winning dream? There are plenty enough dangers in my line of work that chances are I will never need concern myself with an idle retirement."

A flurry of spray landed on them like a swarm of stinging insects and he grinned, displaying large yellowed teeth vaguely reminiscent of the barnacles clinging to the hull below. A velvet arm waved in an expansive gesture across the deck, taking in Donn's bloody nose, Gabriel's red-stained shirt and gunpowder-streaked skin and her own unwholesome, barefoot appearance. "Besides, I should be keen to know in what other walk of life should the likes of me have the pleasure of entertaining such fine company?"

Dinner at the Captain's table was a simple affair, held around the single table in his cabin. Once the rum was flowing freely the cook produce a tureen of porridge from the middle deck. He spooned the grout into bowls, handing them about the table with a faintly apologetic smile.

"Toucan warms up the longer we are into a voyage," said Calderditch with a sideways glance as he took up his spoon.

"That or you've genuinely forgotten what a real meal looks like so a weevil is as good as a hog roast," murmured a sailor on Tara's left.

"The Albatross warms up too, my Lady," Calderditch added after a while, taking in her pale face and untouched bowl. Her legs were folded up tightly before her on the chair, naked toes poking out from the edge of her skirts. "She yaws restless until we're out into open sea, then she can relax."

"That or you've already gobbed up every last morsel in your belly over the rail…" started the man again sardonically until Calderditch frowned, stopping the unhelpful commentary in its tracks.

He addressed his men with an airy wave: "Ain't Blue Tit's kit still down below in the hold? He don't need his boots any more, God rest his soul."

"A- Aye sir, I'll f-f-fetch 'em," said one of the taller men, rising to walk smoothly out of the listing cabin.

"Gull, Toucan, Blue Tit?" Tara raised a questioning eyebrow and swallowed dryly, forcing the bile back to her empty stomach. "Is this a boat or a birdcage?"

Calderditch laughed and settled back in his captain's chair, happy to help with the distraction: "As you might appreciate, Minerva, there are times when a non de plume is useful. None of the lads here've used their given names since their mothers wiped their arses. But the birds, that was Blakelocke's little joke: he said we sang like caged songbirds on our rations of rum."

"So why-?"

"He didn't like me none" he shrugged, guessing at her question. Son-of-a-bitch was the only one without a feathery moniker. "He was my half-brother. Our ma, so the story goes, died for her sins when she birthed me, and Blakelocke couldn't bear that his soft-hearted pa, God rest his soul, kept her bastard for a nourry child. Long time ago now. An' no love lost on either side, although give the man his due, he did for the most part pick a decent alias."

He looked around his men with some satisfaction: "Moorhen's fiery brand is a pretty prominent facial shield, not unlike that belonging to your Red there. Gull's a bad tempered and greedy landlubber, he deserted the navy and's only here with us to pay off a gambling debt he owed our former Captain… Swan's an ugly lobcock and Penguin, surprisingly to take a gander at him, swims like a fish. Parrot stutters, Duck farts and Toucan has a bloody great nose."

The sailors snorted with laughter and bowed with exaggerated flourish as they were each introduced. In a kindred gesture to Moorhen, Donn pushed aside his falling red fringe to reveal the faded but matching scar, prompting more cheers and downed glasses from his fellow criminals. Then, returning from the galley, the tall sailor thrust a small pair of leather boots at her elbow.

"Mi-Minerva," he started.

"Thank you, Parrot, they're perfect."

"You know my secrets, Minerva." Calderditch turned to her in aside as Swan started on a bawdy story of mermaids to the delight of the table. "You wear my shoes and your gentleman bleeds on my decks. We'll put him in a cabin below as soon as he consents to it. Are you going to tell me what you want so badly in Ireland that you'd have me risk my neck for it?"

To tell the truth was to admit treason and Tara thought a moment, watching Donn laugh as she weighed up the chance Calderditch would alert the authorities at the first opportunity. She bought a little time slipping on the boots and tugging the knotted laces tight. They'd clearly belonged to a boy, but something told her not to ask and she satisfied herself by mentally thanking him. Then she felt along the seam of her dress for the hidden placket.

"Our mission is of the utmost secrecy, Captain," she whispered, producing the spidery letter Cromwell had drafted months previous to permit access to the Tower, still tucked tattered inside the folds of her dress. "We travel under the Lord Protector's own orders. We need to get a body off the Althea without alerting attention. I'm not concerned with smuggling so you can relax. We have bigger fish to fry, as it were."

For the longest moment Calderditch scanned the page and Tara affected a general air of importance, praying with every last fibre in her being that he couldn't read. Even though the words themselves would be meaningless the signature was surely recognisable enough, reproduced regularly on posters and proclamations.

Eventually he sniffed and looked at her with a kind of reverenced awe. "Well, I'll be damned."

"It *is* getting rather hot in here." She grinned, unable to contain the relief, and stood to leave, picking up her supper and steadying herself on the table, the chair, the door frame and then the swinging door itself as she headed gingerly out onto deck.

39. THE PAST IS A FOREIGN COUNTRY

"Eat," she said gently, holding the bowl of grout outstretched. "You've lost a lot of blood. His potion, for the pain. Has it worked?"

She tried a smile but it felt hollow and he slowly raised a single eyebrow, taking the bowl from her stiffly to set it down on the deck, before leaning back against a pile of coiled rope.

"You should be below deck," she murmured. "I'll fetch the crew. They're drinking, and we should get their help before they're more sail than ballast…"

"Tara, please. Sit with me a moment."

Please. He'd sought permission, she suddenly realised. Every time he'd touched her, kissed her, held her. Even that night, when she asked for help, she went to him… And each time, in seeking fresh consent, he was quietly setting out the terms of engagement afresh. *Will you be with me for this moment,* he asked. *Mine,* he said, *for now.* For tomorrow? There was no tomorrow. *I can never give you my heart and you would never take it. Whatever you say now, there is too much history between us, and too much future.* She'd already known the rules. For King and country… their King, and their country… The heated desire, even the gentle affection… God knows it had felt real enough but it was unanchored by love she had no right to expect. His possession felt so intense, so all-consuming, but it was a mirage in a desert world; a flicker of his love for Neala Kielty perhaps… Could she blame him for allowing herself, so willingly, to be misled?

She hesitated a moment but sat down next to him, careful to avoid touching him. His eyes were ringed red, his breathing irregular. He shivered and she remembered the cloak she still wore, dropping it around his shoulders. She hugged her arms tight around her chest. She could barely look at him without needing to pull him into her arms and feel the solid reassurance of his body. *Would it always be like this? Even knowing it was all a lie?*

She shook herself mentally: enough. Enough watching, waiting in the shadows. Eddie's trial date was set and he'd release her as soon as it was over, one way or another, and she would disappear as Gabriel predicted. But she would be free of his care, his possession, his plans. Free of the futile distraction clawing at her heart. *It's time.*

The men were willing and able, and she'd heard Hyde's caustic summary, the cause was more urgent than ever. *Cromwell must fall.* She would go immediately to Exeter, to take Eddie's place organising rebellion under the direction of General Monck's inimitable wife.

There was relief in the decision, and strength.

"I'd sooner sleep on deck," she murmured after a while, eyeing the sheen of sweat on his pale skin. "The men below will lie cheaper than beggars but louder than clocks."

He snorted and, after a moment, she started again: "Are you going to tell me how exactly you plan to get three indentured labourers off a naval frigate under the nose of its captain and armed crew without even so much as a fully functioning sword arm? It's suicide. They'll arrest you-"

"I haven't the faintest idea," he interrupted with a rueful smile and an awkward shrug. "But I'll think of something."

No doubt he would think of something, it was just difficult to envisage anything that didn't end with him being captured or killed or, at best, traded for the Kielty prisoners. There was no question that he would do whatever it took to save Donn's family. *They were his family too.* There was every chance that the six-month-old soul boarding the slave ship in Cork was his baby. Faced with a suicidal mission to the French or the probability of court martial in London, here was something worth dying for.

In the darkness, without the distraction of sunlight or coastal view, the Albatross groaned and creaked as if bursting with a restless need to tell its own ghost stories but the waves rolled alongside hushing it, giving them space to talk. They sat in awkward silence and she stilled a moment, grateful for the breeze that settled her stomach and drew away the tears that pricked her eyes. She ran her thumbnail along a deep groove on the deck.

"Tara," Gabriel started finally, making her jump. "You were on the French frigate..."

She glanced at him a moment, long spine stiff, mouth set in a grim line and brown eyes fixed hard on a knot on the wooden deck. "Yes," she said eventually. "I was."

"Why?"

She was still his wife. An uncharitable impulse to remind him of the fact and make him suffer swept through her and she breathed deeply, momentarily unsure if she could bring herself to indulge it. She couldn't. "I was watching the ship from the harbour. The wind changed and someone closed the window to the captain's cabin against the smoke. You wouldn't have been able to get in."

She shrugged helplessly. "The captain had been drinking in the tavern with some of the crew. They were setting off in a row boat back to the ship, fearing the mob when everyone thought the explosion was a French plot. I could think of nothing else to get on board. I told him I was a jilt-"

She felt his flinch as no more than a ripple along the hair on his exposed forearm. She could tell from the ragged sound of his breath that the wound was hurting him but he held himself impassive, fiercely tense. Perhaps it wasn't the wound. She swallowed, her heart close to breaking, and took a deep breath to control her voice.

"I slipped my shoes off in his cabin and complained of the heat. I opened the window wide and when I heard you outside, I begged him to take me on deck for more air. It was dark and he'd already ordered the crew to the gun deck... We went to the bridge and soon he had me hard against the wheel. He nudged my chin to the moon and kissed my neck."

"Ta-"

"Then I remembered one of Marie's stories, and I told him in my finest bawdy house: *It's so mighty a pleasure sir, to be fornicating with such a handsome monsieur.*

"At first, he just grunted, unwilling to waste time on words, so I continued: *My friend Bessy was fair tied up with syphilitic knots in the end. She took an extra dose of the quicksilver sweats and, lifting her face from her upturned hands, she found them cupping her septum!* He seemed confused, so I continued: *Since all whores and all French sailors are riddled with the pox, oh, doesn't it feel good that we should have found each other to make hay while the sun shines?*

"I moved then to kiss him but his eyebrows shot up. *Tout les putains anglais?* I nodded: all the English whores. *Mais tous les marins francaise aussi, non?*" She mimicked a deep French voice, quivering with outrage: "*Absolutement non, Madam.* Not all the French sailors. After that he was in quite a hurry to have me rowed back to dry land."

Tara forced a small light-hearted shrug. The corner of his lips quirked and she felt a small flutter of relief, even though the fledgling grin didn't quite reach his eyes. Then the clouds parted, allowing a shaft of moonlight to illuminate them and Gabriel hung his head again, his features disappearing beneath the dark waves of his hair.

"You might not have... you're fearless," he murmured, reaching clumsily out for her hand and clenching his jaw as the movement aggravated the wound.

Easy, as it turns out, she thought. There's everything to play for. She pulled her fingers gently away and wrapped her arms around her chest again like armour. But now I have nothing to lose.

* * *

In the burgeoning grey of dawn, Tara stirred with the ringing of a hollow bell intoning the ahoy of land. Ireland. She scrambled awkwardly off the pallet without waking him, lifting his heavy arm back onto his own narrow bunk from where it had spilled in the darkness to touch her. Fearful that fever would take hold in his wound, she'd stayed by his side continuously the last two days, above deck and then below when Calderditch finally pulled rank and insisted he rest clear of the myriad activities involved in keeping the Albatross running. The captain was mostly concerned, Tara presumed, by the risk of scuppering the Lord Protector's important plans, but that didn't change the fact he was right: Gabriel had needed rest. He needed it still.

Up on deck, a fat seagull plopped heavily down beside her with a loud braying squawk. Through the rail, Cork's stone-built harbour was coming into sharp relief against the indistinct beiges and greens of land. Calderditch was right about this too: the Althea had beaten them on the clear water straight of the Irish Sea. From a distance, the ship sat like a toad, ready to open her hatches wide and swallow passing insects with a flick of her lashing tongue. Indeed, from this distance she could just make out an open-air holding pen of people on the dockside; slaves waiting for embarkation.

She turned to see Gabriel emerged from the cabin, moving in short purposeful bursts, strapping his sword and pistol holster to his waist with a faint grimace at every jarring movement.

"How is it today?" she asked, slipping quickly behind him and lifting his shirt before he had a chance to protest. He tried to twist to face her but the action was beyond him and he stiffened as her fingers gently traced the wound. Mercifully, there was no fresh blood on Toucan's bandage and the exposed flesh on either side was still no hotter than the normal furnace temperature of his skin.

"Minerva! Sir!" Cadlerditch ambled over with one eye scanning the approaching harbour. "We'll moor up behind the Althea but you'll have to get yourselves off unseen. I can't begin to imagine how you'll extract warm bodies from that navy vessel. I suppose you'd best take Gull along with you for good measure. But I warn you, mind – you get one hour, no more. This is not a port for me to be hanging around in. I won't be waiting long enough for the Harbour Master to notice we've no business being here."

"Understood," said Gabriel but Tara just nodded, wondering abstractly at the speed with which the port wall was approaching.

Minutes later her fingers were white on the rail as the Albatross ground along hewn granite to the audible vocal consternation of Calderditch and his first mate. "Ho! Fucking wretches! Shake a leg!"

Almost at once men leapt onto firm ground, spring ropes in hand, scrabbling on slippery cobbles as they looped the ropes around bollards and braced themselves for purchase against the tug of the moving vessel.

"Hold her, you scurvy bastards! Hold firm!"

Shouts soon echoed back from other crews on the quayside as the lugger came slowly and dangerously close to butting into the rear of the Althea. More sheets were thrown and more bulging arms strained, dragging on the ropes. Every eye in the port was glazed by the spectacle and every breath held to see if the lascivious figurehead on the bow spit of the Albatross would purse her red lips to the Althea's broad rump or knock the living daylights out of her.

"Now," hissed Gabriel and he jumped from the moving stern onto the quayside, holding firmly onto Tara's hand. Gull, the heavyset sailor who'd led her on board two days previous, landed softly behind them with Donn, knives drawn, and they ran, skirting around the customs house, to duck behind a low wall and better survey the scene.

"There are three soldiers around the pen," reported Gull by way of summary. "Each'll be armed, obviously, plus likely 35 or 40 crew already on deck for a ship of that size."

He flicked a pointed glance over the four of them and Gabriel shifted uncomfortably against the wall. Beads of sweat had broken out on his forehead and he snapped through clenched teeth: "No-one asked you to come."

"That ain't strictly true," muttered Gull rebelliously. "Last one on board, says Cap'n, first one sent on the fuckin' fool's errands."

"Who'll be the stiff-lookin' fella comin' off the deck?" whispered Donn quickly, heading off any unhelpful argument.

"That'll be Cap'n Winterton," murmured Gull, slightly appeased by having his expert opinion expressly sought. "The soldiers are handing over to the Navy. Most of the slave ships for this run are from yon Protector's fleet; they ain't exactly immune to the potential for profit but better disciplined for the task than yer average privateer." He shrugged and cast a professional eye over the pens: "Mind you, there'll not be a great deal of profit in this venture by the looks of it. Red, are these your people?"

With his back to the wall and the prisoners, Gabriel had sunk to his haunches, eyes fixed and scanning the entrance to Cork's docks for more soldiers. Finding a knife still clutched in his hand, Gull slid down next to him and worried at the embedded grime beneath his fingernails, head sunk in apparent absorption, content now to the leave the vigilance to others. Tara alone watched Donn as he struggled to hold in the horror of fate, his eyes peering above the stones as he scanned the bedraggled mass for the friends and neighbours he once knew intimately.

At first glance the pen was a static still life canvas, but every now again movement rippled through the throng and the bodies parted, twisted, shifting like a shoal of dull brown fish. New scenes were disgorged. Here a worn barefoot woman, one hand on the shoulder of a skinny teenage boy. Now a middle aged couple, white haired and grey clad. Hollow, expressionless eyes.

"Maire," Donn hissed eventually, his voice thick with the shock of recognition and his muscles taught with the urge to run to her. "An' she's holdin' a bairn."

Gabriel's focus on the gates didn't waiver but Tara flickered her eyes over the wall in the direction of Donn's watery gaze. An elderly woman had collapsed to the dirt floor, clutching a tight bundle of rags. Maire Kielty was the embodiment of exhaustion. She shifted slightly in response to a careless knee and the cloth fell open, revealing a shaft of thick blonde curls. Against the dirty brown tableau of prisoners, the baby's head stood out like a candle in the gloom.

"That'll be fixin' it then, so," muttered Donn blankly. "There's none as I can remember lookin' like that on my side."

They sat in silence for a moment, before Gabriel pulled out his pistol and double checked the lock. He hissed at the awkward movement but his sword was ready in his left hand. Donn frowned momentarily. Glancing at Tara, he pulled a hip flask from his breeches and offered it up: "Luck o' the Irish to ye?"

Gabriel's dark hair shimmered in the early sunlight as he looked up and Tara saw the genesis of a familiar grin beneath the curls. "I suppose every little helps."

She watched as he took a swig of the whisky, head back and throat bobbing as he swallowed. She glanced between Donn and Gull then waited an agonising few moments, until the meaning became thin and his eyes, pupils dark and wide with confusion, fell heavily closed. His shoulders slumped and she reached out to capture his head before it crashed back against the stone.

"Ye could've chose a more convenient fuckin' spot," grumbled Gull as he dragged Gabriel's deadened arm heavily around his neck and braced his legs against the wall to lift him. His thighs shook with the effort of taking the larger man's weight and sweat beaded on his forehead as he half carried, half dragged the prostrate form to where it would be out of sight behind a pile of crates, ready to make progress back to the Albatross. "Go!" he hissed as an afterthought, twisting awkwardly around Gabriel's torso to make the point. "I don't need to remind ye that if anyone sniffs around I'm off."

"Able fer it?" asked Donn quietly, glancing back from his aunt.

Tara nodded. She took a deep breath and stood up, emitting a gut-wrenching scream as she ran directly, unarmed, towards the soldiers.

* * *

On some deeply buried, sub-conscious level, Captain Jeremiah Winterton had decided early on that his current naval posting ferrying bodies to the New World would be infinitely easier if he judged the contents of his hold for what it represented in the cargo ledger: one hundred and twenty beasts of burden. *Nothing more, nothing less.* Still, he'd learned from a number of these voyages that it was better not to see the seething mass of Irish at all if it could be helped. If no overexcited dockside corporal had insisted on dragging him from the comfort of his cabin to witness some fool's woeful attempt at a berthing... Lucky for the fool in question, his fustylugs of a ship ground to a halt in time to avoid damage to the Althea. Hell truly hath no fury like the Lord Protector's fleet admiral.

He stroked his moustache neatly flat and sniffed, regretting it almost immediately when his nostrils took in not sharp brine air but the vile vapours of sweat and excrement. Half-starved, half-decrepit, half-human, the Irish in the pens on this miserable grey morning were the very dregs of a race disposed to violence, idleness and, worse, to ignorant and idolatrous popery. A good number of ships had carried healthier cargo across the oceans, to greater profit, but his was not to query the expediency of his order. They were clear enough, and even supplemented on this voyage by a need to meet with the Spanish out to sea and hand over an important sealed missive, written by Cromwell himself. Winterton's chest puffed imperceptibly. This was the real mission; the stinking slaves were nothing more than an elaborate, expendable sideshow.

On the quayside, observing the pens under heavy brows, he saw nothing but feckless men, rancid women and pathetic children. *Papists.* His orthodox bigotry told him their souls were damned to Hell eternal; little point overanalysing the quality of their next few years on earth. If they were even so lucky as to survive the journey. It mattered not. *For what is your life?* He wanted to scream at the hollow eyes that watched him with the calm stupor of cattle in the slaughterhouse. *It is even a vapour, that appeareth for a little time, and then vanisheth away. James 4:14*, he added, with no small sense of satisfaction for having made another apposite selection from his mental catalogue of righteousness.

It was the silence he really detested. For a man schooled in the considered art of engagement, he had no respect for the sullen, vacant emptiness of acceptance. He hated them. Eyes watching him impassively, judging, waiting. Waiting for what? They drove like geese at the wagging of a hat. If the tables were turned, would he just stand there, relinquish England and allow his cursed fate to unravel at another's will? He would not. Was it really acceptance or was each lost soul busy forging intricate and bloody plans for his own destruction? He had an answer for that too. *Exodus 1:10. Come on, let us deal wisely with them; lest they multiply, and it come to pass, that, when there falleth out any war, they join also unto our enemies, and fight against us, and so get them up out of the land.*

Suddenly one of them was screaming, a noise so unusual that it took a moment to react. He turned his eyes with detached slow motion as a banshee careened pell mell across the cobbles. The Irish were as transfixed by the sight but across the dock yard, Colonel Smith, experienced veteran of torie scraps, dropped to his knees and raised his pistol, aiming it steadily at her head. He followed the Colonel's squinting sight: crazed eyes, streaming tears, hair flying out. Unarmed. Running towards the pen, rather than away from it. Expensive dress.

"Stop!" he barked, pacing forward. "Do not shoot I say!"

Smith snapped his head around and stood smartly to as Winterton hurried down the gang plank put his arms out to catch the girl before she ran headlong into the iron bars of the pen. The screams finally formed urgent, high-pitched words. English words. "My baby! Rupert! She stole my baby!"

"Calm yourself, madam," he started brusquely, pushing her back to arm's length, eyes flicking distastefully over her torn silk and back towards the windswept man who jogged up behind her, auburn hair long and loose and arms raised in supplication. Also unarmed.

"She's taken my Rupert! My baby!" the girl continued, heedless of the Captain's order. He nodded over her head to Colonel Smith, continue loading, who sheathed his weapon and turned back to the pen, barking orders to the Irish to move along the gangplank. A soldier at the back of a pen brandished an iron cattle prod and filthy feet shuffled miserably forward.

"No!" Tara screamed again towards his cargo, struggling against his grip: "Rupert!"

The rabid wench was strong; she might actually knock him over if she kept fighting. Winterton thought a moment before slapping her face hard enough to command her attention and stop the screams. "Who the devil are you, Madam?"

Tara's hand shot to her stinging cheek and her eyes widened with something she hoped approximated a respectful shock. She fell to her knees without warning and looked up over his belly. "Mistress Pitts. This is my brother John. My husband was granted land in Galway for service to the good Lord Protector but he was sent to report to the garrison in Dublin. I was alone with our baby when our farm was intruded by tories. God be thanked the soldiers came to save us but Rupert was gone. Oh, Rupert!"

She grabbed hold of the Captain's sleeve for good measure and jabbed a finger towards Maire Kielty, whose shaded eyes watched them dispassionately from the gangplank: "From the start, she was hanging around him, telling me he was beautiful. We've followed hard upon the troops. She stole my baby, sir! Don't let her take him!"

He shrugged off her hand awkwardly, moustache twitching, and patted on his pocket for the passenger list. Abstract irritation washing over him again that his supposedly experienced quartermaster had mislaid the more impressively neat copy ledger. Forced to brandish a piece of tattered parchment, he flicked it importantly past her eyes. "My orders, Madam, are to load every one of the names on this list into the hold of this ship and this will shortly be done. We counted the heads more than once. There was no additional baby. I cannot simply remove a named Irish on the say so of any wailing woman."

"God's wounds, Rupert is not Irish! Anyone might easily switch or replace an innocent babe in such times as these!" She glanced back at Donn and beneath his heavy fringe, his hooded eyes were rimmed with alarm. The bodies in the pen were slowly thinning. Someone had recognised him, knew him for a collaborator after his years translating orders for Fleetwood, and was calling to attract the soldiers' attention. But without so much as a glance in their direction, someone else elbowed the threat in the face and he collapsed, leaving others to tread slowly over and around his prostrate form. Tara dragged her attention back to the Captain: "Have you not children? Please. Just ask her!"

Captain Winterton considered a moment, running his hand impatiently across his face. No, he had no children. He had no wife. Fickle, superficial creatures, women, too rashly choleric to be use to man or beast. He closed his eyes, as if hoping that this troublesome apparition would disappear as calmly as his cargo dissolved beneath deck. Most of them, anyway, he amended, as he opened them to see Colonel Smith tentatively prod at a fallen Irish man with his boot.

At length, he scanned the deck for the quartermaster. "You have two minutes to convince me, Mistress Pitts. Stubbers! Bring the old Kielty woman to me!"

Tara and Donn followed closely behind Winterton as he paced back up the crew gangplank, barking orders without breaking step at the deck hands busy readying the Althea for departure. Still a proud woman, Maire Kielty held her poise as she was shoved up through a hatch and tugged along by the elbow, skeletal arms still wrapped tightly around the tatty linen bundle.

"Irish!" started the Captain, presiding from the first step to the bridge to emphasise his importance: "This woman says you have stolen her baby. What say you?"

Maire looked deliberately and impassively at Tara and then at Donn before turning back to address the Captain: "Aye. So it is."

The Captain sighed impatiently and leaned forward, gingerly peeling back the coverlet to reveal the shock of bright yellow curls. The quartermaster chimed in, ever unhelpful: "It's not worth 'out to us, Cap'n, sir. If I've told the men once I've told them sundry times: stinkin' babes and kids're more trouble than they're worth. We skimmed off the most likely looking two years ago and they're already in Jamaica. The rest won't sell, even if they make it alive."

Winterton sucked in his cheeks and fingered his list again, biding time. The background economics really were by-the-by when his commands were scratched out in black and white. Stubbers was offering opinions above his station. Again.

"Where's her husband, Stubbers? Patrick…"

"Kielty's dead, Cap'n."

Winterton shook his head, as if this were a minor irritation. "This is extremely serious, Irish. Kidnap is a capital offence. What would possess you to do such a thing?"

Tara felt Donn tense behind her and curled her fists but Maire just shrugged, lips pursed. "Feckin' gobermouch, it's none of yer business. I'm old and riddled with canker. Paddy an' I was figurin' a bairn might be worth hapenny. If not, then the ocean's deep and the land's already so full to bursting with feckin' Englishmen that it would not be much missin' another."

"Unnatural witch!" cried the quartermaster and Winterton put a warning hand on his chest to prevent his stepping any closer towards her.

The Captain considered his options. He looked across at the Englishwoman, eyes rimmed with panic. She would undoubtedly make another scene. He was generally impervious to melodrama but there was something about her, some promise of a steel will beneath immodestly unkempt hair and ragged dress. Some echo of breeding in the way she held herself; some hint of threat that she would not be easily quieted. If called upon to justify his decision the confession must be adequate to settle the matter.

At his nearly imperceptible nod, Tara leant forward to take possession of the baby with the shadow of a squeeze to Maire's cold fingers. Frighteningly insubstantial for the life it contained and thick with the stench of a filthy clout, she clasped it tight against her chest.

A rasping cry rose from the squirming rags in protest at the change of hands, evidence of the unexpected tenacity of its occupant, and instinctively she whispered soothing words, shifting her hold, terrified to hold the bundle too tight and cause pain: "Hush, darling, my darling... it's alright, you'll be alright, everything will be alright... hush."

"He's a bonny lad, sure he is, minds me of little Donnacha," Maire murmured under her breath, before stepping back, a hint of dreaminess about the words: "*Glaoch mé Aodhan air.*"

Tara didn't understand the Gaelic but, without warning, silent tears fell spontaneously and uncontrollably down her cheeks: "Captain, what will happen?"

"You will leave her in Cork to the mercy of the courts, Captain?" interrupted Donn, his first words measured, quiet, carefully constructed in mimic of Tara's own voice without the inflexion of his tell-tale accent.

Winterton drew himself up like Solomon and looked out over the deck. "We are on my ship, sir, and here on these boards I am judge and jury. Rest assured there will be no mercy. *Proverbs 21:15: joy to the just to do judgment. Destruction to the workers of iniquity.*"

Tara froze, heart beating fast but mind blank and body unbiddable. Stubbers understood; he took Maire's elbow to lead her up onto the bridge, calling for attention. Donn touched her arm with tense fingers. There was nothing more to say, nothing they could do, and at Winterton's curt dismissal, they walked back down the crew gangplank to the quayside. Several sailors were loosening the last few mooring warps holding the Althea to the bollards and they fell, slapping against her hull with wet, resounding smacks that made Donn flinch in anticipation of the Captain's justice.

It came before they reached the cobbles. One shot. It was barely loud enough to be heard above the creaking and groaning of the old frigate as it was nudged reluctantly to movement, but still it echoed around her hollow chest. With shaking fingers, she reached out and took Donn's hand in hers, squeezing tightly, her other arm wound securely around Gabriel's son.

* * *

He snapped to without preamble and his body jerked upwards, smacking his head firmly and eye-wateringly into the low beams above his bunk. "Ow!"

"There. He's awake now," said Toucan unnecessarily, plugging the small jar of smelling salts with a rag and moving aside so Tara could sit down on the edge beside him. The cabin titled with the roll of the waves and for a moment she put out a hand to steady herself on his thin mattress.

"Tara! What the Hell? How did I-? What have you-?"

"His name is Aodhan," she whispered, handing the baby over, smiling as predatory fingers gripped hold of the loose curls lying unsuspecting against his jaw, the darkest black wrapping around the palest skin. Gabriel took him instinctively, speechless with wonder, and looked into the wide blue question in his round eyes.

"He's your son, Milord. I'll not be lookin' to confuse the lad." Donn's voice, thick again with the accent of his fathers, rose quietly from the corner and Gabriel tilted his throbbing head to look at him. For a moment their eyes met and both men understood instinctively how things would be. Donn nodded and made to leave, adding before he did: "Aodhan. It means born of fire."

40. THE FRENCH ARE VERY MUCH SHORT WITH US

To Sir William Lockhart, our Ambassador in France
Whitehall, 31 August 1658.

Sir,

I have seen your Letter to Mr. Secretary Thurloe, and although I have no doubt either of your diligence or ability to serve us, the French are very much short with us.

We never were so foolish as to believe that the French and their interests were the same as ours in all things, but we thought to have joint interests as to the Spaniard (the most implacable enemy to France). I am now astonished to learn France thinks we negotiate with the Spanish in defiance of our alliance. What scabrous vermin would spread such lies?

Now I know the startling lack of faith in French hearts, I pray you tell Cardinal Manzini that talking reassuringly of our alliance is a parcel of childish words. I think they will do all to prevent our influence on the continent. We never could have foreseen that we should be failed towards as we are!

I desire that the following is demanded: satisfaction for the expense of our Naval Forces (incurred out of an honourable and honest aim to pursue joint enemies alongside France); and confirmation of how our Men on French soil will be returned to us. Those unable to leave should know the affection and gratitude in the very heart of England.

I would know with some urgency what France saith, and will do. Your very loving friend,
OLIVER P.

41. LIGHT AND DARK

Aodhan peered myopically over his father's shoulder at the pile of fresh linens and threw his head back for a piercing wail, globules of his porridge supper bubbling from his open mouth. Gabriel struggled to hold the convulsing body against him, fingers spread wide across the boy's back while his free hand shook a folded cloth out impatiently and laid it flat on the bed. He turned to retrieve a bowl and balanced it next to the cloth for easy reach, the cold-water sloshing over the sides in his rush and pooling on the coverlet.

Now icy, his touch provoked even greater outrage and Aodhan's balled face turned an indignant puce to match the shade of his inflamed gums. Gabriel had considerable sympathy for the babe at the tortuous sight of a first tooth slowly breaking the skin but the process had other, no less traumatic, side effects. As if on cue, the loose green sludge that Ann swore was normal, imbued as she was with a near mystical knowledge of such things despite being childless, oozed from the sides of Aodhan's heavy clout. It smeared on his shirt.

"Hell's teeth," he muttered with mild irritation as the indelible stain spread with every squirming kick. Unceremoniously he put the squirming bundle down on its back and wrinkled his nose as plump little legs and fists waved energetically in the air, squaring up for a fight.

"Seriously, I've no idea why you should be so upset. Your body servant here is getting you a fresh clout, keeping you clean, attending to your every whim."

Aodhan stopped moving suddenly, ceased the scream and looked up at him with wide blue eyes. Encouraged, Gabriel continued talking with a singsong lilt as he peeled back the soiled linen and dropped it on the floor, wiping awkwardly like an archaeologist to excavate delicate pink skin through the muck.

"Who do you think is going to find me a clean shirt, hmm? Should I perhaps… " At a loss, his mind groped for a rhyme, something Leo had sung, at Treguddick, to little Henry. He picked up a hesitant thread: *"Tommy was a piper's Son, and fell in love when he was young… But all the tunes that he could play, were o'er the hills, and far away…"*

When he'd finished, he stood for a while and just looked at his son, laying in a shaft of late afternoon sun. Patted gently dry and freshly clean, Aodhan's colour had returned to normal. He might have been Rupert, a babe himself when Lucius took him to Tretower Castle that last time, with clear instruction to disassociate himself from the Godlphins before ascending to court in London. That was twenty years ago. With a detached hindsight, he could still see Lucius striding to fetch his whip, disappointed by the affection in the farewell. Offended by his son's weakness. In the darkness of the memory, a babe's blond curls gleamed like a torch.

Gabriel shook his head distractedly and laid a hand lightly across Aodhan's warm belly, enjoying the contented gurgle. In the blessed weeks since their arrival back home, his little chest had filled to a barrel, from which long limbs protruded, podgy and strong.

Home.

They were a long way from Hellens Manor. Its echoing corridors and nervous bevy of servants was softened only by the frosty efficiency of Ann. Well, he thought wryly, there was no change in Ann at least. It was hard to speak of his affection for the woman when Tara asked, not that he really wanted to try. It was not possible to analyse what she had done for him, patching up his wounds and keeping scraps of food safely hidden, not without remembering Lucius.

They were further still from whatever home Aodhan had shared in Ireland with Donn's family. He whispered another silent prayer of thanks for Maire Kielty, a daily occurrence since Cork. Commend her soul to Heaven, Lord. Her sacrifice was so that my innocent son might live. The tightness in his chest only eased when the invocation ended: Help me, Lord. I am blind to your brute purpose but give me the same strength for sacrifice, so that I may deliver them both to safety.

"If there were a chance, I could keep you with me…" he murmured. If circumstances had been different, was it really in him to be a father? In moments like this, it was possible to fantasise that it was. He drew a finger across the naked sole of the babe's foot and smiled as the round eyes creased into gurgling laughter. He felt a rush of tenderness and indulged it, letting it jostle for space with his aching need for Tara before it dissolved into the potent draught of duty and responsibility.

Home. It was no bricks and mortar fantasy. She was his home. She alone had the power to justify him, to give meaning to his life, to banish his nightmares. *Could he be the same for her?* She'd chosen him over running to the anonymous company of a boarding house in London; over his offer of installation in a town house with Rupert and Marie. She held herself carefully apart from him but she was still here; heavy with secrets, painfully preoccupied with the trial, frustrated by her inability to do anything of practical use for Villiers. A series of trips to Temple Bar for legal counsel had proved fruitless; the Tower guards were no doubt pilfering the food parcels she delivered. But at the end of each day she came back to Petersham. To Ham House, to him. *Home.*

For now, it was all he could hope for. He trod carefully; they both did. Neither of them prodded at the delicate house of cards for fear it would topple into the dust. They avoided all talk of the future. Took meaningless distraction in everyday estate running, Slept in separate beds… Yet every wretched moment was as precarious as it was precious. An apparent stay of execution on Cromwell's order to France was no grounds for relief. The Lord Protector was distracted, reported to be devastated after the death of Elizabeth Claypole. He was also no doubt still waiting for a response from the Spanish court, although he might realise any day now that his offer had never been delivered by the Althea.

Fleetwood had meanwhile written first enquiring casually as to his recent whereabouts, expressing surprise that the terms of his house arrest would be so flagrantly ignored. It was a transparent preamble to court martial and another letter had duly arrived this morning: he was now given summons to attend Horse Guard Yard in London on 5 September. His commander would be reluctant to condemn him, but he would have little choice. At least is would be after Villiers' trial tomorrow, he thought, for then it didn't matter. Villiers would be safe. Tara would be safe. Aodhan would be safe, taken back with Rupert and Marie to Treguddick, loved with light touches by the whole Godolphin clan, living the childhood he'd once dreamed of.

A shaft of late evening sunlight bathed the babe with golden warmth as if he were suspended in a delicious honey. He leaned forward gently to kiss the clear, untroubled forehead and stretched down for a moment on the mattress beside him. On impulse he scooped up the perfect body and lifted him overhead, great snorts of giggles falling from on high: "What say you, little piglet, how do you like to fly?"

Aodhan's belly shook with laughter underneath his fingers and a stream of golden urine arced towards him without warning, the yellow line adding more unwarranted decoration to his shirt.

"Give me strength." Finally defeated, Gabriel laughed as he laid the boy gently down to his side and sat up onto the edge of the bed to peel the linen carefully over his head.

"Sir! What the Devil are you doing? You know I'll do his clouts." Ann bustled in, shooing him away as she picked up the baby. Aodhan relaxed immediately against her chest. "Mrs Moore needs you, now. She says she's not strong enough…"

At that he was gone, grabbing at his scabbard and buckling it onto his belt. He ran down the stairs two at a time, only to find her standing on the first-floor landing with her back to him, focused on something outside the window.

"Tara! You're back? What is it?"

"Look." She tapped impatiently on a diamond pane of glass, brows furrowed in concern. Robert Gardener was stripped to the waist, chopping exhaustedly and inaccurately at a dead fruit tree on the far edge of the lawn. "He's losing the light, thank God, but I'm not sure he'll stop. You have to help him. I'm worried he's going to have a heart attack or chop his leg off. "

He smiled, his heart rate returning to normal as he peered at the old man, stubbornly heaving the axe in the vague direction of the gnarled trunk. "What are you doing here? I thought you were to accompany Marie to Richmond this afternoon?"

"Marie sprained her ankle on the cobbles. I promised to sit with her until Rupert can be found."

"Milord?" Donn called up carefully from the bottom of the stairs. "The… the colts have arrived."

She frowned. "More bloody horses? Gabriel, you have to help Robert."

"I will," he insisted, flicking his eyes in the direction of Gardener as he turned to run down the stairs. Tara raised an eyebrow, finally taking in his dishevelled appearance, but there was nothing to rail against bar the thudding sound of his footsteps and the raised afterthought as he disappeared across the chequered hall. "Later. Soon. I'll have him stop for today. Go to Marie!"

* * *

"Look, despite some evident enthusiasm for the idea, there are clearly not enough of us to storm the Tower and just walk out with Villiers. Indeed gentlemen, if that were an option, we might have tried it a little sooner," said Gabriel dryly by way of summary. As usual, Hyde's London men were eagerly committed to whatever fight they could find to vindicate their King. Sensing a whisper of dissent, he raised a warning eyebrow at John Ashton's frown. "It is agreed our best chance is to attack the transport en route to his trial tomorrow."

He surveyed the map rolled out on the kitchen table before them, its corners weighted by a random assortment of mugs and candlesticks, and pointed at the Palace of Westminster: "The High Court of Justice sits in the Painted Chamber. Gurney or coach, we will have a short window to intercept it... There are only two probable routes from the Tower on wheels; the other streets are too narrow and chaotic. John Ashton and John Betterley – you'll wait here, on Thames Street. Rupert and Tom – you'll be on Tower Street. Donn - you're by far the swiftest horseman. Wait by the Tower. When you see which direction they're taking, ride hell-for-leather to tell the men not in its path.

"There should be time enough for the lot of you to convene on Fish Street Hill, to the north here or south here." He pointed at two intersections where London's key east-west thoroughfares passed across the steeply sloping road south to London Bridge and the men nodded.

"Then together, we will have numbers and surprise to carry out the ambush," said Betterley, pursuing his lips in approval.

"How many guards is he likely to have?" Tom asked practically.

"Only one or two, I'd say," said Ashton. "Maybe four. The most I've ever seen is seven."

Rupert rolled his eyes but Gabriel continued: "I need another coach waiting on the north side of the bridge."

John Lockhart nodded, finally breaking his silence. "I'll be there, sir."

"Then Tom, see Villiers installed with Lockhart. Lockhart, you're to drive further on into Kent, to rendezvous with another carriage. You'll see the sign to stop, that we discussed earlier. You will then release Villiers and return to London alone."

"Sir, the lady," said Betterley hesitantly. "Do you need us to-"

"No. There's another driver to take her. You don't know him. If something goes awry tomorrow, I would not have any of you able to find her." He paused. The implication clear enough. If they were captured, tortured, no man would be able unwillingly to betray her route to safety with the Stuarts. By the time Thurloe could trace the plan to Gabriel, she would be clear.

"Tomorrow, then." Gabriel lifted a candlestick and let the map spring from the table before rolling it back up and slipping it inside its casing, dismissing the men with an efficient nod. "Thank you, gentlemen." All three Johns grinned back and filed wordlessly out through the back door, dissolving into the darkening evening.

Rupert clasped his shoulder as he passed. "Does she know yet, cousin?" he asked quietly.

Gabriel shook his head, almost imperceptibly, and Rupert hung his, clearly biting his tongue as he left to head upstairs and attend to his immobile wife.

"Donn," Gabriel said suddenly, stopping him as he was about to leave. "You've been too quiet. Tell me, what're you thinking? I want your opinion: is there a problem with the plan?"

"No Milord. The plan's just grand." Half through the doorway, he paused and turned with some reluctance to speak. "Look, I wasna goin' to be tellin' ye, mind, but aye, since ye asked it needs sayin': yer a feckin' idjit."

Gabriel started but before he could respond, Ann pushed past Donn into the kitchen, shooing the groom back to the stables and exhaling an exaggerated "harrumph" at the state of the table. She muttered reproach as she collected empty mugs and randomly scattered candlesticks: "Little wonder your fine silver is going missing at such an alarming rate, sir. And will you look at the state of your shirt? I can't think it's proper to have-"

"Ann, please, we have matters to discuss." Mechanically, Gabriel turned to the fireplace and stripped off his spoiled linen.

"I must admit I was surprised to see that cantankerous battle-axe still so fighting fit and able," murmured Tom once she'd left with Gabriel's balled shirt. He reached across the table to pour two fresh whiskeys. "She must be well into her sixties."

"I'm beginning to wonder if she's immortal."

"Perhaps she sold her soul to the Devil," Tom replied with a grin, offering one of the glasses.

"Be nice. She could starve us." Gabriel muttered wryly as he took it and sat down in a high armchair by the fire, rolling the liquid around the glass, watching vacantly as it picked up dancing lights. It was a comfortable silence, born from long trust; each man momentarily wrapped in his own assessment of the task ahead. At length, he looked up: "I'm sorry you're here for this, Tom. But by God I'm glad to see you."

Tom shrugged. "Rupert was scared witless when you were arrested, he meant well with his summons. Besides, Leo tells me I'm no use to her during her confinement and she'd rather I spent the month watching your back than gandermooning with the parlour maids."

Gabriel inclined his head with a grin that didn't reach his eyes and they each took a mouthful of whisky in silent toast to Leo and baby Henry.

"Of course, you know Donn's right," said Tom, with considered casualness.

"She's safer with Charlie," Gabriel finally replied, knocking back the glass and its contents, ploughing his fingers through his hair.

"She's a resourceful woman, Gabe, and she's fiercely intelligent. I imagine she's a greater chance of navigating court and Cromwell than most."

"She's unlike anyone I've ever met," Gabriel conceded. "You should have seen her in Portsmouth. She took control of the men without hesitation and organised an attack on a military target without a single casualty. I couldn't have carried out Hyde's orders without her."

"And unless I'm mistaken, since Edward Villiers was arrested, she's been the only link to most of the rebels along the South Coast. Do you know yet how she communicates with them?"

"No," said Gabriel quietly on an exhaled breath. "She won't tell me. She'd convened the meeting in Portsmouth before I could see how she did it. No notes, no envelopes, no scribbles... she pulled their strings without so much as raising a hand. She might as well have drawn a blasted pentagon on the floor and summoned them with a spell."

"Best not mention that to Titus Latimer," Tom laughed before feeling the need to state the obvious: "But you are entirely unable to direct them in the future if she's not here?"

"When we get him free, Villiers will tell us..." Gabriel put his glass down heavily and leant forward, silent a moment, putting his head in his hands while his fingers ran back again through his hair.

"What if we can't... get him free?"

"I'll think of something. Christ, Tom, I have to. The stakes are too high. If I let her stay, she'll get involved... she'll insist on managing the cells directly. You'll have read about the round ups, the executions... Cromwell's net is tightening around us and I can't keep Thurloe at arm's length for much longer. Fleetwood's threatening court martial. When I'm no longer able to protect her, if she's caught..."

Tom thought a while, sipping from his own glass. "That may all be true. But why can I not shake the feeling that what you really mean is that she's safer away from you than from Westminster?"

Gabriel snorted: "I've made some important enemies in the last few months. One way or another, I'm on borrowed time but I've always known how this would end. Charlie said from the start that if I could get Villiers out, he would take her as well. I won't deny her that chance. She wouldn't thank me, for dragging her down into the particular Hell coming for the sake of a passing fancy."

"It's hardly that."

"Do not presume-"

"Hell's teeth, Gabe, remember who you're talking to! I've seen the way you look at her, and the way she looks at you. It's a hunger. There's not a village idiot in all England who couldn't see it's more than a common infatuation. Only a damned fool would let such love slip through his fingers and you would willingly cast it into the ocean! Why are you so damned afraid of baring your soul to her when she's the only thing in the world to satisfy it? You cannot fear rejection?"

"Rejection would be a release!" Gabriel gave a hollow laugh before standing and bracing himself against the mantel, the line of his shoulders stiff, his voice low and strained. "Christ, the very thought of living without her and… But she's risked too much for me already and I can finally get her clear, safe from all this."

Tom shook his head but he thought a moment before he repeated quietly: "You have to tell her. You can't just send her away; she deserves to know what you're planning."

"No. I have to be sure she'll go. It's too late, Tom. I'm decided."

"It's not your decision, Gabe! You want to be punished for your sins? Find me a man in all England who doesn't! But you needn't be your own judge, jury and blasted executioner." Tom downed his whiskey and stared at the empty bottom of the glass a moment. When he finally looked up, he'd almost regained his calm: "Jesus man, just think on it. There aren't many so blessed with-"

"Blessed with what, Tom? An endless supply of snorting ponies? A wizened miracle of a gardener? A tendency to self-righteous stubbornness?"

Tom cocked his head at the sudden arrival of Tara at the kitchen door. "Quite, Gabe. What she said."

Tara frowned as she approached the fire and Tom stood from his chair, dropping a gentle kiss on the top of her head before he slid out of the door, pulling it tactfully closed behind him.

"I'm sorry," she started, momentarily awkward. "I didn't mean to interrupt-"

"You didn't," Gabriel replied quietly, standing to greet her. "Please, sit down. You'd like a drink?"

She sank into Tom's seat as he refreshed the glasses and gave a half-hearted smile as he handed her one. She took a sip and felt a burning line course down her throat before cradling it in her lap.

"How's everyone upstairs?" he started.

"Aodhan's snoring sweetly." She gave a small smile, but her eyes were rimmed red. "Marie's tried to provide distraction from her sick bed but in truth she makes a terrible patient and there are only so many threads I can wind or ribbons I can pair... Thank God, Rupert made a timely reappearance... I... I keep thinking about tomorrow."

Gabriel sank suddenly to his knees beside her and closed his fingers around hers on the glass. They were cold and his brows furrowed, a line appearing at the centre of his forehead. "It'll be alright."

"It won't," she replied quietly, shivering despite the warmth radiating from him. "I've been here before, remember? After Penruddock, when my father... You haven't seen Hyde again, have you?"

He gave a small and truthful shake of his head and she watched abstractly as the firelight picked up screws of red in his twisting black hair. "Then there's no hope. Tomorrow he'll die; I've failed to do anything that might save him."

"You've kept everything he believes in alive. You uncovered Willys for a spy. You saved his men from wasting their lives in a trap... You kept the Sealed Knot-"

"For now, perhaps. And at a price." Ralph's ring flashed with the flames and she frowned. "I keep thinking: what might have happened if I had only married Jack a month earlier? He was keen that we shouldn't wait but I stalled, I was scared of becoming reliant on him after so long living alone. But as his wife, I might not have been so foolish at Westminster... I might not have agreed to Cromwell's plan. People have died, because of me. Tollemache-"

"Stop, Tara. That brute died because of me. You were Tollemache's prize; Cromwell would have found a way to hand you over one way or another. You might even have added the butcher to your list." Gabriel hung his head, his lips grazing her fingers as he fought to control an irrational stab of jealous anger at the thought of Jack Ludlow, unable to speak the wretch's name for fear it would hang in the air between them.

"I was reckless in Cork… I forced Maire Kielty into a position where she could do nothing but sacrifice herself to get us all off the ship. I should have found another way. It was my fault she died-"

"Not a day goes by when I don't thank her from the depths of my heart, but there was nothing else you could have done! I should have been more use, Tara. If it's anyone's fault, it's mine. I could have traded myself. But I've talked it through with Donn, you were so brave. There was nothing else you could have done. You have to know that."

She reached out and ran a gentle finger along the scar on his cheek: "All the things you have had to do, for me, that I've asked of you…"

"Everything, Tara, I'd do it all again a thousand times over and be damned for it. Even after… when I let you think I'd betrayed your men… you saved my son's life. You saved my life; you saved my soul."

"You were my husband," she said simply. Her stomach rolled chill with the memory of the French captain on La Glorieuse; he wouldn't know everything. She drew her hand back to the glass. "Even if it was only make believe -"

"I *am* your husband," he said softly, an intensity in his hazel eyes holding her firm. "Look at me and know this: every minute with you is real Tara. God knows, it's more real than anything I've ever known." She broke the gaze but he gently lifted her chin so there was no escape: "Your courage shines from you like light. But you can see right through me, I know you can, and there's nothing but black… I've lived in the shadows for so long I don't know how to be without them. It's nearly over, the trial is tomorrow, and I can't keep you in this darkness."

"No." Tara frowned, pulling away to stand, struggling to release herself from his disorientating closeness. *Was this the end?* He was trying to tell her that he was ready to let her go, like Hyde said he would, like Henry Godolphin knew he would. She would disappear; go to Exeter in a matter of hours. She took a deep breath. "Gabriel, I know you. I've always known you. I know your nightmares… After tomorrow-"

He hung his head. "After tomorrow, there's to be a summons to Whitehall for court martial. Fleetwood has written. They know I breached the terms of my house arrest, and he wants to see me in three days. Cromwell may yet send me to the French and if by some miracle I survive those odds, Hyde will have another errand. I knew what it meant to give my oath to Charlie."

"You're scaring me." Her stomach lurched and impulsively, she dropped to her knees before him, running a tentative hand along his jaw, pushing back the hair and gently turning his face to look at her. "Must I lose you too? Let's leave. Spain, Italy. Further. I don't care, I can't... I won't..." she whispered, chasing the confession of her need as it slipped away. "I..."

He pulled her hard into him then, his arms encasing her body and his scent enveloping her senses. Her tears were wet against his chest as he pressed his lips to the top of her head. "I can't run. There's no honour in it. There are people who depend on me."

"*I* depend on you. You swore an oath to *me*."

"I swore to keep you safe and I will. I'd give my life to protect you, Tara, willingly, without hesitation. I only wish it were that simple. Whatever happens now..."

"Did you love her?"

He frowned momentarily, pulling back a little in surprise at the question: "Who?"

"Neala, Neala Kielty." She flinched as she whispered the name, feeling immediate shame in the question.

Resting his forehead down against hers, his dark eyes filled her vision. It was a while before he spoke and when the words came, they were cracked, husked. "May God forgive me, I did not. I was... empty and she paid for my weakness with her life. I didn't love her..."

The door slammed abruptly open behind them and Rupert manoeuvred around the kitchen table with a tray of empty glasses and plates balanced precariously in one hand and a bunch of ribbons grasped in the other.

"Ma cherie requires ever more refreshment and freshly washed fancies," he announced unapologetically as he put down the tray with an awkward, twisting bend. "Is Ann about? Forget His Damnable Highness, the only true tyranny a man need concern himself with is love!"

Gabriel frowned but he didn't take his eyes from Tara. Without acknowledging his cousin, he kissed her fiercely, his fingers running through her hair to anchor her head. The taste of salt-water and whiskey passed between them before he spoke again: "I didn't know the meaning of the word."

42. THE PAINTED CHAMBER

"No. Up there." He nodded towards a rickety-looking wooden staircase at the back of the Painted Chamber. It led to a platform gallery, installed to accommodate High Court spectators and leaning hard against walls once alive with vibrant colour. She frowned. Gabriel's selection would give them a view of the entire courtroom, but put them at a distance from Eddie and the Commissioners' bench that sat on the raised dais at the front. But he'd already started towards it and reluctantly she followed.

Spectators were already packed in tightly and excited murmurs buzzed between the four walls like trapped flies. They wove through the stench of unwashed bodies, all sweating impatiently in the heat as they waited for the action to start. There were two large arched windows along the longer external wall, grand and gothic in style, but while they permitted enough daylight to conduct proceedings there was nothing that could be done to increase airflow. Tara felt slick sweat slide down the backs of her legs and scooped drops of perspiration out from the front of her bodice. She wore the pale-yellow dress, scrubbed and mended a dozen times since that day she was to wed Jack. It seemed right somehow, as she'd laced the stays in Petersham, but now she couldn't remember why.

"… struck with the dead palsy on the one side…"

Tara froze. Gabriel had heard it too and he reached back to thread his fingers into hers, pulling her gently along behind him. "Gossips, nothing more," he insisted over his shoulder and under his breath. "He's well enough to stand trial."

Through a crushing rabble she was rubbing shoulders with an

unapologetic collection of all human life. The mildly curious and otherwise unemployed had come for a good old-fashioned gawp at the accused. They jostled for view next to more rabid commonwealth fanatics, who set out their elbows for a pitch as they might have set out a stall selling pamphlets detailing the gruesome tastes of royalist traitors. She read the enthusiasm in their wide-eyed grins and it translated neatly into the certainty of guilt. Edward Villiers roasts the children of honest Commonwealth supporters on a spit. Overcome with disgust, she took no pains to avoid stepping on a few toes, recklessly willing on a chance to fight and take a stand.

A short, balding man finally took the bait, and grabbed at her sleeve to remonstrate: "Oi! Watch it, clumsy stampcrab!"

Gabriel spun immediately back with a warning glare and before she had a chance to engage and the protester dropped his hand, scuttling back into the crowd. Frustrated, she scowled as he manoeuvred her round ahead of him, but he didn't seem to notice. He steered her firmly up the staircase to the gallery, where his imperious glance created space on the front row bench and they sat down.

"He has friends here too," he whispered into her hair as he surveyed the baying crowd beneath them. "He's not alone."

"I can't see any." Anger dissipating in worry, she scanned the assembly futilely for friendly faces. Two of the five Commissioners were now seated behind their long bench, waiting to pass judgment. The sweat froze on her skin when she noticed him: "Why is Titus Latimer here?"

"Titus is everywhere."

"But what business has he acting as a Commissioner?"

Gabriel frowned: "He normally presides over the ecclesiastical courts, but he's got fingers in many pies."

"He's a fifth monarchist…" She stilled as she remembered wilfully antagonizing the man over their impromptu wedding breakfast and then again at Hampton Court. She'd put Eddie on the back foot. Trying not to panic, the practical part of her brain rifled through its complicated catalogue of religious enthusiasms and alliances that shifted like sands. Was a fifth monarchist more or less likely to tolerate Eddie's Quaker leanings? Would he read unholy dissention or brotherly kinship in the followers of George Fox? Might Eddie's stubbornly arcane speech patterns antagonise or make up for the damage she'd done? "He believes that the rule of saints will usher in the imminent reign of Christ on earth…"

"He believes he is one of those saints, and while he lives, it is frankly as fair an assumption for his future as any," Gabriel gave a small wry smile, nodding towards a door behind the bench to watch Thurloe enter, before continuing in a low whisper: "Latimer survived the purge of the Nominated Assembly five years ago somehow. He's since outlived accusations of conspiracy and miraculously avoided the Coleman Street round-up in April. Thurloe's desperate for him to slip up. It may be divine providence… but a betting man might think there's a reasonable chance he has something on Cromwell to have survived this long. Damned if I can find out what it is though."

She felt a small shrug in his arm as she stared down, and her shaking hands busied themselves stroking up and down the rough struts of the balustrade in front of them. The room teamed with enemies. Thurloe had inclined his body towards the back of an unmistakable head; Cromwell was sitting stock still in the front row. Gabriel pulled her hand back from the threat of splinters, his fingers threading through hers, reassuringly warm.

"Latimer is tomorrow's problem, not today's… You'll note His Highness is not yet sitting on his throne," he murmured, nodding to a large object in the front corner of the chamber, covered in a red velvet throw. The corner of his lips quirked gently. "It's not quite finished yet. There is apparently some ongoing discussion as to who is paying for it."

He was trying to distract her, and she appreciated the attempt. She flicked her eyes over the whitewashed walls: "I don't care much for the art, either. This painted chamber promises more than it delivers."

He smiled and kissed her forehead and she leant silently against him for a few minutes, until the door opened again and Edward Villiers limped into view. A shock of silence stilled the crowd for a moment. He was flanked by two large soldiers who led him to an exposed stool in the centre of a cleared area before the Commissioners' bench and she felt Gabriel stiffen as they watched him. Hatless, he was noticeably thinner than he had been in May when she last saw him, and he sat slowly, grimacing a little.

Then the three remaining Commissioners filed in to take their seats. One carried a nosegay, presumably full of aromatic herbs to ward off the threat of typhus. Such close proximity to the accused, so fresh from the Tower, was a risky business. When they were all settled, the man on the far left stood and thoughtfully adjusted glasses that were perhaps a little large for his small features. He looked over the room awaiting its respectful stillness before unrolling a parchment and taking a deep breath to speak with measured emphasis.

"The High Court of Justice is hereby convened this second day of September, one thousand six hundred and fifty-eight with all due Power, given by the Act of Parliament, entitled An Act for Establishing an High Court of Justice, to hear and determine all such Matters, Crimes and Offences contrary to the Articles and Laws or Statutes of this Commonwealth, including the Concealments of Treasons."

He paused to allow the gravity of the proceedings sink in and a few excited whispers hissed from the stools beneath. They ceased when he continued: "This Court is hereby authorised and required to pronounce Judgment, and shall and may Award Execution against such Offenders. And where for Offences of High Treason, and other Crimes, Sentence of Death is to be pronounced, this Court is authorised to cause Sentence of Death to be given and executed, having regard to the nature of the Offence."

Proceedings began with the prosecution's case and Thurloe's angular body feigned leisurely confidence as he approached the bench, laying his drafted speech theatrically aside to speak his heartfelt truth. He waved at Eddie with a flourish: "Commissioners. Loyal subjects of England. This man is an enemy of the state. He is a founding member of the traitorous organisation calling itself the Sealed Knot, which has made contact with the exiled pretender Charles Stuart and is rabble-rousing for his return.

"You will know my Lords that the accused's brother was executed in Exeter three years ago on the very same charges of treason. This is a familiar enterprise! At that time, Edward Villiers escaped justice but new evidence has emerged of a wickedness and devilment in his actions that threatens the very fabric of our Government and our Godly society. I will produce irrefutable evidence-"

"You tortured a mad man! Hewitt was a mad man!"

The lone voice of protest triggered consternation amongst the guards and they moved quickly to expel the interruption. Tara exclaimed with the shock of recognition at the cropped blonde hair bobbing between the cramped rows, undeterred by the threat of violence. Mungo Gordon was a simple creature, he'd helped run the Friends' meetings in Exeter, and she started, ready to defend him but Gabriel gently laid a restraining hand on her forearm. She glanced up at him and he shook his head imperceptibly. When she looked back to the room, Mun was gone.

A Commissioner stood then and gave an impatient flutter of his fingers. "First and last warning. It is of vital importance to our Lord Protector that these trials are held in public so as to avoid the degradations and abuses common under that tyrant monarch Charles Stuart, but another word and I will hold each and every one of you in contempt."

Animated chatter immediately bubbled up and burst on pointed whispers of sshh! and Thurloe waited expansively for total silence to reassert itself before continuing. "I have irrefutable evidence that in the defendant's actions it is possible to observe a design of so-called prince Charles Stuart, to seduce the people of this nation from their due obedience to this present Government. He would invite them, by promoting his pretended Interest, to embroil this nation in new troubles, by bloody and intestine war..."

Eddie was staring blankly ahead, and Tara wondered briefly if he could have heard. Then his head bowed and she realised, desperate tears pricking, that he had indeed suffered a stroke. A mild one perhaps but his left features had slid slightly, his movements were too tightly controlled.

"...I have spent years unmasking the hypocrites of the Sealed Knot organisation, in uncovering its wicked designs, lodged under the specious pretences of loyalty, which would most undoubtedly have ended in the destruction of the truly Godly if the Lord and Justice not prevented it..."

Unfathomable stifling hours passed. Gabriel sat stock sill and expressionless but Tara barely noticed him, engrossed in the speeches and soliloquies that slipped into impenetrable Latin legalese. No defence was permitted; instead Thurloe calmly orchestrated the calling of witnesses whose names she'd never heard, the presentation of exhibits apparently recovered from his house in Exeter that she'd never seen. In the rising heat of the afternoon, the crowd became restless. There were no breaks for food or comfort. Bottoms fidgeted and wriggled on uncomfortable wooden stools, covetous glances thrown pointedly towards those with the forethought to bring a cushion to sit on or a pasty to eat.

At length, Thurloe's prosecution argument drew to a close and Latimer leaned forward: "Edward Villiers, the Secretary of State has made a compelling case concerning your involvement in this radical and wicked

Sealed Knot organisation. I am strongly tempted to agree with his assessment of your pivotal importance, given the circumstantial evidence and witness corroboration, albeit that the prosecution has unfortunately failed to produce direct evidence of your providing orders to bring about your intended mischief."

He paused pointedly to ensure that every spectator knew the architect of the prosecution's failings and Thurloe tensed, rubbing his nails over the red back of his left hand, before Latimer began again. "Edward Villiers, I will ask you directly. Do you believe the execution of the old King saved a people enthralled by tyranny and slavery, as a result of which they were, through the Blessed and Glorious Appearances of God, so happily redeemed?"

Eddie paused, his first words heavy with a lisp. "I believe the past is seldom as we would have it."

Another Commissioner sighed irritably before interjecting: "It's intolerably hot. Too hot for riddles, Villiers. The trials of earlier conspirators were too lengthy and I would not let this drag on for day after miserable day. Let me be plainer than my learned Lord Latimer here. Would you have Charles Stuart's son returned from the Continent and installed on the throne in place of our gracious and merciful Lord Protector, Oliver Cromwell?"

For a minute or two the room was silent, and Tara held her breath.

"Do you believe that restoring the Stuart line justifies the use of violence, taking away all hope of a settled peace in this Commonwealth? Have you incited such violence?" The Commissioner sighed irritably. "Tis a simple question, Villiers. I speak for everyone here in this infernal heat when I say I have neither the energy nor the patience to continue any longer. How do you plead? Be warned the bench will be forced to imply an admission of guilt into any refusal to answer."

The Commissioner bowed his head to receive a word from the court recorder and the accused's shaking voice rose slowly above the judicial whispers: "I do not recognise thy lawful authority. Thou art the pretenders. Charles Stuart is the rightful heir to the throne of England and I recognise him as such. I am a Quaker, a follower of George Fox, and I speak in the grace that cometh by truth and the Lord God will fulfil me. Long live the King!"

Like the thrust of a sword that finds its mark, the words could not have made Edward Villiers' fate clearer. In horror, Tara leaned forward and gripped the rail, knuckles white. She took a sharp intake of breath amid the rising roars and jeers of the spectators. "Eddie, no. No… no… What have you done?"

The Commissioner steepled his fingers on the bench and hung his head momentarily. Then, decided, he pushed his glasses back up his nose, gave a curt nod to his fellows on the bench and proceedings sped up. A guard grabbed at Villiers and hauled him to his feet to hear the sentence. The formal intonation had returned and with it the necessary volume to be heard over the whoops and cries of the crowd: "No pious or judicious person can possibly be Deluded under such gross Deceits as to contribute assistance for the Stuarts and Betray that very Authority we hath been Engaged in for the better Information and Satisfaction of the People of this Land. It is hereby Adjudged and Declared to be the verdict of this Chamber that you are guilty of High Treason and that you shall be proceeded against as a Traitor.

"You shall be led to the place from whence you came, and, on the Morrow, you will be drawn upon a hurdle to the place of Execution. Thereafter, we are resolved that You shall be Hanged by the Neck and, being alive, shall be cut down, and your Entrails be taken out of your body. You living, the same will be Burnt before your eyes, and your Head will be cut off, your Body will be divided into four Quarters, to be disposed of at the Pleasure of the Lord Protector."

No, no, no. He'd condemned himself to martyrdom, to Hell with the consequences, and any last shred of hope dissolved. Tara started forward onto her feet, mouthing the words impotently. *No, no no no. No!* No sound would come and her silent screams fell unheeded on the busy heads below. Her knees threatened to collapse, and Gabriel slipped a firm arm around her waist. She wriggled to get away but his grip tightened and he pulled her back down, into his side.

"And the Lord have mercy on your soul."

A sudden gunshot outside broke through the nightmare and in a split second the chattering courtroom dissolved into chaos. There were unfocused screams and several panicking bodies collapsed to the floor, scrabbling to hide under the rows of stools and knocking them over in the process. A dozen hooded men entered with quick, fluid movements, weapons drawn, to position themselves around the room. Those men whose military drill remained second nature scanned the exits and barked orders to keep down. Others patted frantically for their own weapons before remembering they had handed in what they carried to the guards, in order to be permitted entry.

Most stopped moving altogether, fear rooting them to the spot, and from above Tara could see the intruders' blades glinting as they moved bloodlessly between the bodies.

"Be still!" She could barely hear the voice above the pounding in her chest, but the command hushed the entire room. "Be still! And everyone walks out alive."

It took them less than a minute for one of the men to knock out the one resisting guard and bundle Edward Villiers from the room, the others dissolving behind as swiftly as they had arrived.

"Hyde?" she whispered breathlessly.

Without acknowledging the question, Gabriel scanned the chamber. The Commissioners were scurrying hurriedly out but the Lord Protector was on the floor, flanked by his protection team as they beat a path back to the judicial antechamber. The larger of his personal guards sheltered his body with his own, unwilling to risk that the threat had passed. In the centre of the floor, Thurloe stood exposed, his mouth open and gaping soundlessly. Another gunshot, this time echoing and distant, marked the end of a trance and almost immediately the crowd breathed in unison, unfurling beneath them.

"Quick," Gabriel urged, standing to lead her back along the platform, clearing a path through shocked faces as they descended.

From the corner of his eye, he saw Thurloe spring forward to intercept them at the exit and cursed. He broke step momentarily to spin Tara before him, his eyes begging her for trust as his fingers swiftly curled around her neck, finding the carotid artery beating fast below the surface of her skin. He squeezed momentarily and her brows furrowed but she collapsed, unconscious, and he swung her up into his arms.

The Secretary of State's hand rested nervously on the hilt of his blade as he pulled up before them, blocking the door, his eyes running suspiciously over the limp body gathered against his chest.

"Step aside, Thurloe, my wife has fainted. I would get her into the air, out of this heat." There was nothing for it but to keep moving and he pushed past the man, noting the prostrate guards in the corridor outside. No obvious pools of blood. Tom would have taken pains to avoid any permanent damage. "Talk to me later."

"I will, sir." Thurloe insisted, clearly unconvinced but also unwilling to draw his weapon without ready back up. He contented himself shouting after them down the corridor. "I will come to you very soon!"

Tara's eyelids fluttered with the change of light and she started, squinting across the Whitehall courtyard towards a waiting queue of hackney carriages. "What the Hell?"

"Not yet," he growled, his hold shifting slightly, his arms tightening in warning, and she felt the bounce beneath them as he climbed the steps of the first carriage. He lay her down on the bench and rapped on the ceiling. Once the rhythm of movement was safely established, she opened her eyes again and sat up slowly, rubbing the side of her neck, viewing him narrowly as he balanced on his haunches on the carriage floor.

"Did I hurt you?"

"No... but you planned this?"

"Not quite this," he admitted with a cautious smile, securing the leather blind tightly across the windows and submersing them in a deep gloom before he took a seat beside her. "I'd wanted to intercept his transport en route from the Tower and avoid the trial altogether, but Governor Barkstead sent him straight to custody in Whitehall last night after his stroke. He clearly didn't want a premature death ruining all the fun."

"Where is he now?"

"In a private carriage. Once out of London he'll pass through the Weald, to the Romney Marshes. He's heading to the coast. There'll be a boat waiting in St Mary's Bay."

"The Weald," she said quietly, bracing herself as the carriage took a bumpy corner at speed. In the darkness, Gabriel put a steadying hand across her lap. So much for the hunt he had disappeared on after Mary Cromwell's wedding; liberating Eddie had clearly been months in the planning. "Thomas Belasyse. The alibi he gave you...?"

"Monck is not the only man to hedge his bets. Belasyse saw his uncle beheaded within days of his marriage... it was relatively easy to convince him to gain favour with Charlie."

"Thank you, Gabriel." She crumpled, letting the relief wash across her chest, and put her head in her hands. "God, thank you so much."

He didn't say anything but after a moment the tension in her chest returned as she felt him draw a hand back though his hair. She looked up for him, eyes narrowing but unable to see clearly. There was something else.

"And from St Mary's Bay?"

"From there it's a short passage over the Channel to Wissant, a small fishing village south of Calais. Hyde will be waiting there with a fresh coach, ready to go to the Stuart court in Antwerp. Three, four days at most."

The carriage swayed as the pace changed, clattering hooves slowing their beat until finally there was silence. Nothing but the pounding of her heart. Gabriel pulled aside the blind an inch. "We're here."

"Where?" Tara squinted, frowning, at the sight of St Mary Magdelin's steeple. "Southwark? I thought we were going home... What's going on Gabriel? Tell me now or so help me God, I'll-"

"Tara, Charlie's expecting you both."

He slid off the seat to his knees to face her, and slipped his hand behind her head, his fingers curling possessively around the nape of her neck. She flinched, unwilling to be tricked again into unconsciousness but he shook his head and tilted her face, forcing her to look directly at him. "You're going with Villiers."

She could hear herself giving a hollow laugh as she shook her head: "No, I'm not. I'm going to Exeter-"

"You haven't got a choice. Your involvement in the Sealed Knot, it's over."

"*This* is the end you've been waiting for?" She gave a short bitter snort, eyes flashing as she pulled out of his touch, shifting back on the bench. "I'd thought you might cut me loose, but *this*?"

"*Cut you loose?* You know what faces me here. I told you Fleetwood has already started the process for a court martial. Now Thurloe assumes I'm involved in today's events… you can't think I'll let you be any part of this when I can't protect you from it. I'm getting you clear Tara. You haven't got a choice."

"You didn't think to mention this before?"

"You would have agreed?"

"No! I have a role here. What about Aodhan…"

"I'm sending him back with Rupert and Marie, he'll be raised at Treguddick."

She stilled a moment as everything unravelled. "But the men, my uncle's men… I'm the only link with them! Charlie needs me here. And you would exile me?"

He hung his head momentarily. "Villiers is free now; he'll tell us how messages are sent so Nan can replace the command. He'll agree with me; this is the right thing to do."

"The right thing now I'm no longer of any use?"

"I would keep you safe."

"You would set yourself free!" she snapped.

"Do I look free?" he cried back. Even in the thin light, she could see his dark eyes were hooded, sunken. There was no hint of the playfulness that danced habitually in the corners. Long lashes were brushed with moisture, brows drawn tight into a frown. Unable to stop her hands, they went instinctively to his head, fingers running through his hair, tracing the firmness of his skull, threading into what remained of the gathered braid.

After a heartbeat he mirrored the urgent grasp and closed the gap between them with a kiss, hard, deep and demanding. Their teeth clashed and his fingers tightened almost painfully but he didn't relinquish his hold and neither did she. She could feel the tremor across his chest as it heaved, his chest or maybe hers. Then, as quickly as he had taken her breath, he pulled back, leaving gasps and the faint tang of quicksilver in his place as he turned and left the coach.

The carriage door clicked shut after him and the horses started again with a sudden violence that jerked Tara back to her seat with a curse. She twisted awkwardly onto her knees, screaming at Gabriel's receding form through the rear window before being bumped back about face. Struggling to keep a balance she hammered on the door, the ceiling. She stamped on the floor to make the driver stop. But at each beat she heard a deep voice urging the horses faster and the coach hurtled ever further from London.

It was miles before the roads became easier and the pace slowed sufficiently for Tara to release her bone-white grip on the window rail. She shouted again at the driver, her voice now hoarse, and, finally, heard the whistle of a command to draw up. Mun opened the door, his blonde crop wind-battered into awkward angles and his familiar bland features clearly nervous.

"Mungo Thatcher, you bloody bastard!" she screamed, pushing him back as she half slid, half stumbled from the carriage, batting away his proffered hand. "Why didn't you stop? I know you could hear me."

"I'm sorry Miss Villiers, I am truly," he started, twitching nervously. Hands on hips she was struggling to hide her shaking hands or control her breathing. She paced forward a few steps, blankly surveying the empty countryside around them while he continued. "I was told to drive hard. The tall fella in black said you'd likely yell blue murder but that whatever you said I had to get you here within the hour."

"Where is he?" she demanded, turning back.

"Here, Tammy."

Eddie limped into sight from the behind the carriage and she stumbled a moment before running to him, throwing her arms about his frail frame. Mun had drawn up alongside another coach, and with a silent acknowledgement he swapped positions on the block with the other driver, who turned her Hackney carriage about and headed straight back to London without any hesitation.

"You're really here…" she whispered as Mun flicked the reins and the coach jolted into movement.

"Not a moment too soon, God be praised." Eddie smiled apologetically at the slur in his voice as he took her hand. The pale skin on his face was stretched thinly over his bones in some places and hang slackly in others, drooping a little on the left. Old scabs and bruises were taking time to heal on his neck and fingers, but his hollowed eyes shone with excitement. "All credit to the Earl of Denby for our deliverance. Oh Tammy, I will thank him from the bottom of my soul if providence were ever to put him in my path again. Our young King is wise beyond measure to have sent such a competent guardian angel..."

"He's a consummate professional," she replied quietly, turning away. In the relative luxury of a private coach the windows were covered with modern glass and wide-open fields stretched out before them, glowing fiery orange in the dying evening sun.

"He's thought of everything. There are local men in Romney prepared to testify our boat has sunk and produce flotsam evidence of shipwreck so we aren't pursued. He even gave Mun a bag of thy things," he pointed towards a snapsack in the corner of the coach and waited but she didn't say anything and at length he continued: "Hyde is waiting in France. The Chancellor is mighty impressed with thee, how thee stopped the uprising, and organised the men in Portsmouth-"

"How do you know about that?"

"It's amazing what one might hear in a Tower dungeon," he said unhelpfully, with a small smile. "Good God in Heaven, thou art a clever girl, as brave as any man. Heart and stomach of a commander. I underestimated thee when I sent thee away and I am sorry for it."

"And now I am exiled again."

Eddie gave a small shrug: "Thine father would be mighty proud."

"My father is not here to comment and neither, very nearly, were you. You condemned yourself refusing to admit the court's authority; what were you thinking?" A hint of anger played at the edges of her words.

Eddie shrugged. "I made life a little easier for the Commissioner, that is all. His father was a good man, before the war. With Cromwell watching he had to be brutal. He had no choice but to find against me one way or another." He smiled weakly: "besides, the Society of Friends requireth necessary libation with the blood of a martyr, or what hope have we of standing the test of time? I flattered myself that my death might come to mean something for my fellow enthusiasts as well as our royalist friends."

Tara stiffened as she checked off her mental roll-call. Everyone she'd ever loved had marched off to their glorious martyrdom without a second thought about who might be left behind. Ralph, Angela, Gregory. Eddie was prepared to die. And now she could add Gabriel to the list. He would attend the court martial, be damned for desertion and-

"Tammy, art thou alright? Thy face is pale-"

"I'm fine," she said, shaking off the thought and rolling her eyes at the incongruity of the question, coming from a man mere hours away from being hung, drawn and quartered.

"Thou look ill."

Her stomach lurched as if to prove his point and she lay a hand flat on her belly in a futile bid to settle it. The ride was nausea-inducing.

"I understand my dear," he said. "Rest now. Sleep a little… Thine Earl hath given us what remains of my natural lifetime to talk."

"He's… Eddie, he's not mine." She faltered as she said it but Edward just nodded, picking up her hand and laying a thoughtful kiss on her fingers.

It took little more than the suggestion of sleep to induce the need of it in Eddie. Without further comment he sunk back into the corner and lay his head against a padded wall, closing his eyes. Presumably it took several months in the Tower to consider the bone-rattling seats a luxury however, and Tara sat back restlessly, scanning the darkening horizon. After a while she tugged over the snapsack, curious as to which of her meagre personal possessions Ann might have considered essential enough to have packed. At the top was a small parcel, and she glanced across at Eddie. He was asleep, his mouth opened by the jolting, a snore shuddering staccato as he clung to the edges of whatever sweet dream had taken hold. She extricated it slowly, frowning, turning the weight over and over in her hands. It was a book. Eventually she slid a finger under the edge of the parchment, breaking Gabriel's wax seal and revealing the compendium of Old English from Salisbury market. Opening the cover, a note slid from between the pages into her lap. His generous, looping hand covered the scrap of paper: "Forgive me."

How very wise and keen you are, Gabriel, she recalled ironically, sitting back and closing her eyes. Oh how merciful and mindful and mild. How bloody stupid and foolish you are, Tara, oh how proud and bloody-minded and blind. I can never give you my heart. It really was over.

Suddenly there was a muffled "ho!" from Mun and without warning the world tumbled over and over. Her body was thrown heavily against walls and ceiling, smacking cool walls and warm flesh as her limbs flailed for purchase. She heard the sound of the window smashing, and then the door sprung open to reveal a square of disorientating night sky. She felt only abstractly the rush of cool night breeze and the scrape of mud and glass and gravel as she was flung from the coach. The air left her lungs as she landed with a muffled oompfh and blackness engulfed her.

Her thoughts were too groggy and she groped blindly at the moonlight as arms tightened around her, lifting her clear from the ground.

"I've got you, Tara," he said simply, his face obscured by darkness but his voice as calm as a summer sky.

"No, no..." There was something unfathomable in the shining eyes and through the fog in her brain she scrambled for a foothold on the precipice. "Jack..."

"Relax, my sweeting. He can't get you now."

The words were silky and Jack's lips had curved into a smile that didn't reach his eyes, but Tara had passed out again and didn't see it. ☐

43. THE ROTTEN CORE

She woke with a start in the pitch black, lying on her side, head pounding and stomach churning with hot nausea. The air was unbearably close. Her mind was groggy and her tongue thick, as if she had had too many jugs of raspberry wine. Only she couldn't remember drinking.

It was unbelievably hot, hard. She was sweating. Her last memory... an accident and then Jack. Jack had found her; he had plucked her from the rough verge and carried her, but where to? She tried to turn and sit up, wincing as her head hit something solid almost immediately. Her elbows were constrained, her brows furrowed in confusion. A sudden jolt of the floor threw her whole body upwards and she screamed as she came into contact again with the hard wood above her. A rocking movement she hadn't consciously been aware of ceased.

"She's awake!"

The muffled voice was familiar, but not in a reassuring way. It caught in her mind as the motion jarred her body. A thud, a few heavy, bouncing footsteps and then the wooden roof was lifted and bright sunlight dazzled her eyes. Instinctively her right hand came up for shade and the action sent a sharp pain racing from her wrist, making her gasp.

When the world came slowly into focus it centred on Bulstrode Wortley's leering grin. In confusion she looked instinctively for Gabriel, her eyes searching behind sinewy shoulders as he placed a hand on her chest, holding her awkwardly down on her back, pinning her in the trunk.

"He can't help you now." His laugh was hollow and mocking as he guessed what she wanted. His giggle was childishly dirty: "He'll never come for you again."

A horrible realisation rose from deep within her stomach: it wasn't an accident. No. No, no, no. Terror sliced through her and her chest tightened as her mind hovered on the edge of control.

"Did you sleep well, my sweeting?" Jack's gentle voice was the very parody of concern, as he entered the carriage, his blue eyes filled with feinted empathy. His fingers calmly stroked his stubbled chin. "You've been out for the count all day! I was beginning to wonder if, well, you might be done for."

Tearing her eyes from Jack she realised that she was still in the same carriage taking them to the south coast. Taking her and Eddie. There was a familiar rip on the leather seat pad where Eddie had sat, and a small tear in the window curtain. The fabric billowed faintly where a breeze had found its way through broken glass. When she didn't speak, Jack raised an eyebrow. "Do you know what, Bul, I think she's still sleepy, perhaps we should leave her a while longer?"

"Wait!" Tara croaked. Heart hammering, she gritted her teeth and pushed back against Bulstrode's rigid fist, hitting the sides of a trunk. He looked to Jack for direction and upon receiving a small nod of consent, his fingers twisted into the front of her stays, pulling her roughly up to sitting. She felt the sweat run down her back as her position shifted. Her legs straightened and a fresh chill of terror rose up her spine when she saw that her ankles were chained together.

Oh God. A metallic clanking filled the air as she scrabbled to pull her knees up and her breathing became rapid. On the edge of a chasm, she crossed her arms, adrenaline dulling the screaming in her wrist, and dug her fingernails into what flesh they could find beneath her sleeves, as if clinging to a sheer wall would stop her falling.

Jack laughed: "Sweeting, all this frowning won't do at all. Why, you look just as you did on our wedding day! Look at the lovely dress you're wearing… was that not bought with the wages of my honest labour?"

"I… I don't…" Tara stammered, her throat painfully dry, her mind recoiling at the dangerous edge in Jack's voice. "Water."

"Allow me," Jack casually lifted the heavy chains from her feet to make it easier for her to shift position and smiled as if this were a perfectly natural turn of events. "You'll appreciate we couldn't take any chances."

He leaned in to slowly peel the fingers of her right hand from her left arm, holding up the arm to inspect it in the light and she winced at the pain. Her right wrist was already black from bruising and his index finger gently traced the blooming stain.

"You would be chained here too, but it looked sore," he whispered conspiratorially, close enough to let his breath warm the vulnerable skin on her neck and she turned away, straining to avoid his mouth. "You know, I'm not a complete brute; I can be exceptionally tender."

He leaned back and watched her for a moment before unstoppering a leather water bottle and offering it up. Desperately thirsty, Tara leant forward to take a long draught. He pulled it away before the water was finished and small rivulets ran down her chin. "Enough."

Then he pulled back, casually plunked himself on the bench next to Wortley and winked at her, his lips curling, a hint of a dimple forming on his right cheek. She had kissed that divut; recently enough that she remembered the rough feel of his blonde stubble on her lips. *Who is he?* The two men exchanged glances she couldn't understand and when he stood up to go, her voice wavered with a plea not to leave. *Keep him talking.*

"Jack, please, where's my uncle?"

Wortley settled back to worry at an embedded thorn on his hand with a small blade while Jack replied: "The traitor Edward Villiers is on his way back to London. Straight to the Tower; a nice surprise for the Secretary of State, a little proof that I was worth his faith after all."

"But how? Who with-?"

"I know what you planned," he interrupted. "I've had my eye on your Earl for months. I know he has dirty little secrets. Abi told me everything."

"Abi? Abigail Hardwick?"

"Oh, it's always the quiet ones you have to watch, Tamara, you should know that! But then you're not a complete dalcop, are you? Of course, she's not from the same political stock as myself and Bulstrode here. We are driven by high-minded ideals... She did it because she loves me... a damn site more than you ever did. She'd do anything for me." He gave an exaggerated wink and she stared for a moment, incredulous. The nervous, blank-eyed mouse of a maid had delivered his notes and returned with snatches of their lives. Did Gabriel know?

"Where is Mungo Thatcher?" she asked flatly.

"Your driver? He's dead, my sweeting. In the accident he came a little unstuck and fell awkwardly from his perch. Quite tragic, although of course he's a traitor so... so we strapped him to the roof of your uncle's coach. They'll be needing his head for the gate."

Jack's tone remained conversational, as if they were discussing the weather, or the packaging of pork loin, and she bit her lip as tears gathered behind her eyelids. Once they fell, they would pour endlessly and she couldn't afford to cry. She wouldn't do it. She forced herself to focus on the feel of her fingertips, pushing hard against the wood and running along the splinters. She had to bury Mun deep inside, for now, and focus on working out how long she needed to keep alive, to keep Eddie alive, until help would come. Perhaps there were witnesses.

"Was anyone else hurt?" she asked quietly, trying to keep the hitch of emotion from her voice.

He gave a smug smile. "Here's news, my sweeting: there was no one else. The carriage simply hit a... a rock, shall we say, then overturned! Pesky things these modern carriages, so unstable. Thanks be to God for your deliverance and the astonishing coincidence that we were passing by, no?"

A shiver rippled across her chest as her mind raced to piece together the only logical explanation. Jack had set the whole thing up. No-one knew about the coach accident. No-one would even know she had even been kidnapped. Gabriel would be back at Ham House, utterly preoccupied in saying goodbye to Aodhan; preparing for Fleetwood's court martial; waiting for the formal news that his wife's boat had sunk to the bottom of the Channel... Ready to fake the right amount of grief. In any case, he would not expect to hear anything for another week at least and it might be days before news of Eddie's recapture reached him. She was on her own.

"That's right!" Jack's knack of reading her thoughts as if they were written out plainly on her face had not been dented with time. "The Lord of the Manor, so masterful, so full of vim, hasn't the faintest idea. In fact, by the time someone sees fit to mention in passing that your precious uncle has been executed I'm quite sure he'll struggle to remember to ask: 'and whatever happened to that traitor's hussy niece?'" His expression darkened and he enunciated all the words, spitting venom. "You know the one, he'll say. That stinking wanton whore."

She rose defiant eyes to give him a level look; "And just what is going to happen to her?"

"Wouldn't you rather the surprise? I do remember how you loved surprises. Come on, my sweeting, be honest with me. I'll wager you were thrilled with the surprise we had on our wedding day!"

He put his hand out and cupped her cheek, the calloused pad of his thumb dragging across her bottom lip. "So pretty," he murmured, to himself as much as her. "Such kissable lips. So nearly mine."

"Jack," She forced herself not to bite down, to withstand his touch as she whispered his name, waiting breathlessly for him to hear the love she had born him on the morning of their wedding. To come to his senses. "Jack, where are we?"

Another second and the spell was broken. His voice was lighter, conversational again: "Actually we're on our way back to London too. Not fifteen miles hence as we stand. Petts Wood. We're running a little behind schedule, since it took longer to right the carriage than I'd hoped. Bul is surprisingly strong though, as luck would have it. It's funny how the fates align. I decided we'd travel separately with you, because, well… never mind, you'll find out soon enough."

"Save me the punchline."

Jack laughed aloud, and a thought appeared to occur to him: "Do you want to hear something really amusing, Tara? Do you know that Gabriel Moore married you on orders from Charles Stuart?"

Her gut flipped as if he'd punched her but she nodded mutely; there seemed little point now in denying it.

"Well, it's a rather delicious coincidence that our marriage would have been a sham too."

"What do you mean?"

"Edward Villiers was never meant to be arrested. He's not the big fish. Thurloe wants someone who calls himself Lord Carnage and thought your simple uncle might lead us to him. He wanted me close to the last Villiers, to learn as much as we could about the Sealed Knot. Until His Highness busied himself in John Hewitt's interrogation, the plan was really very simple. I was to marry you, relocate you to Devon and become so deeply embedded in your treacherous lives no one would bother to hide anything from me. Your uncle would have been as free and easy with his confidences, his contacts, as you would doubtless have been with your favours."

"But Cromwell thought to marry me to Silus Tollemache," she whispered.

Jack shrugged. "Neither here nor there. You don't seriously think Thurloe tells the old man all his plans? Thurloe is the future. He's the kingmaker. I say that rather ironically, you understand." He giggled at his own joke before looking back at her. "You could have been part of it with me, Tara."

"But-"

"Ha! You don't think I actually…? My sweeting, I was being paid!" Jack laughed again, nudging Bul to share in the joke.

So, Jack was an agent of parliament, paid to infiltrate and deceive. There had been no loving romance, no whirlwind proposal. And now he was not battling with a lover's agony at their aborted wedding, not simply settling a score against Gabriel. The knot in her stomach tightened; she'd been used by both sides, and of all people it had taken Jack to peel back her life like an onion, exposing each layer as a translucent sham until, at its heart, there was nothing more than a rotten core.

"'Til death do us part," he mused, pushing a hand up her leg and under her skirts until she twisted him loose.

"Don't get me wrong," he added, withdrawing the explorative fingers without complaint and hooking a stray curl behind her ear, a spontaneously tender gesture. "I never liked the idea of him being paid to want you as well. He had no right to touch you after you promised to wed me."

She stiffened. *Keep him talking.* He'd yet to give her anything she could use. "You aren't even a butcher, are you?"

Wortley snorted but Jack replied almost apologetically, his head swinging from side to side as if he was dealing with a particularly slow child. "No. sweeting, I was just hacking away at dead beasts. I wouldn't know an arse from an elbow."

He jabbed sharply at her elbow and then her bottom to prove his point and she flinched, her eyes misting as she looked away from him. "You only came to Petersham to lay a trap for my uncle?"

"Oh come on, Tara, you're better than this. I never thought you dumb witted, but this is taking too long." He rolled his eyes, finally bored with the effort of explaining, and rose from the seat to take hold of the door handle.

A bird squawked outside as if startled by a passer-by and Tara's eyes widened at the slither of a chance. Jack had heard it too but before he could turn back to clamp his hand over her mouth she was screaming as loud as she could. This time Wortley didn't wait to be told, he snapped forward and backhanded her without warning. Her temple struck the side of the trunk in a hammer blow as her head snapped around and she felt the blood seeping through her hairline as zigzags of light and pain filled her vision.

"I owed you that, Milady," he laughed, shifting his weight to leave.

Hell hath no fury, hissed a detached part of her mind, no fury like a bitter, jealous weasel, not fit to breath the same air as the man whose household he had so incompetently infiltrated. She swallowed an urge to wipe the smile from his face, tell him that all along Gabriel knew and had turned the tables to mislead Thurloe. *Move*. She struggled dizzily. Her scalp flared with stinging pain but her good hand reached to scratch at him even as the chains dragged her back down. He made it out unhindered and slammed the door shut behind him, trapping her again.

Time passed, no telling how much, until she was galvanised to drag herself onto the back bench. She found herself looking directly at the oak trunk she'd been lying in, filling the floor where a row of facing seats had been only yesterday. It was Eddie's chest from Exeter, of all things. Gabriel's eye on the detail as he arranged for their new life. It must have been on the roof. In Exeter, it contained nothing more than linen and a few changes of clothes though, didn't it? Not that it mattered now; the contents were clearly gone. Dumped or maybe even hidden by the roadside for a later pick up. The quality was good; they'd fetch decent coin at market.

It occurred to her with a sudden fearful stab that Jack had removed the contents simply in order to bundle her in. To force her body in and close the lid. Such a damn fool. It wasn't a clothes trunk. *It was a coffin*. And they had left her in there as if she were already dead, or soon would be. The sweat on her body now felt ice cold. A fly knocked itself senseless against the coach door, seeking its own escape. Outside, muffled voices made noises about preparing to leave and an overwhelming terror filled her chest, drowning her lungs. She couldn't control it anymore. The weight of fear was dragging her under. She slid to the floor, crawled to the door and threw herself against the hard wood, hammering and screaming for air, gagging as nausea rolled over her in waves. Laughter behind the door heightened her hysteria and she clawed at the wood.

Without warning it swung open and she fell forwards. The steps had been unfolded and as her body slid awkwardly down the metal treads, Jack bent to catch her. Without pride, she clung desperately around his neck as he hoisted her to standing, his scent strangely familiar. A wave of cooling air opened her lungs and she breathed in, her sobbing and heartrate slowly subsiding. She closed her eyes as he whispered in her ear, almost tenderly: "What on earth's the matter, my sweeting?"

Out of the dark coach, under the sunshine, drowsy bees buzzed about them without any sense of urgency and in Jack's arms she wondered briefly if she'd imagined everything. After a moment, he pulled back and tilted his head, gently tucking a stray twist of hair behind her ear while he waited for an answer. But then she met his eyes and a fresh wave of sickness rolled upwards from her stomach. There was no warmth in the familiar gesture, just an objective detachment that made her shiver. *Run. Hide.*

"Please, it's too hot. I have to be sick, and I have to pee." She bobbed briefly, looking a little embarrassed, trying not to pay too much obvious attention to the surroundings. They were in a wood. Oak trees, no, chestnut trees, beech, birch, ash, all fanned out in every direction away from the dirt trail. A willow. *Was there water nearby?* He'd said Petts Wood. No rivers that she could remember…

Jack nodded towards a clump of bushes behind the coach. Her spine stiffened and she shuffled in the direction he had indicated, praying that he would leave her alone for a few minutes, long enough perhaps to find a way of removing the anklets and running, or climbing, or untethering one of the horses from the coach struts and riding away at speed. From the position of the sun it was late-afternoon; long fingers of shade were already spreading across the ground. A couple of hours and it would be dark.

She was conscious to turn back and give him a grateful smile as she went.

44. GREAT EXPECTATIONS

By dawn, Gabriel had long since given up on any notion of sleep. He paced the hard wood of the long gallery, kicking at shadows and measuring time with heavy footsteps. At the south window he paused again, scanning the approach carriageway through the dimpled, diamond glass. Habit more than hope. *Nothing.*

He laced his fingers behind his head and raised weary eyes towards heaven. "God, please, tell me she's made it to Otford."

A small village just outside Sevenoaks, Otford was chosen for its distance from London and its quiet alehouse sat squarely on the point at which her path to the coast would intersect with the Pilgrim's Way. The tavern was called The Tabard, after its namesake in the Canterbury Tales, and planning the route he'd thought privately it might make her smile, remembering the stubborn nag she had nicknamed Jankyn. *Fool.* As if she would likely be in any mood for frivolity. *Are you cursing me now, Tara?*

He growled aloud with frustration, bracing himself against the window, shaking his head at Donn's brutally accurate assessment but unable to stop it echoing around his brain. *Feckin' idjit.*

He had placed men sporadically along the route, each ready to ride back reports on the progress of the coach. John Ashton had already confirmed they'd passed through Petts Wood as planned, but Otford? Donn was due back hours ago. There would be no rest until he knew she was safely with Hyde in France, and then, then his only hope would be to bury himself in duty, to try and forget. He would attend to the urgent summons that had arrived from Fleetwood. The nightmares would return and then news would reach London that their boat had sunk. That she was lost at sea. His wife, she had had no chance, she couldn't swim. *His wife.*

His heart jolted with the sound of frantic banging downstairs. Someone was here, early. Donn. *At last.* He down ran to meet him, overtaking his yawning housekeeper as he took the stairs two at a time. "Back abed, Ann."

"Word's come of her?" She hovered for a moment, uncertain, but turned to climb the stairs back to her room for another hour or so of precious sleep if she could manage it before the babe woke. "I'll send Abigail down to get you coffee, assuming she's not had the gall to desert us again. Too delicate that one, too-"

"Milord, I'm feckin' sorry." The words spilled out between panting breaths even before Gabriel had fully opened the door.

"What? Why?" he demanded, reading the panic in Donn's clear blue eyes as a ball of ice settled in his stomach.

"I waited as ye said, so I did. The Tabard in Otford. They should have been there by eleven by my reckonin'. But I waited an' there was nothin'. They didna come. I went to the stables an' asked about..."

"And?" A thin wail bounced along the corridors and down the staircase. Aodhan was awake. Gabriel tugged Donn into the kitchen where there was less chance of disturbing the entire household further.

"An' a fella told me as how he'd seen a coach overturned on the road from London, not two miles outside the village. Some passers-by'd already stopped to help. But the driver told them it was under control an' sent them on their way."

"And?"

"I went ridin' back along the road, Milord. I've been on it all night, retracin' the route ye'd planned yerself back an' fro. "

"And?"

"Nothin'. It was gone."

"What the hell do you mean?"

"The coach. I couldna see sign of it anywhere, and they certainly didna reach the inn. It disappeared."

Gabriel gripped the edge of the kitchen table as the news sunk in. She was alive. She must be. If it had been an accident, Donn would have found her. There would have been no need to clear up the evidence on the road and they would have continued on to Otford; the good Samaritans would have taken them on to the inn. Highwaymen? Perhaps, but still no reason for the entire coach to dissolve; no common thief would have the stomach for abduction. They'd been ambushed; no other reason for a coach to disappear. Frozen fingers climbed his spine. Where the Hell are you, Tara?

"Milord?"

"Sir?" Ann drifted into the kitchen like a ghost in her housecoat. Her face was pallid and her hair pushed roughly back under a homespun coif. Aodhan squirmed in her arms. He half tilted his drowsy head towards the male voices and Gabriel moved towards him, leaning in instinctively to kiss the top of his head.

"Go back to sleep my sweetheart, Papa has to go out a while, 'tis all." He flicked his eyes up at Ann and frowned at the confusion clouding her blank eyes. "Where's Abigail?"

"Passed over," said Ann blankly.

"What?"

"God save her soul."

"Her lad, John, he'll be in the stables," murmured Donn quickly and he headed out of the back door. "I'll fetch him."

"How? The pox?" Gabriel lifted Aodhan from her shaking arms. "She wasn't ill, was she?"

Ann sat down heavily at the table and hung her head: "Poison. I found an empty bottle of Robert's arsenic on the floor by her bed…"

The kitchen door swung open before he could reply and John rushed in, ashen faced, ahead of Donn: "W-where's ma?"

"Wait, John" said Gabriel softly.

"She's killed herself, hasn't she?" the boy demanded, wide eyed, hesitating to run past the men.

"What reason could she have to do something so terrible? If she's done for herself her soul will burn for all..." whispered Ann, stopping abruptly when Gabriel put a warning hand on her shoulder.

"She's killed herself... I knew it... that fucking b-bastard!"

The curse snapped Ann from her shock: "Language, John! You'll remember, you're in the company of your Lord."

"What do you mean, John? Who are you talking about?" Gabriel put Aodhan back in his housekeeper's lap and took the boys' matchstick shoulders gently, crouching down until he could look directly at him. He waited, watching the internal battle cloud red rimmed eyes that flashed with anger. The boy didn't want to betray his mother; whatever the reason, it was bad.

"I meant the b-butcher."

"She's been stepping out with Ned Gibbons," explained Ann, distastefully. "Someone should fetch him."

"He b-beats her." The boy shrugged, as if that by itself were of little consequence. "I meant the other one, Jack Ludlow. He's had her fetchin' stuff from here. Silver. Candlesticks and such..."

"Don't worry about that," said Gabriel as the boys eyes narrowed with fear.

"He said when she'd got enough, he'd t-take her away. Then he took off last n-night. Left a n-note that he'd not be b-back. B-broke her heart... I'm s-s-sorry Milord, I didn't mean-."

Ann exhaled noisily but Gabriel pulled the child into his arms. He murmured something soothing, feeling John's stiff, brittle frame wrack with silent sobs, but the pit of his own stomach clenched in fear as fury sharpened his senses. The butcher had Tara. His hand patted instinctively for the reassurance of his sword at his waist and he caught Donn's eye above the boy's head: "Fetch Tom and Ru-"

"Present and correct, sir," Rupert snapped his heels to as Tom manoeuvred around his younger brother, laying his pistol flat on the table and frowning slightly at the sight of the stable lad.

Gabriel looked over at his cousins, each dressed and armed. Ready. He nodded, releasing the boy but bending down to make sure his words were heard: "John, listen to me. You must go now to rouse Minister Fielding at St Peter's Church. This is important. Tell him that the Earl of Denby is certain there is something he can do for her soul, a special prayer he can say quickly to send her to Heaven. Remind him that he once told me all things are possible with God." He flicked his eyes up. "Ann, have Robert lay Mistress Hardwick in the blue room to receive her son and the Minister when he returns. Donn, saddle the horses. We'll leave immediately."

Donn's red hair flickered in a low ray of dawn light as he hesitated by the door: "Will ye not be waitin' here yerself Milord, for news to come from the Three Cups, just in case they're movin' straight there by some other road?"

"I'm no good at waiting."

45. TAKES ONE TO KNOW ONE

Tara peered through the leaves as she spat out the remnants of a foul bile, breathing heavily. Jack and Bulstrode stamped out the remains of a cooking fire and she cursed herself for the time wasted. Once back on the road, her opportunities to escape would be limited. Now or never.

But she couldn't run. Not for long with shoes missing and the chains around her ankles. It hadn't taken long to realise she couldn't break them loose. She'd have to take a horse, and she looked about frantically for a distraction. On her knees she scrabbled to free some large stones hard baked in the dry dirt. How many? Three, four. If she could throw them far enough, would the men fear they had company? They would surely leave the coach to scout for threats at least.

Her fingers shook as she lifted her arm for the first throw. Please, please, please. She counted to three and released the stone. It hit a tree to the north behind the coach and a bird squawked. Jack stopped still, alert to the movement. She saw him lift a finger to his lips to silence Bulstrode and motion towards the noise. The second rock hit another tree, further away to the south, behind them. She held her breath and watched Jack through the branches. He seemed to think for a moment, and then muttered something. Both men drew their daggers and nodded briefly at each other before slipping silently away, dividing as each took a different thud to investigate.

Now. Tara gathered up the heavy chains and skirted the bushes, half jogging, half stumbling towards the horses. Fingers fumbling, she unbuckled the carriage yoke from the grey's bridle and slid out the long straps, willing it with as gentle a whisper as she could manage to stay silent as it nudged a questioning nose in her direction. With a supreme effort she took up the weight of the chain again and hoisted one foot onto the narrow limber shaft to mount. Chest heaving, she brought her other foot up onto the unsteady beam and dragged herself half across the horse's rump.

It whinnied in surprise as the chains thudded heavily against its belly and, as it skittered forward, she laced the fingers of her left hand awkwardly into its mane for purchase. She had intended to pull up somehow into side saddle position but putting distance between herself and Jack was more important. Laying awkwardly across its back, she punched the horse's side with her right fist to set it into a determined canter, screaming at the jagged pain in her wrist. The grey obliged immediately, its movement nearly winding her as she bounced against its knobbly back, clinging to every strands of hair and leather she could grasp to stop herself being dragged off sideways by the weight of the chains.

"Ho!"

With a threatening crack of his coach whip, Wortley stepped into the path of the horse and it reared, throwing her off to the hard ground before clattering off through the trees. She had no time to register the hurt or take a deep breath before he dragged her to her feet but she squealed at a flash of pain as he took hold of a leather belt strap that was caught between his teeth and yanked her hands behind her back. The strap wrapped around her upper arms and he pulled it tight. She spat at his face between pants and braced herself for the impact but he smiled.

"I should thank you, Milady. Jack didn't think you needed teaching a lesson but we know better about what you need, don't we?"

He pulled a stocky blade from his boot and she let out a panicked sound but he put a finger to his lips in warning and moved to slice through the ribbon still somehow holding back the bulk of her hair. His fingers threaded gently through the dark waves, arranging them thoughtfully around her shoulders like a dutiful lady's maid before tightly wrapping the whole length slowly around his hand and tugging it roughly back, forcing her chin up.

She yelped before clamping her mouth shut, her nostrils flaring. Too close. A small whimper escaped as Wortley's tongue furred a line up her neck from her collarbone. She was shaking when he nipped at her ear, a jolt of pain pricking her eyes with tears. "I've been waiting a long time to have some fun with you."

"We've discussed this, Wortley, she's not here for your amusement." The point of Jack's dagger dented the loose skin of man's neck and he stepped back slowly, releasing her hair. He lifted his hands into the air in a gesture of supplication before slowly sheathing his own blade.

"Humble apologies Jack." His scowl bordered on just the right side of deference. "I didn't know she actually holds meaning for you."

"She doesn't hold meaning," said Jack with an indifferent shrug. His vacant eyes bore holes into her as he felt along the sharp edges of his blade, but it slipped into its sheath untested. He turned away a moment, eyeing the woods to the south, before spinning back. "But she owes me a wedding night and I'll not take my turn after your filthy spigot. Perhaps you're right though. No sense in waiting."

He grabbed her upper arm and eyed the loose straps on the carriage, adding practically: "She's fucked it. You'll have to do something with the shafts so the weight is balanced for one horse."

"But Jack-"

"No interruptions!" Jack barked over his shoulder.

He yanked her away from the coach as Wortley turned his miserable face back to it. Hampered by the weight at her ankles, her feet kept getting stuck but he half-dragged, half-carried her anyway, forcing her to keep pace, sweeping down with a grunt to free the chain when it got caught on fallen branches or around tussocks of long grass.

When they tumbled through branches into the peace of an ancient clearing, it was as if time were momentarily suspended. A calm washed over her. She knew it would come to this, ever since the first moment she had gained consciousness and looked into his vacant eyes. She observed Jack objectively, realising she must be heavy. He was panting hard, doubled over and clutching his waist. She peered back and, in the distance, between the trees, she could still just see Wortley. He sat high on the carriage block, a wide hat shading his eyes from the sunlight, waiting for his turn, filing his nails with the edge of his glinting dagger.

She glanced back at the haphazard path they had taken, the trampled route marked with bloody trails. Momentarily confused, she looked down and realised the blood was hers; the skin on her ankles torn by the chains. Odd, she thought blankly, it doesn't hurt anymore. But she could feel a tickling sensation as bright red dripped wet, smudging on her naked feet, rivulets reaching the dirt below. And she could hear the horse chestnut leaves whispering like Roman spectators at an arena, baying for even more blood. *Did it have to hurt?*

"You're a filthy whore." Jack had recovered sufficiently to pace a tight circle around her, as if she were on trial and he the prosecution and judge.

"Takes one to know one," she muttered recklessly, "You sold your favours to Thurloe - ah!"

He slapped her hard then and she could taste the metallic tang of blood on the inside of her mouth. Instinctively she tried to draw her arms protectively about her, but the bonds were too tight, there was no purchase, no movement. She gritted her teeth as her cheek reddened, forcing her breath to calm. *It'll be over soon.*

"Sweeting, you never did tell me what he did to you, that day I found you cursing his name in your hovel," said Jack, his tone changing again. He came close, his hand cupping her face and forcing her to look at him, his eyes as cold and clear as the water on a January morning. She tried to wriggle free but his grip tightened, tipping her face further up, painful dents on her neck where his fingernails dug into the flesh.

"Nor will I," she panted, green eyes stormy.

"You don't need to," he shrugged. "I already know everything. That devil enslaved you, bound you, made you submit to his coarse rutting. He has tainted you with his sin. I saw, Tara. I was there."

"It was you…" she whispered. "You told Thurloe about my message to Lord Carnage; you had Gabriel arrested."

"It was always me." He released her head and dragged a finger along the top edge of her stays as he walked around her.

"Wortley is a liability if you hope for a long career as one of Thurloe's agents."

"He's as predictable as a cockroach and as loyal as a dog." She felt him shrug hard against her back and his chin came to rest on her shoulder, his hands running unhindered down her sides, over her hips, tracing the shape of her flesh between her legs. "I like to keep a pet."

"Get your hands off me," she hissed.

"But sweeting, I've saved you from the Stuart scum! I'll mask his sin on your flesh."

As he spoke, he came around in front of her again. His left hand fumbled for the clasp at his waist and he opened his breeches. His large cockstand sprung free and he forcibly tilted her head down to look at it, quivering and pale in the sunlight. *No*. Revulsion pulsed in her stomach. *No, no, no*. She tried to step back but he put a heavy foot on the chain between her ankles, pinning her to the spot. The pad of his thumb dragged across her lower lip, forcing her mouth open for his rough kiss. Then he pulled back and smiled calmly as she spat on his shirt, leaving a bloody circle of saliva.

"Temper, temper," he chided with a humourless smile and undeterred his left hand moved up to her chest, kneading her breast to the point of pain. "Is this very much like the little games he has you play? When he tastes you and touches you and fucks you in my place? Do you play at being the little traitor, for the excitement of being punished?"

Those stakes were real. The thought jolted through her like a wake-up call. "Jack, please, I have to find Eddie."

"Oh, please Jack," he mimicked, breathless with a grotesque passion. "Forget the old man, sweeting! If Edward Villiers is not already admiring the sight of his own bowels he soon will be."

"Please."

"Oh, you'll beg me. You'll beg me to end it all, to make it stop, and when you do I shall be only too happy to give you salvation." His fingers shifted and both hands curled about her throat. "It's a kindness you don't deserve. But I am soft-hearted. If you are especially good to me, I will save your body from Bul."

"Jack, you don't have to do this…" She was at the edge of the chasm again, her gasps for breath increasingly frantic.

"When I report to Thurloe, I will tell him you found some way of hanging yourself in the woods here. Perhaps you were racked with guilt or terrified of a traitor's death. Perhaps after seeing me again you realised you couldn't live without me. Perhaps you just couldn't run the risk of returning to a brutalised life with your depraved Earl. I haven't decided yet. It doesn't matter. Any which way, my sweeting, your pretty neck will just snap."

Slowly, he pulled upwards until she was on tip toes, squeezing gently as if to prove how little effort was required to break her bones, as cleanly as if she were a poached pheasant. He tested her weight, observing the rise and fall of her body, rubbing her belly against his cockstand with a peculiar, almost scientific, detachment. She bit down hard on her bottom lip. His arousal was fed by the promise of violence and her limbs trembled with the realisation that before her last breath, Jack would take his time breaking her body for the sheer amusement of it.

I don't have to make it easy. She glanced back towards the carriage. Wortley was gone, no telling where. She snatched a deeper breath and straightened her spine, preparing for a single shot before she lost her remaining strength. *I will not lay down for you.* The best outcome was a blow that tipped him into killing her immediately.

She bought her knee up, making thudding contact with his exposed groin. He buckled and clutched at his crotch as the heavy ankle chain swung in an arc, slapping hard against his shin, but her wave of satisfaction was short lived. She took a half step backwards as he lurched at her legs from the floor, face contorted with rage, and she stumbled back, landing heavily with a scream on her bound arms.

He was on top of her then, his weight pinning her down, pushing her harder onto her arms as he yanked her skirts past her knees. Her right wrist flashed blinding agony and her shoulders felt like they would dislocate, wrenched from their sockets. She yelped with the pain, tears finally flowing uncontrollably free, defeated sobs racking her chest. Her body had flattened the tall grass but all around her it stood, untouched and untroubled, waving gently in the warm breeze, and all she could see was Jack. He yanked at the lacing of her stays, his sweaty fingers too eager to gain proper purchase on the slippery ribbon. His head bowed in concentration, blonde hair slipping forward into his eyes, and he shook with frustration.

Gabriel... Gabriel... She was whispering his name as an incantation on rasping breath. She'd failed him. It was all she could think. He'd learn of her death, if he learned of it at all, and know she had failed to get Eddie safely to the boat. After everything he'd done, everything he'd risked.

"Hell's teeth, shut the fuck up!" he cursed, dispensing with the stays and shifting on his knees to separate her thighs as he dragged and clawed her skirts out of his way. The fabric ripped and he became more desperate, hampered by unwieldy folds of linen. "Shut up! Shut up! He is not-"

He stopped suddenly, leaving the words hanging, and looked down at his chest, his brows furrowed in confusion at the shiny point that had appeared between in the centre of his shirt. Silently, he raised cold blue eyes to hers and blood bloomed on his lips. Tara's eyes widened in horror and her ears filled with a relentless, high-pitched scream. Jack was trying to speak.

"Tara, look at me! Tara!"

No, not Jack. Another voice. *Another man.* Firm hands pulled her out from underneath Jack's slumped body. An arm around her waist took her weight and she was lifted upright. She flinched when a knife flashed in the setting sun but it sliced though the leather strap behind her back, letting the blood flow back into her arms as they fell painfully and heavily forward. Free. *Free.*

"Tara, I have you. Breathe. You're safe, my darling. I have you. God's blood, forgive me, I should never have left you. I have you now. *Sssh.* Breathe, please, God, breathe."

Her body responded instinctively to his instruction and she breathed deeply, dragging in air and the scent of him until the screams stopped. Gabriel. He'd found her. Somehow. He was here and she was safe. She sobbed in relief and wound a throbbing arm around his neck, letting the security of his size envelope her, laughing at the euphoria of relief that swept through her chest as he wrapped strong arms around her.

It was a fleeting sensation. She screeched with pain and her arm recoiled in a burning instant. Sharp tears sprang to her eyes and she looked down to realise she was cradling a bleeding hand. She caught Gabriel's livid frown as he pushed her unceremoniously back to the ground and she landed with a thump beside Jack's crumpled body, realising with horror that shallow breaths still gurgled quietly in his chest.

"No... *no...*"

She scrabbled her bound feet against the grass to put some distance between them and scrambled awkwardly to stand, pushing herself up with deadened, unbiddable arms. She looked to Gabriel but he had already spun away and she screamed as he reached out and caught the coachwhip on its second crack, grunting as the leather bit into his fingers but quickly twisting it around his hand. He gritted his teeth, giving it a firm yank, and Wortley staggered towards them, only catching himself as he dropped the handle.

Tara shuffled back instinctively but, unthreatened, Gabriel slowly unwound the lash from his hand and balled it experimentally into a fist. Wortley froze; not twelve feet away, he was close enough to see Jack's immobile form on the trampled grass and for a split second he hovered, weighing up his chances of running back into the trees. His features wavered visibly until the sinking realisation that he would have to fight.

Still when Gabriel squared and took a couple of steps towards him, Wortley panicked, running forward and lunging for the first blood. The blow was incompetent and Gabriel blocked before seizing the recoiling fist, twisting it up behind the man's back. There was a horrible, strangely feminine scream of pain and a crunch of bone echoed in the clearing. Wortley's other hand swung instinctively round to claw at Gabriel' face, but he couldn't get purchase and when Gabriel buried his fist in Wortley's stomach the man folded. His contorted face met Gabriel's knee as he fell, his whole body snapping back to land heavily on the grass. His head thudded on the ground a split second later, lying at an awkward angle from the top of a broken neck.

Gabriel turned around immediately. He had already pulled his pistol from its holster at his waist and sparked the fuse by the time he reached her side and he raised the barrel as Jack's hand rolled heavily to grasp towards her bare foot. *No.* He frowned but with mechanical purpose Tara moved forward to take the weapon from him. Left arm extended, she took aim. It was heavier than she expected and the barrel wavered momentarily.

"You don't have to do this."

"I do." She squeezed the cold trigger without further hesitation, barely flinching as the explosion echoed across the clearing and blood from the close impact splattered across her skirt.

It took a while to realise the sounds of hammering hoof beats were not her heart and Donn slid from his mount beside them before it drew to a snorting, sweating halt. Her ears were ringing and Gabriel gently unclenched her fingers from the smoking pistol as Donn placed a supportive arm about her back and gently lifted a water bottle to her lips. She drank deeply but kept her eyes on Jack, searching for the rise and fall of a laboured breath. His chest was still.

46. THE SCORE

"Ready?"

With Gabriel's warm breath in her ear and his arms securely around her, Tara nodded. He nudged Rowley forward into a gentle walk and she winced as the movement jolted her limbs, nudging bruises against the saddle. But she kept her eyes on Donn, unable to turn away from the sight of him. He'd unstrapped the spade from the side of the coach, the one intended for freeing the vehicle from mud, and he was digging. He didn't break pace: one strong stroke after another. A deep chasm yawned slowly in the grassy clearing.

All that fear and pain, and in a matter of hours it would be just another patch of scarred earth, in just another wood. Rain would wash away the blood but first Donn would make them disappear. *No more Bulstrode. No more Jack.* Both would be buried with the manacles Gabriel had hammered free from her ankles with a dark curse. Then Donn would take the battered coach to Maidstone and sell it for scrap. *No more coach.* No trace would remain.

"How did you find me?" she asked quietly as Rowley's hooves found an ancient pathway and their route diverged from the main carriage track, back between the trees.

Gabriel hesitated as the light breeze lifted a curl of her hair, bringing a wave of her scent to him. With some effort he buried a memory of kissing her pale skin, breathing a line south from her collarbone to a place where the heady perfume intensified. "I had men waiting along the route to report on your progress to the coast. You were supposed to be in Otford the day before yesterday. Donn was waiting for you. When you didn't turn up, we came looking."

She shivered despite the heat and a soundless sob racked her body. His stomach lurched and he nuzzled her neck, tightening his hold on her instinctively, unable to reveal the truth of the matter: I was lucky. What could he tell her about what it would have done to him if he hadn't found her in time? How could he explain the pounding in his heart as he galloped non-stop towards the Weald, alive to any broken branch or flattened grass that might be the only signpost to her location? With Donn, he had scanned the route twice over, seeing nothing until, finally, a chance shaft of sunlight glinted on white linen. It was a pile of clothes, stashed in leafy undergrowth but clearly disturbed by some creature overnight. In the woods, Villiers' shirt was as good as a flag.

"They have Eddie."

"They don't. He's with Tom and Rupert and he's back on the road to the coast."

"Oh, thank God… how?" she half turned in the saddle and he met her eyes with what he sincerely hoped was a reassuring smile.

"They put him in a second coach and sent him off to London, with a single drunken lad as driver and guard. The authorities might want your uncle but I'll wager that bastard thought he had the real prize here." His throat tightened and he paused briefly before continuing. "We met the coach just outside Bromley and saw the boy off-"

"You mean-" Some tortuous impulse insisted that she keep a tally of the deaths around her.

"No." He shook his head, cutting her off, and the corners of his mouth twitched unwittingly. "We sent him to an alehouse with a purse of coin. He was just a kid; he didn't know his cargo and we strongly suspected that with the means for a few more jugs of ale he would barely know his own name."

"Mun?"

"He got a nasty bang on the head and he's a bit bruised, but he'll live."

"Jack told me he'd died."

"Then he can add lying to his collection of deadly sins. I'll see him safely back to the West Country after we've met your uncle in St Mary's Bay."

"We're still meeting the boat," she said, the words hollow, more statement than question.

Gabriel paused a moment, controlling his voice for the reply: "We can take a more direct route on horseback. We'll likely arrive around the same time as your uncle's coach."

She exhaled, unsure what to say. *Then the plan hasn't changed.* And neither his desire to exile her. She tried for a while to hold herself apart from him but, gradually, the swaying motion undid her wary resolve. She leaned back finally against the warm solidity of his chest, surrendering for the short time left to the security of his arms, and they continued for couple of hours into the warm evening, barely speaking but no longer with any use for words.

* * *

Gabriel unbuttoned his doublet, shrugging it off onto the riverbank. They'd pulled up by the River Medway to rest for the night and he lifted her gently down to sit on the bank, wrapped in his cloak. With Rowley safely hobbled behind them, his long nose merrily sunk in the long grass for his supper, Gabriel sat down beside her and pulled off his boots, throwing them into a pile with the horse's tack. His shirt followed and he ripped it swiftly into long lengths for bandages.

"We should assess the damage," he said softly, holding her gaze in his as he pulled her gently to standing.

Instinctively, she bent her head to his hand, turning it over to look at the risen red welt from the whip and his knuckles, raw from the impact on Wortley. On his upper arm a dark line of blood traced the impact of the first stroke, where it had ripped through his sleeve. He smiled at her frown. "I think we both know I'll live."

"I… what happens now, Gabriel? What happens when Thurloe finds that Jack is dead?" Her voice rose in panic, some after-tremor of shock. "He'll come for you again–"

"Tara, you're hurt," he interrupted, cupping her face and gently drawing her eyes back towards his. His brows slanted with concern and his voice was soft but urgent. "I need to see how badly."

She nodded mutely, too exhausted not to relinquish herself to his care. Still she looked away as he gently lifted his cloak off her shoulders. He searched her face for any flicker of fear as he began to unlace her stays, letting them fall away to the ground before slowly untying the waist band holding her skirt up. She stiffened as it bunched at her feet and he held her elbow to steady her as she stepped out from the fabric puddle wearing only her shift.

"Look at me. I need to see how badly you are hurt but I don't want you to be afraid." His eyes sought hers again, scanning for the truth, checking that, after everything she had been through, she did not fear his touch. "Tell me to stop at any time, we can take this at your pace."

She shook her head briefly and he smiled gently in response. His eyes held hers as his fingers began to trace her hairline, feeling gently for the source of the blood that had dried along her cheek. She winced when he found the gash at her temple and his mouth hardened into a grim line as he examined it. Not deep enough for stitches but still nasty, jagged.

"What happened here?"

"I fell. Bul... He, he hit me. But Gabriel, they'll come for you. Jack was working for Thurloe the whole time. How will you explain the fact that he..."

She couldn't bring herself to say it. Even after everything. His stomach lurched but he refocused on his task, ignoring the intelligence. Thurloe was already coming. Slowly, he lifted her wrists, turning them over in his hands one by one, his jaw tightening at the sight of the purple bruising and the feel of her flinch. "And this?"

"I think I sprained it when the coach turned. It wasn't too bad, but then, when I tried to get away... I fell."

It was badly swollen. He felt tenderly along the bone, nothing obviously broken, then unable to stop himself he pressed the inside of the damaged wrist gently to his lips. Battlefield training, he thought ruefully after a moment, not something he ever thought to employ with his wife. He wrapped it round with a stabilising strip of linen before lowering it back to her side. He should have been there. He should have protected her.

He ran his hands up her arms and over her shoulders, down across the curves of her body. A practical assessment. "Does it hurt here? Here? Ribs? Spine?"

She shook her head, avoiding his eyes as her teeth worried her bottom lip. He read the preoccupation and ached to take away the pain; even now she cared more for his welfare than her own: "Tara, darling, look at me. Don't worry. I won't have to explain anything. As far as anyone's concerned, that bastard's not dead, he's just missing."

"*He was watching me...*" she whispered quietly, all traces of anger dissolved in a solution of defeat and disbelief. "It was Thurloe's design, to get unfettered access to Eddie and infiltrate the Sealed Knot. *He was under orders to marry me.*"

"I doubt he considered it a major hardship..." he started sarcastically, tailing off awkwardly when he realised the parallels she would have drawn.

"A minor inconvenience perhaps," she shrugged, her voice vacant and quiet.

His hands had come to rest on her hips. He dropped to his knees and hung his head for a moment, unable to find the words. How could he tell her, now? How could he possibly say that yes, he'd pulled her from the church that day on the orders of his Prince; yes, he married her for, what, duty? He'd used his name and position to draw her to him. But all the time he'd been so preoccupied building a secure fortress around her for the sake of his orders, that the defences around his heart stood wide open. But it was his mistake and he had to live with the consequences. *Damned fool.* Every schoolboy knows never to leave your citadel exposed; he deserved to watch it turn to dust.

Besides, even if he confessed it all now from his knees, what earthly good could come of it, just hours before she finally sailed to safety? He should have protected her and he'd failed. How could he possibly watch her from the stand at a court martial or keep her safe while he was fighting with the French? He couldn't. *He wouldn't.* She had to get on that damned boat.

Tara caught the tension along his shoulder blades but after a moment his fingers moved on behind to trace her bottom gently and her breath hitched.

"Sore?"

Yes. *Very.* The shift was doubtless covering numerous bumps and bruises. But his dark head was too close; his warm breath teased her sex through the thin linen and her insides quivered into rebellious life. Her fingers ached to bury themselves in his thick hair, still loosely gathered in a braid but falling free to frame his jawline. Damn the man; her body responded to him as it always had, without sense or warning, only it was too late now. She shook her head too quickly, refusing to look at him.

"My feet hurt," she whispered.

"Really?" Gabriel glanced up, the hint of a grin chastising her attempt to deflect his attention. But a blush had risen in her cheeks and the sight of it struck him harder than the whip. He'd wanted to know that the bond between them was not irrevocably broken. It could not be forced, or faked, and there it was. *Congratulations, you selfish fucking lobcock,* he screamed at himself, *happy now?*

He refocused on the inventory, flicking his eyes up to her profile so he wouldn't miss a tell-tale grimace or hiss of pain. His hands slid around her thighs, sweeping gently downwards over grazes.

"Here?" A particularly large bruise showed hazy through the shift.

"I tried to get away. I untethered a horse from the carriage."

"Quite the horsewoman these days."

"Apparently not," she murmured sardonically, "I fell off."

He raised his eyebrows with a gentle grin: "Let's work up to bareback stunts, my Lady."

He took a sharp intake of breath when he finally looked properly and saw the damage to her ankles. Earlier, all of his attention had been on breaking off the chain. Now he could see that the manacles had cut welts into the flesh, bright crimson rings in otherwise dark purple bruising. Dried blood caked the skin on her naked feet.

"The chains," he whispered hoarsely and she nodded. "God, Tara, I'm so sorry."

"It's not your fault," she said simply.

After a moment, he swallowed. "Did he…?"

Tara shook her head and he could hear the enormous effort of control in her simple answer. "He didn't have time. You found me…"

Gabriel waited a moment to compose himself so she wouldn't see the fury clouding his features. The worthless bastard was dead and, by now, buried in an unmarked grave. But still Jack Ludlow threatened to destabilise him. He could have seen him hang for poaching three months ago, what possessed him to leave him be? Her explanations had been straightforward but Tara's bruised and damaged body spoke volumes. For the pain and fear he had caused her, the man deserved to be killed again. *And again.* Running him through had been too easy. God, he wanted to hurt something badly.

But would that be too easy for him, as well… The wrenching of his gut knew the very worst of it was the knowledge that beneath the damage he should have protected her from, underneath the tremors of a need he recognised all too well, there was a deeper hurt that wouldn't heal so quickly. No amount of vengeance exerted on Ludlow's ghost could rid him of that guilt. She'd opened herself to him, to their marriage; she'd saved his life and his son's. And he'd abandoned her to abduction, to brutal ravishment, to death.

He took a deep breath and sat back on his heels: "I need to wash these wounds before I can bind them."

She put a tentative hand on his shoulder to pause him a second. "But… why would they give Jack up as missing?"

"You of all people know how sides can be turned on a sixpence," he looked up, unable to stop himself placing a gentle kiss on her fingers. "I'm sure the authorities will assume that he took advantage of the chaos caused by your uncle's escape to steal away with his one true love."

"You mean me? Thurloe will never believe that. He paid him to pretend to love me, remember? But it was more than the wage; he told me he was committed to the cause."

"Bastard should have been committed to Bethlem."

He stood and lifted her gently into his arms, turning towards the river. He picked a path down to where it lapped at a sandy slope, wading in without hesitation until the water reached his chest. She squealed, the water cold and stinging on her damaged skin, so he held her safe and still for a moment, waiting for the coolness to numb the pain. In a minute or so she had acclimatised and the dragging current slowly worked its magic. Her ankles no longer throbbed and the dull aches of her legs and bottom were eased. She closed her eyes and leaned against his chest; her right arm wound loosely around his neck to keep the bandaged wrist out of the water.

"Tara, I need to set you down so I can wash the gash on your head."

His gentle tone took a while to pierce her reverie, but as he started to shift his hold the blissful sense of weightlessness morphed into the threat of lost control. The current was too strong to get purchase on the shifting riverbed and she panicked, green eyes startled wide as she wriggled to face him and reached desperately to tighten both arms around his neck. "No! I can't swim!"

"I know, my darling. I know. I have you." The water crept up the linen and her shift clung as tightly to her body as he did, so that he could feel every contour against his chest and legs. "Tara, I won't let you go."

She didn't answer at first, but gritted her teeth, tensing uncomfortably as he wiped clean the blood from her face with a pad made from more of his ripped shirt. After a while, she opened her eyes: "We both know that isn't true."

"God help me." His chest constricted violently and he leaned down to take her mouth.

In the cool water she could feel his deep, dark heat pour into her. Every sensation held her suspended. She wasn't conscious of him walking from the water but became aware obliquely that she was laid back on a soft mossy bank that yielded to her weight. She was drowning in the blue dusk that crept up to cover her skin like a blanket and yet he had peeled back the sodden shift. Her limbs were unbelievably heavy but she dragged her arms about his neck and wrapped her legs up around his waist, revelling in the solid wall of his body as he slowly entered her, a granite anchor holding them firm to a blissful dream.

He moved with tenderness, taking his weight on his elbows and painstakingly avoiding contact with the bruises on her skin, but the price of his control was the utter loss of her own. His lips moved over her, laying down warm kisses that might have been whispers of desire, demand or apology, drawing together threads of a response from her body. His hands stroked her skin, caressing, healing. Gradually, his pace created in her a taut echo of her need. And when the mounting tension finally snapped, it brought waves of heart-breaking sensation. She arched her back to scream and she could taste the salty tang of tears in his own shuddering groan.

"I didn't know it could be like this," he whispered, his breath raising more goose bumps along her slickened neck and sending an exquisite after-shudder down through her body.

She had virtually passed out when he wrapped protective lengths of linen around her ankles, but as the night pressed on they slept fitfully, wound so tightly together beneath his cloak that their flesh felt pressed into one mould. Each was so aware of the other it was as though every breath, every heartbeat, every fluttered eyelash might have belonged to him, or her, or both.

"What were you dreaming about?" he whispered as she stirred with the insistent coo of a wood pigeon. Fat feathers eyed them indifferently from a nearby branch, which bounced when its incumbent gave way to a flock of lighter birds, each taking up its tentative morning song. They knew the score.

"My new life."

"You have a plan?" he queried mildly, his fingers stroking her bottom with a casual possession.

"Of course," she said simply, arching instinctively towards him. "Mmm."

"Tell me?" He traced shapes on her flesh and kissed her slowly, deeply, before giving her a chance to answer. There was all the time in the world in his question, and yet no time at all. Dawn was lurking and it crept around them, tugging at their elbows and their ankles, nagging for acknowledgement.

She raised an eyebrow and eyed him suspiciously in the cool half-light. It was surely obvious that having seen Eddie with her own eyes, she would not get on the boat. If Gabriel thought otherwise, she would do it without him: find Lady Monck; get to her men in the southwest; avenge her family… relieve Cromwell of his invisible crown.

"What does any woman want to do?" she asked at length, uncertain if this was a game. "I'll find a companionable man with all his own teeth; have some children; and sit by the fireside with my needlework."

"Well, assuming you can snare such a catch that all sounds rather lovely. You are clearly very fond of sewing…" He slipped his hand over her hip and his fingers into hair, smiling as she squirmed against his touch. He nuzzled into her neck to find the pulse point, beating loud and fast. "Besides, I have never met a woman more suited to a lifetime of wifely obedience and placid domestic servitude. Ow!"

He laughed as she elbowed him in the ribs, and together they settled back. Tara let her left hand meander across the sloping plane of his stomach, her fingers spreading wide on the hair roughened skin. "I get the impression you're not taking me seriously."

"My sincere apologies. It's a marvellous plan." His fingers closed over her hand. "What future would you formulate for me, my Lady?"

"Alongside your traitorous liaison with our exiled King, you mean?" She stilled a moment. This was a horrible game. They both knew that Gabriel's fate was entirely in the hands of Cromwell and Fleetwood. She took a deep breath and lifted his fingers to press her lips against the damaged skin. "You should do what you were born to do, my Lord. Since you refuse to claim your inheritance at Hellen's Manor, you will just have to establish yourself and your dynasty in Petersham. There's a lifetime of game to hunt, a sizable estate to remodel and, I assure you, endless village squabbles to mediate. Robert may retire but Aodhan will grow lusty and strong, and Ann will live forever."

She gave a small smile and stared upwards at the sky. Faded pinpricks of starry light were still visible beneath the creeping rays of the sun. She'd always found a peaceful strength in the speckled eternity of night but wrapped in Gabriel's heat, there was an additional thrill in knowing how alone they were together, lying before the heavens. The distant constellations had looked down for countless millennia before her heart existed and they would surely burn ever after. Leo's courage. The scales of Libra. Venus.

"You'll remarry," she added quietly, swallowing the hollow, gaping lurch her stomach gave at the thought of any other woman lying sated and secure in his arms, in her place.

"I won't."

"But as far as the world is concerned, you showed immeasurable patience for my rehabilitation into Cromwell's Godly court but still I ran off with my commoner sweetheart and my convicted uncle. Your treacherous whore of a wife callously abandoned you and is now, rather conveniently, dead, don't forget, sunk in swirling seas. You'll have a broken heart ripe for mending. Besides..."

"Besides what?" he raised an eyebrow and unfurled his hand from hers. Without warning his fingers ran possessively across her belly, curling back towards her sex, making her gasp.

"Oh Gabriel, as if, as if you... as if you'd have to win over society's finest ladies through pity alone. Ah! I'm sure they'll all swoon at the very idea of... of you being a widower. I... I..."

"So," he grinned, jutting out his chin before sliding an arm beneath her and pulling her back to curl tightly against him, one thumb stroking her forearms while his fingers continued exploring, deeper, between her legs. Her bottom nestled against his lap and its firm evidence that, for now at least, society's finest ladies would have to wait their turn. "You think me handsome?"

"You'll do," she retorted, twisting reluctantly away to roll onto her front. Handsome? Still almost aggressively so. "But your pretty face is merely window dressing for your title, rank and fortune."

"Then it's a fine plan," he conceded, settling back and lacing his fingers behind his head with a deep sigh of contentment. After a moment, the first drops of rain fell on his nose and seriousness swept his dark brows: "The only problem is that before I can enjoy the novelty of a second wife, I must send my first off to certain doom at the bottom of the Channel. Even if we both know she's actually awaited by a lifetime's gentle industry by the fireplace."

He moved suddenly to cover her back, taking his weight back onto his elbows and she frowned in unseen question as he gently kissed the back of her neck. Her fingers laced through his, twisting and turning through his grasp, testing the strength of his resolve to keep her, the depth of his need for her. *Say you love me, Gabriel, let me stay with you.*

He hesitated a moment, rolling her onto her back beneath him to search the depths of her eyes with keen intensity, driven by some tortuous impulse to know the full extent of his sacrifice. It might be there, a flickering lamp light in the stormy sea of green, but by God he had to hear it; he had to hear her say the words, to shout them from the rocks. He had to know that she thought their connection was deeper than a physical demand. His body throbbed with need of her but even sheathed deep in her heat, he would never be sated. She was under his skin, burrowed deep within his soul.

Unable to bear the silence a moment longer, his mouth came down on hers, possessive and urgent with the need to draw from her a confession that would at once justify his existence and destroy it. *Say it, Tara, God damn you, say it.*

47. THE BEGINNING

Once the worst of the rain ceased, they set out again and Rowley picked a soft and steady path east from Appledore, along the grass track on the raised Rhee Wall towards New Romney on the coast. On either side of its parallel earth banks, the marsh land fanned out, flat green, veined with centuries-old sewers. And between heavy grey clouds, intermittent sunshine picked out the watercourses and floods, giving flashes of glistening sparkle to an otherwise desolate landscape. Moonlight would do the same with more drama, she thought abstractly, leaning back against Gabriel's chest to imagine the smugglers' bargeboards and row boats drifting quietly along the ancient routes under cover of darkness.

There was nothing for miles in any direction save the squat turret of St Thomas a Becket, which stood alone a few hundred yards off the causeway, maybe half a mile to the south. It was an unusual church, nave and chancel roofs gabled, but tainted by the air of abandonment. Its one-time village was long lost with the plague and there were no parishioners for miles. No signs of life.

She started with the sudden peal of its bells and Gabriel's hand went to his pistol, holstered ready against Rowley's neck. the warhorse danced awkwardly to the discordant clanking, muscles twitching and nostrils flaring under the sweating black coat. Gabriel swiftly lit a match and reined off towards the church without further hesitation, pulling her tight against him and leaning back as Rowley stretched his long fore legs down the bank and squelched heavily into the field. His pistol remained raised, tilted sideward to prevent misfire, and his other arm held firm around her waist.

"Tara, is the splint on your wrist still tight? You must be ready to ride hard to the Bay. Find Tom and get on the boat."

The bells stopped and the large church door crashed open. Gabriel cocked his pistol, twitching the rein to turn Rowley and take her out of the direct firing line but Tara twisted back and put a restraining hand on his arm, pushing the barrel away. "Wait!"

"He's dead!" A ragged peasant, old eyes rimmed red with marsh fever and homebrew, danced drunkenly out of the church and into the long grass to greet them.

"Who's dead?" Tara demanded.

"The tyrant's dead! We are celebrating!"

"Dead?" Gabriel's eyes narrowed but his posture relaxed a little and he sprung down from the saddle, glancing back at Tara as a blonde flash barrelled out behind the bare-legged stranger, landing headlong into him for a bear-sized hug that made him stumble to keep his balance and struggle to safely holster the weapon. "Oof!"

"Ho, Gabe! You found her! Jesus, we only bloody did it!"

"Rupert, careful! This is loaded, man!"

"Thank God. Tara, I can't tell you what a sight you are for sore eyes." Tom appeared in the doorway, laughing as he waved welcome and jogged forward to clasp Gabriel's arm. "And I see you've met our new friend already. We took shelter from the worst of the rain and came across him, deep in an old bottle of alter wine."

Donn stepped out behind him with a relaxed grin, holding a chunk of bread aloft. "Ye took yer time, Milord. I've a shirt ye can be wearin' in my bag. Milady, have ye eaten?"

"Where's Eddie-" she started only for Rupert to interrupt, frowning: "Gabe, where is your shirt?"

"Dead! Dead! Do you hear me?" The peasant was insistent, nodding frantically at Tara, his gesticulating hands noticeably shaking.

He moved towards the giant horse. Rowley stepped restlessly sideways once he was at close quarters with the dancing mad man and Gabriel instinctively moved to block him, one hand resting on the hilt of his sword. The man took no offence at the warning, softly taking up the chorus of an impromptu ballad as he spun around in his private party: "Nine years' mischiefs, tumults and rage, are the only memorials of this Commonwealth's age…"

"Tom, where's Eddie?" Tara slipped awkwardly down from Rowley's back, cradling her bound right wrist and manoeuvring in front of Gabriel as Edward Villiers emerged slowly from the church. He was limping, wrapped in a thick woollen cloak that might have belonged to Tom. They had found him a hat, its brim not quite covering a bandage wrapped around his scalp like a young girl's cap. She ran to him with an unrestrained squeal of relief, wrapping her arms about him.

"Oh, blessed be God!" He whispered, hoarse. The slurring seemed more pronounced than it had been but perhaps she just noticed it more. "Thou art a marvellous sight, Tammy."

"Is it true?" said Gabriel, turning back to Tom and Rupert.

"It's true," said Tom, eyebrows raised. "God has apparently achieved what countless men could not. Cromwell died yesterday. Thurloe's moved quickly and put Tumbledown Dick in his place."

"Then he's backed the wrong horse. Richard's not strong enough."

Tom nodded: "There are rumours already that Charles Fleetwood is considering a move."

"Fleetwood won't support Richard's appointment as Commander-in-Chief. He hasn't the iron fist of his father or even the limited experience of his brother Henry." Gabriel gave a hollow snort of laughter. "Ruthless bastard. I'm summoned to attend him at Whitehall tomorrow. I'd assumed it was to pre-empt a court martial but perhaps it's more likely he's planning his next move."

"Jesus, Gabe. Is it possible Fleetwood could have…?" Tom frowned and caught Gabriel's eye as both men realised the dangerous truth of it: the summons was sent before Cromwell's death.

Habitually, Gabriel looked to the peasant, calculating if he was within earshot, and Rupert changed the subject loudly: "Cousin, you should come inside and see this place. It's got stained glass, and a rail! It somehow survived parliament's ordinance during the first war. I can't remember ever seeing anything like it in England. Marie would be amazed; it's like the Catholic churches in France."

"Well, yes, quite, Mr Godolphin," said Edward, shaking his head distractedly as he released Tara and started thoughtfully on a lesson. "That's exactly the problem. That is one thing parliament must be given credit for and I look forward to discussing this with the Prince. Each s-steeple house filled with monuments of superstition or idolatry is a deceiver, deflecting attention from the truth that cometh by Jesus."

Rupert looked confused but the peasant meandered back across the grass, still preoccupied. "Dead! And the rising has started!"

"A rising?" Tara turned to the peasant, jogging a few steps to reach him. "What do you mean a rising?"

"The keeper of the Mermaid Inn in Rye had the word of a traveller from Winchester." He half-hummed and half sang the revelation to the approximate tune of his ballad. "They say there are bonfires lit all along the south coast like it's Fifth November. Fireworks burning orange and white like comets! Explosions! All the ports are calling to Charles Stuart over the waves, bidding him home. It's only a matter of time!"

Tara felt the sudden closeness of Gabriel as a heated tremor across her back. He murmured into her ear: "More fireworks? Your men are confident."

She turned enough to see the corners of his mouth quirk and shrugged. "You wouldn't begrudge my men a party?"

They watched as the peasant danced quickly away from Rowley's thudding sidestep, squealing in his excitement: "It's all over!"

"I doubt very much that's the case," she observed quietly, her voice a thoughtful whisper.

Gabriel's arms came solidly around her then and his chin nodded where it rested above her head. "It's only just begun."

"We need to cut straight across the marsh from here," interrupted Tom practically, eyeing a grey mist rolling towards them from the direction of the coast. "The boat's due in two hours. We've dallied too long; we should keep moving."

* * *

The beach slung a flat beige band along the width of St Mary's Bay, and in the distance, anchored while it waited, a compact caravel lurched on dull green waves. Its three masts stood black, pointing at the grey mizzle like wavering compass needles looking for true north.

"Fairly typical beach weather, I see," Rupert muttered as the men silently dismounted and Gabriel lifted Tara gently down. He shuddered as splatters of sea spray landed on his nose, carried on bursts of chill breeze. "At least Marie will not be jealous of our day trip."

Leaving them to secure the horses, Tara stepped silently towards the water, over lines of seashell detritus, and sat down on damp sand beside Eddie. He was still huddled in Tom's cloak, eyes firmly on the waiting vessel. It swept slowly around its anchor and she caught sight of its name: The New World.

Rupert snorted as he stopped behind them. "Lead skies, drizzle… the new world looks much the same as the old one to me," he said wryly, an attempt to lighten the mood as Gabriel strode past them down the beach to signal readiness.

In the distance, the captain gave a short wave in their direction and they watched as he hooked his leg over the gunnel to climb down a stern ladder, dropping into a shallow rowing tender beside a crewmate.

"The Lord's providence is to be trusted, Tammy. You must know he sent an angel to you." Eddie murmured suddenly, as he pulled off his shoes and stockings, ready to wade into the sea. He leant over and squeezed her hand a moment, then his tone changed: "We'll be in Antwerp with the Prince before the week is out."

"Yes, I know Eddie, you told me."

"Then we shall have peace and quiet by the fireside, while the strong men here determine our fate."

She shot Eddie a sideways glance. He shrugged, innocent enough, and she gave a small smile, drawing a deliberate circle in the sand with her bare toes as the tender washed swiftly closer on the waves. The rolling tide was coming in; there was barely any work for the sailor to do on the oars. In deeper waters, the larger vessel bobbed insubstantially on its pewter platter but Eddie was clearly nonplussed. She laid a hand flat upon her stomacher to quell the squirming in her belly at the thought of boarding it.

"A day or two on The New World here. Carriage to where Charlie sits waiting," she mused. "Easy."

Gabriel had arrived back from the water's edge and bent to lift her into his arms a last time before turning to wade into the sea through foamy grey rolls of tide. A few yards along the beach, Edward was picking his own way out towards the boat. He smiled across at the two of them and made an exaggerated shudder at the ice-cold brine.

"Are you comfortable?" Gabriel asked at length, rearranging his grasp to better support her bandaged ankles and keep them dry against the spray.

The tenderness of his actions threatened to unravel her resolve and she took a deep breath, looking up into Eddie's watery eyes, catching his imperceptible nod before he turned to wave at the captain. It was time. She steeled her rolling stomach for the truth.

"Are you?" she replied quietly. "There is comfort to be had in following orders,"

A heartbeat passed and then he stopped, the water lapping above his knees.

"Tara, look at me. I'm not putting you on a boat to The blasted Netherlands because Charlie ordered me to. I am doing it because I can't think of another way to-"

She twisted without warning and dropped out of his arms, the force of her anger impervious to the shock of cold water reaching to the top of her thighs. A brisk breeze whipped dark curls in front of her face and she shoved them back. "Enough. I won't do this."

"You will."

"I'm not a child, Gabriel, stop trying to turn me into one. How dare you deign to decide what's best for me? Who in God's name gave you that right, you arrogant bastard?"

"That right is mine. I'm your husband," he started. His fingers twitched to take her upper arms, but he thought better of it.

"No, for the record, you're not! You committed to me 'til death do us part. And here, now, I'm poised to drown. You are freed of the bargain. This is the end. I'm master of my own fate. Christ, Gabriel, it's one thing to fake a temporary affection, quite another to assume eternal dominion-"

"Fake an affection? Dear God, are you serious?" he shouted, voice raised against the wind and the waves and hoarse with anger, not caring any more whether Edward Villiers could hear, or Tom or Rupert or Donn back on the beach or even the captain leaning over the edge of his boat, hand outstretched, poised to haul the first half of his cargo aboard. His eyes flashed and, exasperated, he stabbed his fingers back through his hair: "Years, Tara, years, I've lived a sword's breadth from discovery and a traitor's death; you can't think I would willingly sit you on that knife-edge beside me? With Cromwell dead, it will only get more dangerous! Loyalties will shift like sands-"

"But there will be no orders for France now. And Fleetwood will not follow through with a court martial." she interrupted.

"Only to hand me the burden of knowing I owe him my life and to tie me to open rebellion against Richard Cromwell. There is still a very good chance I am about to fall."

"Then for Christ's sake, let me catch you!" Impulsively she cupped his head and turned his face to look at her, pushing aside the sea-splatted locks of hair that stuck to his skin. "Let me work with you! Gabriel, I understand. I know what it means to you, after everything that happened in Ireland. I know the guilt in you, why you feel that you must keep me safe... but I'm staying here. I am useful to Charlie here. I've proved it time and again and with Eddie abroad there is a place for me-"

"Guilt? You think this is guilt, when I would crumble my whole world between my hands, if it would only keep you safe. I would lay it at your feet, if only I thought it were worth having!"

"There you go again!" she shouted back, unwilling to hear the pain in his words. Hot tears pricked and she shook her head, unable to look into the intensity in his dark eyes. "How the Hell dare you decide what is worth my having?"

A rolling wave shoved at her legs, pushing her momentarily off balance and he caught her against him as she gasped. He tilted up her chin, forcing her to look directly into his gaze, before twisting his fingers into her hair and angling her head back to kiss her mouth thoroughly, with unexpected tenderness.

"When this is over, I will find you," he whispered urgently, his voice low. "I'm yours, only yours, and I always will be. It doesn't matter where you are, I will find you. If there is no path to find, I will make one. But you have to go to Charlie now, Tara, I will not stake you in this bloody game. I will not lose you, do you hear me?"

"No!" Panting hard, she put a hand against his chest. "You listen to me. Put me on that boat if you must but I'll come straight back. I won't sit idly in an exiled court while Eddie's men are left to someone they don't trust. I will not live another half-life in the shadows, praying for the chance of some second resurrection, fearing every packet should it bring news of your death, terrified to wake into a world without you—"

He took her mouth again, a kiss savage now with need and anger, his tongue speaking wordless volumes on possession. Rippling waves dragged her skirts around him, forcing her legs to part around one of his solid thighs and snatching her footing. One firm hand was curled around the nape of her neck but he relinquished this hold in order to lift her clear of the destabilising waves. She wrapped her heavy, wet legs around his waist and her arms wound around his neck.

From the beach there were distant whoops of encouragement. Rupert had cupped his hands to project an excited whistle across the sand and over Rowley's agitated whinny: "*A fine catch, Gabe!*"

"*Careful cousin, your feet are getting wet!*" added Tom, his shout muffled by the sound of waves and gusts of wind.

She gasped for breath when he released her mouth, his own chest heaving: "You exasperating, headstrong woman. You're as deaf as a fencepost and as stubborn as an ass…"

"Quite the smallest compliments I ever heard."

"But I love you. God help me, Tara Moore, you've stolen my mind, my heart and my soul. You took them piece by piece until there was nothing left that belongs to me. You're a thief, and may you be damned for it."

"And I mean to take your world as well, whether you would like it or not, Gabriel Moore for it's my world too." Tara started to shrug, as casually as she could while her heart pounded, but it wasn't enough. She grasped his head in her cold fingers, keeping her eyes firmly on his. "I'm dammed if I belong in any place without you in it."

"Milord! There's heavy clouds on the horizon!"

She glanced over a moment to see that Eddie was already on board, and that he was exchanging a silent, satisfied glance with Tom back on the beach. He sensed her watching and tilted his hat in her direction.

The captain leant over the rail of the creaking tender to yell, the boat rocking with his shifting weight. "Probably nout more than a squall," he shouted awkwardly. "But we've to leave now to stand a chance of clearing the headland. Milady?"

Gabriel searched her clear gaze as it retuned to him. He had to give her every chance. "The country is on fire, Tara, but this may be the best chance Charlie has to take it back. If war comes again… this, all of this, everything we are fighting for… history may burn us from its pages."

"You thought we would live forever?" She gave a small smile and ran her thumb softly across the scar on his cheek, wiping away cool moisture that might have been sea spray, her fingers feeling the determination in the set of his jawline.

"I will burn for you for all eternity." He frowned and rested his forehead forward onto hers, kissing her again with an urgent tenderness until she could hear nothing but the vital rhythm of blood in their veins, love promising its own immortality.

"Milord!"

"Thurloe, Richard, even Latimer… all the men like them… It's life and death now, a matter of sheer survival as everything unravels. Without Cromwell they're weakened and they're cornered but they have everything to gain, they'll behave like wounded beasts."

"Do I need to tell you again?"

"They'll do whatever they can to stop us."

"Let them try." Her lips twitched and the corners of his eyes creased, the first hint of a grin tugging at his mouth.

"*God speed, Captain!*" he yelled towards the boat, without taking his eyes from hers. "Villiers! Tell Charlie we'll be ready for him!"

Without the necessity of further encouragement, the sailor made heavy drags on the oars to turn the tender in the right direction and, taking its cue, the front sail of the caravel fell out with a thwack and a crack as it caught the wind.

ACKNOWLEDGEMENTS

In the mid seventeenth century, our ancestors tore England apart. Whole families and communities were divided and dislocated for a radical idea that severed the head of God's anointed monarch and promised to redefine the relationship between power and people. Only by the summer of 1658, when the main action of *The Sealed Knot* takes place, Oliver Cromwell's constitutional experiment is failing with his health and he was getting desperate. Abroad, control of the sugar trade was the only hope for his empty coffers, but this relied on winning foreign battles and building political allegiances on shifting sands. At home, the weeds of factionalism grew faster than he could pull them out.

I've devoured books on this period for decades, too many to count, but in truth I'm far more interested in its familiarity than its foreignness. It only takes a glance at recent events to see that, as a nation, we're not quite as pathologically stable as we might like to believe. So while my main characters are a fiction, a nod to the passions and weaknesses that make us eternal, they stand for everyone trying to navigate echoes of conflict while staying true to their own path. For everyone fighting to make sense of a world turned upside down. There are plenty of characters here based on real people, although I've necessarily overlaid a fair amount of imagination to tell their histories and describe their foibles.

In writing this, I've used lots of contemporary sources and language (and curses). An excerpt from Robert Herrick's 1648 poem *Corinna's Going a-Maying* is used in Chapter 33. I can't take credit for the bawdy *Oyster Nan* ballad set out in Chapters 3 and 6. The Oliver Cromwell Association (http://www.olivercromwell.org/wordpress) meanwhile reproduces plenty of his original letters and together with *The State Papers Online – Highlights of SPO III* (http://gale.cengage.co.uk/state-papers-online-15091714.aspx) these were useful in crafting the "original sources" littered throughout.

I'm an ex-journalist, current lawyer with three young children, who remain stubbornly impervious to all and any attempts to inspire a love for and fascination with history. I currently live just outside London and spend a lot of time in the same haunts as Gabriel and Tara, albeit with fewer swords.

London, October 2022

Printed in Great Britain
by Amazon